Dinah Maria Mulock Craik

Mistress and Maid

A Household Story

Dinah Maria Mulock Craik

Mistress and Maid
A Household Story

ISBN/EAN: 9783337396992

Printed in Europe, USA, Canada, Australia, Japan

Cover: Foto ©Andreas Hilbeck / pixelio.de

More available books at **www.hansebooks.com**

MISTRESS AND MAID.

A Household Story.

BY THE AUTHOR OF

"JOHN HALIFAX, GENTLEMAN," "THE WOMAN'S KINGDOM,"
"HANNAH," "A BRAVE LADY," "THE OGILVIES,"
"OLIVE," "AGATHA'S HUSBAND," &c.

HARPER & BROTHERS, PUBLISHERS,
NEW YORK AND LONDON,
1899.

MISTRESS AND MAID.

CHAPTER I.

SHE was a rather tall, awkward, and strongly-built girl
of about fifteen. This was the first impression the "maid"
gave to her "mistresses," the Misses Leaf, when she entered their kitchen accompanied by her mother, a widow and
washerwoman, by name Mrs. Hand. I must confess, when
they saw the damsel, the ladies felt a certain twinge of
doubt as to whether they had not been rash in offering to
take her; whether it would not have been wiser to have
gone on in their old way—now, alas! grown into a very
old way, so as almost to make them forget they had ever
had any other—and done without a servant still.

Many consultations had the three sisters held before
such a revolutionary extravagance was determined on.
But Miss Leaf was beginning both to look and to feel "not
so young as she had been;" Miss Selina ditto; though,
being still under forty, she would not have acknowledged
it for the world. And Miss Hilary, young, bright and active as she was, could by no possibility do every thing that
was to be done in the little establishment; be, for instance,
in three places at once—in the school-room teaching little
boys and girls, in the kitchen cooking dinner, and in the
rooms up stairs busy at house-maid's work. Besides, much
of her time was spent in waiting upon "poor Selina," who
frequently was, or fancied herself, too ill to take any part
in either the school or house duties.

Though, the thing being inevitable, she said little about

it, Miss Leaf's heart was often sore to see Hilary's pretty hands smeared with blacking of grates, and roughened with scouring of floors. To herself this sort of thing had become natural—but Hilary!

All the time of Hilary's childhood the youngest of the family had, of course, been spared all house-work; and afterward her studies had left no time for it. For she was a clever girl, with a genuine love of knowledge; Latin, Greek, and even the higher branches of arithmetic and mathematics, were not beyond her range; and this she found much more interesting than washing dishes or sweeping floors. True, she always did whatever domestic duty she was told to do; but her bent was not in the household line. She had only lately learned to " see dust," to make a pudding, to iron a shirt; and, moreover, to reflect, as she woke up to the knowledge of how these things should be done, and how necessary they were, what must have been her eldest sister's lot during all these twenty years! What pains, what weariness, what eternal toil must Johanna have silently endured in order to do all those things which till now had seemed to do themselves!

Therefore, after much cogitation as to the best and most prudent way to amend matters, and perceiving with her clear common-sense that, willing as she might be to work in the kitchen, her own time would be much more valuably spent in teaching their growing school, it was Hilary who, these Christmas holidays, first started the bold idea, " We must have a servant;" and therefore, it being necessary to begin with a very small servant on very low wages (£3 per annum was, I fear, the maximum), did they take this Elizabeth Hand.

So, hanging behind her parent, an anxious-eyed and rather sad-voiced woman, did Elizabeth enter the kitchen of the Misses Leaf.

The ladies were all there. Johanna arranging the table for their early tea; Selina lying on the sofa trying to cut bread and butter; Hilary on her knees before the fire, making the bit of toast—her eldest sister's one luxury.

This was the picture that her three mistresses presented to Elizabeth's eyes; which, though they seemed to notice nothing, must in reality have noticed every thing.

"I've brought my daughter, ma'am, as you sent word you'd take on trial," said Mrs. Hand, addressing herself to Selina, who, as the tallest, the best dressed, and the most imposing, was usually regarded by strangers as the head of the family.

"Oh, Johanna, my dear."

Miss Leaf came forward, rather uncertainly, for she was of a shy nature, and had been so long accustomed to do the servant's work of the household that she felt quite awkward in the character of mistress. Instinctively she hid her poor hands, that would at once have betrayed her to the sharp eyes of the working-woman, and then, ashamed of her momentary false pride, laid them outside her apron and sat down.

"Will you take a chair, Mrs. Hand? My sister told you, I believe, all our requirements. We only want a good, intelligent girl. We are willing to teach her every thing."

"Thank you, kindly; and I be willing and glad for her to learn, ma'am," replied the mother, her sharp and rather free tone subdued in spite of herself by the gentle voice of Miss Leaf. Of course, living in the same country town, she knew all about the three school-mistresses, and how till now they had kept no servant. "It's her first place, and her'll be awk'ard at first, most like. Hold up your head, Lizabeth."

"Is her name Elizabeth?"

"Far too long and too fine," observed Selina from the sofa. "Call her Betty."

"Any thing you please, miss; but I call her Lizabeth. It wor my young missis's name in my first place, and I never had a second."

"We will call her Elizabeth," said Miss Leaf, with the gentle decision she could use on occasion.

There was a little more discussion between the mother and the future mistress as to holidays, Sundays, and so on,

during which time the new servant stood silent and im-
passive in the door-way between the back kitchen and the
kitchen, or, as it is called in those regions, the house-place.

As before said, Elizabeth was by no means a personable
girl, and her clothes did not set her off to advantage. Her
cotton frock hung in straight lines down to her ankles,
displaying her clumsily shod feet and woolen stockings;
above it was a pinafore—a regular child's pinafore, of the
cheap, strong, blue-speckled print which in those days was
generally worn. A little shabby shawl, pinned at the
throat, and pinned very carelessly and crookedly, with an
old black bonnet much too small for her large head and
her quantities of ill-kept hair, completed the costume. It
did not impress favorably a lady who, being, or rather
having been, very handsome herself, was as much alive to
appearances as the second Miss Leaf.

She made several rather depreciatory observations, and
insisted strongly that the new servant should only be
taken " on trial," with no obligation to keep her a day longer than they wished. Her feeling on the matter commu-
nicated itself to Johanna, who closed the negotiation with
Mrs. Hand by saying,

" Well, let us hope your daughter will suit us. We will
give her a fair chance, at all events."

" Which is all I can ax for, Miss Leaf. Her bean't much
to look at, but her's willin' and sharp, and her's never told
me a lie in her life. Courtesy to thy missis, and say thee'lt
do thy best, Lizabeth."

Pulled forward, Elizabeth did courtesy, but she never
offered to speak. And Miss Leaf, feeling that for all parties the interview had better be shortened, rose from her
chair.

Mrs. Hand took the hint and departed, saying only
" Good-by, Elizabeth," with a nod half encouraging, half
admonitory, which Elizabeth silently returned. That was
all the parting between mother and daughter; they neither kissed nor shook hands, which undemonstrative farewell somewhat surprised Hilary.

Now Miss Hilary Leaf had all this while gone on toast-ing. Luckily for her bread, the fire was low and black: meantime, from behind her long drooping curls (which Johanna would not let her "turn up," though she was twenty), she was making her observations on the new servant. It might be that, possessing more head than the one and more heart than the other, Hilary was gifted with deeper perception of character than either of her sisters, but certainly her expression, as she watched Elizabeth, was rather amused and kindly than dissatisfied.

"Now, girl, take off your bonnet," said Selina, to whom Johanna had silently appealed in her perplexity as to the next proceeding with regard to the new member of the household.

Elizabeth obeyed, and then stood, irresolute, awkward, and wretched to the last degree, at the farthest end of the house-place.

"Shall I show you where to hang up your things?" said Hilary, speaking for the first time; and at the new voice, so quick, cheerful, and pleasant, Elizabeth visibly started.

Miss Hilary rose from her knees, crossed the kitchen, took from the girl's unresisting hands the old black bonnet and shawl, and hung them up carefully on a nail behind the great eight-day clock. It was a simple action, done quite without intention, and accepted without acknowledgment, except one quick glance of that keen yet soft gray eye; but years and years after Elizabeth reminded Hilary of it.

And now Elizabeth stood forth in her own proper likeness, unconcealed by bonnet or shawl, or maternal protection. The pinafore scarcely covered her gaunt neck and long arms: that tremendous head of rough, dusky hair was evidently for the first time gathered into a comb. Thence elf-locks escaped in all directions, and were forever being pushed behind her ears, or rubbed (not smoothed; there was nothing smooth about her) back from her forehead, which, Hilary noticed, was low, broad, and full. The rest of her face, except the before-mentioned eyes, was abso-

lutely and undeniably plain. Her figure, so far as the pinafore exhibited it, was undeveloped and ungainly, the chest
being contracted and the shoulders rounded, as if with carrying children or other weights while still a growing girl.
In fact, nature and circumstances had apparently united in
dealing unkindly with Elizabeth Hand.

Still here she was; and what was to be done with her?

Having sent her with the small burden, which was apparently all her luggage, to the little room—formerly a
box-closet—where she was to sleep, the Misses Leaf—or, as
facetious neighbors called them, the Miss Leaves—took serious counsel together over their tea.

Tea itself suggested the first difficulty. They were always in the habit of taking that meal, and, indeed, every
other, in the kitchen. It saved time, trouble, and fire, besides leaving the parlor always tidy for callers, chiefly pupils' parents, and preventing these latter from discovering
that the three orphan daughters of Henry Leaf, Esq., so-
licitor, and sisters of Henry Leaf, Junior, Esq., also solicit-
or, but whose sole mission in life seemed to have been to
spend every thing, make every body miserable, marry, and
die, that these three ladies did always wait upon themselves at meal-times, and did sometimes breakfast without
butter, and dine without meat. Now this system would
not do any longer.

"Besides, there is no need for it," said Hilary, cheerfully.
"I am sure we can well afford both to keep and to feed a
servant, and to have a fire in the parlor every day. Why
not take our meals there, and sit there regularly of evenings?"

"We must," added Selina, decidedly. "For my part, I
couldn't eat, or sew, or do any thing with that great hulk-
ing girl sitting staring opposite, or standing; for how could
we ask her to sit with us? Already, what must she have
thought of us—people who take tea in the kitchen?"

"I do not think that matters," said the eldest sister,
gently, after a moment's silence. "Every body in the
town knows who and what we are, or might if they chose

to inquire. We can not conceal our poverty if we tried; and I don't think any body looks down upon us for it. Not even since we began to keep school, which you thought was such a terrible thing, Selina."

"And it was. I have never reconciled myself to teach ing the baker's two boys and the grocer's little girl. You were wrong, Johanna; you ought to have drawn the line somewhere, and it ought to have excluded trades-people."

"Beggars can not be choosers," began Hilary.

"Beggars!" echoed Selina.

"No, my dear, we never were that," said Miss Leaf, interposing against one of the sudden storms that were often breaking out between these two. "You know well we have never begged nor borrowed from any body, and hardly ever been indebted to any body, except for the extra lessons that Mr. Lyon would insist upon giving to Ascott at home."

Here Johanna suddenly stopped, and Hilary, with a slight color rising in her face, said,

"I think, sisters, we are forgetting that the staircase is quite open, and though I am sure she has an honest look, and not that of a listener, still Elizabeth might hear. Shall I call her down stairs, and tell her to light a fire in the parlor?"

While she is doing it—and in spite of Selina's forebodings to the contrary, the small maiden did it quickly and well, especially after a hint or two from Hilary—let me take the opportunity of making a little picture of this same Hilary.

Little it should be, for she was a decidedly little woman; small altogether, hands, feet, and figure being in satisfactory proportion. Her movements, like those of most little women, were light and quick rather than elegant; yet every thing she did was done with a neatness and delicacy which gave an involuntary sense of grace and harmony. She was, in brief, one of those people who are best described by the word "harmonious;" people who never set your teeth on edge, or rub you up the wrong way, as very

excellent people occasionally do. Yet she was not over
meek or unpleasantly amiable; there was a liveliness and
even briskness about her, as if the every-day wine of her
life had a spice of Champagniness, not frothiness, but natural effervescence of spirit, meant to "cheer but not ine-
briate" a household.

And in her own household this gift was most displayed.
No centre of a brilliant, admiring circle could be more
charming, more witty, more irresistibly amusing than was
Hilary sitting by the kitchen fireside, with the cat on her
knee, between her two sisters, and the school-boy Ascott
Leaf, their nephew—which four individuals, the cat being
not the least important of them, constituted the family.

In the family Hilary shone supreme. All recognized her
as the light of the house, and so she had been ever since
she was born, ever since her

> "Dying mother mild,
> Said, with accents undefiled,
> 'Child, be mother to this child.'"

It was said to Johanna Leaf — who was not Mrs. Leaf's
own child. But the good step-mother, who had once taken
the little motherless girl to her bosom, and never since
made the slightest difference between her and her own
children, knew well whom she was trusting.

From that solemn hour, in the middle of the night, when
she lifted the hour-old baby out of its dead mother's bed
into her own, it became Johanna's one object in life.
Through a sickly infancy, for it was a child born amidst
trouble, her sole hands washed, dressed, fed it: night and
day it "lay in her bosom, and was unto her as a daughter."

She was then just thirty; not too old to look forward to
woman's natural destiny, a husband and children of her
own. But years slipped by, and she was Miss Leaf still.
What matter! Hilary was her daughter.

Johanna's pride in her knew no bounds. Not that she
showed it much: indeed, she deemed it a sacred duty not
to show it, but to make believe her "child" was just like

other children. But she was not. Nobody ever thought
she was—even in externals. Fate gave her all those gifts
which are sometimes sent to make up for the lack of worldly prosperity. Her brown eyes were as soft as doves' eyes,
yet could dance with fun and mischief if they chose; her
hair, brown also, with a dark red shade in it, crisped itself
in two wavy lines over her forehead, and then tumbled
down in two glorious masses, which Johanna, ignorant,
alas! of art, called "very untidy," and labored in vain to
quell under combs, or to arrange in proper, regular curls.
Her features—well, they too were good; better than these
unartistic people had any idea of—better even than Selina's, who in her youth had been the belle of the town. But,
whether artistically correct or not, Johanna, though she
would on no account have acknowledged it, believed solemnly that there was not such a face in the world as little
Hilary's.

Possibly a similar idea dawned on the apparently dull
mind of Elizabeth Hand, for she watched her youngest mistress intently, from kitchen to parlor, and from parlor back
to kitchen; and once, when Miss Hilary stood giving information as to the proper abode of broom, bellows, etc., the
little maid gazed at her with such admiring observation
that the scuttle she carried was tilted, and the coals were
strewn all over the kitchen floor. At which catastrophe
Miss Leaf looked miserable, Miss Selina spoke crossly, and
Ascott, who just then came into his tea, late as usual, burst
into a shout of laughter.

It was as much as Hilary could do to help laughing herself, she being too near her nephew's own age always to
maintain a dignified, aunt-like attitude; but nevertheless,
when, having disposed of her sisters in the parlor, she
coaxed Ascott into the school-room, and insisted upon his
Latin being done—she helping him, Aunt Hilary scolded
him well, and bound him over to keep the peace toward
the new servant.

"But she is such a queer one. Exactly like a South-Sea
Islander. When she stood with her grim, stolid, despair-

ing countenance, contemplating the coals — oh, Aunt Hilary, how killing she was!"

And the regular, rollicking, irresistible boy-laugh broke
out again.

"She will be great fun. Is she really to stay?"

"I hope so," said Hilary, trying to be grave. "I hope
never again to see Aunt Johanna cleaning the stairs, and
getting up to light the kitchen fire of winter mornings, as
she will do if we have not a servant to do it for her. Don't
you see, Ascott?"

"Oh, I see," answered the boy, carelessly. "But don't
bother me, please. Domestic affairs are for women, not
men." Ascott was eighteen, and just about to pass out of
his caterpillar state as a doctor's apprentice-lad into the
chrysalis condition of a medical student in London. "But,"
with sudden reflection, "I hope she won't be in my way.
Don't let her meddle with any of my books and things."

"No; you need not be afraid. I have put them all into
your room. I myself cleared your rubbish out of the box-
closet—"

"The box-closet! Now, really, I can't stand—"

"She is to sleep in the box-closet; where else could she
sleep?" said Hilary, resolutely, though inwardly quaking a
little; for somehow the merry, handsome, rather exacting
lad had acquired considerable influence in this household
of women. "You must put up with the loss of your 'den,'
Ascott: it would be a great shame if you did not, for the
sake of Aunt Johanna and the rest of us."

"Um!" grumbled the boy, who, though he was not a
bad fellow at heart, had a boy's dislike to "putting up"
with the slightest inconvenience. "Well, it won't last
long. I shall be off shortly. What a jolly life I'll have in
London, Aunt Hilary! I'll see Mr. Lyon there too."

"Yes," said Aunt Hilary, briefly, returning to Dido and
Æneas; humble and easy Latinity for a student of eighteen;
but Ascott was not a brilliant boy, and, being apprenticed
early, his education had been much neglected, till Mr. Lyon
came as usher to the Stowbury Grammar-school, and hap-

pening to meet and take an interest in him, taught him and his Aunt Hilary Latin, Greek, and mathematics together, of evenings.

I shall make no mysteries here. ˙Human nature is human nature all the world over. A tale without love in it would be unnatural, unreal—in fact, a simple lie; for there are no histories and no lives without love in them; if there could be, Heaven pity and pardon them, for they would be mere abortions of humanity.

Thank Heaven, we, most of us, do not philosophize: we only live. We like one another, we hardly know why; we love one another, we still less know why. If on the day she first saw—in church it was—Mr. Lyon's grave, heavy-browed, somewhat severe face—for he was a Scotsman, and his sharp, strong Scotch features did look "hard" beside the soft, rosy, well-conditioned Saxon youth of Stowbury—if on that Sunday any one had told Hilary Leaf that the face of this stranger was to be the one face of her life, stamped upon brain, and heart, and soul with a vividness that no other impressions were strong enough to efface, and retained there with a tenacity that no vicissitudes of time, or place, or fortunes had power to alter, Hilary would —yes, I think she would—have quietly kept looking on. She would have accepted her lot, such as it was, with its shine and shade, its joy and its anguish: it came to her without her seeking, as most of the solemn things in life do; and, whatever it brought with it, it could have come from no other source than that from which all high, and holy, and pure loves ever must come—the will and permission of GOD.

Mr. Lyon himself requires no long description. In his first visit he had told Miss Leaf all about himself that there was to be known; that he was, as they were, a poor teacher, who had altogether "made himself," as so many Scotch students do. His father, whom he scarcely remembered, had been a small Ayrshire farmer; his mother was dead, and he had never had either brother or sister.

Seeing how clever Miss Hilary was, and how much as a

school-mistress she would need all the education she could get, he had offered to teach her along with her nephew; and she and Johanna were only too thankful for the advantage. But during the teaching he had also taught her another thing, which neither had contemplated at the time— to respect him with her whole soul, and to love him with her whole heart.

Over this simple fact let no more be now said. Hilary said nothing. She recognized it herself as soon as he was gone; a plain, sad, solemn truth, which there was no deceiving herself did not exist, even had she wished its nonexistence. Perhaps Johanna also found it out in her darling's extreme paleness and unusual quietness for a while; but she, too, said nothing. Mr. Lyon wrote regularly to Ascott, and once or twice to her, Miss Leaf; but, though every one knew that Hilary was his particular friend in the whole family, he did not write to Hilary. He had departed rather suddenly, on account of some plan which, he said, affected his future very considerably, but which, though he was in the habit of telling them his affairs, he did not further explain. Still Johanna knew he was a good man, and, though no man could be quite good enough for her darling, she liked him, she trusted him.

What Hilary felt none knew. But she was very girlish in some things; and her life was all before her, full of infinite hope. By-and-by her color returned, and her merry voice and laugh were heard about the house just as usual.

This being the position of affairs, it was not surprising that after Ascott's last speech Hilary's mind wandered from Dido and Æneas to vague listening, as the lad began talking of his grand future—the future of a medical student, all expenses being paid by his godfather, Mr. Ascott, the merchant, of Russell Square, once a shop-boy of Stowbury. Nor was it unnatural that all Ascott's anticipations of London resolved themselves, in his aunt's eyes, into the one fact that he would "see Mr. Lyon."

But in telling thus much about her mistresses, I have for the time being lost sight of Elizabeth Hand.

Left to herself, the girl stood for a minute or two look-ing around her in a confused manner; then, rousing her fac-ulties, began mechanically to obey the order with which her mistress had quitted the kitchen, and to wash up the tea-things. She did it in a fashion that, if seen, would have made Miss Leaf thankful the ware was only the common set, and not the cherished china belonging to former days: still she did it, noisily it is true, but actively, as if her heart were in the work. Then she took a candle and peer-ed about her new domains.

These were small enough, at least they would have seem-ed so to other eyes than Elizabeth's; for, until the school-room and box-closet above had been kindly added by the landlord, who would have done any thing to show his re-spect for the Misses Leaf, it had been merely a six-roomed cottage — parlor, kitchen, back kitchen, and three upper chambers. It was a very cozy house notwithstanding, and it seemed to Elizabeth's eyes a perfect palace.

For several minutes more she stood and contemplated her kitchen, with the fire shining on the round oaken stand in the centre, and the large wooden-bottomed chairs, and the loud-ticking clock, with its tall case, the inside of which, with its pendulum and weights, had been a perpetual mys-tery and delight, first to Hilary's, and then to Ascott's childhood. Then there was the sofa, large and ugly, but oh! so comfortable, with its faded, flowered chintz, wash-ed and worn for certainly twenty years. And, over all, Elizabeth's keen observation was attracted by a queer ma-chine apparently made of thin rope and bits of wood, which hung up to the hooks on the ceiling — an old-fashioned baby's swing. Finally, her eye dwelt with content on the blue and red diamond-tiled floor, so easily swept and mop-ped, and (only Elizabeth did not think of that, for her hard childhood had been all work and no play) so beautiful to whip tops upon! Hilary and Ascott, condoling together over the new servant, congratulated themselves that their delight in this occupation had somewhat faded, though it was really not so many years ago since one of the former's pupils, coming suddenly out of the school-room, had caught her in the act of whipping a meditative top round this same kitchen floor.

Meantime Elizabeth penetrated farther, investigating the back kitchen, with its various conveniences; especially the pantry, every shelf of which was so neatly arranged and so beautifully clean. Apparently this neatness impressed the girl with a sense of novelty and curiosity; and though she could hardly be said to meditate—her mind was not sufficiently awakened for that—still, as she stood at the kitchen fire, a slight thoughtfulness deepened the expression of her face, and made it less dull and heavy than it had at first appeared.

"I wonder which on 'em does it all. They must work pretty hard, I reckon; and two o' them's such little uns."

She stood a little while longer; for sitting down appeared to be to Elizabeth as new a proceeding as thinking; then she went up stairs, still literally obeying orders, to shut windows and pull down blinds at nightfall. The bedrooms were small, and insignificantly, nay, shabbily furnished; but the floors were spotless—ah! poor Johanna! —and the sheets, though patched and darned to the last extremity, were white and whole. Nothing was dirty, nothing untidy. There was no attempt at picturesque poverty—for, whatever novelists may say, poverty can not be picturesque; but all things were decent and in order. The house, poor as it was, gave the impression of belonging to "real ladies;" ladies who thought no manner of work beneath them, and who, whatever they had to do, took the pains to do it as well as possible.

Mrs. Hand's roughly brought-up daughter had never been in such a house before, and her examination of every new corner of it seemed quite a revelation. Her own little sleeping nook was fully as tidy and comfortable as the rest, which fact was not lost upon Elizabeth. That bright look of mingled softness and intelligence— the only thing which beautified her rugged face—came into the girl's eyes as she "turned down" the truckle-bed, and felt the warm blankets and sheets, new and rather coarse, but neatly sewed.

"Her's made 'em hersel', I reckon. La!" Which of her mistresses the "her" referred to remained unspecified; but Elizabeth, spurred to action by some new idea, went briskly back into the bedrooms, and looked about to see if there was any thing she could find to do. At last, with a sudden inspiration, she peered into a wash-stand, and found there an empty ewer. Taking it in one hand and the candle in the other, she ran down stairs.

Fatal activity! Hilary's pet cat, startled from sleep on the kitchen hearth, at the same instant ran wildly up stairs; there was a start—a stumble—and then down came the candle, the ewer, Elizabeth, and all.

It was an awful crash. It brought every member of the family to see what was the matter.

"What has the girl broken?" cried Selina.

"Where has she hurt herself?" anxiously added Johanna.

Hilary said nothing, but ran for a light, and then picked up first the servant, then the candle, and then the fragments of crockery.

"Why, it's my ewer, my favorite ewer, and it's all smashed to bits, and I never can match it. You careless, clumsy, good-for-nothing creature!"

"Please, Selina," whispered her distressed elder sister.

"Very well, Johanna. You are the mistress, I suppose; why don't you speak to your servant?"

Miss Leaf, in a humbled, alarmed way, first satisfied herself that no bodily injury had been sustained by Elizabeth, and then asked her how this disaster had happened. For a serious disaster she felt it was. Not only was the present loss annoying, but a servant with a talent for crockery breaking would be a far too expensive luxury for them to think of retaining. And she had been listening in the solitude of the parlor to a long lecture from her always dissatisfied younger sister on the great doubts Selina had about Elizabeth's "suiting."

"Come, now," seeing the girl hesitated, "tell me the plain truth. How was it?"

"It was the cat!" sobbed Elizabeth.

"What a barefaced falsehood!" exclaimed Selina. "You wicked girl, how could it possibly be the cat? Do you know you are telling a lie, and that lies are hateful, and that all liars go to—"

"Nonsense! hush!" interrupted Hilary, rather sharply; for Selina's "tongue," the terror of her childhood, now merely annoyed her. Selina's temper was a long understood household fact—they did not much mind it, knowing her bark was worse than her bite—but it was provoking that she should exhibit herself so soon before the new servant.

The latter first looked up at the lady with simple surprise: then as, in spite of the other two, Miss Selina worked herself up into a downright passion, and unlimited abuse fell upon the victim's devoted head, Elizabeth's manner changed. After one dogged repetition of "It was the cat!" not another word could be got out of her. She stood, her eyes fixed on the kitchen floor, her brows knitted, and her under lip pushed out—the very picture of sullenness. Young as she was, Elizabeth evidently had, like her unfortunate mistress, "a temper of her own" — a spiritual deformity that some people are born with, as others with hare-lip or club-foot; only, unlike these, it may be conquered, though the battle is long and sore, sometimes ending only with life.

It had plainly never commenced with poor Elizabeth Hand. Her appearance, as she stood under the flood of sharp words poured out upon her, was absolutely repulsive. Even Miss Hilary turned away, and began to think it would have been easier to teach all day and do housework half the night, than have the infliction of a servant— to say nothing of the disgrace of seeing Selina's "peculiarities" so exposed before a stranger.

She knew of old that to stop the torrent was impracticable. The only chance was to let Selina expend her wrath and retire, and then to take some quiet opportunity of explaining to Elizabeth that sharp language was only "her way," and must be put up with. Humiliating as this was, and fatal to domestic authority that the first thing to be taught a new servant was to "put up with" one of her mistresses, still there was no alternative. Hilary had already foreboded and made up her mind to such a possibility, but she had hoped it would not occur the very first evening.

It did, however, and its climax was worse even than she anticipated. Whether, irritated by the intense sullenness of the girl, Selina's temper was worse than usual, or whether, as is always the case with people like her, something else had vexed her, and she vented it upon the first cause of annoyance that occurred, certain it is that her tongue went on unchecked till it failed from sheer exhaustion. And then, as she flung herself on the sofa—oh, sad mischance!—she caught sight of her nephew standing at the school-room door, grinning with intense delight, and making faces at her behind her back.

It was too much. The poor lady had no more words left to scold with; but she rushed up to Ascott, and, big lad as he was, she soundly boxed his ears.

On this terrible climax let the curtain fall.

CHAPTER II.

COMMON as were the small feuds between Ascott and his Aunt Selina, they seldom reached such a catastrophe as that described in my last chapter. Hilary had to fly to the rescue, and literally drag the furious lad back into the school-room; while Johanna, pale and trembling, persuaded Selina to quit the field and go and lie down. This was not difficult; for the instant she saw what she had done, how she had disgraced herself and insulted her nephew, Selina felt sorry. Her passion ended in a gush of "nervous" tears, under the influence of which she was led up stairs and put to bed, almost like a child—the usual termination of these pitiful outbreaks.

For the time, nobody thought of Elizabeth. The hapless cause of all stood "spectatress of the fray" beside her kitchen fire. What she thought history saith not. Whether in her own rough home she was used to see brothers and sisters quarreling, and mothers boxing their children's ears, can not be known; whether she was or was not surprised to see the same proceedings among ladies and gentlemen, she never betrayed; but certain it is that the little servant became uncommonly serious — yes, serious rather than sulky, for her "black" looks vanished gradually—as soon as Miss Selina left the kitchen.

On the reappearance of Miss Hilary it had quite gone. But Hilary took no notice of her; she was in search of Johanna, who, shaking and cold with agitation, came slowly down stairs.

"Is she gone to bed?"

"Yes, my dear. It was the best thing for her; she is not at all well to-day."

Hilary's lip curled a little, but she replied not a word. She had not the patience with Selina that Johanna had. She drew her elder sister into the little parlor, placed her in the arm-chair, shut the door, came and sat beside her, and took her hand.

Johanna pressed it, shed a quiet tear or two, and wiped them away. Then the two sisters remained silent, with hearts sad and sore.

Every family has its skeleton in the house; this was theirs. Whether they acknowledged it or not, they knew quite well that every discomfort they had, every slight jar which disturbed the current of household peace, somehow or other originated in "poor Selina." They often called her "poor" with a sort of pity—not unneeded, Heaven knows! for if the unhappy are to be pitied, ten times more so are those who make others miserable.

This was Selina's case, and had been all her life. And, sometimes, she herself knew it. Sometimes, after an especially bad outbreak, her compunction and remorse would be almost as terrible as her passion, forcing her sisters to make every excuse for her; she "did not mean it;" it was only "ill health," or "nerves," or her "unfortunate way of taking things."

But they knew in their hearts that not all their poverty and the toils it entailed, not all the hardships and humiliations of their changed estate, were half so bitter to bear as this something—no moral crime, and yet in its results as fatal as crime—which they called Selina's "way."

Ascott was the only one who did not attempt to mince matters. When a little boy he had openly declared he hated Aunt Selina; when he grew up he as openly defied her; and it was a most difficult matter to keep even decent peace between them. Hilary's wrath had never gone farther than wishing Selina was married, that appearing the easiest way to get rid of her. Latterly she had ceased this earnest aspiration, it might be because, learning to think more seriously of marriage, she felt that a woman who is no blessing in her own household is never likely much to bless a husband's; and that, looking still farther forward, it was, on the whole, a mercy of Providence which made Selina not the mother of children.

Yet her not marrying had been somewhat a surprise, for she had been attractive in her day, handsome and agreeable in society. But perhaps, for all that, the sharp eye of the opposite sex had discovered the cloven foot, since, though she had received various promising attentions, poor Selina had never had an offer; nor, fortunately, had she ever been known to care for any body. She was one of those women who would have married as a matter of course, but who never would have been guilty of the weakness of falling in love. There seemed small probability of shipping her off, to carry into a new household the restlessness, the fretfulness, the captious fault-finding with others, the readiness to take offense at what was done and said to herself, which made poor Selina Leaf the unacknowledged grief and torment of her own.

Her two sisters sat silent. What was the use of talking? It would be only going over and over again the old thing; trying to ease and shift a little the long-familiar burden, which they knew must be borne. Nearly every household has, near or remote, some such burden, which Heaven only can lift off or help to bear. And sometimes, looking round the world outside, these two congratulated themselves, in a half sort of way, that theirs was as light as it was; that Selina was, after all, a well-meaning, well-principled woman, and, in spite of her little tempers, really fond of her family, as she truly was, at least as fond as a nature which has its centre in self can manage to be.

Only when Hilary looked, as to-night, into her eldest sister's pale face, where year by year the lines were deepening, and saw how every agitation such as the present shook her more and more—she who ought to have a quiet life and a cheerful home, after so many hard years—then Hilary, fierce in the resistance of her youth, felt as if what she could have borne for herself she could not bear for Johanna, and, at the moment, sympathized with Ascott in actually " hating" Aunt Selina.

"Where is that boy? He ought to be spoken to," Johanna said, at length, rising wearily.

"I have spoken to him; I gave him a good scolding. He is sorry, and promises never to be so rude again."

"Oh no; not till the next time," replied Miss Leaf, hopelessly. "But, Hilary," with a sudden consternation, "what are we to do about Elizabeth?"

The younger sister had thought of that. She had turned over in her mind all the pros and cons, the inevitable " worries" that would result from the presence of an additional member of the family, especially one from whom the family skeleton could not be hid—to whom it was already only too fatally revealed.

But Hilary was a clear-headed girl, and she had the rare faculty of seeing things as they really were, undistorted by her own likings or dislikings—in fact, without reference to herself at all. She perceived plainly that Johanna ought

not to do the house-work; that Selina would not, and that
she could not: *ergo*, they must keep a servant. Better,
perhaps, a small servant, over whom they could have the
same influence as over a child, than one older and more independent, who would irritate her mistresses at home, and
chatter of them abroad. Besides, they had promised Mrs.
Hand to give her daughter a fair trial. For a month, then,
Elizabeth was bound to stay; afterward, time would show.
It was best not to meet troubles half way.

This explained, in Hilary's cheerful voice, seemed greatly
to reassure and comfort her sister.

"Yes, love, you are right; she must remain her month
out, unless she does something very wrong. Do you think
that really was a lie she told?"

"About the cat? I don't quite know what to think.
Let us call her, and put the question once more. Do you
put it, Johanna. I don't think she could look at you and
tell you a story."

Other people, at sight of that sweet, grave face, its bloom
faded, and hairs silvered long before their time, yet beautiful, with an almost childlike simplicity and childlike peace
—most other people would have been of Hilary's opinion.

"Sit down; I'll call her. Dear me, Johanna, we shall
have to set up a bell as well as a servant, unless we had
managed to combine the two."

But Hilary's harmless little joke failed to make her sister smile, and the entrance of the girl seemed to excite positive apprehension. How was it possible to make excuse
to a servant for her mistress's shortcomings? how scold
for ill-doing this young girl, to whom, ere she had been a
night in the house, so bad an example had been set? Johanna half expected Elizabeth to take a leaf out of Selina's
book, and begin abusing herself and Hilary.

No; she stood very sheepish, very uncomfortable, but
not in the least bold or sulky—on the whole, looking rather penitent and humble.

Her mistress took courage.

"Elizabeth, I want you to tell me the truth about that
B

unfortunate breakage. Don't be afraid. I had rather you broke every thing in the house than have told me what was not true."

"It *was* true; it was the cat."

"How could that be possible? You were coming down stairs with the ewer in your hand."

"He got under my feet, and throwed me down, and so I tumbled, and smashed the thing agin the floor."

The Misses Leaf glanced at each other. This version of the momentous event was probable enough, and the girl's eager, honest manner gave internal confirmatory evidence pretty strong.

"I am sure she is telling the truth," said Hilary. "And remember what her mother said about her word being always reliable."

This reference was too much for Elizabeth. She burst out, not into actual crying, but into a smothered choke.

"If you donnot believe me, missus, I'd rather go home to mother."

"I do believe you," said Miss Leaf, kindly; then waited till the pinafore, used as a pocket-handkerchief, had dried up grief and restored composure.

"I can quite well understand the accident now; and I am sure, if you had put it as plainly at first, my sister would have understood it too. She was very much annoyed, and no wonder. She will be equally glad to find she was mistaken."

Here Miss Leaf paused, somewhat puzzled how to express what she felt it her duty to say, so as to be comprehended by the servant, and yet not to let down the dignity of the family. Hilary came to her aid.

"Miss Selina is sometimes hasty; but she means kindly always. You must take care not to vex her, Elizabeth; and you must never answer her back again, however sharply she speaks. It is not your business; you are only a child, and she is your mistress."

"Is her? I thought it was this 'un."

The subdued clouding of Elizabeth's face, and her blunt

pointing to Miss Leaf as "this 'un," were too much for Hilary's gravity. She was obliged to retreat to the press, and begin an imaginary search for a book.

"Yes, I am the eldest, and I suppose you may consider me specially as your mistress," said Johanna, simply. "Remember always to come to me in any difficulty; and, above all, to tell me every thing outright, as soon as it happens. I can forgive you almost any fault if you are truthful and honest; but there is one thing I never could forgive, and that is deception. Now go with Miss Hilary, and she will teach you how to make the porridge for supper."

Elizabeth obeyed silently: she had apparently a great gift for silence. And she was certainly both obedient and willing: not stupid, either, though a nervousness of temperament which Hilary was surprised to find in so big and coarse-looking a girl made her rather awkward at first. However, she succeeded in pouring out, and carrying into the parlor without accident, three platefuls of that excellent condiment which formed the frugal supper of the family, but which they ate, I grieve to say, in an orthodox Southern fashion, with sugar or treacle, until Mr. Lyon—greatly horrified thereby—had instituted his national custom of "supping" porridge with milk.

It may be a very unsentimental thing to confess, but Hilary, who, even at twenty, was rather practical than poetical, never made the porridge without thinking of Robert Lyon, and the day when he first staid to supper and ate it, or, as he said, and was very much laughed at, ate "them" with such infinite relish. Since then, whenever he came, he always asked for his porridge, saying it carried him back to his childish days. And Hilary, with that curious pleasure that women take in waiting upon any one unto whom the heart is ignorantly beginning to own the allegiance, humble yet proud, of Miranda to Ferdinand:

"To be your fellow
You may deny me; but I'll be your servant
Whether you will or no."

Hilary contrived always to make his supper herself.

Those pleasant days were now over; Mr. Lyon was gone. As she stood alone over the kitchen fire, she thought—as now and then she let herself think for a minute or two in her busy prosaic life — of that August night, standing at the front door, of his last "good-by," and last hand-clasp, tight, warm, and firm; and somehow she, like Johanna, trusted in him.

Not exactly in his love; it seemed almost impossible that *he* should love *her*, at least till she grew much more worthy of him than now; but in himself, that he would never be less himself, less thoroughly good and true than now. That, some time, he would be sure to come back again, and take up his old relations with them, brightening their dull life with his cheerfulness; infusing in their feminine household the new element of a clear, strong, energetic, manly will, which sometimes made Johanna say that instead of twenty-five the young man might be forty; and, above all, bringing into their poverty the silent sympathy of one who had fought his own battle with the world — a hard one, too, as his face sometimes showed — though he never said much about it.

Of the results of this pleasant relation — whether she, being the only truly marriageable person in the house, Robert Lyon intended to marry her, or was expected to do so, or that society would think it a very odd thing if he did not do so—this unsophisticated Hilary never thought at all. If he had said to her that the present state of things was to go on forever; she to remain always Hilary Leaf, and he Robert Lyon, the faithful friend of the family, she would have smiled in his face and been perfectly satisfied.

True, she had never had any thing to drive away the smile from that innocent face; no vague jealousies aroused; no maddening rumors afloat in the small world that was his and theirs. Mr. Lyon was grave and sedate in all his ways; he never paid the slightest attention to, or expressed the slightest interest in, any woman whatsoever.

And so this hapless girl loved him—just himself; without the slightest reference to his " connections," for he had none; or his " prospects," which, if he had any, she did not know of. Alas! to practical and prudent people I can offer no excuse for her, except, perhaps, what Shakspeare gives in the creation of his poor Miranda.

When the small servant re-entered the kitchen, Hilary, with a half sigh, shook off her dreams, called Ascott out of the school-room, and returned to the work-a-day world and the family supper.

This being ended, seasoned with a few quiet words administered to Ascott, and which, on the whole, he took pretty well, it was nearly ten o'clock.

"Far too late to have kept up such a child as Elizabeth; we must not do it again," said Miss Leaf, taking down the large Bible with which she was accustomed to conclude the day — Ascott's early hours at school and their own house-work making it difficult of mornings. Very brief the reading was, sometimes not more than half a dozen verses, with no comment thereon; she thought the Word of God might safely be left to expound itself. Being a very humble-minded woman, she did not feel qualified to lead long devotional " exercises," and she disliked formal written prayers. So she merely read the Bible to her family, and said after it the Lord's Prayer.

But, constitutionally shy as Miss Leaf was, to do even this in presence of a stranger cost her some effort ; and it was only a sense of duty that made her say " yes" to Hilary's suggestion, " I suppose we ought to call in Elizabeth ?"

Elizabeth came.

" Sit down," said her mistress; and she sat down, staring uneasily round about her, as if wondering what was going to befall her next. Very silent was the little parlor ; so small, that it was almost filled up by its large square piano, its six cane-bottomed chairs, and one easy-chair, in the which sat Miss Leaf, with the great Book in her lap.

"Can you read, Elizabeth?"

"Yes, ma'am."

"Hilary, give her a Bible."

And so Elizabeth followed, guided by her not too clean finger, the words, read in that soft, low voice, somewhere out of the New Testament; words simple enough for the comprehension of a child or a heathen. The "South-Sea Islander," as Ascott long persisted in calling her, then, doing as the family did, turned round to kneel down; but in her confusion she knocked over a chair, causing Miss Leaf to wait a minute till reverent silence was restored. Elizabeth knelt, with her eyes fixed on the wall: it was a green paper, patterned with bunches of nuts. How far she listened, or how much she understood, it was impossible to say; but her manner was decent and decorous.

"*Forgive us our trespasses, as we forgive those that trespass against us.*" Unconsciously Miss Leaf's gentle voice rested on these words, so needed in the daily life of every human being, and especially of every family. Was she the only one who thought of "poor Selina?"

They all rose from their knees, and Hilary put the Bible away. The little servant "hung about," apparently uncertain what was next to be done, or what was expected of her to do. Hilary touched her sister.

"Yes," said Miss Leaf, recollecting herself, and assuming the due authority, "it is quite time for all the family to be in bed. Take care of your candle, and mind and be up at six to-morrow morning."

This was addressed to the new maiden, who dropped a courtesy, and said, almost cheerfully, "Yes, ma'am."

"Very well. Good-night, Elizabeth."

And, following Miss Leaf's example, the other two, even Ascott, said civilly and kindly, "Good-night, Elizabeth."

CHAPTER III.

THE Christmas holidays ended, and Ascott left for London. It was the greatest household change the Misses Leaf had known for years, and they missed him sorely. Ascott was not exactly a lovable boy, and yet, after the fashion of womankind, his aunts were both fond and proud of him; fond, in their childless old-maidenhood, of any sort of nephew, and proud, unconsciously, that the said nephew was a big fellow, who could look over all their heads, besides being handsome and pleasant-mannered, and, though not clever enough to set the Thames on fire, still sufficiently bright to make them hope that in his future the family star might again rise.

There was something pathetic in these three women's idealization of him—even Selina's, who, though quarreling with him to his face, always praised him behind his back—that great, good-looking, lazy lad; who, every body else saw clearly enough, thought more of his own noble self than of all his aunts put together. The only person he stood in awe of was Mr. Lyon, for whom he always protested unbounded respect and admiration. How far Robert Lyon liked Ascott even Hilary could never quite find out; but he was always very kind to him.

There was one person in the house who, strange to say, did not succumb to the all-dominating youth. From the very first there was a smouldering feud between him and Elizabeth. Whether she overheard, and slowly began to comprehend his mocking jibes about the "South-Sea Islander," or whether her sullen and dogged spirit resisted the first attempts the lad made to "put upon her"—as he did upon his aunts, in small daily tyrannies—was never found out; but certainly Ascott, the general favorite, found little favor with the new servant. She never answered

when he "hollo'd" for her; she resisted blacking his boots
more than once a day; and she obstinately cleared the
kitchen fireplace of his "messes," as she ignominiously
termed various pots and pans belonging to what *he* called
his "medical studies."

Although the war was passive rather than aggressive,
and sometimes a source of private amusement to the aunts,
still, on the whole, it was a relief when the exciting cause
of it departed; his new and most gentlemanly portman-
teau being carried down stairs by Elizabeth herself, of her
own accord, with an air of cheerful alacrity, foreign to her
mien for some weeks past, and which, even in the midst of
the dolorous parting, amused Hilary extremely.

"I think that girl is a character," she said afterward to
Johanna. "Anyhow she has curiously strong likes and
dislikes."

"You may say that, my dear; for she brightens up
whenever she looks at you."

"Does she? Oh, that must be because I have most to
do with her. It is wonderful how friendly one gets over
saucepans and brooms, and what reverence one inspires in
the domestic mind when one really knows how to make a
bed or a pudding."

"How I wish you had to do neither!" sighed Johanna,
looking fondly at the bright face and light little figure that
was flitting about, putting the school-room to rights before
the pupils came in.

"Nonsense — I don't wish any such thing. Doing it
makes me not à whit less charming and lovely." She oft-
en applied these adjectives to herself, with the most perfect conviction that she was uttering a fiction patent to
every body. "I must be very juvenile also, for I'm certain
the fellow-passenger at the station to-day took me for Ascott's sweetheart. When we were saying good-by, an old
gentlemen who sat next him was particularly sympathetic,
and you should have seen how indignantly Ascott replied,
·'It's only *my aunt !*'"

Miss Leaf laughed, and the shadow vanished from her

face, as Hilary had meant it should. She only said, caress-
ing her,

" Well, my pet, never mind. I hope you may have a
real sweetheart some day."

" I'm in no hurry, thank you, Johanna."

But now was heard the knock after knock of the little
boys and girls, and there began that monotonous daily
round of school labor, rising from the simplicities of c, a, t,
cat, and d, o, g, dog, to the sublime heights of Pinnock
and Lennie, Télémaque and Latin Delectus. No loftier:
Stowbury being well supplied with first-class schools, and
having a vague impression that the Misses Leaf, born ladies and not brought up as governesses, were not competent educators except of very small children.

Which was true enough until lately. So Miss Leaf kept
contentedly to the c, a, t, cat, and d, o, g, dog, of the little
butchers and bakers, as Miss Selina, who taught only sewing, and came into the school-room but little during the
day, scornfully termed them. The higher branches, such
as they were, she left gradually to Hilary, who, of late,
possibly out of sympathy with a friend of hers, had begun
to show an actual gift for teaching school.

It is a gift, all will allow, and chiefly those who have,
it not, among which was poor Johanna Leaf. The admiring envy with which she watched Hilary moving briskly
about from class to class, with a word of praise to one and
rebuke to another, keeping every one's attention alive,
spurring on the dull, controlling the unruly, and exercising
over every member in this little world that influence, at
once the strongest and most intangible and inexplicable—
personal influence—was only equaled by the way in which,
at pauses in the day's work, when it grew dull and monotonous, or when the stupidity of the children ruffled her
own quiet temper beyond endurance, Hilary watched Johanna.

The time I am telling of is now long ago. The Stowbury
children, who were then little boys and girls, are now fathers
and mothers—doubtless a large proportion being decent

B 2

tradesfolk in Stowbury still; though, in this locomotive quarter, many must have drifted off elsewhere — where, Heaven knows! But not a few of them may still call to mind Miss Leaf, who first taught them their letters—sitting in her corner between the fire and the window, while the blind was drawn down to keep out, first the light from her own fading eyes, and, secondly, the distracting view of green fields and trees from the youthful eyes by her side. They may remember still her dark plain dress and her white apron, on which the primers, torn and dirty, looked half ashamed to lie; and, above all, her sweet face, and sweeter voice, never heard in any thing sharper than that grieved tone which signified their being "naughty children." They may recall her unwearied patience with the very dullest and most wayward of them; her unfailing sympathy with every infantile pleasure and pain. And I think they will acknowledge that whether she taught them much or little —in this advancing age it might be thought little—Miss Leaf taught them one thing—to love her; which, as Ben Jonson said of the Countess of Pembroke, was in itself a "liberal education."

Hilary, too. Often, when Hilary's younger and more restless spirit chafed against the monotony of her life; when, instead of wasting her days in teaching small children, she would have liked to be learning, learning—every day growing wiser and cleverer, and stretching out into that busy, bright, active world of which Robert Lyon had told her—then the sight of Johanna's meek face bent over those dirty spelling-books would at once rebuke and comfort her. She felt, after all, that she would not mind working on forever, so long as Johanna still sat there.

Nevertheless, that winter seemed to her very long, especially after Ascott was gone. For Johanna, partly for money and partly for kindliness, had added to her day's work four evenings a week, when a half-educated mother of one of her little pupils came to be taught to write a decent hand, and to keep the accounts of her shop. Upon which Selina, highly indignant, had taken to spending her evenings in the school-room, interrupting Hilary's solitary studies there by many a lamentation over the peaceful days when they all sat in the kitchen together and kept no servant. For Selina was one of those who never saw the bright side of any thing till it had gone by.

"I'm sure I don't know how we are to manage with Elizabeth. That greedy—"

"And growing," suggested Hilary.

"I say, that greedy girl eats as much as any two of us. And as for her clothes—her mother does not keep her even decent."

"She would find it difficult upon three pounds a year."

"Hilary, how dare you contradict me! I am only stating a plain fact."

"And I another. But, indeed, I don't want to talk, Selina."

"You never do, except when you are wished to be silent, and then your tongue goes like any race-horse."

"Does it? Well, like Gilpin's,

"'It carries weight, it rides a race,
'Tis for a thousand pound!'

—and I only wish it were. Heigh-ho! if I could but earn a thousand pounds!"

Selina was too vexed to reply; and for five quiet minutes Hilary bent over her Homer, which Mr. Lyon had taken such pleasure in teaching her, because, he said, she learned it faster than any of his grammar-school boys. She had forgotten all domestic grievances in a vision of Thetis and the water-nymphs, and was repeating to herself, first in the sonorous Greek, and then in Pope's small but sweet English, that catalogue of oceanic beauties ending with

"Black Janira and Janassa fair,
And Amatheia with her amber hair."

"Black, did you say? I'm sure she was as black as a chimney-sweep all to-day. And her pinafore—"

"Her what? Oh, Elizabeth, you mean—"

"Her pinafore had three rents in it, which she never thinks of mending, though I gave her needles and thread myself a week ago. But she does not know how to use them any more than a baby."

"Possibly nobody ever taught her."

"Yes; she went for a year to the National School, she says, and learned both marking and sewing."

"Perhaps she has never practiced them since. She could hardly have had time, with all the little Hands to look after, as her mother says she did. All the better for us. It makes her wonderfully patient with our troublesome brats. It was only to-day, when that horrid little Jacky Smith hurt himself so, that I saw Elizabeth take him into the kitchen, wash his face and hands, and cuddle him up and comfort him, quite motherly. Her forte is certainly children."

"You always find something to say for her."

"I should be ashamed if I could not find something to say for any body who is always abused."

Another pause—and then Selina returned to the charge.

"Have you ever observed, my dear, the extraordinary way she has of fastening, or, rather, not fastening her gown behind? She just hooks it together at the top and at the waist, while between there is a—"

"*Hiatus valde deflendus.* Oh dear me! what shall I do? Selina, how can I help it if a girl of fifteen years old is not a paragon of perfection? as of course *we* all are, if we only could find it out."

And Hilary, in despair, rose to carry her candle and books into the chilly but quiet bedroom, biting her lips the while lest she should be tempted to say something which Selina called "impertinent," which perhaps it was, from a younger sister to an elder. I do not set Hilary up as a perfect character. Through sorrow only do people go on to perfection; and sorrow, in its true meaning, this cherished girl had never known.

But that night, talking to Johanna before they went to sleep—they had always slept together since the time when the elder sister used to walk the room of nights with that puling, motherless infant in her arms—Hilary anxiously started the question of the little servant.

"I am afraid I vexed Selina greatly about her to-night; and yet what can one do? Selina is so very unjust—always expecting impossibilities. She would like to have Elizabeth at once a first-rate cook, a finished house-maid, and an attentive lady's-maid, and all without being taught! She gives her things to do, neither waiting to see if they are comprehended by her, nor showing her how to do them. Of course the girl stands gaping and staring, and does not do them, or does them so badly that she gets a thorough scolding."

"Is she very stupid, do you think?" asked Johanna, in unconscious appeal to her pet's stronger judgment.

"No, I don't. Far from stupid; only very ignorant, and—you would hardly believe it—very nervous. Selina frightens her. She gets on extremely well with me."

"Any one would, my dear. That is," added the conscientious elder sister, still afraid of making the "child" vain, "any one whom you took pains with. But do you think we ever can make any thing out of Elizabeth? Her month ends to-morrow. Shall we let her go?"

"And perhaps get in her place a story-teller—a tale-bearer—even a thief. No, no; let us

"'Rather bear the ills we have,
Than fly to others that we know not of;'

and a thief would be worse than even a South-Sea Islander."

"Oh yes, my dear," said Johanna, with a shiver.

"By-the-by, the first step in the civilization of the Polynesians was giving them clothes. And I have heard say that crime and rags often go together; that a man unconsciously feels he owes something to himself and society in the way of virtue when he has a clean face and clean shirt, and a decent coat on. Suppose we try the experiment of dressing Elizabeth. How many old gowns have we?"

The number was few. Nothing in the Leaf family was ever cast off till its very last extremity of decay; the talent that

"Gars auld claes look amaist as gude 's the new"

being especially possessed by Hilary. She counted over
her own wardrobe and Johanna's, but found nothing that
could be spared.

"Yes, my love, there is one thing. You certainly shall
never put on that old brown merino again, though you
have laid it so carefully by, as if you meant it to come out
as fresh as ever next winter. No, Hilary, you must have a
new gown, and must give Elizabeth your brown merino."

Hilary laughed, and replied not.

Now it might be a pathetic indication of a girl who had
very few clothes, but Hilary had a superstitious weakness
concerning hers. Every dress had its own peculiar chron-
icle of the scenes where it had been, the enjoyments she
had shared in it. Particular dresses were special memo-
rials of her loves, her pleasures, her little passing pains: as
long as a bit remained of the poor old fabric, the sight of
it recalled them all.

This brown merino—in which she had sat two whole
winters over her Greek and Latin by Robert Lyon's side,
which he had once stopped to touch and notice, saying
what a pretty color it was, and how he liked soft-feeling
dresses for women—to cut up this old brown merino seemed to hurt her so she could almost have cried.

Yet what would Johanna think if she refused? And
there was Elizabeth absolutely in want of clothes. "I
must be growing very wicked," thought poor Hilary.

She lay a good while silent in the dark, while Johanna
planned and replanned—calculating how, even with the
addition of an old cape of her own, which was out of the
same piece, this hapless gown could be made to fit the
gaunt frame of Elizabeth Hand. Her poor kindly brain
was in the last extremity of muddle, when Hilary, with a
desperate effort, dashed in to the rescue, and soon made all
clear, contriving body, skirt, sleeves, and all.

"You have the best head in the world, my love. I don't
know whatever I should do without you."

"Luckily you are never likely to be tried. So give me
a kiss; and good-night, Johanna."

I misdoubt many will say I am writing about small, ridiculously small things. Yet is not the whole of life made up of infinitesimally small things? And in its strange and solemn mosaic, the full pattern of which we never see clearly till looking back on it from far away, dare we say of any thing which the hand of Eternal Wisdom has put together that it is too common or too small?

CHAPTER IV.

WHILE her anxious mistresses were thus talking her over the servant lay on her humble bed and slept. They knew she did, for they heard her heavy breathing through the thin partition-wall. Whether, as Hilary suggested, she was too ignorant to notice the days of the week or month, or, as Selina thought, too stupid to care for any thing beyond eating, drinking, and sleeping, Elizabeth manifested no anxiety about herself or her destiny. She went about her work just as usual; a little quicker and readier, now she was becoming familiarized to it; but she said nothing. She was undoubtedly a girl of silent and undemonstrative nature.

"Sometimes still waters run deep," said Miss Hilary.

"Nevertheless, there are such things as canals," replied Johanna. "When do you mean to have your little talk with her?"

Hilary did not know. She was sitting, rather more tired than usual, by the school-room fire, the little people having just departed for their Saturday half-holiday. Before clearing off the *débris* which they always left behind, she stood a minute at the window, refreshing her eyes with the green field opposite, and the far-away wood, crowned by a dim white monument, visible in fair weather, on which those bright brown eyes had a trick of lingering, even in the middle of school-hours. For the wood and the hill beyond belonged to a nobleman's "show" estate five miles off—the only bit of real landscape beauty that Hilary had ever beheld. There, during the last holidays but one, she, her sisters, her nephew, and, by his own special request, Mr. Lyon, had spent a whole long, merry, midsummer day. She wondered whether such a day would ever come again.

But spring was coming again, anyhow : the field looked smiling and green, speckled here and there with white dots, which, she opined, might possibly be daisies. She half wished she was not too old and dignified to dart across the road, leap the sunk fence, and run to see.

"I think, Johanna—Hark ! what can that be ?"

For at this instant somebody came tearing down the stairs, opened the front door, and did—exactly what Hilary had just been wishing to do.

"It's Elizabeth, without her bonnet or shawl, with something white flying behind her. How she is dashing across the field ! What can she be after ? Just look."

But loud screams from Selina's room—the front one—where she had been lying in bed all morning, quite obliterated the little servant from their minds. The two sisters ran hastily up stairs.

Selina was sitting up, in undisguised terror and agitation.

"Stop her ! Hold her ! I'm sure she has gone mad. Lock the door—or she'll come back and murder us all."

"Who—Elizabeth ? Was she here ? What has been the matter ?"

But it was some time before they could make out any thing. At last they gathered that Elizabeth had been waiting upon Miss Selina, putting vinegar-cloths on her head, and doing various things about the room. "She is very handy when one is ill," even Selina allowed.

"And I assure you I was talking most kindly to her: about the duties of her position, and how she ought to dress better, and be more civil-behaved, or else she never could expect to keep any place. And she stood in her usual sulky way of listening, never answering a word— with her back to me, staring right out of window. And I had just said, ' Elizabeth, my girl'—indeed, Hilary, I was talking to her in my very kindest way—"

"I've no doubt of it—but do get on."

"When she suddenly turned round, snatched a clean towel from a chair-back, and another from my head—actually from my very head, Johanna—and out she ran. I called after her, but she took no more notice than if I had been a stone. And she left the door wide open—blowing upon me. Oh, dear; she has given me my death of cold." And Selina broke into piteous complainings.

Her elder sister soothed her as well as she could, while Hilary ran down to the front door and looked, and inquired every where for Elizabeth. She was not to be seen on field or road; and along that quiet terrace not a soul had even perceived her quit the house.

"It's a very odd thing," said Hilary, returning. "What can have come over the girl? You are sure, Selina, that you said nothing which—"

"Now I know what you are going to say. You are going to blame me. Whatever happens in this house you always blame me. And perhaps you're right. Perhaps I am a nuisance—a burden—would be far better dead and buried. I wish I were!"

When Selina took this tack, of course her sisters were silenced. They quieted her a little, and then went down and searched the house all over.

All was in order—at least in as much order as was to be expected the hour before dinner. The bowl of half-peeled potatoes stood on the back kitchen "sink;" the roast was down before the fire; the knives were ready for cleaning. Evidently Elizabeth's flight had not been premeditated.

"It's all nonsense about her going mad. She has as sound a head as I have," said Hilary to Johanna, who began to look seriously uneasy. "She might have run away in a fit of passion, certainly; and yet that is improbable; her temper is more sullen than furious. And, having no lack of common sense, she must know that doing a thing like this is enough to make her lose her place at once."

Yes," said Johanna, mournfully, "I'm afraid after this she must go."

" Wait and see what she has to say for herself," pleaded Hilary. "She will surely be back in two or three minutes."

But she was not, nor even in two or three hours.

Her mistresses' annoyance became displeasure, and that again subsided into serious apprehension. Even Selina ceased talking over and over the incident which gave the sole information to be arrived at; rose, dressed, and came down to the kitchen. There, after long and anxious consultation, Hilary, observing that "somebody had better do something," began to prepare the dinner, as in pre-Elizabethan days; but the three ladies' appetites were small.

About three in the afternoon, Hilary, giving utterance to the hidden alarm of all, said,

" I think, sisters, I had better go down as quickly as I can to Mrs. Hand's."

This agreed, she stood consulting with Johanna as to what could possibly be said to the mother in case that unfortunate child had not gone home, when the kitchen door opened, and the culprit appeared.

Not, however, with the least look of a culprit. Hot she was, and breathless; and with her hair down about her ears, and her apron rolled up round her waist, presented a most forlorn and untidy aspect; but her eyes were bright, and her countenance glowing.

She took a towel from under her arm. "There's one on 'em—and you'll get back—the other—when it's washed."

Having blurted out this, she leaned against the wall, trying to recover her breath.

" Elizabeth ! Where have you been ? How dared you go ? Your behavior is disgraceful — most disgraceful, I say. Johanna, why don't you speak to your servant ?" (When, for remissness in reproving others, the elder sister fell herself under reproof, it was always emphatically "*your* sister"—"*your* nephew"—"*your* servant.")

But, for once, Miss Selina's sharp voice failed to bring the customary sullen look to Elizabeth's face, and when

Miss Leaf, in her milder tones, asked where she had been, she answered unhesitatingly,

"I've been down the town."

"Down the town!" the three ladies cried, in one chorus of astonishment.

"I've been as quick as I could, missis. I runned all the way, there and back; but it was a good step, and he was some'at heavy, though he is but a little 'un."

"He! who on earth is *he?*"

"Deary me! I never thought of axing; but his mother lives in Hall Street. Somebody saw me carrying him to the doctor, and went and told her. Oh! he was welly killed, Miss Leaf—the doctor said so; but he'll do now, and you'll get your towel clean washed to-morrow."

While Elizabeth spoke so incoherently, and with such unwonted energy and excitement, Johanna looked as if she thought her sister's fears were true, and the girl had really gone mad; but Hilary's quicker perceptions jumped at a different conclusion.

"Quiet yourself, Elizabeth," said she, taking a firm hold of her shoulder, and making her sit down, when the rolled-up apron dropped, and showed itself all covered with blood-spots. Selina screamed outright.

Then Elizabeth seemed to become half conscious that she had done something blamable, or was at least a suspected character. Her warmth of manner faded; the sullen cloud of dogged resistance to authority was raging in her poor dirty face, when Hilary, beginning with "Now, we are not going to scold you, but we must hear the reason of this," contrived by adroit questions, and not a few of them, to elicit the whole story.

It appeared that, while standing at Miss Selina's window, Elizabeth had watched three little boys apparently engaged in a very favorite amusement of little boys in that field—going quickly behind a horse, and pulling out the longest and handsomest hairs in his tail to make fishing-lines of. She saw the animal give a kick, and two of the boys ran away; the other did not stir. For a minute or so she noticed a black lump lying in the grass; then, with the quick instinct for which nobody had ever given her credit, she guessed what had happened, and did immediately the wisest and only thing possible under the circumstances, namely, to snatch up a towel, run across the field, bind up the child's head as well as she could, and carry it, bleeding and insensible, to the nearest doctor, who lived nearly a mile off.

She did not tell—and they only found it out afterward —how she had held the boy while under the doctor's hands, the skull being so badly fractured that the frightened mother fainted at the sight; how she had finally carried him home, and left him comfortably settled in bed, his senses returned, and his life saved.

"Ay, my arms do ache above a bit," she said, in answer to Miss Leaf's questions. "He wasn't quite a baby—nigh upon twelve, I reckon; but then he was very small of his age. And he looked just as if he was dead—and he bled so."

Here, just for a second or two, the color left the big girl's lips, and she trembled a little. Miss Leaf went to the kitchen cupboard, and took out their only bottle of wine—administered in rare doses, exclusively as medicine.

"Drink this, Elizabeth; and then go and wash your face and eat your dinner. We will talk to you by-and-by."

Elizabeth looked up with a long, wistful stare of intense surprise, and then added, "Have I done any thing wrong, missis?"

"I did not say so. But drink this, and don't talk, child."

She was obeyed. By-and-by Elizabeth disappeared into the back kitchen, emerged thence with a clean face, hands, and apron, and went about her afternoon business as if nothing had happened.

Her mistresses' threatened "talk" with her never came about. What, indeed, could they say? No doubt the little servant had broken the strict letter of domestic law by running off in that highly eccentric and inconvenient way; but, as Hilary tried to explain by a series of most ingenious ratiocinations, she had fulfilled, in the spirit of it, the very highest law—that of charity. She had also shown prompt courage, decision, practical and prudent forethought, and, above all, entire self-forgetfulness.

"And I should like to know," said Miss Hilary, warming with her subject, "if those are not the very qualities which go to constitute a hero."

"But we don't want a hero; we want a maid-of-all-work."

"I'll tell you what we want, Selina. We want a *woman*—that is, a girl with the making of a good woman in her. If we can find that, all the rest will follow. For my part, I would rather take this child, rough as she is, but with her truthfulness, conscientiousness, kindliness of heart, and evident capability of both self-control and self-devotedness, than the most finished servant we could find. My advice is—keep her."

This settled the matter, since it was a curious fact that the "advice" of the youngest Miss Leaf was, whether they knew it or not, almost equivalent to a family ukase.

When Elizabeth had brought in the tea-things, which she did with especial care, apparently wishing to blot out the memory of the morning's escapade by astonishingly good behavior for the rest of the day, Miss Leaf called her, and asked if she knew that her month of trial ended this day.

"Yes, ma'am," with the strict formal courtesy, something between that of the old-world family domestic—as her mother might have been to the Miss Elizabeth Something she was named after—and the abrupt "dip" of the modern national school-girl, which constituted Elizabeth Hand's sole experience of manners.

"If you had not been absent I should have gone to speak to your mother to-day. Indeed, Miss Hilary was going when you came in; but it would have been with a very different intention from what we had in the morning. However, that is not likely to happen again."

"Eh?" said Elizabeth, inquiringly.

Miss Leaf hesitated, and looked uneasily at her two sisters.   It was always a trial to her shy nature to find herself the mouth-piece of the family; and this same shyness made it still more difficult to break through the stiff barriers which seemed to rise up between her, a gentlewoman well on in years, and this coarse working-girl.   She felt, as she often complained, that with the kindest intentions she did not quite know how to talk to Elizabeth.

"My sister means," said Hilary, "that as we are not likely to have little boys half killed in the field every day, she trusts you will not be running away again as you did this morning.   She feels sure that you would not do such a thing, putting us all to so great annoyance and uneasiness, for any less cause than such as happened to-day.   You promise that?"

"Yes, Miss Hilary."

"Then we quite forgive you as regards ourselves.   Nay"—feeling, in spite of Selina's warning nudge, that she had hardly been kind enough—"we rather praise than blame you, Elizabeth.   And if you like to stay with us, and will do your best to improve, we are willing to keep you as our servant."

"Thank you, ma'am.   Thank you, Miss Hilary.   Yes, I'll stop."

She said no more, but sighed a great sigh, as if her mind were relieved—("So," thought Hilary, "she was not so indifferent to us as we imagined")—and bustled back into her kitchen.

"Now for the clothing of her," observed Miss Leaf, also looking much relieved that the decision was over.   "You know what we agreed upon, and there is certainly no time to be lost.   Hilary, my dear, suppose you bring down your brown merino?"

Hilary went without a word.

People who inhabit the same house, eat, sit, and sleep together—loving one another and sympathizing with one another ever so deeply and dearly—nevertheless inevitably have momentary seasons when the intense solitude in

which we all live, and must expect ever to live, at the
depth of our being, forces itself painfully upon the heart.
Johanna must have had many such seasons when Hilary
was a child; Hilary had one now.

She unfolded the old frock, and took out, of its pocket—
a hiding-place at once little likely to be searched and harmless if discovered, a poor little memento of that happy midsummer day:

"*Dear Miss Hilary,—To-morrow, then, I shall come.
Yours truly, Robert Lyon.*"

The only scrap of note she had ever received; he always wrote to Johanna—as regularly as ever, or more so,
now Ascott was gone—but only to Johanna. She read
over the two lines, wondered where she should keep them
now that Johanna might not notice them, and then recoiled, as if the secret were a wrong to that dear sister who
loved her so well.

"But nothing makes me love her less; nothing ever
could. She thinks me quite happy; so I am; and yet—
oh, if I did not miss him so!"

And the aching, aching want which sometimes came
over her began again. Let us not blame her. God made
all our human needs. God made love; not merely affection, but actual *love*—the necessity to seek and find out
some other being; not another, but the complement of
one's self—the "other half" who brings rest and strength
for weakness, sympathy in aspiration, and tenderness for
tenderness, as no other person ever can. Perhaps, even in
marriage, this love is seldom found, and it is possible in all
lives to do without it. Johanna had done so. But then
she had been young, and was now growing old; and Hilary was only twenty, with a long life before her. Poor
child! let us not blame her.

She was not in the least sentimental, her natural disposition inclining her to be more than cheerful—actually gay.
She soon recovered herself; and when, a short time after,
she stood, scissors in hand, demonstrating how very easy
it was to make something out of nothing, her sisters never

suspected how very near tears had lately been to those bright eyes, which were always the sunshine of the house.

"You are giving yourself a world of trouble," said Selina. "If I were you I would just make over the dress to Elizabeth, and let her do what she could with it."

"My dear, I always find I give myself twice the trouble by expecting people to do what they can't do. I have to do it myself afterward. Prove how a child who can't even handle a needle and thread is competent to make a gown for herself, and I shall be most happy to secede in her favor."

"Nay," put in the eldest sister, afraid of a collision of words, "Selina is right; if you do not teach Elizabeth to make her own gowns, how can she learn ?"

"Johanna, you are the brilliantest of women! and you know you don't like the parlor littered with rags and cuttings. You wish to get rid of me for the evening? Well, I'll go! Hand me the work-basket and the bundle, and I'll give my first lesson in dress-making to our South-Sea Islander."

But Fate stood in the way of Miss Hilary's good intentions.

She found Elizabeth, not as was her wont, always busy over the perpetual toil of those who have not yet learned the mysterious art of arrangement and order, nor, as sometimes, hanging sleepily over the kitchen fire, waiting for bedtime, but actually sitting—sitting down at the table. Her candle was flaring on one side of her; on the other was the school-room ink-stand, a scrap of waste paper, and a pen. But she was not writing; she sat with her head on her hands, in an attitude of disconsolate idleness, so absorbed that she seemed not to hear Hilary's approach.

"I did not know you could write, Elizabeth."

"No more I can," was the answer, in the most doleful of voices. "It bean't no good. I've forgotten all about it. T' letters wonna join."

"Let me look at them." And Hilary tried to contemplate gravely the scrawled and blotted page, which looked very much as if a large spider had walked into the ink-bottle and then walked out again on a tour of investigation. "What did you want to write?" asked she, suddenly.

Elizabeth blushed violently. "It was the woman, Mrs. Cliffe, t' little lad's mother, you know; she wanted somebody to write to her husband as is at work in Birmingham, and I said I would. I'd learned at the National, but I've forgotten it all. I'm just as Miss Selina says—I'm good for nowt."

"Come, come, never fret;" for there was a sort of choke in the girl's voice. "There's many a good person who never learned to write. But I don't see why you should not learn. Shall I teach you?"

Utter amazement, beaming gratitude, succeeded one another plain as light in Elizabeth's eyes; but she only said, "Thank you, Miss Hilary."

"Very well. I have brought you an old gown of mine, and was going to show you how to make it up for yourself, but I'll look over your writing instead. Sit down, and let me see what you can do."

In a state of nervous trepidation pitiful to behold, Elizabeth took the pen. Terrible scratching resulted; blots innumerable; and one fatal deluge of ink, which startled from their seats both mistress and maid, and made Hilary thankful that she had taken off her better gown for a common one, as, with sad thriftiness, the Misses Leaf always did of evenings.

When Elizabeth saw the mischief she had done, her contrition and humility were unbounded. "No, Miss Hilary, you can't make nothin' of me. I be too stupid. I'll give it up."

"Nonsense!" And the bright, active little lady looked steadily into the heavy face of this undeveloped girl, half child, half woman, until some of her own spirit seemed to be reflected there. Whether the excitement of the morning had roused her, or her mistresses' kindness had touched Elizabeth's heart, and—as in most women—the heart was

C

the key to the intellect; or whether the gradual daily influence of her changed life during the last month had been
taking effect, now for the first time to appear, certain it is
that Hilary had never perceived before what an extremely
intelligent face it was—what good sense was indicated in
the well-shaped head and forehead—what tenderness and
feeling in the deep-set gray eyes.

"Nonsense," repeated she. "Never give up any thing;
I never would. We'll try a different plan, and begin from
the beginning, as I do with my little scholars. Wait while
I fetch a copy-book out of the parlor press."

She highly amused her sisters with a description of what
she called "her newly-instituted Polynesian Academy," returned, and set to work to guide the rough, coarse hand
through the mysteries of caligraphy.

To say this was an easy task would not be true. Nature's own laws and limits make the using of faculties
which have been unused for generations very difficult at
first. To suppose that a working man, the son of working
men, who applies himself to study, does it with as little
trouble as your upper-class children, who have been unconsciously undergoing education ever since the cradle, is a
great mistake. All honor, therefore, to those who do attempt, and to ever so small a degree succeed in the best
and surest culture of all, self-culture.

Of this honor Elizabeth deserved her share.

"She is stupid enough," Hilary confessed, after the lesson was over; "but there is a dogged perseverance about
the girl which I actually admire. She blots her fingers,
her nose, her apron, but she never gives in; and she sticks
to the grand principle of one thing at a time. I think she
did two whole pages of a's, and really performed them satisfactorily, before she asked to go on to b's. Yes, I believe she will do."

"I hope she will do her work, any how," said Selina,
breaking into the conversation rather crossly. "I'm sure
I don't see the good of wasting time over teaching Elizabeth to write when there's so much to be done in the house

by one and all of us from Monday morning till Saturday night."

"Ay, that's it," answered Hilary, meditatively. "I don't see how I ever shall get time to teach her, and she is so tired of nights when the work is all done; she'll be dropping asleep with the pen in her hand—I have done it myself before now."

Ay, in those days when, trying so hard to "improve her mind," and make herself a little more equal and companionable to another mind she knew, she had, after her daily house cares and her six hours of school-teaching, attempted at nine P.M. to begin close study on her own account. And though with her strong will she succeeded tolerably, still, as she told Johanna, she could well understand how slow was the "march of intellect" (a phrase which had just then come up) among day-laborers and the like; and how difficult it was for these Mechanics' Institutions, which were now talked so much of, to put any new ideas into the poor tired heads, rendered sluggish and stupid with hard bodily labor.

"Suppose I were to hold my Polynesian Academy on a Sunday?" and she looked inquiringly at her sisters, especially Johanna.

Now the Misses Leaf were old-fashioned country-folk, who lived before the words Sabbatarian and un-Sabbatarian had ever got into the English language. They simply "remembered the Sabbath-day to keep it holy;" they arranged so as to make it for all the household a day of rest; and they went regularly to church once—sometimes Selina and Hilary went twice. For the intervening hours, their usual custom was to take an afternoon walk in the fields: begun chiefly for Ascott's sake, to keep the lad out of mischief, and put into his mind better thoughts than he was likely to get from his favorite Sunday recreation of sitting on the wall throwing stones. After he left for London there was Elizabeth to be thought of; and they decided that the best Sabbath duty for the little servant was to go and see her mother. So they gave her every Sunday aft-

ernoon free, only requiring that she should be at home
punctually after church-time, at eight o'clock. But from
thence till bedtime was a blank two hours, which, Hilary
had noticed, Elizabeth not unfrequently spent in dozing
over the fire.

"And I wonder," said she, giving the end of her long
meditation out loud, "whether going to sleep is not as
much Sabbath-breaking as learning to write? What do
you say, Johanna?"

Johanna, simple, God-fearing woman as she was, to whom
faith and love came as natural as the breath she drew, had
never perplexed herself with the question. She only smiled
acquiescence. But Selina was greatly shocked. Teaching
to write on a Sunday! Bringing the week-day work into
the day of rest! Doing one's own pleasure on the holy
day! She thought it exceedingly wrong. Such a thing
had never been heard of in their house. Whatever else
might be said of them, the Leafs were always a respectable family as to keeping Sunday. Nobody could say that
even poor Henry—

But here Selina's torrent of words stopped.

When conversation revived, Hilary, who had been at
first half annoyed and half amused, resumed her point seriously.

"I might say that writing isn't Elizabeth's week-day
work, and that teaching her is not exactly doing my own
pleasure; but I won't creep out of the argument by a quib-
ble. The question is, *What* is keeping the Sabbath-day
'holy?' I say—and I stick to my opinion—that it is by
making it a day of worship, a rest day—a cheerful and
happy day—and by doing as much good in it as we can;
and, therefore, I mean to teach Elizabeth on a Sunday."

"She'll never understand it. She'll consider it 'work.'"

"And if she did, work is a more religious thing than
idleness. I am sure I often feel that, of the two, I should
be less sinful in digging potatoes in my garden, or sitting
mending stockings in my parlor, than in keeping Sunday
as some people do—going to church genteelly in my best

clothes, eating a huge Sunday dinner, and then nodding over a good book, or taking a regular Sunday nap, till bedtime."

"Hush, child!" said Johanna, reprovingly; for Hilary's cheeks were red, and her voice angry. She was taking the hot, youthful part, which, in its hatred of shams and forms, sometimes leads—and not seldom led poor Hilary—a little too far on the other side. "I think," Miss Leaf added, "that our business is with ourselves, and not with our neighbors. Let us keep the Sabbath according to our conscience. Only, I would take care never to do any thing which jarred against my neighbor's feelings. I would, like Paul, 'eat no meat while the world standeth' rather than 'make my brother to offend.'"

Hilary looked in her sister's sweet, calm face, and the anger died out of her own.

"Shall I give up my academy?" she said, softly.

"No, my love. It is lawful to do good on the Sabbath-day, and teaching a poor ignorant girl to write is an absolute good. Make her understand that, and you need not be afraid of any harm ensuing."

"You never will make her understand," said Selina, sullenly. "She is only a servant."

"Nevertheless, I'll try."

Hilary could not tell how far she succeeded in simplifying to the young servant's comprehension this great question, involving so many points—such as the following of the spirit and the letter, the law of duty and the compulsion of love, which, as she spoke, seemed opening out so widely and awfully that she herself involuntarily shrank from it, and wondered that poor finite creatures should ever presume to squabble about it at all.

But one thing the girl did understand—her young mistress's kindness. She stood watching the little delicate hand that had so patiently guided hers, and now wrote copy after copy for her future benefit. At last she said,

"You're taking a deal o' trouble wi' a poor wench, and it's very kind in a lady like you."

Miss Hilary was puzzled what answer to make. True enough, it was "kind," and she was a "lady;" and between her and Mrs. Hand's rough daughter was an unmistakable difference and distinction. That Elizabeth perceived it was proved by her growing respectfulness of manner—the more respectful, it seemed, the more she herself improved. Yet Hilary could not bear to make her feel more sharply than was unavoidable the great gulf that lies, and ever must lie—not so much between mistress and servant, in their abstract relation—(and yet that is right, for the relation and authority is ordained of God)—but between the educated and the ignorant, the coarse and the refined.

"Well," she said, after a pause of consideration, "you always have it in your power to repay my 'kindness,' as you call it. The cleverer you become, the more useful you will be to me; and the more good you grow, the better I shall like you."

Elizabeth smiled—that wonderfully bright, sudden smile which seemed to cover over all her plainness of feature.

"Once upon a time," Hilary resumed by-and-by, "when England was very different from what it is now, English ladies used to have what they call 'bower-women,' whom they took as girls, and brought up in their service; teaching them all sorts of things—cooking, sewing, spinning, singing, and, probably, except that the ladies of that time were very ill educated themselves, to read and write also. They used to spend part of every day among their bower-women; and as people can only enjoy the company of those with whom they have some sympathy in common, we must conclude that—"

Here Hilary stopped, recollecting she must be discoursing miles above the head of *her* little bower-maiden, and that, perhaps, after all, her theory would be best kept to herself, and only demonstrated practically.

"So, Elizabeth, if I spend a little of my time in teaching you, you must grow up my faithful and attached bower-maiden."

"I'll grow up any thing, Miss Hilary, if it's to please

you," was the answer, given with a smothered intensity that quite startled the young mistress.

"I do believe the girl is getting fond of me," said she, half touched, half laughing, to Johanna. "If so, we shall get on. It is just as with our school-children, you know. We have to seize hold of their hearts first, and their heads afterward. Now Elizabeth's head may be uncommonly tough, but I do believe she likes me."

Johanna smiled; but she would not for the world have said—never encouraging the smallest vanity in her child —that she did not think this circumstance so very remarkable.

CHAPTER V.

A HOUSEHOLD exclusively composed of women has its advantages and its disadvantages. It is apt to become somewhat narrow in judgment, morbid in feeling, absorbed in petty interests, and bounding its vision of outside things to the small horizon which it sees from its own fireside. But, on the other hand, by this fireside often abides a settled peace and purity, a long-suffering, generous forbearance, and an enduring affectionateness which the other sex can hardly comprehend or credit. Men will not believe, what is nevertheless the truth, that we can "stand alone" much better than they can; that we can do without them far easier, and with less deterioration of character, than they can do without us; that we are better able to provide for ourselves interests, duties, and pleasures; in short, strange as it may appear, that we have more real self-sustaining independence than they.

Of course, that the true life, the highest life, is that of man and woman united, no one will be insane enough to deny; I am speaking of the substitute for it, which poor humanity has so often to fall back upon and make the best of —a better best very frequently than what appears best in the eyes of the world. In truth, many a troubled, care-ridden, wealthy family, torn with dissensions, or frozen up in

splendid formalities, might have envied that quiet, humble
maiden household of the Misses Leaf, where their only trial
was poverty, and their only grief the one which they knew
the worst of, and had met patiently for many a year—poor
Selina's " way."

I doubt not it was good for Elizabeth Hand that her first
place—the home in which she received her first impressions
—was this feminine establishment, simple and regular, in
which was neither waste nor disorder allowed. Good, too,
that while her mistresses' narrow means restricted her in
many things enjoyed by servants in richer families, their
interests, equally narrow, caused to be concentrated upon
herself a double measure of thought and care. She became
absolutely " one of the family," sharing in all its concerns.
From its small and few carnal luxuries—such as the cake,
fruit, or pot of preserves, votive offerings from pupils' parents—up to the newspaper and the borrowed book, nothing was either literally or metaphorically "locked up"
from Elizabeth.

This grand question of locking-up had been discussed in
full conclave the day after her month of probation ended,
the sisters taking opposite sides, as might have been expected. Selina was for the immediate introduction of a
locksmith and a key-basket.

" While she was only on trial it did not so much signify; besides, if it did, we had only buttons on the press-
doors; but now she is our regular servant we ought to in-
stitute a regular system of authority. How can she respect a family that never locks up any thing ?"

" How can we respect a servant from whom we lock up
every thing ?"

" Respect a servant !   What do you mean, Hilary ?"

" I mean that if I did not respect a servant I would be
very sorry to keep her one day in any house of mine."

" Wait till you've a house of your own to keep, miss,"
said Selina, crossly. " I never heard such nonsense. Is
that the way you mean to behave to Elizabeth ? leave every thing open to her—clothes, books, money; trust her

with all your secrets; treat her as your most particular friend?"

"A girl of fifteen would be rather an inconvenient particular friend! And I have happily few secrets to trust her with. But if I could not trust her with our coffee, tea, sugar, and so on, and bring her up from the very first in the habit of being trusted, I would recommend her being sent away to-morrow."

"Very fine talking; and what do you say, Johanna?— if that is not an unnecessary question after Hilary has given her opinion."

"I think," replied the elder sister, taking no notice of the long-familiar innuendo, "that in this case Hilary is right. How people ought to manage in great houses I can not say, but in our small house it will be easier and better not to alter our simple ways. Trusting the girl, if she is a good girl, will only make her the more trustworthy; if she is bad, we shall the sooner find it out and let her go."

But Elizabeth did not go. A year passed; two years; her wages were raised, and with them her domestic position. From a "girl" she was converted into a regular servant; her pinafores gave place to grown-up gowns and aprons, and her rough head, at Miss Selina's incessant instance, was concealed by a cap—caps being considered by that lady as the proper and indispensable badge of servanthood.

To say that during her transition state, or even now that she had reached the cap era, Elizabeth gave her mistresses no trouble, would be stating a self-evident improbability. What young lass under seventeen, of any rank, does not cause plenty of trouble to her natural guardians? Who can "put an old head on young shoulders?" or expect from girls at the most unformed and unsatisfactory period of life that complete moral and mental discipline, that unfailing self-control, that perfection of temper and every thing else, which, of course, all mistresses always have?

I am obliged to confess that Elizabeth had a few—nay,

C 2

not a few—most obstinate faults; that no child tries its
parents, no pupil its school-teachers, more than she tried
her three mistresses at intervals. She was often thoughtless and careless, brusque in her manner, slovenly in her
dress; sometimes she was downright "bad"—filled full, as
some of her elders and betters are at all ages, with absolute
naughtiness; when she would sulk for hours and days together, and make the whole family uncomfortable, as many
a servant can make many a family small as that of the
Misses Leaf.

But still they never lost what Hilary termed their "respect" for Elizabeth; they never found her out in a lie, a
meanness, or an act of deception or dishonesty. They took
her faults as we must take the surface-faults of all connected with us—patiently rather than resentfully, seeking to
correct rather than to punish. And though there were
difficult elements in the household, such as there being
three mistresses to be obeyed—the youngest mistress a
thought too lax, and the second one undoubtedly too severe—still no girl could live with these high-principled,
much-enduring women without being impressed with two
things which the serving class are slowest to understand
—the dignity of poverty, and the beauty of that which is
the only effectual law to bring out good and restrain evil,
the law of loving-kindness.

Two fracases, however, must be chronicled, for after both
the girl's dismissal hung on a thread. The first was when
Mrs. Cliffe, mother of Tommy Cliffe, who was nearly killed
in the field, being discovered to be an ill sort of woman,
and in the habit of borrowing from Elizabeth stray shillings which were never returned, was forbidden the house,
Elizabeth resented it so fiercely that she sulked for a whole
week afterward.

The other and still more dangerous crisis in Elizabeth's
destiny was when a volume of Scott's novels, having been
missing for some days, was found hidden in her bed, and
she lying awake reading it, was thus ignominiously discovered at eleven P.M. by Miss Selina, in consequence of the
gleam of candle-light from under her door.

It was true, neither of these errors were actual moral crimes. Hilary even roused a volley of sharp words upon herself by declaring they had their source in actual virtues; that a girl who would stint herself of shillings, and hold resolutely to any liking she had, even if unworthy, had a creditable amount of both self-denial and fidelity in her disposition. Also that a tired-out maid-of-all-work, who was kept awake of nights by her ardent appreciation of the "Heart of Mid-Lothian," must possess a degree of both intellectual and moral capacity which deserved cultivation rather than blame. And though this surreptitious pursuit of literature under difficulties could not, of course, be allowed, I grieve to say that Miss Hilary took every opportunity of not only giving the young servant books to read, but of talking to her about them. And also that a large proportion of these books were, to Miss Selina's unmitigated horror, absolutely fiction!—stories, novels, even poetry—books that Hilary liked herself—books that had built up in her her own passionate dream of life; wherein all the women were faithful, tender, heroic, self-devoted, and all the men were—something not unlike Robert Lyon.

Did she do harm? Was it, as Selina and even Johanna said sometimes, "dangerous" thus to put before Elizabeth a standard of ideal perfection, a Quixotic notion of life— life in its full purpose, power, and beauty—such as otherwise never could have crossed the mind of this poor working-girl, born of parents who, though respectable and worthy, were in no respect higher than the common working class? I will not argue the point: I am not making Elizabeth a text for a sermon; I am simply writing her story.

One thing was certain—that by degrees the young woman's faults lessened; even that worst of them, the unmistakable bad temper, not aggressive, but obstinately sullen, which made her and Miss Selina sometimes not on speaking terms for a week together. But she simply "sulked;" she never grumbled or was pert; and she did her work just as usual, with a kind of dogged struggle not only against the superior powers, but against something within herself much harder to fight with.

"She makes me feel more sorry for her than angry with her," Miss Leaf would sometimes say, coming out of the kitchen with that grieved face which was the chief sign of displeasure her sweet nature ever betrayed. "She will have up-hill work through life, like us all, and more than many of us, poor child!"

But gradually Elizabeth, too, copying involuntarily the rest of the family, learned to put up with Miss Selina, who, on her part, kept a sort of armed neutrality. And once, when a short but sharp illness of Johanna's shook the household from its even tenor, startled every body out of their little tempers, and made them cling together and work together in a sort of fear-stricken union against one common grief, Selina allowed that they might have gone farther and fared worse on the day they engaged Elizabeth.

After this illness of his aunt Ascott came home. It was his first visit since he had gone to London; Mr. Ascott, he said, objected to holidays. But now, from some unexplained feeling, Johanna in her convalescence longed after the boy—no longer a boy, however, but nearly twenty, and looking fully his age. How proud his aunts were to march him up the town, and hear every body's congratulations on his good looks and polished manners! It was the old story—old as the hills! I do not pretend to invent any thing new. Women, especially maiden aunts, will repeat the tale till the end of time, so long as they have youths belonging to them on whom to expend their natural tendency to clinging fondness, and ignorant, innocent hero-worship. The Misses Leaf—ay, even Selina, whose irritation against the provoking boy was quite mollified by the elegant young man—were no wiser than their neighbors.

But there was one person in the household who still obstinately refused to bow the knee to Ascott. Whether it was, as psychologists might explain, some instinctive polarity in their natures, or whether, having once conceived a prejudice, Elizabeth held on to it like grim death, still there was the same unspoken antagonism between them. The young fellow took little notice of her except to observe "that she hadn't grown any handsomer;" but Elizabeth watched him with a keen severity that overlooked nothing, and resisted, with a passive pertinacity that was quite irresistible, all his encroachments on the family habits, all the little self-pleasing ways which Ascott had been so used to of old that neither he nor his aunts apparently recognized them as selfish.

"I canna bear to see him" ("*can not*," suggested her mistress, who, not seeing any reason why Elizabeth should not speak the Queen's English as well as herself, had instituted *h's*, and stopped a few more glaring provincialisms). "I can not bear to see him, Miss Hilary, lolling on the arm-chair when missis looks so tired and pale, and sitting up o' nights, burning double fires, and going up stairs at last with his boots on, waking every body. I dunnot like it, I say."

"You forget; Mr. Ascott has his studies. He must work for his next examination."

"Why doesn't he get up of a morning, then, instead of lying in bed, and keeping the breakfast about till ten? Why can't he do his learning by daylight? Daylight's cheaper than mould candles, and a deal better for the eyes."

Hilary was puzzled. A truth was a truth, and to try and make it out otherwise, even for the dignity of the family, was something from which her honest nature revolted. Besides, the sharp-sighted servant would be the first to detect the inconsistency of one law of right for the parlor and another for the kitchen. So she took refuge in silence and in the apple-pudding she was making.

But she resolved to seize the first opportunity of giving Ascott, by way of novelty, the severest lecture that tongue of aunt could bestow. And this chance occurred the same afternoon, when the other two aunts had gone out to tea to a house which Ascott voted "slow," and declined going to. She remained to make tea for him, and in the mean time took him for a constitutional up and down the public walks hard by.

Ascott listened at first very good-humoredly, once or twice calling her "a dear little prig" in his patronizing way—he was rather fond of patronizing his Aunt Hilary. But when she seriously spoke of his duties, as no longer a boy, but a man, who ought now to assume the true, manly right of thinking for and taking care of other people, especially his aunts, Ascott began to flush up angrily.

"Now stop that, Aunt Hilary; I'll not have you coming Mr. Lyon over me."

"What do you mean?"

For of late Ascott had said very little about Mr. Lyon —not half so much as Mr. Lyon, in his steadily persistent letters to Miss Leaf, told her about her nephew Ascott.

"I mean that I'll not be preached to like that by a woman. It's bad enough to have to stand it from a man; but then Lyon's a real sharp fellow, who knows the world, which women don't, Aunt Hilary. Besides, he coaches me in my Latin and Greek; so I let him pitch into me now and then. But I won't let *you;* so just stop it, will you?"

Something new in Ascott's tone—speaking more of the resentful fierceness of the man than the pettishness of the boy—frightened his little aunt, and silenced her. By-and-by she took comfort from the reflection that, as the lad had in his anger betrayed, he had beside him in London a monitor whose preaching would be so much wiser and more effectual than her own that she determined to say no more.

The rare hearing of Mr. Lyon's name—for, time and absence having produced their natural effect, except when his letters came, he was seldom talked about now—set Hilary thinking.

"Do you go to see him often?" she said at last.

"Who — Mr. Lyon?" And Ascott, delighted to escape into a fresh subject, became quite cheerful and communicative. "Oh, bless you! he wouldn't care for my going to him. He lives in a two-pair back, only one room, 'which serves him for kitchen, and parlor, and all;' dines at a cook-shop for ninepence a day, and makes his own porridge night and morning. He told me so once, for he isn't a bit ashamed of it. But he must be precious hard up some-times. However, as he contrives to keep a decent coat on his back, and pay his classes at the University, and carry off the very best honors going there, nobody asks any questions. That's the good of London, Aunt Hilary," said the young fellow, drawing himself up with great wisdom. " Only look like a gentleman, behave yourself as such, and nobody asks any questions."

" Yes," vaguely acquiesced Aunt Hilary. And then her mind wandered yearningly to the solitary student in the two-pair back. He might labor and suffer; he might be ill; he might die, equally solitary, and " nobody would ask any questions." This phase of London life let a new light in upon her mind. The letters to Johanna had been chief-ly filled with whatever he thought would interest them. With his characteristic Scotch reserve he had said very lit-tle about himself, except in the last, wherein he mentioned that he had " done pretty well" at college this term, and meant to " go in for more work" immediately.

What this work entailed — how much more toil, how much more poverty—Hilary knew not. Perhaps even his successes, which Ascott went on to talk of, had less place in her thoughts than the picture of the face she knew, sharpened with illness, wasted with hard work and soli-tary care.

" And I can not help him—I can not help him !" was her bitter cry; until, passing from the dream-land of fancy, the womanly nature asserted itself. She thought if it had been, or if it were to be, her blessed lot to be chosen by Robert Lyon, how she would take care of him ! what an utter slave she would be to him ! How no penury would frighten her, no household cares oppress or humble her, if done for him and for his comfort. To her brave heart no battle of life seemed too long or too sore, if only it were fought for him and at his side. And as the early-falling leaves were blown in gusts across her path, and the misty autumn night began to close in, nature herself seemed to plead in unison with the craving of her heart, which sighed that youth and summer last not always; and that, "be it ever so humble," as the song says, there is no place so bright and beautiful as the fireside of a loveful home.

While the aunt and nephew were strolling thus, thinking of very different things, their own fire, newly lit—Ascott liked a fire—was blazing away in solitary glory for the benefit of all passers-by. At length one—a gentleman —stopped at the gate, and looked in, then took a turn to the end of the terrace, and stood gazing in once more. The solitude of the room apparently troubled him; twice his hand was on the latch before he opened it and knocked at the front door.

Elizabeth appeared, which seemed to surprise him.

"Is Miss Leaf at home?"

"No, sir."

"Is she well? Are all the family well?" and he stepped right into the passage, with the freedom of a familiar foot.

("I should ha' slammed the door in his face," was Elizabeth's comment afterward, "only, you see, Miss Hilary, he looked a real gentleman.")

The stranger and she mutually examined one another.

"I think I have heard of you," said he, smiling. "You are Miss Leaf's servant—Elizabeth Hand."

"Yes, sir," still grimly, and with a determined grasp of the door-handle.

"If your mistresses are likely to be home soon, will you allow me to wait for them? I am an old friend of theirs. My name is Lyon."

Now Elizabeth was far too much one of the family not to have heard of such a person. And his knowing her was a tolerable proof of his identity; besides, unconsciously, the girl was influenced by that look and mien of true gentlemanhood, as courteous to the poor maid-of-all-work as he would have been to any duchess born; and by that bright, sudden smile, which came like sunshine over his face, and, like sunshine, warmed and opened the heart of every one that met it.

It opened that of Elizabeth. She relaxed her Cerberus keeping of the door, and even went so far as to inform him that Miss Leaf and Miss Selina were out to tea, but Miss Hilary and Mr. Ascott would be at home shortly. He was welcome to wait in the parlor if he liked.

Afterward, seized with mingled curiosity and misgiving, she made various errands to go in and look at him; but she had not courage to address him, and he never spoke to her. He sat by the window, gazing out into the gloaming. Except just turning his head at her entrance, she did not think he had once stirred the whole time.

Elizabeth went back to her kitchen, and stood listening for her young mistress's familiar knock. Mr. Lyon seemed to have listened too, for before she could reach it the door was already opened.

There was a warm greeting—to her great relief; for she knew she had broken the domestic laws in admitting a stranger unawares—and then Elizabeth heard them all three go into the parlor, where they remained talking, without ringing for either tea or candles, a full quarter of an hour.

Miss Hilary at last came out, but, much to Elizabeth's surprise, went straight up into her bedroom, without entering the kitchen at all.

It was some minutes before she descended; and then, after giving her orders for tea, and seeing that all was arranged with special neatness, she stood absently by the kitchen fire. Elizabeth noticed how wonderfully bright her eyes were, and what a soft, happy smile she had. She noticed it, because she had never seen Miss Hilary look exactly like that before; and she never did again.

"Don't you be troubling yourself with waiting about here," she said; and her mistress seemed to start at being spoken to. "I'll get the tea all right, Miss Hilary. Please go back into the parlor."

Hilary went in.

CHAPTER VI.

ELIZABETH got tea ready with unwonted diligence and considerable excitement. Any visitor was a rare occurrence in this very quiet family; but a gentleman visitor— a young gentleman too—was a remarkable fact, arousing both interest and curiosity. For in the latter quality this girl of seventeen could scarcely be expected to be deficient; and as to the former, she had so completely identified herself with the family she served, that all their concerns were her concerns also. Her acute comments on their few guests and on their little scholars sometimes amused Hilary as much as her criticisms on the books she read; but, as neither were ever put forward intrusively or impertinently, she let them pass, and only laughed over them with Johanna in private.

In speaking of these said books, and the questions they led to, it was not likely but that mistress and maid—one aged twenty-two, and the other seventeen—should occasionally light upon a subject rather interesting to women of their ages, though not commonly discussed between mistresses and maids. Nevertheless, when it did come in the way, Miss Hilary never shirked it, but talked it out, frankly and freely, as she would to any other person.

"The girl has feelings and notions on the matter, like all other girls, I suppose," reasoned she to herself: "so it is important that her notions should be kept clear, and her feelings right. It may do her some good, and save her from much harm."

And so it befell that Elizabeth Hand, whose blunt ways, unlovely person, and temperament so oddly nervous and reserved kept her from attracting any "sweetheart" of her own class, had unconsciously imbibed her mistress's theory of love. Love, pure and simple, the very deepest and highest, sweetest and most solemn thing in life: to be

believed in devoutly until it came, and when it did come,
to be held to firmly, faithfully, with a single-minded, settled constancy, till death—a creed quite impossible, many
will say, in this ordinary world, and most dangerous to be
put into the head of a poor servant. Yet a woman is but
a woman, be she maid-servant or queen; and if, from
queens to maid-servants, girls were taught thus to think
of love, there might be a few more "broken" hearts perhaps, but there would certainly be fewer wicked hearts;
far fewer corrupted lives of men and degraded lives of
women; far fewer unholy marriages, and desolated, dreary, homeless homes.

Elizabeth, having cleared away her tea-things, stood listening to the voices in the parlor, and pondering.

She had sometimes wondered in her own mind that no
knight ever came to carry off her charming princess—her
admired and beloved Miss Hilary. Miss Hilary, on her
part, seemed totally indifferent to the youth at Stowbury,
who indeed were, Elizabeth allowed, quite unworthy her
regard. The only suitable lover for her young mistress
must be somebody exceedingly grand and noble—a com-
pound of the best heroes of Shakspeare, Scott, Fenimore
Cooper, Maria Edgeworth, and Harriet Martineau. When
this strange gentleman appeared—in ordinary coat and
hat, or rather Glengary bonnet, neither particularly handsome nor particularly tall, yet whose coming had evidently given Miss Hilary so much pleasure, and who, once or
twice while waiting at tea, Elizabeth fancied she had seen
looking at Miss Hilary as nobody ever looked before—
when Mr. Robert Lyon appeared on the horizon, the faithful "bower-maiden" was a good deal disappointed.

She had expected something better; at all events, something different. Her first brilliant castle in the air fell,
poor lass! but she quickly built it up again, and, with the
vivid imagination of her age, she mapped out the whole
future, ending by a vision of Miss Hilary, all in white,
sweeping down the Terrace in a carriage and pair—to fortune and happiness; leaving herself, though with a sore

want at her heart, and a great longing to follow, to devote
the remainder of her natural life to Miss Johanna.

"Her couldna do without somebody to see to her—and
Miss Selina do worrit her so," muttered Elizabeth, in the
excitement of this Alnaschar vision, relapsing into her old
provincialisms.   "So, even if Miss Hilary axes me to come,
I'll stop, I reckon.   Ay, I'll stop wi' Miss Leaf."

This valorous determination taken, the poor maid-servant's dream was broken by the opening of the parlor door,
and an outcry of Ascott's for his coat and gloves, he having to fetch his aunts home at nine o'clock, Mr. Lyon ac-
companying him.   And as they all stood together at the
front door, Elizabeth overheard Mr. Lyon say something
about what a beautiful night it was.

"It would do you no harm, Miss Hilary; will you walk
with us?"

"If you like."

Hilary went up stairs for her bonnet and shawl; but
when, a minute or two after, Elizabeth followed her with
a candle, she found her standing in the centre of the room,
all in the dark, her face white, and her hands trembling.

"Thank you—thank you!" she said, mechanically, as
Elizabeth folded and fastened her shawl for her, and descended immediately.   Elizabeth watched her take, not
Ascott's arm, but Mr. Lyon's, and walk down the terrace
in the starlight.

"Some'at's wrong.   I'd like to know who's been a-vexin'
of her," thought fiercely the young servant.

No, nobody had been "a-vexin'" her mistress.   There
was nobody to blame; only there had happened to Hilary
one of those things which strike like a sword through a
young and happy heart, taking all the life and youth out
of it.

Robert Lyon had, half an hour ago, told her—and she
had had to hear it as a piece of simple news, to which she
had only to say "Indeed!"—that to-day and to-morrow
were his two last days at Stowbury—almost his last in England.   Within a week he was to sail for India.

There had befallen him what most people would have considered a piece of rare good fortune. At the London University, a fellow-student, whom he had been gratuitously "coaching" in Hindostanee, fell ill, and was "thrown upon his hands," as he briefly defined services which must have been great, since they had resulted in this end. The young man's father, a Liverpool and Bombay merchant, made him an offer to go out there to their house, at a rising salary of 300 rupees a month for three years; after the third year to become a junior partner, remaining at Bombay in that capacity for two years more.

This he told to Hilary and Ascott in almost as few words as I have here put it, for brevity seemed a refuge to him: it was also to one of them. But Ascott asked so many questions that his aunt needed to ask none. She only listened, and tried to take all in, and understand it—that is, in a consecutive, intelligent, business shape, without feeling it. She dared not let herself feel it, not for a second, till they were out, arm-in-arm, under the quiet winter stars. Then she heard his voice asking her,

"So you think I was right?"

"Right?" she echoed, mechanically.

"I mean, in accepting that sudden chance, and changing my whole plan of life. I did not do it—believe me—without a motive."

What motive? she would once unhesitatingly have asked; now she could not.

Robert Lyon continued speaking, distinctly and yet in an undertone, that, though Ascott was walking a few yards off, Hilary felt was meant for her alone to hear.

"The change is, you perceive, from the life of a student to that of a man of business. I do not deny that I preferred the first. Once upon a time, to be a fellow in a college, or a professor, or the like, was my utmost aim; and I would have half killed myself to attain it. Now, I think differently."

He paused, but did not seem to require an answer, and it did not come.

"I want not to be rich, but to get a decent competence, and to get it as soon as I can. I want not to ruin my health with incessant study. I have already injured it a good deal."

"Have you been ill? You never said so."

"Oh no, it was hardly worth while. And I knew an active life would soon set me right again. No fear! there's life in the old dog yet. He does not wish to die. But," Mr. Lyon pursued, "I have had a 'sair fecht' the last year or two. I would not go through it again, nor see any one dear to me go through it. It is over, but it has left its scars. Strange! I have been poor all my life, yet I never till now felt an actual terror of poverty."

Hilary shrank within herself, less even at the words than at something in their tone—something hard, nay, fierce; something at once despairing and aggressive.

"It is strange," she said; "such a terror is not like you. I feel none; I can not even understand it."

"No; I knew you could not," he muttered, and was silent.

So was Hilary. A vague trouble came over her. Could it be that he, Robert Lyon, had been seized with the *auri sacra fames*, which he had so often inveighed against and despised?—that his long battle with poverty had caused in him such an overweening desire for riches that, to obtain them, he would sacrifice every thing else, exile himself to a far country for years, selling his very life and soul for gold?

Such a thought of him was so terrible—that is, would have been were it tenable—that Hilary for an instant felt herself shiver all over. The next she spoke out—in justice to him she forced herself to speak out—all her honest soul.

"I do believe that this going abroad to make a fortune, which young men so delight in, is often a most fatal mistake. They give up far more than they gain—country, home, health. I think a man has no right to sell his life any more than his soul for so many thousands a year."

Robert Lyon smiled. "No; and I am not selling mine.

With my temperate habits I have as good a chance of health at Bombay as in London—perhaps better. And the years I must be absent I would have been absent almost as much from you—I mean they would have been spent in work as engrossing and as hard. They will soon pass, and then I shall come home rich—rich. Do you think I am growing mercenary?"

"No."

"Tell me what you do think about me."

"I—can not quite understand."

"And I can not make you understand. Perhaps I will, some day, when I come back again. Till then, you must trust me, Hilary."

It happens occasionally, in moments of all but intolerable pain, that some small thing—a word, a look, a touch of a hand, lets in such a gleam of peace that nothing ever extinguishes the light of it: it burns on for years and years, sometimes clear, sometimes obscured, but as ineffaceable from life and memory as a star from its place in the heavens. Such, both then and through the lonely years to come, were those five words, "You must trust me, Hilary."

She did; and in the perfectness of that trust her own separate identity, with all its consciousness of pain, seemed annihilated: she did not think of herself at all, only of him, and with him, and for him. So, for the time being, she lost all sense of personal suffering, and their walk that night was as cheerful and happy as if they were to walk together for weeks, and months, and years in undivided confidence and content, instead of its being the last—the very last.

Some one has said that all lovers have, soon or late, to learn to be only friends : happiest and safest are those in whom the friendship is the foundation—always firm and ready to fall back upon long after the fascination of passion dies. It may take a little from the romance of these two if I own that Robert Lyon talked to Hilary not a word about love, and a good deal about pure business, telling her all his affairs and arrangements, and giving her as clear ·

an idea of his future life as it was possible to do within the limits of one brief half hour.

Then casting a glance round, and seeing that Ascott was quite out of earshot, he said, with that tender fall of the voice that felt, as some poet hath it,

" Like a still embrace,"

" Now tell me as much as you can about yourself."

At first there seemed nothing to tell, but gradually he drew from Hilary a good deal. Johanna's feeble health, which caused her continuing to teach to be very unadvisable ; and the gradual diminishing of the school—from what cause they could not account—which made it very doubtful whether some change would not soon or late be necessary.

What this change should be she and Mr. Lyon discussed a little—as far as, in the utterly indefinite position of affairs, was possible. Also, from some other questions of his, she spoke to him about another dread which had lurked in her mind, and yet to which she could give no tangible shape—about Ascott. He could not remove it, he did not attempt; but he soothed it a little, advising her as to the best way of managing the willful lad. His strong, clear sense, just judgment, and, above all, a certain unspoken sense of union, as if all that concerned her and hers he took naturally upon himself as his own, gave Hilary such comfort that, even on this night, with a full consciousness of all that was to follow, she was happy—nay, she had not been so happy for years. Perhaps (let the truth be told, the glorious truth of true love, that its recognition, spoken or silent, constitutes the only perfect joy of life—that of two made one)—perhaps she had never been so really happy since she was born.

The last thing he did was to make her give him an assurance that in any and all difficulty she would apply to him.

" To me, and to no one else, remember. No one but myself must help you. And I will, so long as I am alive. Do you believe this?"

She looked up at him by the lamp-light, and said, " I do."
" And you promise ?"
" Yes."

Then they loosed arms, and Hilary knew that they should
never walk together again till—when, and how ?

Returning, of course he walked with Miss Leaf; and
throughout the next day, a terribly wet Sunday, spent by
them entirely in the little parlor, they had not a minute of
special or private talk together. He did not seem to wish
it—indeed, almost avoided it.

Thus slipped away the strange, still day—a Sunday never to be forgotten. At night, after prayers were over, Mr.
Lyon rose suddenly, saying he must leave them now; he
was obliged to start from Stowbury at daybreak.

" Shall we not see you again ?" asked Johanna.

" No. This will be my last Sunday in England. Good-
by !"

He turned excessively pale, shook hands silently with
them all—Hilary last—and almost before they recognized
the fact he was gone.

With him departed, not all Hilary's peace, or faith, or
courage of heart—for to all who love truly, while the best
beloved lives, and lives worthily, no parting is hopeless
and no grief overwhelming—but all the brightness of her
youth, all the sense of joy that young people have in loving and in being loved again, in fond meetings and fonder
partings, in endless walks and talks, in sweet kisses and
clinging arms. Such happiness was not for her; when she
saw it the lot of others, she said to herself, sometimes with
a natural sharp sting of pain, but oftener with a solemn .
acquiescence, " It is the will of God; it is the will of
God."

Johanna, too, who would have given her life almost to
bring some color back to the white face of her darling, of
whom she asked no questions, and who never complained
nor confessed any thing, many and many a night, when
Hilary either lay awake by her side, or tossed and moaned
in her sleep till the elder sister took her in her arms like a

D

baby—Johanna, too, said to herself, "This is the will of God."

I have told thus much in detail the brief, sad story of Hilary's youth, to show how impossible it was that Elizabeth Hand could live in the house with these two women without being strongly influenced by them, as every person—especially every woman—influences for good or for evil every other person connected with her or dependent upon her.

Elizabeth was a girl of close observation and keen perception. Besides, to most people, whether or not their sympathy be universal, so far as the individual is concerned, any deep affection generally lends eyes, tact, and delicacy.

Thus when, on the Monday morning at breakfast, Miss Selina observed "what a fine day Mr. Lyon was having for his journey; what a lucky fellow he was; how he would be sure to make a fortune, and if so, she wondered whether they should ever see or hear any thing of him again"—Elizabeth, from the glimpse she caught of Miss Hilary's face, and from the quiet way in which Miss Leaf merely answered, "Time will show," and began talking to Selina about some other subject—Elizabeth resolved never in any way to make the smallest allusion to Mr. Robert Lyon. Something had happened, she did not know what, and it was not her business to find out; the family affairs, so far as she was trusted with them, were warmly her own, but into the family secrets she had no right to pry.

Yet, long after Miss Selina had ceased to "wonder" about him, or even to name him—his presence or absence did not touch her personally, and she was always the centre of her own small world of interest—the little maid-servant kept in her mind, and pondered over at odd times every possible solution of the mystery of this gentleman's sudden visit; of the long, wet Sunday when he sat all day talking with her mistresses in the parlor; of the evening prayer, when Miss Leaf had twice to stop, her voice faltered so; and of the night when, long after all the others had gone to bed, Elizabeth, coming suddenly into the parlor, had found Miss Hilary sitting alone over the embers of the fire, with the saddest, saddest look! so that the girl had softly shut the door again without ever speaking to "missis."

Elizabeth did more, which, strange as it may appear, a servant who is supposed to know nothing of any thing that has happened can often do better than a member of the family who knows every thing, and this knowledge is sometimes the most irritating consciousness a sufferer has. She followed her young mistress with a steady watchfulness, so quiet and silent that Hilary never found it out— saved her every little household care, gave her every little household treat. Not much to do, and less to be chronicled; but the way in which she did it was all.

During the long, dull winter days, to come in and find the parlor fire always bright, the hearth clean swept, and the room tidy; never to enter the kitchen without the servant's face clearing up into a smile; when her restless irritability made her forget things and grow quite vexed in the search after them, to see that somehow her shoes were never misplaced, and her gloves always came to hand in some mysterious manner—these trifles, in her first heavy days of darkness, soothed Hilary more than words could tell.

And the sight of Miss Hilary going about the house and school-room as usual, with that poor white face of hers; nay, gradually bringing to the family fireside, as usual, her harmless little joke, and her merry laugh at it and herself —who shall say what lessons may not have been taught by this to the humble servant, dropping deep-sown into her heart, to germinate and fructify, as her future life's needs required?

It might have been so—God knows! He alone can know, who, through what (to us) seem the infinite littlenesses of our mortal existence, is educating us into the infinite great-ness of his and our immortality.

CHAPTER VII.

Autumn soon lapsed into winter; Christmas came and
went, bringing, not Ascott, as they hoped and he had promised, but a very serious evil in the shape of sundry bills of .
his, which, he confessed in a most piteous letter to his Aunt
Hilary, were absolutely unpayable out of his godfather's
allowance. They were not large—or would not have seemed so to rich people—and they were for no more blamable
luxuries than horse-hire, and a dinner or two to friends out
in the country; but they looked serious to a household
which rarely was more than five pounds beforehand with
the world.

He had begged Aunt Hilary to keep his secret, but that
was evidently impossible; so, on the day the school-ac-
counts were being written out and sent in, and their amount
anxiously reckoned, she laid before her sisters the lad's letter, full of penitence and promises:

"I will be careful—I will indeed—if you will help me
this once, dear Aunt Hilary; and don't think too ill of me.
I have done nothing wicked. And you don't know London
—you don't know, with a lot of young fellows about one,
how very hard it is to say no."

At that unluckly postscript the Misses Leaf sorrowfully
exchanged looks. Little the lad thought about it—but
these few words were the very sharpest pang Ascott had
ever given to his aunts.

"What's bred in the bone will come out in the flesh."
"Like father, like son." "The sins of the parents shall be
visited on the children." So runs many a proverb; so confirms the unerring decree of a just God, who would not be
a just God did he allow himself to break his own righteous
laws for the government of the universe; did he falsify the
requirements of his own holy and pure being by permitting
any other wages for sin than death. And though, through

his mercy, sin forsaken escapes sin's penalty, and every human being has it in his power to modify, if not to conquer, any hereditary moral as well as physical disease, thereby avoiding the doom and alleviating the curse, still the original law remains in force, and ought to remain, an example and a warning. As true as that every individual sin which a man commits breeds multitudes more, is it that every individual sinner may transmit his own peculiar type of weakness or wickedness to a whole race, disappearing in one generation, reappearing in another, exactly the same as physical peculiarities do, requiring the utmost caution of education to counteract the terrible tendencies of nature—the " something in the blood" which is so difficult to eradicate ; which may even make the third and fourth generations execrate the memory of him or her who was its origin.

The long life-curse of Henry Leaf the elder, and Henry Leaf the younger, had been—the women of the family well knew—that they were men " who couldn't say No." So keenly were the three sisters alive to this fault—it could hardly be called a crime, and yet, in its consequences, it was so — so sickening the terror of it which their own wretched experience had implanted in their minds, that during Ascott's childhood and youth his very fractiousness and roughness, his little selfishness, and his persistence in his own will against theirs, had been hailed by his aunts as a good omen that he would grow up " so unlike his poor father."

If the two unhappy Henry Leafs—father and son—could have come out of their graves that night and beheld these three women, daughters and sisters, sitting with Ascott's letter on the table, planning how the household's small expenses could be contracted, its still smaller luxuries relinquished, in order that the boy might honorably pay for pleasures he might so easily have done without ! If they could have seen the weight of apprehension which then sank like a stone on these long-tried hearts, never to be afterward quite removed ; lightened sometimes, but always— however Ascott might promise and amend—always there!

On such a discovery, surely, these two "poor ghosts" would have fled away moaning, wishing they had died childless, or that during their mortal lives any amount of self-restraint and. self-compulsion had purged from their natures the accursed thing—the sin which had worked itself out in sorrow upon every one belonging to them years after their own heads were laid in the quiet dust.

"We must do it," was the conclusion the Misses Leaf unanimously came to—even Selina, who, with all her faults, had a fair share of good feeling and of that close clinging to kindred which is found in fallen households, or households whom the sacred bond of common poverty has drawn together in a way that large, well-to-do home circles can never quite understand. "We must not let the boy remain in debt; it would be such a disgrace to the family."

"It is not the remaining in debt, but the incurring of it, which is the real disgrace to Ascott and the family."

"Hush, Hilary!" said Johanna, pointing to the opening door; but it was too late.

Elizabeth, coming suddenly in—or else the ladies had been so engrossed with their conversation that they had not noticed her—had evidently heard every word of the last sentence. Her conscious face showed it—more especially the bright scarlet which covered both her cheeks when Miss Leaf said "Hush!" She stood, apparently irresolute as to whether she should run away again; and then her native honesty got the upper hand, and she advanced into the room.

"If you please, missis, I didn't mean to — but I've heard—"

"What have you heard—that is, how much?"

"Just what Miss Hilary said. Don't be afeared. I sha'n't tell. I never chatter about the family. Mother told me not."

"You owe a great deal, Elizabeth, to your good mother. Now go away."

"And another time," said Miss Selina, "knock at the door."

This was Elizabeth's first initiation into what many a servant has to share—the secret burden of the family. After that day, though they did not actually confide in her, her mistresses used no effort to conceal that they had cares; that the domestic economies must, this winter, be especially studied; there must be no extra fires, no candles left burning to waste; and, once a week or so, a few butterless breakfasts or meatless dinners must be partaken of cheerfully in both parlor and kitchen. The Misses Leaf never stinted their servant in any thing in which they did not stint themselves.

Strange to say, in spite of Miss Selina's prophecies, the girl's respectful conduct did not abate; on the contrary, it seemed to increase. The nearer she was lifted to her mistresses' level, the more her mind grew, so that she could better understand her mistresses' cares, and the deeper became her consciousness of the only thing which gives one human being any real authority over another—personal character.

Therefore, though the family means were narrowed, and the family luxuries few, Elizabeth cheerfully put up with all; she even felt a sort of pride in wasting nothing and in making the best of every thing, as the others did. Perhaps, it may be said, she was an exceptional servant; and yet I would not do her class the wrong to believe so—I would rather believe that there are many such among it; many good, honest, faithful girls, who only need good mistresses unto whom to be honest and faithful, and they would be no less so than Elizabeth Hand.

The months went by—heavy and anxious months; for the school gradually dwindled away, and Ascott's letter— now almost the only connection his aunts had with the outer world, for poverty necessarily diminished even their small Stowbury society—became more and more unsatisfactory; and the want of information in them was not supplied by those other letters, which had once kept Johanna's heart easy concerning the boy.

Mr. Lyon had written once before sailing, nay, after sailing, for he had sent it home by the pilot from the English Channel; then there was, of course, silence. October, November, December, January, February, March—how often did Hilary count the months, and wonder how soon a letter could come—whether a letter ever would come again. And sometimes—the sharp present stinging her with its small daily pains, the future looking dark before her and them all—she felt so forlorn, so forsaken, that but for a certain tiny well-spring of hope, which rarely dries up till long after three-and-twenty, she could have sat down and sighed, "My good days are done."

Rich people break their hearts much sooner than poor people; that is, they more easily get into that morbid state which is glorified by the term "a broken heart." Poor people can not afford it. Their constant labor "physics pain." Their few and narrow pleasures seldom pall. Holy poverty! black as its dark side is, it has its bright side too, that is, when it is honest, fearless, free from selfishness, wastefulnesses, and bickerings; above all, free from the terror of debt.

"We'll starve—we'll go into the workhouse rather than we'll go into debt!" cried Hilary once, in a passion of tears, when she was in sore want of a shawl, and Selina urged her to get it, and wait till she could pay for it. "Yes; the workhouse! It would be less shame to be honorably indebted to the laws of the land than to be meanly indebted, under false pretenses, to any individual in it."

And when, in payment for some accidental lessons, she got next month enough money to buy a shawl, and a bonnet too—nay, by great ingenuity, another bonnet for Johanna—Hilary could have danced and sang—sang, in the gladness and relief of her heart, the glorious euthanasia of poverty.

But these things happened only occasionally; the daily life was hard still—ay, very hard, even though at last came the letter from "foreign parts;" and following it, at regular intervals, other letters. They were full of facts rather than feelings—simple, straightforward; worth little as literary compositions; school-master and learned man as he was, there was nothing literary or poetical about Mr. Lyon; but what he wrote was like what he spoke, the accurate reflection of his own clear, original mind, and honest, tender heart.

His letters gave none the less comfort because, nominally, they were addressed to Johanna. This might have been from some crotchet of over-reserve, or delicacy, or honor—the same which made him part from her for years with no other word than "You must trust me, Hilary;" but, whatever it was, she respected it, and she did trust him. And whether Johanna answered his letters or not, month by month they unfailingly came, keeping her completely informed of all his proceedings, and letting out, as epistles written from over the seas often do, much more of himself and his character than he was probably aware that he betrayed.

And Hilary, whose sole experience of mankind had been the scarcely remembered father, the too well remembered brother, and the anxiously watched nephew, thanked God that there seemed to be one man in the world whom a woman could lean her heart upon, and not feel the support break like a reed beneath her—one man whom she could entirely believe in, and safely and sacredly trust.

CHAPTER VIII.

TIME slipped by. Robert Lyon had been away more than three years. But in the monotonous life of the three sisters at Stowbury nothing was changed — except, perhaps, Elizabeth, who had grown quite a woman; might have passed almost for thirty, so solidly old-fashioned were her figure and her manners.

Ascott Leaf had finished his walking the hospitals and his examinations, and was now fitted to commence practice for himself. His godfather had still continued his allowance, though once or twice, when he came down to

Stowbury, he had asked his aunts to help him in some
small debts—the last time in one a little more serious;
when, after some sad and sore consultation, it had been resolved to tell him he must contrive to live within his own
allowance.   For they were poorer than they used to be;
many more schools had arisen in the town, and theirs had
dwindled away.   It was becoming a source of serious anxiety whether they could possibly make ends meet; and
when, the next Christmas, Ascott sent them a five-pound
note—an actual five-pound note, together with a fond,
grateful letter that was worth it all, the aunts were deeply thankful, and very happy.

But still the school declined.   One night they were speculating upon the causes of this, and Hilary was declaring,
in a half jocular, half earnest way, that it must be because
a prophet is never a prophet in his own country.

"The Stowbury people will never believe how clever I
am.   Only it is a useless sort of cleverness, I fear.   Greek,
Latin, and mathematics are no good to infants under sev-
en, such as Stowbury persists in sending to us."

"They think I am only fit to teach little children—and
perhaps it is true," said Miss Leaf.

"I wish you had not to teach at all.   I wish I was a
daily governess—I might be, and earn enough to keep the
whole family; only, not here."

"I wonder," said Johanna, thoughtfully, "if we shall
have to make a change!"

"A change!"   It almost pained the elder sister to see
how the younger brightened up at the word.   "Where to
—London?   Oh, I have so longed to go and live in London!   But I thought you would not like it, Johanna."

That was true.   Miss Leaf, whom feeble health had
made prematurely old, would willingly have ended her
days in the familiar town; but Hilary was young and
strong.   Johanna called to mind the days when she too
had felt that rest was only another name for dullness, and
when the most difficult thing possible to her was what
seemed now so easy—to sit down and endure.

Besides, unlike herself, Hilary had her life all before her. It might be a happy life, safe in a good man's tender keeping; those unfailing letters from India seemed to prophesy that it would. But no one could say. Miss Leaf's own experience had not led her to place much faith in either men or happiness.

Still, whatever Hilary's future might be, it would likely be a very different one from that quiet, colorless life of hers. And as she looked at her young sister, with the twilight glow on her face—they were taking an evening stroll up and down the terrace—Johanna hoped and prayed it might be so. Her own lot seemed easy enough for herself; but for Hilary—she would like to see Hilary something better than a poor school-mistress at Stowbury.

No more was said at that time, but Johanna had the deep, still, Mary-like nature which "kept" things, and "pondered them in her heart;" so that when the subject came up again she was able to meet it with that sweet calmness which was her especial characteristic—the unruffled peace of a soul which no worldly storms could disturb overmuch, for it had long since cast anchor in the world unseen.

The chance which revived the question of the Great Metropolitan Hegira, as Hilary called it, was a letter from Mr. Ascott, as follows:

"Miss Leaf:

"Madam,—I shall be obliged by your informing me if it is your wish, as it seems to be your nephew's, that, instead of returning to Stowbury, he should settle in London as a surgeon and general practitioner?

"His education complete, I consider that I have done my duty by him; but I may assist him occasionally still, unless he turns out—as his father did before him—a young man who prefers being helped to helping himself, in which case I shall have nothing more to do with him.

"I remain, madam, your obedient servant,
"Peter Ascott."

The sisters read this letter, passing it round the table,

none of them apparently liking to be the first to comment upon it. At length Hilary said, "I think that reference to poor Henry is perfectly brutal."

"And yet he was very kind to Henry. And if it had not been for his common sense in sending poor little Ascott and the nurse down to Stowbury, the baby might have died. But you don't remember any thing of that time, my dear," said Johanna, sighing.

"He has been kind enough, though he has done it in such a patronizing way," observed Selina. "I suppose that's the real reason of his doing it. He thinks it fine to patronize us, and show kindness to our family; he, the stout, bullet-headed grocer's boy, who used to sit and stare at us all church-time."

"At you, you mean. Wasn't he called your beau?" said Hilary, mischievously, upon which Selina drew herself up in great indignation.

And then they fell to talking of that anxious question—Ascott's future. A little they reproached themselves that they had left the lad so long in London—so long out of the influence that might have counteracted the evil, sharply hinted in his godfather's letter. But once away, to lure him back to their poor home was impossible.

"Suppose we were to go to him," suggested Hilary.

The poor and friendless possess one great advantage—they have nobody to ask advice of; nobody to whom it matters much what they do or where they go. The family mind has but to make itself up, and act accordingly. Thus, within an hour or two of the receipt of Mr. Ascott's letter, Hilary went into the kitchen, and told Elizabeth that as soon as her work was done Miss Leaf wished to have a little talk with her.

"Eh! what's wrong? Has Miss Selina been a-grumbling at me?"

Elizabeth was in one of her old humors, which, though of course they never ought to have, servants do have as well as their superiors. Hilary perceived this by the way she threw the coals on, and tossed the chairs about. But to-day her heart was far more full of serious cares than Elizabeth's ill temper. She replied, composedly,

"I have not heard that either of my sisters is displeased with you. What they want to talk to you about is for your own good. We are thinking of making a great . change. We intend leaving Stowbury and going to live in London."

"Going to live in London!"

Now, quick as her tact and observation were—her heart taught her these things—Elizabeth's head was a thorough Saxon one, slow to receive impressions. It was a family saying that nothing was so hard as to put a new idea into Elizabeth except to get it out again.

For this reason Hilary preferred paving the way quietly before startling her with the sudden intelligence of their contemplated change.

"Well, what do you say to the plan?" asked she, good-humoredly.

"I dunnot like it at all," was the brief, gruff answer of Elizabeth Hand.

Now it was one of Miss Hilary's doctrines that no human being is good for much unless he or she has what is called "a will of one's own." Perhaps this, like many another creed, was with her the result of circumstances. But she held it firmly, and with that exaggerated one-sidedness of feeling which any bitter family or personal experience is sure to leave behind—a strong will was her first attraction to every body. It had been so in the case of Robert Lyon, and not less in Elizabeth's.

But this quality has its inconveniences. When the maid began sweeping up her hearth with a noisy, angry gesture, the mistress did the wisest and most dignified thing a mistress could do under the circumstances, and which she knew was the sharpest rebuke she could administer to the sensitive Elizabeth—she immediately quitted the kitchen.

For an hour after the parlor-bell did not ring; and though it was washing-day, no Miss Hilary appeared to

help in folding up the clothes. Elizabeth, subdued and
wretched, waited till she could wait no longer, then knocked at the door, and asked humbly if she could bring in
supper.

The extreme kindness of the answer—to the effect that
she must come in, as they wanted to speak to her, crushed
the lingering fragments of ill humor out of the girl.

"Miss Hilary has told you our future plans, Elizabeth;
now we wish to have a little talk with you about yours."

"Eh?"

"We conclude you will not wish to go with us to London, and it would be hardly advisable you should. You
can get higher wages now than any we can afford to give
you; indeed, we have more than once thought of telling
you so, and offering you your choice of trying for a better
place."

"You're very kind," was the answer, stolid rather than
grateful.

"No; I think we are merely honest. We should never
think of keeping a girl upon lower wages than she was
worth. Hitherto, however, the arrangement has been quite
fair; you know, Elizabeth, you have given us a deal of
trouble in the teaching of you." And Miss Leaf smiled,
half sadly, as if this, the first of the coming changes, hurt
her more than she liked to express. "Come, my girl," she
added, "you needn't look so serious. We are not in the
least vexed with you; we shall be very sorry to lose you,
and we will give you the best of characters when you
leave."

"I dunnot—mean—to leave."

Elizabeth threw out the words like pellets, in a choked
fashion, and disappeared suddenly from the parlor.

"Who would have thought it!" exclaimed Selina; "I
declare the girl was crying."

No mistake about that; though when, a few minutes
after, Miss Hilary entered the kitchen, Elizabeth tried in a
hurried, shamefaced way to hide her tears by being very
busy over something. Her mistress took no notice, but

began, as usual on washing-days, to assist in various domestic matters, in the midst of which she said, quietly,

"And so, Elizabeth, you would really like to go to London?"

"No, I shouldn't like it at all—never said I should. But if you go, I shall go too—though missis is so ready to get shut o' me."

"It was for your own good, you know."

"You always said it was for a girl's good to stop in one place; and if you think I am going to another—I aren't, that's all."

Rude as the form of the speech was—almost the first rude speech that Elizabeth had ever made to Miss Hilary, and which, under other circumstances, she would have felt bound severely to reprove—the mistress passed it over. That which lay beneath it, the sharpness of wounded love, touched her heart. She felt that, for all the girl's rough manner, it would have been hard to go into her London kitchen and meet a strange London face, instead of that fond, homely one of Elizabeth Hand's.

Still, she thought it right to explain to her that London life might have many difficulties; that, for the present at least, her wages could not be raised, and the family might at first be in even more straitened circumstances than they were at Stowbury.

"Only at first, though, for I hope to find plenty of pupils. And by-and-by our nephew will get into practice."

"Is it on account of him you're going, Miss Hilary?"

"Chiefly."

Elizabeth gave a grunt, which said as plainly as words could say, "I thought so;" and relapsed into what she, no doubt, believed to be virtuous indignation, but which, as it was testified against the wrong parties, was open to the less favorable interpretation of ill humor—a small injustice not uncommon with us all.

I do not pretend to paint this young woman as a perfect character. She had her fierce dislikes as well as her strong fidelities; her faults within and without, which had to be struggled with, as all of us have to struggle to the very end of our days. Oftentimes not till the battle is nigh over—sometimes not till it is quite over—does God give us the victory?

Without more discussion on either side, it was agreed that Elizabeth should accompany her mistresses. Even Mrs. Hand seemed to be pleased thereat, her only doubt being lest her daughter should meet and be led astray by that bad woman Mrs. Cliffe, Tommy Cliffe's mother, who was reported to have gone to London. But Miss Hilary explained that this meeting was about as probable as the rencontre of two needles in a hay-rick; and, besides, Elizabeth was not the sort of girl to be easily "led astray" by any body.

"No, no; her's a good wench, though I says it," replied the mother, who was too hard worked to have much sentiment to spare. "I wish the little 'uns may take pattern by our Elizabeth. You'll send her home, maybe, in two or three years' time, to let us have a look at her?"

Miss Hilary promised, and then took her way back through the familiar old town—so soon to be familiar no more—thinking anxiously, in spite of herself, upon those two or three years, and what they might bring.

It happened to be a notable day—that sunshiny 28th of June — when the little round - cheeked damsel, who is a grandmother now, had the crown of three kingdoms first set upon her youthful head, and Stowbury, like every other town in the land, was a perfect bower of green arches, garlands, banners; white-covered tables were spread in the open air down almost every street, where poor men dined, or poor women drank tea; and every body was out and abroad, looking at or sharing in the holiday-making, wild with merriment, and brimming over with passionate loyalty to the Maiden Queen.

That day is now twenty-four years ago; but all those who remember it must own there never has been a day like it, when, all over the country, every man's heart throbbed with chivalrous devotion, every woman's with womanly tenderness, toward this one royal girl, who—God bless her!—has lived to retain and deserve it all.

Hilary called for, and protected through the crowd the little, timid widow lady who had taken off the Misses Leaf's hands their house and furniture, and whom they had made very happy—as the poor often can make those still poorer than themselves—by refusing to accept any thing for the "good-will" of the school. Then she was fetched by Elizabeth, who had been given a whole afternoon's holiday; and mistress and maid went together home, watching the last of the festivities, the chattering groups that still lingered in the twilight streets, and listening to the merry notes of the "Triumph" which came down through the lighted windows of the Town Hall, where the open-air tea-drinkers had adjourned to dance country dances, by civic permission, and in perfectly respectable jollity.

"I wonder," said Hilary — while, despite some natural regret, her spirit stretched itself out eagerly from the narrowness of the place where she was born into the great wide world; the world where so many grand things were thought, and written, and done; the world Robert Lyon had so long fought with, and was fighting bravely still— "I wonder, Elizabeth, what sort of place London is, and what our life will be in it?"

Elizabeth said nothing. For the moment her face seemed to catch the reflected glow of her mistress's, and then it settled down into that look of mingled resistance and resolution which was habitual to her. For the life that was to be, which neither knew—oh, if they had known !— she also was prepared.

CHAPTER IX.

THE day of the grand hegira came.

"I remember," said Miss Leaf, as they rumbled for the last time through the empty morning streets of poor old Stowbury—"I remember my grandmother telling me that

when my grandfather was courting her, and she out of co-
quetry refused him, he set off on horseback to London, and
she was so wretched to think of all the dangers he ran on
the journey, and in London itself, that she never rested till
she got him back, and then immediately married him."

"No such catastrophe is likely to happen to any of us,
except, perhaps, to Elizabeth," said Miss Hilary, trying to
get up a little feeble mirth, any thing to pass away the
time and lessen the pain of parting, which was almost too
much for Johanna. "What do you say? Do you mean
to get married in London, Elizabeth?"

But Elizabeth could make no answer, even to kind Miss
Hilary. They had not imagined she felt the leaving her
native place so much. She had watched intently the last
glimpse of Stowbury church tower, and now sat with red-
dened eyes, staring blankly out of the carriage window,

"Silent as a stone."

Once or twice a large slow tear gathered on each of her
eyes, but it was shaken off angrily from the high cheek-
bones, and never settled into absolute crying. They
thought it best to take no notice of her. Only, when reach-
ing the new small station, where the "resonant steam-ea-
gles" were, for the first time, beheld by the innocent Stowbury ladies, there arose a discussion as to the manner of
traveling. Miss Leaf said decidedly, "Second-class; and
then we can keep Elizabeth with us." Upon which Elizabeth's mouth melted into something between a quiver and
a smile.

Soon it was all over, and the little household was com-
pressed into the humble second-class carriage, cheerless
and cushionless, whirling through indefinite England in a
way that confounded all their geography and topography.
Gradually, as the day darkened into heavy, chilly July
rain, the scarcely kept-up spirits of the four passengers began to sink. Johanna grew very white and worn; Selina
became, to use Ascott's phrase, "as cross as two sticks;"
and even Hilary, turning her eyes from the gray, sodden-

looking landscape without, could find no spot of comfort to rest on within the carriage except that round rosy face of Elizabeth Hand's.

Whether it was from the spirit of contradiction existing in most such natures, which, especially in youth, are more strong than sweet, or from a better feeling, the fact was noticeable, that when every one else's spirits went down Elizabeth's went up. Nothing could bring her out of a "grumpy" fit so satisfactorily as her mistresses falling into one. When Miss Selina now began to fidget hither and thither, each tone of her fretful voice seeming to go through her eldest sister's every nerve, till even Hilary said, impatiently, "Oh, Selina, can't you be quiet?" then Elizabeth rose from her depth of gloomy discontent up to the surface immediately.

She was only a servant; but Nature bestows that strange vague thing that we term "force of character" independently of position. Hilary often remembered afterward how much more comfortable the end of the journey was than she had expected—how Johanna lay at ease, with her feet on Elizabeth's lap, wrapped in Elizabeth's best woolen shawl; and how, when Selina's whole attention was turned to an ingenious contrivance with a towel, and fork, and Elizabeth's basket, for stopping the rain out of the carriage-roof—she became far less disagreeable, and even a little proud of her own cleverness. And so there was a temporary lull in Hilary's cares, and she could sit quiet, with her eyes fixed on the rainy landscape, which she did not see, and her thoughts wandering toward that unknown place and unknown life into which they were sweeping, as we all sweep, ignorantly, unresistingly, almost unconsciously, into new destinies. Hilary, for the first time, began to think of theirs. Anxious as she had been to go to London, and wise as the proceeding appeared, now that the die was cast and the cable cut, the old, simple, peaceful life at Stowbury grew strangely dear.

"I wonder if we shall ever go back again, or what is to happen to us before we do go back," she thought, and turned, with a half-defined fear, toward her eldest sister, who looked so old and fragile beside that sturdy, healthy servant-girl. "Elizabeth!" Elizabeth, rubbing Miss Leaf's feet, started at the unwonted sharpness of Miss Hilary's tone. "There; I'll do that for my sister. Go and look out of the window at London."

For the great smoky cloud which began to rise in the rainy horizon was indeed London. Soon through the thickening nebula of houses they converged to what was then the nucleus of all railway traveling, the Euston Terminus, and were hustled on to the platform, and jostled helplessly to and fro—these poor country ladies! Anxiously they scanned the crowd of strange faces for the one only face they knew in the great metropolis—which did not appear.

"It is very strange—very wrong of Ascott. Hilary, you surely told him the hour correctly. For once, at least, he might have been in time."

So chafed Miss Selina, while Elizabeth, who, by some miraculous effort of intuitive genius, had succeeded in collecting the luggage, was now engaged in defending it from all comers, especially porters, and making of it a comfortable seat for Miss Leaf.

"Nay, have patience, Selina. We will give him just five minutes more, Hilary."

And Johanna sat down, with her sweet, calm, long-suffering face turned upward to that younger one, which was, as youth is apt to be, hot, and worried, and angry. And so they waited till the terminus was almost deserted, and the last cab had driven off, when, suddenly, dashing up the station-yard out of another, came Ascott.

He was so sorry, so very sorry, downright grieved, at having kept his aunts waiting. But his watch was wrong —some fellows at dinner detained him—the train was before its time, surely. In fact, his aunts never quite made out what the excuse was; but they looked into his bright, handsome face, and their wrath melted like clouds before the sun. He was so gentlemanly, so well dressed—much better dressed than even at Stowbury, and he seemed so unfeignedly glad to see them. He handed them all into the cab—even Elizabeth, though whispering meanwhile to his Aunt Hilary, "What on earth did you bring her for?" —and then was just going to leap on to the box himself, when he stopped to ask "Where he should tell cabby to drive to?"

"Where to?" repeated his aunts, in undisguised astonishment. They had never thought of any thing but of being taken home at once by their boy.

"You see," Ascott said, in a little confusion, "you wouldn't be comfortable with me. A young fellow's lodgings are not like a house of one's own, and, besides—"

"Besides, when a young fellow is ashamed of his old aunts, he can easily find reasons."

"Hush, Selina!" interposed Miss Leaf. "My dear boy, your old aunts would never let you inconvenience yourself for them. Take us to an inn for the night, and to-morrow we will find lodgings for ourselves."

Ascott looked greatly relieved.

"And you are not vexed with me, Aunt Johanna?" said he, with something of his old childish tone of compunction, as he saw—he could not help seeing—the utter weariness which Johanna tried so hard to hide.

"No, my dear, not vexed. Only I wish we had known this a little sooner, that we might have made arrangements. Now, where shall we go?"

Ascott mentioned a dozen hotels, but they found he only knew them by name. At last Miss Leaf remembered one which her father used to go to on his frequent journeys to London, and whence, indeed, he had been brought home to die. And though all the recollections about it were sad enough, still it felt less strange than the rest in this dreariness of London. So she proposed going to the "Old Bell," Holborn.

· "A capital place!" exclaimed Ascott, eagerly. "And I'll take and settle you there; and we'll order supper, and make a jolly night of it. All right. Drive on, cabby!"

He jumped on the box, and then looked in mischievous·

ly, flourishing his lit cigar, and shaking his long hair—his aunt Selina's two great abominations—right in her indignant face, but withal looking so merry and good-tempered that she shortly softened into a smile.

"How handsome the boy is growing!"

"Yes," said Johanna, with a sigh; "and, did you notice? how exceedingly like his—"

The sentence was left unfinished. Alas! if every young man who believes his faults and follies injure himself alone could feel what it must be, years afterward, to have his nearest kindred shrink from saying, as the saddest, most ominous thing they could say of his son, that the lad is growing "so like his father!"

It might have been—they assured each other that it was—only the incessant roll, roll of the street sounds below their windows which kept the Misses Leaf awake half the night of this their first night in London. And when they sat down to breakfast—having waited an hour vainly for their nephew—it might have been only the gloom of the little parlor which cast a slight shadow over them all. Still the shadow was there.

It deepened, despite the sunshiny morning into which the last night's rain had brightened until Holborn Bars looked cheerful, and Holborn pavement actually clean, so that, as Elizabeth said, "you might eat your dinner off it," which was the one only thing she condescended to approve in London. She had sat all evening mute in her corner, for Miss Leaf would not send her away into the *terra incognita* of a London hotel. Ascott, at first considerably annoyed at the presence of what he called a "skeleton at the feast," had afterward got over it, and run on with a mixture of childish glee and mannish pomposity about his plans and intentions: how he meant to take a house, he thought, in one of the squares, or a street leading out of them; how he would put up the biggest of brass plates, with "Mr. Leaf, surgeon," and soon get an extensive practice, and have all his aunts to live with him. And his aunts had smiled and listened, forgetting all about the silent figure in the corner, who, perhaps, had gone to sleep, or had also listened.

"Elizabeth, come and look out at London."

So she and Miss Hilary whiled away another heavy three quarters of an hour in watching and commenting on the incessantly shifting crowd which swept past Holborn Bars. Miss Selina sometimes looked out too, but more often sat fidgeting, and wondering why Ascott did not come; while Miss Leaf, who never fidgeted, became gradually more and more silent. Her eyes were fixed on the door with an expression which, if Hilary could have remembered so far back, would have been to her something not painfully new, but still more painfully old—a look branded into her face by many an hour's anxious listening for the footsteps that never came, or only came to bring distress. It was the ineffaceable token of that long, long struggle between affection and conscience, pity and scarcely repressible contempt, which for more than one generation had been the appointed burden of this family—at least the women of it, till sometimes it seemed to hang over them almost like a fate.

About noon Miss Leaf proposed calling for the hotel bill. Its length so alarmed the country ladies that Hilary suggested not staying to dine, but going immediately in search of lodgings.

"What, without a gentleman! Impossible! I always understood ladies could go nowhere in London without a gentleman!"

"We shall come very ill off, then, Selina. But, anyhow, I mean to try. You know the region where, we have heard, lodgings are cheapest and best—that is, best for us. It can not be far from here. Suppose I start at once?"

"What, alone?" cried Johanna, anxiously.

"No, dear. I'll take the map with me, and Elizabeth. She is not afraid."

Elizabeth smiled, and rose, with that air of dogged devotedness with which she would have prepared to follow Miss Hilary to the North Pole if necessary. So, after a

few minutes of arguing with Selina, who did not press her
point overmuch, since she herself had not to commit the
impropriety of the expedition; after a few minutes more
of hopeless lingering about, till even Miss Leaf said they
had better wait no longer, mistress and maid took a farewell nearly as pathetic as if they had been in reality Arc-
tic voyagers, and plunged right into the dusty glare and
hurrying crowd of the " sunny side" of Holborn in July.

A strange sensation, and yet there was something exhil-
arating in it. The intense solitude that there is in a London crowd these country girls—for Miss Hilary herself
was no more than a girl—could not as yet realize. They
only felt the life of it; stirring, active, incessantly moving
life, even though it was of a kind that they knew as little
of it as the crowd did of them. Nothing struck Hilary
more than the self-absorbed look of passers-by; each so
busy on his own affairs that, in spite of Selina's alarm, for
all notice taken of them, they might as well be walking
among the cows and horses in Stowbury field.

Poor old Stowbury ! They felt how far away they were
from it when a ragged, dirty, vicious-looking girl offered
them a moss rose-bud for " one penny, only one penny,"
which Elizabeth, lagging behind, bought, and found it only
a broken-off bud stuck on to a bit of wire.

" That's London ways, I suppose," said she, severely, and
became so misanthropic that she would hardly vouchsafe a
glance to the handsome square they turned into, and merely observed of the tall houses—taller than any Hilary had
ever seen, that she " wouldn't fancy running up and down
them stairs."

But Hilary was cheerful in spite of all. She was glad to
be in this region, which theoretically she knew by heart—
glad to find herself in the body where in the spirit she had
come so many a time. The mere consciousness of this
seemed to refresh her. She thought she would be much
happier in London; that in the long years to come that
must be borne, it would be good for her to have something
to do as well as to hope for, something to fight with as

well as to endure. Now more than ever came pulsing in
and out of her memory a line once repeated in her hearing,
with an observation of how "true" it was. And though
originally it was applied by a man to a woman, and she
smiled sometimes to think how "unfeminine" some people
—Selina, for instance—would consider her turning it the
other way, still she did so. She believed that, for woman
as for man, that is the purest and noblest love which is the
most self-existent, most independent of love returned, and
which can say each to the other equally on both sides that
the whole solemn purpose of life is, under God's service,

"If not to win, to feel more worthy thee."

Such thoughts made her step firmer and her heart lighter, so that she hardly noticed the distance they must have
walked till the close London air began to oppress her, and
the smooth glaring London pavements made her Stowbury
feet ache sorely.

"Are you tired, Elizabeth? Well, we'll rest soon. There
must be lodgings near here. Only I can't quite make
out—"

As Miss Hilary looked up to the name of the street, the
maid noticed what a glow came into her mistress's face,
pale and tired as it was. Just then a church clock struck
the quarter hour.

"That must be St. Pancras. And this—yes, this is Burton Street, Burton Crescent."

"I'm sure missis wouldn't like to live there," observed
Elizabeth, eying uneasily the gloomy *rez-de-chaussée*, familiar to many a generation of struggling respectability,
where, in the decadence of the season, every second house
bore the announcement "apartments furnished."

"No," Miss Hilary replied, absently. Yet she continued to walk up and down the whole length of the street;
then passed out into the dreary, deserted-looking Crescent,
where the trees were already beginning to fade; not, however, into the bright autumn tint of country woods, but
into a premature withering, ugly and sad to behold.

E

"I am glad he is not here—glad, glad!" thought Hilary, as she realized the unutterable dreariness of those years when Robert Lyon lived and studied in his garret from month's end to month's end—these few dusty trees being the sole memento of the green country life in which he had been brought up, and which she knew he so passionately loved. Now she could understand that "calenture" which he had sometimes jestingly alluded to, as coming upon him at times, when he felt literally sick for the sight of a green field or a hedge full of birds. She wondered whether the same feeling would ever come upon her in this strange desert of London, the vastness of which grew upon her every hour.

She was glad he was away—yes, heart-glad! And yet, if this minute she could only have seen him coming round the Crescent; have met his smile, and the firm, warm clasp of his hand—

For an instant there rose up in her one of those wild, rebellious outcries against fate, when to have to waste years of this brief life of ours in the sort of semi-existence that living is, apart from the treasure of the heart and delight of the eyes, seems so cruelly, cruelly hard!

"Miss Hilary—"

She started, and "put herself under lock and key" immediately.

"Miss Hilary, you do look so tired!"

"Do I? Then we will go and sit down in this baker's shop, and get rested and fed. We can not afford to wear ourselves out, you know. We have a great deal to do to-day."

More indeed than she calculated, for they walked up one street and down another, investigating at least twenty lodgings before any appeared which seemed fit for them. Yet some place must be found where Johanna's poor tired head could rest that night. At last, completely exhausted, with that oppressive exhaustion which seems to crush mind as well as body after a day's wandering in London, Hilary's courage began to ebb. Oh for an arm to lean on, a voice to listen for, a brave heart to come to her side, saying, "Do not be afraid, there are two of us!" And she yearned, with an absolutely sick yearning such as only a woman who now and then feels the utter helplessness of her womanhood can know, for the only arm she cared to lean on, the only voice dear enough to bring her comfort, the only heart she felt she could trust.

Poor Hilary! And yet why pity her? To her three alternatives could but happen: were Robert Lyon true to her, she would be his, entirely and devotedly, to the end of her days; did he forsake her, she would forgive him; should he die, she would be faithful to him eternally. Love of this kind may know anguish, but not the sort of anguish that lesser and weaker loves do. If it is certain of nothing else, it can always be certain of itself.

> " Its will is strong:
> It suffers: but it can not suffer long."

And even in its utmost pangs is an underlying peace which often approaches to absolute joy.

Hilary roused herself, and bent her mind steadily on lodgings till she discovered one, from the parlor of which you could see the trees of Burton Crescent and hear the sound of Saint Pancras's clock.

"I think we may do here—at least for a while," said she, cheerfully; and then Elizabeth heard her inquiring if an extra bedroom could be had if necessary.

There was only one small attic. "Ascott never could put up with that," said Hilary, half to herself. Then suddenly—"I think I will see Ascott before I decide. Elizabeth, will you go with me, or remain here?"

"I'll go with you if you please, Miss Hilary."

"If *you* please" sounded not unlike "if *I* please," and Elizabeth had gloomed over a little. "Is Mr. Ascott to live with us?"

"I suppose so."

No more words were interchanged till they reached Gower Street, when Miss Hilary observed, with evident surprise, what a handsome street it was.

" I must have made some mistake.   Still we will find out
Mr. Ascott's number, and inquire."

No, there was no mistake.   Mr. Ascott Leaf had lodged
there for three months, but had given up his rooms that
very morning.

" Where had he gone to ?"

The servant—a London lodging-house servant all over
—didn't know; but she fetched the landlady, who was aft-.
er the same pattern of the dozen London landladies with
whom Hilary had that day made acquaintance, only a little
more Cockney, smirking, dirty, and tawdrily fine. .

" Yes, Mr. Leaf had gone, and he hadn't left no address.
Young college gentlemen often found it convenient to leave
no address.   P'raps he would if he'd known there would
be a young lady a-calling to see him."

" I am Mr. Leaf's aunt," said Hilary, turning as hot as fire.

" Oh, in-deed," was the answer, with civil incredulous-
ness.

But the woman was sharp of perception, as often-cheat-
ed London landladies learn to be.   After looking keenly at
mistress and maid, she changed her tone, nay, even launch-
ed out in praises of her late lodger: what a pleasant gentleman he was; what good company he kept, and how he
had promised to recommend her apartments to his friends.

" And as for the little some'at of rent, miss, tell him it
makes no matter; he can pay me when he likes.   If he
don't call soon, p'raps I might make bold to send his trunk
and his books over to Mr. Ascott's of—dear me, I forget
the number and the square."

Hilary unsuspiciously supplied both.

" Yes, that's it—the old gen'leman as Mr. Leaf went to
dine with every other Sunday—a very rich old gentleman,
who, he says, is to leave him all his money.   Maybe a relation of yours, miss ?"

" No," said Hilary; and adding something about the
landlady's hearing from Mr. Leaf very soon, she hurried out
of the house, Elizabeth following.

" Won't you be tired if you walk so fast, Miss Hilary ?"

Hilary stopped, choking. Helplessly she looked up and down the forlorn, wide, glaring, dusty street, now sinking into the dull shadow of a London afternoon.

"Let us go home!" And at the word a sob burst out— just one passionate pent-up sob. No more. She could not afford to waste strength in crying.

"As you say, Elizabeth, I am getting tired, and that will not do. Let me see; something must be decided." And she stood still, passing her hand over her hot brow and eyes. "I will go back and take the lodgings, leave you there to make all comfortable, and then fetch my sisters from the hotel. But stay first; I have forgotten something."

She returned to the house in Gower Street, and wrote on one of her cards an address—the only permanent address she could think of—that of the city broker who was in the habit of paying them their yearly income of £50.

"If any creditors inquire for Mr. Leaf, give them this. His friends may always hear of him at the London University."

"Thank you, ma'am," replied the now civil landlady. "Indeed, I wasn't afraid of the young gentleman giving us the slip; for, though he was careless in his bills, he was every inch the gentleman. And I wouldn't object to take him in again. Or p'raps you yourself, ma'am, might be a-wanting rooms."

"No, I thank you. Good morning." And Hilary hurried away.

Not a word did she say to Elizabeth, or Elizabeth to her, till they got into the dull, dingy parlor—henceforth to be their sole apology for "home;" and then she only talked about domestic arrangements—talked fast and eagerly, and tried to escape the affectionate eyes which she knew were so sharp and keen. Only to escape them—not to blind them; she had long ago found out that Elizabeth was too quick-witted for that, especially in any thing that concerned "the family." She felt convinced the girl had heard every syllable that passed at Ascott's lodgings: that she knew all that was to be known, and guessed what was to be feared as well as Hilary herself.

"Elizabeth"—she hesitated long, and doubted whether she should say the thing before she did say it—"remember we are all strangers in London, and family matters are best kept within the family. Do not mention either in writing home, or to any body here about—about—"

She could not name Ascott, she felt so horribly ashamed.

CHAPTER X.

LIVING in lodgings, not temporarily, but permanently, sitting down to make one's only "home" in Mrs. Jones's parlor or Mrs. Smith's first-floor, of which not a stick or a stone that one looks at is one's own, and whence one may be evicted or evade, with a week's notice or a week's rent, any day—this sort of life is natural and even delightful to some people. There are those who, like strawberry plants, are of such an errant disposition, that, grow them where you will, they will soon absorb all the pleasantness of their habitat, and begin casting out runners elsewhere; nay, if not frequently transplanted, would actually wither and die. Of such are the pioneers of society—the emigrants, the tourists, the travelers round the world; and great is the advantage the world derives from them, active, energetic, and impulsive as they are—unless, indeed, their talent for incessant locomotion degenerates into rootless restlessness, and they remain forever rolling stones, gathering no moss, and acquiring gradually a smooth, hard surface, which adheres to nothing, and to which nobody dare venture to adhere.

But there are others possessing in a painful degree this said quality of adhesiveness, to whom the smallest change is obnoxious; who like drinking out of a particular cup, and sitting in a particular chair; to whom even a variation in the position of furniture is unpleasant. Of course, this peculiarity has its bad side, and yet it is not in itself mean or ignoble. For is not adhesiveness, faithfulness, constancy—call it what you will—at the root of all citizenship, clanship, and family love? Is it not the same feel-

ing which, granting they remain at all, makes old friendships dearer than any new? Nay, to go to the very sa-
credest and closest bond, is it not that which makes an
old man see to the last in his old wife's faded face the
beauty which perhaps nobody ever saw except himself,
but which he sees and delights in still, simply because it
is familiar and his own?

To people who possess a large share of this rare—shall
I say fatal?—characteristic of adhesiveness, living in lodgings is about the saddest life under the sun. Whether
some dim foreboding of this fact crossed Elizabeth's mind
as she stood at the window watching for her mistresses'
first arrival at " home," it is impossible to say. She could
feel, though she was not accustomed to analyze her feelings. But she looked dull and sad—not cross; even Ascott could not have accused her of " savageness."

And yet she had been somewhat tried. First, in going
out what she termed " marketing," she had traversed a
waste of streets, got lost several times, and returned with
light weight in her butter, and sand in her moist sugar;
also with the conviction that London tradesmen were the
greatest rogues alive. Secondly, a pottle of strawberries,
which she had bought with her own money to grace the
tea-table with the only fruit Miss Leaf cared for, had turned out a large delusion, big and beautiful at top, and all
below small, crushed, and stale. She had thrown it indignantly, pottle and all, into the kitchen fire.

Thirdly, she had a war with the landlady, partly on the
subject of their fire—which, with her Stowbury notions on
the subject of coals, seemed wretchedly mean and small
—and partly on the question of table-cloths at tea, which
Mrs. Jones had " never heard of," especially when the use
of plate and linen was included in the rent. And the din-
giness of the article produced at last out of an omnium-
gatherum sort of kitchen cupboard made an ominous impression upon the country girl, accustomed to clean, tidy
country ways—where the kitchen was kept as neat as the
parlor, and the bedrooms were not a whit behind the sit-

ting-rooms in comfort and orderliness. Here it seemed as if, supposing people could show a few respectable living-rooms, they were content to sleep any where, and cook any how, out of any thing, in the midst of any quantity of confusion and dirt. Elizabeth set all this down as "London," and hated it accordingly.

She had tried to ease her mind by arranging and rearranging the furniture—regular lodging-house furniture—table, six chairs, horse-hair sofa, a what-not, and the chiffonnier, with a tea-caddy upon it, of which the respective keys had been solemnly presented to Miss Hilary. But still the parlor looked homeless and bare; and the yellowish paper on the walls, the large-patterned, many-colored Kidderminster on the floor, gave an involuntary sense of discomfort and dreariness. Besides, No. 15 was on the shady side of the street—cheap lodgings always are; and no one who has not lived in the like lodgings—not a house —can imagine what it is to inhabit perpetually one room where the sunshine just peeps in for an hour a day, and vanishes by eleven A.M., leaving behind in winter a chill dampness, and in summer a heavy, dusty atmosphere, that weighs like lead on the spirits in spite of one's self. No wonder that, as is statistically known and proved, cholera stalks, fever rages, and the registrar's list is always swelled along the shady side of a London street.

Elizabeth felt this, though she had not the dimmest idea why. She stood watching the sunset light fade out of the topmost windows of the opposite house—ghostly reflection of some sunset over fields and trees far away; and she listened to the long, monotonous cry melting away round the Crescent, and beginning again at the other end of the street —"Straw-ber-ries—straw-ber-ries!" Also, with an eye to to-morrow's Sunday dinner, she investigated the cart of the tired costermonger, who crawled along beside his equally tired donkey, reiterating at times, in tones hoarse with a day's bawling, his dreary "Cauli-flow-er! cauli-flower!—Fine new pease, sixpence peck!"

But, alas! the pease were neither fine nor new; and the

cauliflowers were regular Saturday night's cauliflowers.
Besides, Elizabeth suddenly doubted whether she had any
right, unordered, to buy these things, which, from being
common garden necessaries, had become luxuries. This
thought, with some others that it occasioned, her unwonted
state of idleness, and the dullness of every thing about her
—what is so dull as a "quiet" London street on a summer
evening?—actually made Elizabeth stand, motionless and
meditative, for a quarter of an hour.

Then she started to hear two cabs drive up to the door;
the "family" had at length arrived.

Ascott was there too. Two new portmanteaus and a
splendid hat-box cast either ignominy or glory upon the
poor Stowbury luggage; and—Elizabeth's sharp eyes noticed—there was also his trunk, which she had seen lying
detained for rent in his Gower-Street lodgings. But he
looked quite easy and comfortable; handed out his Aunt
Johanna, commanded the luggage about, and paid the cab-
men with such a magnificent air that they touched their
hats to him, and winked at one another, as much as to say,
"That's a real gentleman!"

In which statement the landlady evidently coincided, and
courtesied low when Miss Leaf, introducing him as "my
nephew," hoped that a room could be found for him,
which at last there was, by his appropriating Miss Leaf's,
while she and Hilary took that at the top of the house.
But they agreed Ascott must have a good airy room to
study in.

"You know, my dear boy," said his Aunt Johanna to
him—and at her tender tone he looked a little downcast,
as when he was a small fellow and had been forgiven something—"you know you will have to work very hard."

"All right, aunt! I'm your man for that! This will be
a jolly room; and I can smoke up the chimney capitally."

So they came down stairs quite cheerfully, and Ascott
applied himself with the best of appetites to what he called a "hungry" tea. True, the ham, which Elizabeth had
to fetch from an eating-house some streets off, cost two

shillings a pound, and the eggs, which caused her another war below over the relighting of a fire to boil them, were dismissed by the young gentleman as "horrid stale." Still, woman-like, when there is a man in the question, his aunts let him have his way. It seemed as if they had resolved to try their utmost to make the new home to which he came, or rather was driven, a pleasant home, and to bind him to it with cords of love, the only cords worth any thing, though sometimes—Heaven knows why—even they fail, and are snapped and thrown aside like straws.

Whenever Elizabeth went in and out of the parlor she always heard lively talk going on among the family: Ascott making his jokes, telling about his college life, and planning his life to come, as a surgeon in full practice, on the most extensive scale. And when she brought in the chamber candles, she saw him kiss his aunts affectionately, and even help his Aunt Johanna—who looked frightfully pale and tired, but smiling still—to her bedroom door.

"You'll not sit up long, my dear? No reading tonight?" said she, anxiously.

"Not a bit of it. And I'll be up with the lark to-morrow morning. I really will, auntie. I'm going to turn over a new leaf, you know."

She smiled again at the immemorial joke, kissed and blessed him, and the door shut upon her and Hilary.

Ascott descended to the parlor, threw himself on the sofa with an air of great relief, and an exclamation of satisfaction that "the women" were all gone. He did not perceive Elizabeth, who, hidden behind, was kneeling to arrange something in the chiffonnier, till she rose up and proceeded to fasten the parlor shutters.

"Hollo! are you there? Come, I'll do that when I go to bed. You may 'slope,' if you like."

"Eh, sir?"

"Slope, mizzle, cut your stick; don't you understand? Anyhow, don't stop here bothering me."

"I don't mean to," replied Elizabeth, gravely rather than gruffly, as if she had made up her mind to things as

they were, and was determined to be a belligerent party
no longer. Besides, she was older now—too old to have
things forgiven to her that might be overlooked in a child;
and she had received a long lecture from Miss Hilary on
the necessity of showing respect to Mr. Ascott, or Mr. Leaf,
as it was now decided he was to be called, in his dignity
and responsibility as the only masculine head of the family.

As he lay and lounged there, with his eyes lazily shut,
Elizabeth stood a minute gazing at him. Then, steadfast
in her new good behavior, she inquired "if he wanted any
thing more to-night."

"Confound you, no! Yes; stop." And the young man
took a furtive investigation of the plain, honest face, and
not over-graceful, ultra-provincial figure which still char-
acterized his aunt's "South-Sea Islander."

"I say, Elizabeth, I want you to do something for me."
He spoke so civilly, almost coaxingly, that Elizabeth turned round surprised. "Would you just go and ask the landlady if she has got such a thing as a latch-key?"

"A what, sir?"

"A latch-key—a—oh, she knows. Every London house
has it. Tell her I'll take care of it, and lock the front door
all right. She needn't be afraid of thieves."

"Very well, sir."

Elizabeth went, but shortly reappeared with the information that Mrs. Jones had gone to bed—in the kitchen,
she supposed, as she could not get in. But she laid on the
table the large street-door key.

"Perhaps that's what you wanted, Mr. Leaf. Though I
think you needn't be the least afraid of robbers, for there's
three bolts, and a chain besides."

"All right!" cried Ascott, smothering down a laugh.
"Thank you! That's for you," throwing a half crown
across the table.

Elizabeth took it up demurely, and put it down again.
Perhaps she did not like him enough to receive presents
from him; perhaps she thought, being an honest-minded
girl, that a young man who could not pay his rent had no

business to be giving away half crowns; or else she herself
had not been, so much as many servants are, in the habit
of taking them.   For Miss Hilary had put into Elizabeth
some of her own feeling as to this habit of paying an in-
ferior with money for any little civility or kindness which,
from an equal, would be accepted simply as kindness, and
only requited with thanks.   Anyhow, the coin remained
on the table, and the door was just shutting on Elizabeth,
when the young gentleman turned round again.

"I say, since my aunts are so horridly timid of robbers
and such like, you'd better not tell them any thing about
the latch-key."

Elizabeth stood a minute perplexed, and then replied
briefly, "Miss Hilary isn't a bit timid; and I always tells
Miss Hilary every thing."

Nevertheless, though she was so ignorant as never to have
heard of a latch-key, she had the wit to see that all was not
right.   She even lay awake, in her closet off Miss Leaf's
room, whence she could hear the murmur of her two mistresses talking together long after they retired—lay broad
awake for an hour or more, trying to put things together
—the sad things that she felt certain must have happened
that day, and wondering what Mr. Ascott could possibly
want with the key.   Also, why he had asked her about it,
instead of telling his aunts at once; and why he had treated her in the matter with such astonishing civility.

It may be said a servant had no business to think about
these things, to criticise her young master's proceedings, or
wonder why her mistresses were sad: that she had only to
go about her work like an automaton, and take no interest
in any thing.   I can only answer to those who like such
service, let them have it; and as they sow they will as-
suredly reap.

But long after Elizabeth, young and hearty, was soundly snoring on her hard, cramped bed, Johanna and Hilary
Leaf, after a brief mutual pretense of sleep soon discovered
by both, lay consulting together over ways and means.
How could the family expenses, beginning with twenty-

five shillings per week as rent, possibly be met by the only actual certain family income, their £50 per annum from a mortgage? For the Misses Leaf were of that old-fashioned stamp which believed that to reckon an income by mere probabilities is either insanity or dishonesty.

Common arithmetic soon proved that this £50 a year could not maintain them; in fact, they must soon draw on the little sum—already dipped into to-day for Ascott—which had been produced by the sale of the Stowbury furniture. That sale, they now found, had been a mistake; and they half feared whether the whole change from Stowbury to London had not been a mistake—one of those sad errors in judgment which we all commit sometimes, and have to abide by, and make the best of, and learn from if we can. Happy those to whom "Dinna greet ower spilt milk"—a proverb wise as cheerful, which Hilary, knowing well who it came from, repeated to Johanna to comfort her —teaches a second brave lesson, how to avoid spilling the milk a second time.

And then they consulted anxiously about what was to be done to earn money.

Teaching presented itself as the only resource. In those days women's work and women's rights had not been discussed so freely as at present. There was a strong feeling that the principal thing required was our duties—owed to ourselves, our home, our family and friends. There was a deep conviction—now, alas! slowly disappearing—that a woman, single or married, should never throw herself out of the safe circle of domestic life till the last extremity of necessity; that it is wiser to keep or help to keep a home, by learning how to expend its income, cook its dinners, make and mend its clothes, and, by the law that "prevention is better than cure," studying all those preservative means of holding a family together—as women, and women alone can—than to dash into men's sphere of trades and professions, thereby in most instances fighting an unequal battle, and coming out of it maimed, broken, unsexed; turned into beings that are neither men nor women, with the faults and corresponding sufferings of both, and the compensations of neither.

"I don't see," said poor Hilary, "what I can do but teach. And oh, if I could only get daily pupils, so that I might come home of nights, and creep into the fireside, and have time to mend the stockings and look after Ascott's linen, so that he need not be so awfully extravagant!"

"It is Ascott who ought to earn the family income, and have his aunt to keep house for him," observed Johanna. "That was the way in my time, and I believe it is the right way. The man ought to go out into the world and earn the money; the woman ought to stay at home and wisely expend it."

"And yet that way is not always possible. We know of ourselves instances where it was not."

"Ah! yes," assented Johanna, sighing; for she, far more than Hilary, viewed the family circumstances in the light of its past history—a light too sad almost to bear looking at. "But in ours, as in most similar cases, was something not right, something which forced men and women out of their natural places. It is a thing that may be sometimes a mournful, inevitable necessity; but I never can believe it a right thing, or a thing to be voluntarily imitated, that women should go knocking about the world like men—and—"

"And I am not meaning to do any such thing," said Hilary, half laughing. "I am only going to try every rational means of earning a little money to keep the family going till such time as Ascott can decide on his future, and find a suitable opportunity for establishing himself in practice. In some of the new neighborhoods about London he says he has a capital chance; he will immediately set about inquiries. A good idea, don't you think?"

"Yes," said Johanna, briefly. But they did not discuss this as they had discussed their own plans; and it was noticeable they never even referred to, as a portion of the family finances, that pound a week which, with many re-

grets that it was so small, Ascott had insisted on paying to
his aunts as his contribution to the expenses of the household.

And now the dawn was beginning to break, and the
lively London sparrows to chirp in the chimneys. So Hilary insisted on their talking no more, but going to sleep,
like Christians.

"Very well.   Good-night, my blessing!" said Johanna,
softly.   And perhaps, indeed, her "blessing," with that
strange, bright courage of her own—years after, when Hilary looked back upon her old self, how utterly mad this
courage seemed!—had taken the weight of care from the
elder and feebler heart, so that Johanna turned round and
soon slept.

But long after, till the dawn melted into perfect daylight,
did Hilary lie, open-eyed, listening to quarter after quarter
of the loud St. Pancras clock.   Brave she was, this little
woman, fully as brave and cheerful-hearted as, for Johanna's sake, she made herself out to be; and now that the
paralyzed monotony of her Stowbury life was gone, and
that she was in the midst of the whirl of London, where
he used to work and struggle, she felt doubly bright and
brave.   The sense of resistance, of dogged perseverance, of
"fighting it out" to the last, was strong in her, stronger
than in most women, or else it was the reflection in her
own of that nature which was her ideal of every thing
great and good.

"No," she said to herself, after thinking over for the hundredth time every difficulty that lay before them all —
meeting and looking in the face every wild beast in the
way, even that terrible beast which, happily, had often approached but never yet visited the Leaf family, "the wolf
at the door"—"no, I don't think I am afraid.   I think I
shall never be afraid of any thing in this world if only—
only—"

"If only he loves me."   That was it which broke off unspoken; the helpless woman's cry—the cruel craving for
the one deepest want of a woman's life—deeper than the

same want in man's, or in most men's, because it is more individual; not "if only I am loved," but "if only *he* loves me." And as Hilary resolutely shut her eyes, and forced her aching head into total stillness, sharper than ever, as always was the case when she felt weary, mentally or physically, came her longing for the hand to cling to, the breast to lean against—the heart at once strong and tender, which even the bravest woman feels at times she piteously needs. A heart which can comfort and uphold her, with the strength not of another woman like herself, but of a man, encouraging her, as perhaps her very weakness encourages him, to "fight it out," the sore battle of life, a little longer. But this support, in any shape, from any man, the women of the Leaf family had never known.

The nearest approach to it were those letters from India, which had become, Johanna sometimes jestingly said, a family institution. For they were family letters; there was no mystery about them; they were passed from one to the other, and commented on in perfect freedom—so freely, indeed, that Selina had never penetrated into the secret of them at all. But their punctuality, their faithful remembrance of the smallest things concerning the past, their strong interest in any thing and every thing belonging to the present of these his old friends, were to the other two sisters confirmation enough as to how they might believe in Robert Lyon.

Hilary did believe, and in her perfect trust was perfect rest. Whether he ever married her or not, she felt sure—surer and surer every day—that to her had been sent that best blessing—the lot of so few women—a thoroughly good man to love her and to love.

So with his face in her memory, and the sound of his voice in her ear as distinctly as if it had been only yesterday that he said "You must trust me, Hilary," she whispered to herself, "I do, Robert, I do!" and went to sleep peacefully as a child.

CHAPTER XI.

With a sublime indifference to popular superstition, or, rather, because they did not think of it till all their arrange- ments were completed, the Misses Leaf had accomplished their grand hegira on a Friday. Consequently, their first day at No. 15 was Sunday.

Sunday in London always strikes a provincial person considerably. It has two such distinct sides. First, the eminently respectable, decorous, religious side, which Hila- ry and Selina observed when, about 11 A.M., they joined the stream of well-dressed, well-to-do-looking people, soli- tary or in families, who poured forth from handsome houses in streets or squares, to form the crowded congregation of St. Pancras's Church. The opposite side Hilary also saw when Ascott, who, in spite of his declaration, had not risen in time for breakfast, penitently coaxed his "pretty aunt" to let him take her to the afternoon service in Westmin- ster Abbey. They wended their way through Tottenham Court Road, Oxford Street, Regent Street, and across the park, finding shops open or half open, vehicles plying, and people streaming down each side of the streets.

Hilary did not quite like it, and yet her heart was tender over the poor, hard-worked-looking Cockneys, who seemed so excessively to enjoy their Sunday stroll, their Sunday mouthful of fresh air; or the small Sunday treat their sick- ly, under-sized children had in lying on the grass, and feed- ing the ducks in St. James's Park.

She tried to talk the matter out with Ascott, but, though he listened politely for a minute or two, he evidently took no interest in such things. Nor did he even in the grand old Abbey, with its tree-like, arched avenues of immemori- al stone, its painted windows, through which the colored sunshine made a sort of heavenly mist of light, and its in- numerable graves of generations below. Hilary woke from her trance of solemn delight to find her nephew amusing himself with staring at the people about him, making *sotto voce* quizzical remarks upon them in the intervals of the service, and, finally, the instant it was ended, starting up in extreme satisfaction, evidently feeling that he had done his duty, and that it had been, to use his own phrase, "a confounded bore."

Yet he meant to be kind to his pretty aunt—told her he liked to walk with her because she was so pretty, praised her dress, so neat and tasteful, though a little old-fashioned. But he would soon alter that, he said; he would dress all his aunts in silk and satin, and give them a carriage to ride in; there should be no end to their honor and prosperity. Nay, coming home, he took her a long way round—or she thought so, being tired—to show her the sort of house he meant to have. Very grand it seemed to her Stowbury eyes, with pillars and a flight of steps up to the door— more fit, she ventured to suggest, for a retired merchant than a struggling young surgeon.

"Oh, but we dare not show the struggle, or nobody would ever trust us," said Ascott, with a knowing look. "Bless you, many a young fellow sets up a house, and even a carriage, on tick, and drives and drives about till he drives himself into a practice. The world's all a make-believe, and you must meet humbug with humbug. That's the way, I assure you, Aunt Hilary."

Aunt Hilary fixed her honest eyes on the lad's face—the lad, so little younger than herself, and yet who at times, when he let out sayings such as this, seemed so awfully, so pitifully old; and she felt thankful that, at all risks and costs, they had come to London to be beside him, to help him, to save him, if he needed saving, as women only can. For, after all, he was but a boy. And though, as he walked by her side, stalwart and manly, the thought smote her painfully that many a young fellow of his age was the stay and bread-winner of some widowed mother or sister, nay, even of wife and child, still she repeated, cheerfully, "What can one expect from him? He is only a boy."

God help the women who, for those belonging to them —husbands, fathers, brothers, lovers, sons — have ever so tenderly to *apologize.*

When they came in sight of St. Pancras's Church, Ascott said, suddenly, " I think you'll know your way now, Aunt Hilary."

" Certainly. Why ?"

" Because—you wouldn't be vexed if I left you? I have an engagement — some fellows that I dine with, out at Hampstead, or Richmond, or Blackwall, every Sunday. Nothing wicked, I assure you. And you know it's capital for one's health to get a Sunday in fresh air."

" Yes; but Aunt Johanna will be sorry to miss you."

" Will she ? Oh, you'll smooth her down. Stay ! Tell her I'll be back to tea."

" We shall be having tea directly."

" I declare I had quite forgotten. Aunt Hilary, you must change your hours. They don't suit me at all. No men can ever stand early dinners. By, by ! You are the very prettiest auntie. Be sure you get home safe. Hollo, there ! That's my omnibus."

He jumped on the top of it and was off.

Aunt Hilary stood, quite confounded, and with one of those strange sinkings of the heart which had come over her several times this day. It was not that Ascott showed any unkindness—that there was any actual badness in his bright and handsome young face. Still there was a want there—want of earnestness, steadfastness, truthfulness, a something more discoverable as the lack of something else than as aught in itself tangibly and perceptibly wrong. It made her sad ; it caused her to look forward to his future with an anxious heart. It was so different from the kind of anxiety, and yet settled repose, with which she thought of the only other man in whose future she felt the smallest interest. Of Robert Lyon she was certain that whatever misfortune visited him he would bear it in the best way it could be borne ; whatever temptation assailed him he would fight against it, as a brave and good Christian should fight. But Ascott ?

Ascott's life was yet an unanswered query. She could but leave it in Omnipotent hands.

So she found her way home, asking it once or twice of civil policemen, and going a little distance round—dare I make this romantic confession about so sensible and practical a little woman?—that she might walk once up Burton Street and down again. But nobody knew the fact, and it did nobody any harm.

Meantime at No. 15 the afternoon had passed heavily enough. Miss Selina had gone to lie down—she always did of Sundays, and Elizabeth, after making her comfortable by the little attentions the lady always required, had descended to the dreary wash-house, which had been appropriated to herself under the name of a "private kitchen," in the which, after all the cleanings and improvements she could achieve, she sat like Marius among the ruins of Carthage, and sighed for the tidy bright house-place at Stowbury. Already, from her brief experience, she had decided that London people were horrid shams, because they did not in the least care to have their kitchens comfortable. She wondered how she should ever exist in this one, and might have carried her sad and sullen face up stairs if Miss Leaf had not come down stairs, and glancing about, with that ever-gentle smile of hers, said kindly, "Well, it is not very pleasant, but you have made the best of it, Elizabeth. We must all put up with something, you know. Now, as my eyes are not very good to-day, suppose you come up and read me a chapter." ·

So, in the quiet parlor, the maid sat down opposite her mistress, and read aloud out of that Book which says distinctly,

"*Servants, be obedient to them that are your masters according to the flesh, with fear and trembling, in singleness of heart, as unto Christ: knowing that whatsoever good thing any man doeth, the same shall he receive of the Lord, whether he be bond or free.*"

And yet says immediately after,

"*Ye masters, do the same things unto them, forbearing*

threatening: knowing that your Master also is in heaven; neither is there respect of persons with him."

And I think that Master whom Paul served, not in preaching only, but also in practice, when he sent back the slave Onesimus to Philemon, praying that he might be received, "not now as a servant, but above a servant, a brother beloved," that divine Master must have looked tenderly upon these two women—both women, though of such different age and position, and taught them through his Spirit in his Word, as only he can teach.

The reading was disturbed by a carriage driving up to the door, and a knock, a tremulously grand and forcible footman's knock, which made Miss Leaf start in her easy chair.

"But it can't be visitors to us. We know nobody. Sit still, Elizabeth."

It was a visitor, however, though by what ingenuity he found them out remained, when they came to think of it, a great puzzle. A card was sent in by the dirty servant of Mrs. Jones, speedily followed by a stout, bald-headed, round-faced man—I suppose I ought to write "gentleman" —in whom, though she had not seen him for years, Miss Leaf found no difficulty in recognizing the grocer's 'prentice-boy, now Mr. Peter Ascott, of Russell Square.

She rose to receive him: there was always a stateliness in Miss Leaf's reception of strangers; a slight formality belonging to her own past generation, and to the time when the Leafs were a "county family." Perhaps this extra dignity, graceful as it was, overpowered the little man, or else, being a bachelor, he was unaccustomed to ladies' society; but he grew red in the face, twiddled his hat, and then cast a sharp inquisitive glance toward her.

"Miss Leaf, I presume, ma'am. The eldest?"

"I am the eldest Miss Leaf, and very glad to have an opportunity of thanking you for your long kindness to my nephew. Elizabeth, give Mr. Ascott a chair."

While doing so, and before her disappearance, Elizabeth took a rapid observation of the visitor, whose name and

history were perfectly familiar to her. Most small towns
have their hero, and Stowbury's was Peter Ascott, the grocer's boy, the little fellow who had gone up to London to
seek his fortune, and had, strange to say, found it. Whether by industry or luck—except that industry is luck, and
luck is only another word for industry—he had gradually
risen to be a large city merchant, a drysalter I conclude it
would be called, with a handsome house, carriage, etc. He
had never revisited his native place, which indeed could
not be expected of him, as he had no relations, but when
asked, as was not seldom, of course he subscribed liberally
to its charities.

Altogether he was a decided hero in the place; and
though people really knew very little about him, the less
they knew the more they gossiped, holding him up to the rising generation as a modern Dick Whittington, and reveren-
cing him extremely as one who had shed glory on his native
town. Even Elizabeth had conceived a great idea of Mr.
Ascott. When she saw this little fat man, coarse and common-looking in spite of his good clothes and diamond ring,
and in manner a curious mixture of pomposity and awkwardness, she laughed to herself, thinking what a very uninteresting individual it was about whom Stowbury had
told so many interesting stories.

However, she went up to inform Miss Selina, and prevent her making her appearance before him in the usual
Sunday dishabille in which she indulged when no visitors
were expected.

After the first awkwardness, Mr. Peter Ascott became
quite at his ease with Miss Leaf. He began to talk—not
of Stowbury, that was tacitly ignored by both—but of
London, and then of "my house in Russell Square," "my
carriage," "my servants"—the inconvenience of keeping
coachmen who would drink, and footmen who would not
clean the plate properly; ending by what was a favorite
moral axiom of his, that "wealth and position are heavy
responsibilities."

He himself seemed, however, not to have been quite

overwhelmed by them; he was fat and flourishing—with
an acuteness and power in the upper half of his face which
accounted for his having attained his present position. The
lower half—somehow Miss Leaf did not like it, she hardly
knew why, though a physiognomist might have known.
For Peter Ascott had the underhanging, obstinate, sensual
lip, the large throat—bull-necked, as it has been called—
indications of that essentially animal nature which may be
born with the nobleman as with the clown; which no education can refine, and no talent, though it may coexist with
it, can ever entirely remove. He reminded one, perforce,
of the rough old proverb, "You can't make a silk purse out
of a sow's ear."

Still, Mr. Ascott was not a bad man, though something
deeper than his glorious indifference to grammar, and his
dropped h's— which, to steal some one's joke, might have
been swept up in bushels from Miss Leaf's parlor—made
it impossible for him ever to be, by any culture whatever,
a gentleman.

They talked of Ascott, as being the most convenient
mutual subject; and Miss Leaf expressed the gratitude
which her nephew felt, and she earnestly hoped would ever
show, toward his kind godfather.

Mr. Ascott looked pleased.

"Um—yes, Ascott's not a bad fellow—believe he means
well; but weak, ma'am, I'm afraid he's weak. Knows
nothing of business—has no business habits whatever.
However, we must make the best of him; I don't repent
any thing I've done for him."

"I hope not," said Miss Leaf, gravely.

And then there ensued an uncomfortable pause, which
was happily broken by the opening of the door, and the
sweeping in of a large, goodly figure.

"My sister, Mr. Ascott; my sister Selina."

The little stout man actually started, and, as he bowed,
blushed up to the eyes.

Miss Selina was, as I have stated, the beauty of the family, and had once been an acknowledged Stowbury belle.

Even now, though nigh upon forty, when carefully and becomingly dressed, her tall figure, and her well-featured, fair-complexioned, unwrinkled face made her still appear a very personable woman.   At any rate, she was not faded enough, nor the city magnate's heart cold enough, to prevent a sudden revival of the vision which—in what now seemed an almost antediluvian stage of existence—had dazzled, Sunday after Sunday, the eyes of the grocer's lad. If there is one pure spot in a man's heart—even the very worldliest of men—it is usually his boyish first love.

So Peter Ascott looked hard at Miss Selina, then into his hat, then, as good luck would have it, out of the window, where he caught sight of his carriage and horses.   These revived his spirits, and made him recognize what he was— Mr. Ascott of Russell Square, addressing himself in the character of a benevolent patron to the fallen Leaf family.

"Glad to see you, miss.   Long time since we met— neither of us so young as we have been—but you do wear well, I must say."

Miss Selina drew back; she was within an inch of being highly offended, when she too happened to catch a glimpse of the carriage and horses.   So she sat down and entered into conversation with him; and when she liked, nobody could be more polite and agreeable than Miss Selina.

So it happened that the handsome equipage crawled round and round the Crescent, or stood pawing the silent Sunday street before No. 15 for very nearly an hour, even till Hilary came home.

It was vexatious to have to make excuses for Ascott, particularly as his godfather said with a laugh that "young fellows would be young fellows;" they needn't expect to see the lad till midnight, or till to-morrow morning.

But though in this and other things he somewhat annoyed the ladies from Stowbury, no one could say he was not civil to them—exceedingly civil.   He offered them Botanical Garden tickets — Zoological Garden tickets; he even, after some meditation and knitting of his shaggy gray eyebrows, bolted out with an invitation for the whole family to dinner at Russell Square the following Sunday.

"I always give my dinners on Sunday. I've no time any other day," said he, when Miss Leaf gently hesitated. "Come or not, just as you like."

Miss Selina, to whom the remark was chiefly addressed, bowed the most gracious acceptance.

The visitor took very little notice of Miss Hilary. Probably, if asked, he would have described her as a small, shabbily - dressed person, looking very like a governess. Indeed the fact of her governess-ship seemed suddenly to recur to him; he asked her if she meant to set up another school, and being informed that she rather wished private pupils, promised largely that she should have the full benefit of his "patronage" among his friends. Then he departed, leaving a message for Ascott to call next day, as he wished to speak to him.

"For you must be aware, Miss Leaf, that though your nephew's allowance is nothing—a mere drop in the bucket out of my large income—still, when it comes year after year, and no chance of his shifting for himself, the most benevolent man in the world feels inclined to stop the supplies. Not that I shall do that—at least not immediately: he is a fine young fellow, whom I'm rather proud to have helped a step up the ladder, and I've a great respect"—here he bowed to Miss Selina—"a great respect for your family. Still there must come a time when I shall be obliged to shut up my purse-strings. You understand, ma'am."

"I do," Miss Leaf answered, trying to speak with dignity, and yet patience, for she saw Hilary's face beginning to flame. "And I trust, Mr. Ascott, my nephew will soon cease to be an expense to you. It was your own voluntary kindness that brought it upon yourself, and I hope you have not found, never will find, either him or us ungrateful."

"Oh, as to that, ma'am, I don't look for gratitude. Still, if Ascott does work his way into a good position—and

F

he'll be the first of his family that ever did, I reckon—but I beg your pardon, Miss Leaf. Ladies, I'll bid you good day. Will your servant call my carriage?"

The instant he was gone Hilary burst forth—

"If I were Ascott, I'd rather starve in a garret, break stones in the high-road, or buy a broom and sweep a cross-'ing, than I'd be dependent on this man, this pompous, purse-proud, illiterate fool!"

"No, not a fool," reproved Johanna. "An acute, clear-headed, nor, I think, bad-hearted man. Coarse and common, certainly; but if we were to hate every thing coarse or common, we should find plenty to hate. Besides, though he does his kindness in an unpleasant way, think how very, very kind he has been to Ascott."

"Johanna, I think you would find a good word for the de'il himself, as we used to say," cried Hilary, laughing. "Well, Selina, and what is your opinion of our stout friend?"

Miss Selina, bridling a little, declared that she did not see so much to complain of in Mr. Ascott. He was not ed-ucated certainly, but he was a most respectable person. And his calling upon them so soon was most civil and at-tentive. She thought, considering his present position, they should forget—indeed, as Christians they were bound to forget—that he was once their grocer's boy, and go to dine with him next Sunday.

"For my part, I shall go, though it is Sunday. I con-sider it quite a religious duty—my duty toward my neigh-bor."

"Which is to love him as yourself. I am sure, Selina, I have no objection. It would be a grand romantic wind-up to the story which Stowbury used to tell—of how the 'prentice-boy stared his eyes out at the beautiful young lady; and you would get the advantage of 'my house in Russell Square,' 'my carriage and servants,' and be able to elevate your whole family. Do, now! set your cap at Peter Ascott."

Here Hilary, breaking out into one of her childish fits

of irrepressible laughter, was startled to see Selina's face in one blaze of indignation.

"Hold your tongue, you silly chit, and don't chatter about things you don't understand."

And she swept majestically from the room.

"What have I done? Why, she is really vexed. If I had thought she would have taken it in earnest I would never have said a word. Who would have thought it!"

But Miss Selina's fits of annoyance were so common that the sisters rarely troubled themselves long on the matter. And when at tea-time she came down in the best of spirits, they met her half way, as they always did, thankful for these brief calms in the family atmosphere, which never lasted too long.

It was a somewhat heavy evening. They waited supper till after ten, and yet Ascott did not appear. Miss Leaf read the chapter as usual; and Elizabeth was sent to bed, but still no sign of the absentee.

"I will sit up for him. He can not be many minutes now," said his Aunt Hilary, and settled herself in the solitary parlor, which one candle and no fire made as cheerless as could possibly be.

There she waited till midnight before the young man came in. Perhaps he was struck with compunction by her weary white face—by her silent lighting of his candle, for he made her a thousand apologies.

"'Pon my honor, Aunt Hilary, I'll never keep you up so late again. Poor dear auntie, how tired she looks!" and he kissed her affectionately. "But if you were a young fellow, and got among other young fellows, and they over-persuaded you."

"You should learn to say No."

"Ah!"—with a sigh—"so I ought, if I were as good as my Aunt Hilary."

CHAPTER XII.

Months slipped by; the trees in Burton Crescent had long been all bare; the summer cries of itinerant vegetable dealers and flower-sellers had vanished out of the quiet street. The three sisters almost missed them, sitting in that one dull parlor from morning till night, in the intense solitude of people who, having neither heart nor money to spend in gayeties, live forlorn in London lodgings, and knowing nobody, have nobody to visit, nobody to visit them—

Except Mr. Ascott, who still called, and occasionally staid to tea. The hospitalities, however, were all on their side. The first entertainment—to which Selina insisted upon going, and Johanna thought Hilary and Ascott had better go too—was splendid enough, but they were the only ladies present; and though Mr. Ascott did the honors with great magnificence, putting Miss Selina at the head of his table, where she looked exceedingly well, still the sister agreed it was better that all further invitations to Russell Square should be declined. Miss Selina herself said it would be more dignified and decorous.

Other visitors they had none. Ascott never offered to bring any of his friends, and gradually they saw very little of him. He was frequently out, especially at meal-times, so that his aunts gave up the struggle to make the humble dinners better and more to his liking, and would even have hesitated to take the money which he was understood to pay for his board, had he offered it, which he did not. Yet still, whenever he did happen to remain with them a day or an evening, he was good and affectionate, and always entertained them with descriptions of all he would do as soon as he got into practice.

Meantime they kept house as economically as possible

upon the little ready money they had, hoping that more would come in—that Hilary would get pupils.

But Hilary never did.   To any body who knows London this will not be surprising.   The wonder was in the Misses Leaf being so simple as to imagine that a young country lady, settling herself in lodgings in an obscure metropolitan street, without friends or introduction, could ever expect such a thing.   Nothing but her own daring, and the irrepressible well-spring of hope that was in her healthy youth, could have sustained her in what, ten years after, would have appeared to her, as it certainly was, downright insanity.   But Heaven takes care of the mad, the righteously and unselfishly mad, and Heaven took care of poor Hilary.

The hundred labors she went through—weariness of body and travail of soul, the risks she ran, the pitfalls she escaped—what need to record here?   Many have recorded the like, many more have known them, and acknowledged that when such histories are reproduced in books how utterly imagination fades before reality.   Hilary never looked back upon that time herself without a shuddering wonder how she could have dared all and gone through all.   Possibly she never could but for the sweet old face, growing older yet sweeter every day, which smiled upon her the minute she opened the door of that dull parlor, and made even No. 15 look like home.

When she told, sometimes gayly, sometimes with burning, bursting tears, the tale of her day's efforts and day's failures, it was always comfort to feel Johanna's hand on her hair, Johanna's voice whispering over her, "Never mind, my child, all will come right in time.   All happens for good."

And the face, withered and worn, yet calm as a summer sea, full of the "peace which passeth all understanding," was a living comment on the truth of these words.

Another comfort Hilary had—Elizabeth.   During her long days of absence, wandering from one end of London to the other, after advertisements that she had answered,

or governess institutions that she had applied to, the domestic affairs fell almost entirely into the hands of Elizabeth. It was she who bought in, and kept a jealous eye,
not unneeded, over provisions; she who cooked and waited, and sometimes even put a helping hand, coarse, but
willing, into the family sewing and mending. This had
now become so vital a necessity that it was fortunate Miss
Leaf had no other occupation, and Miss Selina no other entertainment, than stitch, stitch, stitch, at the ever-begin-
ning, never-ending wardrobe wants which assail decent
poverty every where, especially in London.

"Clothes seem to wear out frightfully fast," said Hilary
one day, when she was putting on her oldest gown, to suit
a damp, foggy day, when the streets were slippery with
the mud of settled rain.

"I saw such beautiful merino dresses in a shop in Southampton Row," insinuated Elizabeth; but her mistress shook
her head.

"No, no; my old black silk will do capitally, and I can
easily put on two shawls. Nobody knows me; and people may wear what they like in London. Don't look so
grave, Elizabeth. What does it signify if I can but keep
myself warm? Now run away."

Elizabeth obeyed, but shortly reappeared with a bundle
—a large, old-fashioned thick shawl.

"Mother gave it me; her mistress gave it her; but
we've never worn it, and never shall. If only you didn't
mind putting it on, just this once—this terrible soaking
day!"

The scarlet face, the entreating tones—there was no re-
sisting them. One natural pang Hilary felt—that in her
sharp poverty she had fallen so low as to be indebted to
her servant, and then she too blushed, less for shame at accepting the kindness than for her own pride that could not
at once receive it as such.

"Thank you, Elizabeth," she said, gravely and gently,
and let herself be wrapped in the thick shawl. Its gor-
geous reds and yellows would, she knew, make her notice-

able, even though "people might wear any thing in London." Still, she put it on with a good grace; and all through her peregrinations that day it warmed, not only her shoulders, but her heart.

Coming home, she paused wistfully before a glittering shoe-shop—her poor little feet were so soaked and cold. Could she possibly afford a new pair of boots? It was not a matter of vanity—she had passed that. She did not care now how ugly and shabby looked the "wee feet" that had once been praised; but she felt it might be a matter of health and prudence. Suppose she caught cold—fell ill—died — died, leaving Johanna to struggle alone—died before Robert Lyon came home. Both thoughts struck sharp. She was too young still, or had not suffered enough, calmly to think of death and dying.

"It will do no harm to inquire the price. I might stop it out in omnibuses."

For this was the way every new article of dress had to be procured—"stopping it out" of something else.

After trying several pairs—with a fierce, bitter blush at a small hole which the day's walking had worn in her well-darned stockings, and which she was sure the shopman saw, as well as an old lady who sat opposite — Hilary bought the stoutest and plainest of boots. The bill overstepped her purse by sixpence, but she promised that sum on delivery, and paid the rest. She had got into a nervous horror of letting any account stand over for a single day.

Look tenderly, reader, on this picture of struggles so small, of sufferings so uninteresting and mean. I paint it not because it is original, but because it is so awfully true. Thousands of women, well born, well reared, know it to be true—burned into them by the cruel conflict of their youth; happy they if it ended in their youth, while mind and body had still enough vitality and elasticity to endure! I paint it because it accounts for the accusation sometimes made —especially by men—that women are naturally "stingy." Possibly so; but in many instances may it not have been this petty struggle with petty wants, this pitiful calculating of penny against penny, how best to save here and spend there, which narrows a woman's nature in spite of herself? It sometimes takes years of comparative ease and freedom from pecuniary cares to counteract the grinding, lowering effects of a youth of poverty.

And I paint this picture, too, literally, and not on its picturesque side—if, indeed, poverty has a picturesque side—in order to show another side which it really has—high, heroic, made up of dauntless endurance, self-sacrifice, and self-control. Also to indicate that blessing which narrow circumstances alone bestow, the habit of looking more to the realities than to the shows of things, and of finding pleasure in enjoyments mental rather than sensuous, inward rather than external. When people can truly recognize this they cease either to be afraid or ashamed of poverty.

Hilary was not ashamed—not even now, when hers smote sharper and harder than it had ever done at Stowbury. She felt it a sore thing enough; but it never humiliated nor angered her. Either she was too proud or not proud enough; but her low estate always seemed to her too simply external a thing to affect her relations with the world outside. She never thought of being annoyed with the shopkeeper, who, though he trusted her with the sixpence, carefully took down her name and address; still less to suspecting the old lady opposite, who sat and listened to the transaction—apparently a well-to-do customer, clad in a rich black silk and handsome sable furs—of looking down upon her and despising her. She herself never despised any body except for wickedness.

So she waited contentedly, neither thinking of herself nor of what others thought of her, but with her mind quietly occupied by the two thoughts, which in any brief space of rest always recurred, calming down all annoyances, and raising her above the level of petty pains—Johanna, and Robert Lyon. Under the influence of these her tired face grew composed, and there was a wishful, far-away, fond look in her eyes, which made it not wonder

ful that the said old lady—apparently an acute old soul in
her way—should watch her, as we do occasionally watch
strangers in whom we have become suddenly interested.

There is no accounting for these interests, or to the
events to which they give rise. Sometimes they are pooh-
pooh-ed as "romantic," "unnatural," "like a bit in a novel;" and yet they are facts continually occurring, especially to people of quick intuition, observation, and sympathy.
Nay, even the most ordinary people have known or heard
of such, resulting in mysterious, life-long loves; firm friendships; strange yet often wonderful happy marriages; sudden revolutions of fortune and destiny: things utterly un-
accountable for, except by the belief in the unscrutable
Providence which

> "Shapes our ends,
> Rough-hew them as we will."

When Hilary left the shop she was startled by a voice
at her elbow.

"I beg your pardon, but if your way lies up Southampton Row, would you object to give an old woman a share
of that capital umbrella of yours?"

"With pleasure," Hilary answered, though the oddness
of the request amused her. And it was granted really
with pleasure, for the old lady spoke with those "accents
of the mountain tongue" which this foolish Hilary never
recognized without a thrill at the heart.

"Maybe you think an old woman ought to take a cab,
and not be intruding upon strangers; but I am hale and
hearty, and, being only a street's length from my own door,
I dislike to waste unnecessary shillings."

"Certainly," acquiesced Hilary, with a half sigh: shillings were only too precious to her.

"I saw you in the boot-shop, and you seemed the sort
of young lady who would do a kindness to an old body
like me, so I said to myself, 'I'll ask her.'"

"I am glad you did." Poor girl! she felt unconsciously pleased at finding herself still able to show a kindness
to any body.

F 2

They walked on and on—it was certainly a long street's length—to the stranger's door, and it took Hilary a good way round from hers; but she said nothing of this, concluding, of course, that her companion was unaware of where she lived—in which she was mistaken. They stopped at last before a respectable house near Brunswick Square, bearing a brass plate, with the words "Miss Balquidder."

"That is my name, and very much obliged to you, my dear. How it rains! Ye're just droukit."

Hilary smiled and shook her damp shawl. "I shall take no harm. I am used to going out in all weathers."

"Are you a governess?" The question was so direct and kindly that it hardly seemed an impertinence.

"Yes; but I have no pupils, and fear I shall never get any."

"Why not?"

"I suppose, because I know nobody here. It seems so very hard to get teaching in London. But I beg your pardon."

"I beg yours," said Miss Balquidder—not without a certain dignity—"for asking questions of a stranger. But I was once a stranger here myself, and had a 'sair fecht,' as we say in Scotland, before I could earn even my daily bread. Though I wasn't a governess, still I know pretty well what the sort of life is, and if I had daughters who must work for their bread, the one thing I would urge upon them should be—'Never become a governess.'"

"Indeed. For what reason?"

"I'll not tell you now, my dear, standing with all your wet clothes on; but as I said, if you will do me the favor to call—"

"Thank you!" said Hilary, not sufficiently initiated in London caution to dread making a new aquaintance. Besides, she liked the rough-hewn, good-natured face, and the Scotch accent was sweet to her ear.

Yet when she reached home she was half shy of telling her sisters the engagement she had made. Selina was ex-

tremely shocked, and considered it quite necessary that
the London Directory—the nearest clergyman—or perhaps Mr. Ascott, who, living in the parish, must know—
should be consulted as to Miss Balquidder's respectability.

"She has much more reason to question ours," recollected Hilary, with some amusement, "for I never told her my
name or address. She does not know a single thing about
me."

Which fact, arguing the matter energetically two days
after, the young lady might not have been so sure of, could
she have penetrated the ceiling overhead. In truth, Miss
Balquidder, a prudent person, who never did things by
halves, and, like most truly generous people, was cautious
even in her extremest fits of generosity, at that very moment was sitting in Mrs. Jones's first floor, deliberately discovering every thing possible to be learned about the Leaf
family.

Nevertheless, owing to Selina's indignant pertinacity,
Hilary's own hesitation, and a dim hope of a pupil which
rose up and faded like the rest, the possible acquaintance
lay dormant for two or three weeks; till, alas! the fabulous wolf actually came to the door; and the sisters, after
paying their week's rent, looked aghast at one another, not
knowing where in the wide world the next week's rent was
to come from.

"Thank God, we don't owe any thing—not a penny!"
gasped Hilary.

"No; there is comfort in that," said Johanna. And the
expression of her folded hands and upward face was not
despairing, even though that of the poor widow, when her
barrel of meal was gone, and her cruse of oil spent, would
hardly have been sadder.

"I am sure we have wasted nothing, and cheated nobody
—surely God will help us."

"I know he will, my child."

And the two sisters, elder and younger, kissed one another, cried a little, and then sat down to consider what
was to be done.

Ascott must be told how things were with them. Hitherto they had not troubled him much with their affairs;
indeed, he was so little at home. And, after some private
consultation, both Johanna and Hilary decided that it was
wisest to let the lad come and go as he liked, not attempting—as he once indignantly expressed it—"to tie him to
their apron-strings." For instinctively these maiden ladies felt that with men, and, above all, young men, the only
way to bind the wandering heart was to leave it free, except by trying their utmost that home should be always a
pleasant home.

It was touching to see their efforts, when Ascott came in
of evenings, to enliven for his sake the dull parlor at No.
15. How Johanna put away her mending, and Selina
ceased to grumble, and Hilary began her lively chat, that
never failed to brighten and amuse the household. Her
nephew even sometimes acknowledged that wherever he
went, he met nobody so "clever" as Aunt Hilary.

So, presuming upon her influence with him, on this night,
after the rest were gone to bed, she—being always the
boldest to do any unpleasant thing—said to him,

"Ascott, how are your business affairs progressing?
When do you think you will be able to get into practice?"

"Oh, presently. There's no hurry."

"I am not so sure of that. Do you know, my dear boy"
—and she opened her purse, which contained a few shillings—"that this is all the money we have in the world?"

"Nonsense," said Ascott, laughing. "I beg your pardon," he added, seeing it was with her no laughing matter;
"but I am so accustomed to be hard up that I don't seem
to care. It always comes right somehow—at least with
me."

"How?"

"Oh, I don't exactly know; but it does. Don't fret,
Aunt Hilary. I'll lend you a pound or two."

She drew back. These poor, proud, fond women, who,
if their boy, instead of a fine gentleman, had been a helpless invalid, would have tended him, worked for him, nay,

begged for him—cheerfully, oh! how cheerfully; wanting nothing in the whole world but his love—they could not ask him for his money. Even now, offered thus, Hilary felt as if to take it would be intolerable.

Still the thing must be done.

"I wish, Ascott"—and she nerved herself to say what somebody *ought* to say to him—"I wish you would not lend, but pay us the pound a week you said you could so easily spare."

"To be sure I will. What a thoughtless fellow I have been! But—but—I fancied you would have asked me if you wanted it. Never mind, you'll get it all in a lump. Let me see—how much will it come to? You are the best head going for arithmetic, Aunt Hilary. Do reckon it all up!"

She did so, and the sum total made Ascott open his eyes wide.

"Upon my soul I had no idea it was so much. I'm very sorry, but I seem fairly cleaned out this quarter—only a few sovereigns left to keep the mill going. You shall have them, or half of them, and I'll owe you the rest. Here!"

He emptied on the table, without counting, four or five pounds. Hilary took two, asking him gravely "if he was sure he could spare so much. She did not wish to inconvenience him."

"Oh, not at all; and I wouldn't mind if it did; you have been good aunts to me."

He kissed her, with a sudden fit of compunction, and bade her good-night, looking as if he did not care to be "bothered" any more.

Hilary retired, more sad, more hopeless about him than if he had slammed the door in her face, or scolded her like a trooper. Had he met her seriousness in the same spirit, even though it had been a sullen or angry spirit—and little as she said he must have felt—she wished him to feel— that his aunts were displeased with him; but that utterly unimpressible light-heartedness of his—there was no doing any thing with it. There was, so to speak, "no catching

hold" of Ascott. He meant no harm. She repeated over
and over again that the lad meant no harm. He had no
evil ways; was always pleasant, good-natured, and affectionate, in his own careless fashion, but was no more to be
relied on than a straw that every wind blows hither and
thither, or, to use a common simile, a butterfly that never
sees any thing farther than the nearest flower. His was,
in short, the pleasure-loving temperament, not positively
sinful or sensual, but still holding the pleasure as the greatest good; and regarding what deeper natures call "duty,"
and find therein their strong-hold and consolation, as a
mere bugbear, or a sentimental theory, or an impossible
folly.

Poor lad! and he had the world to fight with; how
would it use him? Even if no heavy sorrows for himself
or others smote him, his handsome face would have to
grow old, his strong frame to meet sickness—death. How
would he do it? That is the thought which always re-
curs. What is *the end* of such men as these? Alas! the
answer would come from hospital wards, alms-houses and
work-houses, debtors' prisons and lunatic asylums.

To apprehensions like this—except the last, happily it
was as yet too far off—Hilary had been slowly and sadly
arriving about Ascott for weeks past; and her conversation
with him to-night seemed to make them darken down upon
her with added gloom. As she went up stairs she set her
lips together hard.

"I see there is nobody to do any thing except me. But
I must not tell Johanna."

She lay long awake, planning every conceivable scheme
for saving money, till at length, her wits sharpened by
the desperation of the circumstances, there flashed upon
her an idea that came out of a talk she had had with Elizabeth that morning. True, it was a perfectly new and un-
tried chance—and a mere chance; still it was right to
overlook nothing. She would not have ventured to tell
Selina of it for the world, and even to Johanna she only
said—finding her as wakeful as herself—said it in a care-

less manner, as if it had relation to nothing, and she expected nothing from it—

"I think, as I have nothing else to do, I will go and see Miss Balquidder to-morrow morning."

CHAPTER XIII.

Miss Balquidder's house was a handsome one, handsomely furnished, and a neat little maid-servant showed Hilary at once into the dining-parlor, where the mistress sat before a business-like writing-table covered with letters, papers, etc., all arranged with that careful order in disorder which indicates, even in the smallest things, the possession of an accurate, methodical mind, than which there are few greater possessions either to its owner or to the world at large.

Miss Balquidder was not a personable woman ; she had never been so even in youth ; and age had told its tale upon those large, strong features—" thoroughly Scotch features" they would have been called by those who think all Scotch-women are necessarily big, raw-boned, and ugly, and have never seen that wonderfully noble beauty—not prettiness, but actual beauty in its highest physical as well as spiritual development—which is not seldom found across the Tweed.

But, while there was nothing lovely, there was nothing unpleasant or uncomely in Miss Balquidder. Her large figure, in its plain black silk dress ; her neat white cap, from under which peeped the little round curls of flaxen hair, neither gray nor snowy, but real " lint-white locks" still ; and her good-humored, motherly look — motherly rather than old-maidish—gave an impression which may be best described by the word " comfortable." She was a " comfortable" woman. She had that quality—too rare, alas ! in all people, and rarest in women going solitary down the hill of life—of being able, out of the deep content of her own nature, to make other people the same.

Hilary was cheered in spite of herself; it always conveys hope to the young, when in sore trouble, if they see the old looking happy.

"Welcome, my dear! I was afraid you had forgotten your promise."

"Oh no," said Hilary, responding heartily to the hearty clasp of a hand large as a man's, but soft as a woman's.

"Why did you not come sooner?"

More than one possible excuse flashed through Hilary's mind, but she was too honest to give it. She gave none at all. Nor did she like to leave the impression that this was merely a visit, when she knew she had only come from secondary and personal motives.

"May I tell you why I came to-day? Because I want advice and help, and I think you can give it, from something I heard about you yesterday."

"Indeed! From whom?"

"In rather a roundabout way; from Mrs. Jones, who told our maid-servant."

"The same girl I met on the staircase at your house? I beg your pardon, but I know where you live, Miss Leaf; your landlady happens to be an acquaintance of mine."

"So she said; and she told our Elizabeth that you were a rich and benevolent woman, who took a great interest in helping other women; not in money"—blushing scarlet at the idea—"I don't mean that, but in procuring them work. I want work—oh! so terribly. If you only knew—"

"Sit down, my dear"—for Hilary was trembling much, her voice breaking, and her eyes filling in spite of all her self-command.

Miss Balquidder—who seemed accustomed to wait upon herself—went out of the room, and returned with cake and glasses; then she took the wine from the sideboard, poured some out for herself and Hilary, and began to talk.

"It is nearly my luncheon-time, and I am a great friend to regular eating and drinking. I never let any thing interfere with my own meals, or other folks' either, if I can help it. I would as soon expect that fire to keep itself up

without coals, as my mind to go on working if I don't look
after my body. You understand? You seem to have good
health, Miss Leaf. I hope you are a prudent girl, and take
care of it."

"I think I do"—and Hilary smiled. "At any rate, my
sister does for me, and also Elizabeth."

"Ah! I liked the look of that girl. If families did but
know that the most useful patent of respectability they
can carry about with them is their maid-servant! That is
how I always judge my new acquaintances."

"There's reason in it too," said Hilary, amused and drawn
out of herself by the frank manner and the cordial voice—
I use the adjective advisedly: none the less sweet because
its good terse English had a decided Scotch accent, with
here and there a Scotch word. Also there was about Miss
Balquidder a certain dry humor essentially Scotch—neither Irish "wit" nor English "fun," but Scotch humor; a
little ponderous, perhaps, yet sparkling; like the sparkles
from a large lump of coal, red-warm at the heart, and capable of warming a whole household, as many a time it had
warmed the little household at Stowbury, for Robert Lyon
had it in perfection. Like a waft as from old times, it
made Hilary at once feel at home with Miss Balquidder.

Equally, Miss Balquidder might have seen something in
this girl's patient, heroic, forlorn youth which reminded her
of her own. Unreasoning as these sudden attractions appear, there is often a hidden something beneath which in
reality makes them both natural and probable, as was the
case here. In half an hour these two women were sitting
talking like old friends, and Hilary had explained her present position, needs, and desires. They ended in the one
cry — familiar to how many thousands more of helpless
young women—"I want work!"

Miss Balquidder listened thoughtfully. Not that it was
a new story—alas! she heard it every day; but there was
something new in the telling of it; such extreme directness
and simplicity, such utter want of either false pride or false
shame. No asking of favors, and yet no shrinking from

well-meant kindness; the poor woman speaking freely to
the rich one, recognizing the common womanhood of both,
and never supposing for an instant that mere money or position could make any difference between them.

The story ended, both turned, as was the character of
both, to the practical application of it—what it was exactly that Hilary needed, and what Miss Balquidder could
supply.

The latter said, after a turn or two up and down the
room with her hands behind her—the only masculine trick
she had—

"My dear, before going farther, I ought to tell you one
thing—I am not a lady."

Hilary looked at her in no little bewilderment.

"That is," explained Miss Balquidder, laughing, "not an
educated gentlewoman like you. I made my money myself—in trade. I kept an outfitter's shop."

"You must have kept it uncommonly well," was the involuntary reply, which, in its extreme honesty and *naïveté*,
was perhaps the best thing that Hilary could have said.

"Well, perhaps I did," and Miss Balquidder laughed her
hearty laugh, betraying one of her few weaknesses—a consciousness of her own capabilities as a woman of business,
and a pleasure at her own deserved success.

"Therefore, you see, I can not help you as a governess.
Perhaps I would not if I could, for, so far as I see, a good
clearance of one half the governesses into honest trades
would be for their own benefit, and greatly to the benefit
of the other half. But that's not my affair. I only meddle with things I understand. Miss Leaf, would you be
ashamed of keeping a shop?"

It is no reflection upon Hilary to confess that this point-
blank question startled her. Her bringing up had been
strictly among the professional class; and in the provinces
sharper than even in London is drawn the line between the
richest tradesman who "keeps a shop," and the poorest
lawyer, doctor, or clergyman who ever starved in decent
gentility. It had been often a struggle for Hilary Leaf's

girlish pride to have to teach A B C to little boys and girls whose parents stood behind counters; but as she grew older she grew wiser, and intercourse with Robert Lyon had taught her much. She never forgot one day, when Selina asked him something about his grandfather or great-grandfather, and he answered quickly, smiling, "Well, I suppose I had one, but I really never heard." Nevertheless, it takes long to conquer entirely the class prejudices of years, nay, more, of generations. In spite of her will, Hilary felt herself wince, and the color rush all over her face, at Miss Balquidder's question.

"Take time to answer, and speak out, my dear. Don't be afraid. You'll not offend me."

The kindly, cheerful tone made Hilary recover her balance immediately.

"I never thought of it before; the possibility of such a thing did not occur to me; but I hope I should not be ashamed of any honest work for which I was competent. Only—to serve in a shop—to wait upon strangers—I am so horribly shy of strangers." And again the sensitive color rushed in a perfect tide over cheeks and forehead.

Miss Balquidder looked, half amused, compassionately at her.

"No, my dear, you would not make a good shop-woman —at least there are many who are better fitted for it than you; and it is my maxim that people should try to find out, and to do, only that which they are best fitted for. If they did we might not have so many cases of proud despair and ambitious failure in the world. It looks very grand and interesting sometimes to try and do what you can't do, and then tear your hair, and think the world has ill used you—very grand, but very silly; when all the while, perhaps, there is something else you can do thoroughly well, and the world will be exceedingly obliged to you for doing it, and *not* doing the other thing. As doubtless the world was to me, when, instead of being a mediocre musician, as I once wished to be—it's true, my dear—I took to keeping one of the best ladies' outfitting warehouses in London."

While she talked her companion had quite recovered herself, and Miss Balquidder then went on to explain, what I will tell more briefly, if less graphically, than the good Scotchwoman, who, like all who have had a hard struggle in their youth, liked a little to dilate upon it in easy old age.

Hard as it was, however, it had ended early, for at fifty she found herself a woman of independent property, without kith or kin, still active, energetic, and capable of enjoying life. She applied her mind to find out what she could best do with herself and her money.

"I might have bought a landed estate to be inherited by—nobody; or a house in Belgravia, and an opera-box, to be shared by—nobody. We all have our pet luxuries; none of these were exactly mine."

"No," assented Hilary, somewhat abstractedly. She was thinking—if *she* could make a fortune, and—and give it away!—if, by any means, any honorable, upright heart could be made to understand that it did not signify, in reality, which side the money came from; that it sometimes showed deeper, the very deepest attachment, when a proud, poor man had self-respect and courage enough to say to a woman, "I love you, and I will marry you; I am not such a coward as to be afraid of your gold."

But, oh! what a ridiculous dream!—and she sat there, the penniless Hilary Leaf, listening to Miss Balquidder, the rich lady, whose life seemed so easy. For the moment, perhaps, her own appeared hard. But she had hope, and she was young. She knew nothing of the years and years that had had to be lived through before those kind eyes looked as clear and cloudless as now; before the voice had gained the sweet evenness of tone which she liked to listen to, and felt that it made her quiet and "good," almost like Johanna's.

"You see, my dear," said Miss Balquidder, "when one has no duties, one must just make them; when we have nobody to care for us, we must take to caring for every body. I suppose"—here a slight pause indicated that this life, like all women's lives, had had its tale, now long, long told—"I suppose I was not meant to be a wife, but I am quite certain I was meant to be a mother. And"—with her peculiar, bright, humorous look—"you'd be astonished, Miss Leaf, if you knew what lots of 'children' I have in all parts of the world."

Miss Balquidder then went on to explain, that finding, from her own experience, how great was the number, and how sore the trial, of young women who nowadays are obliged to work—obliged to forget that there is such a thing as the blessed privilege of being worked for—she had set herself, in her small way, to try and help them. Her pet project was to induce educated women to quit the genteel starvation of governess-ships for some good trade, thereby bringing higher intelligence into a class which needed, not the elevation of the work itself, which was comparatively easy and refined, but of the workers. She had therefore invested sum after sum of her capital in setting up various small shops in the environs of London, in her own former line, and others—stationers, lace-shops, etc. —trades which could be well carried on by women. Into the management of these she put as many young girls as she could find really fitted for it, or willing to learn, paying them regular salaries, large or small, according to their deserts.

"Fair work, fair pay; not one penny more or less; I never do it; it would not be honest. I overlook each business myself, and it is carried on in my name. Sometimes it brings me in a little profit, sometimes not. Of course," she added, smiling, "I would rather have profits than losses; still, I balance one against the other, and it leaves me generally a small interest for my money—two or three per cent., which is all I care about. Thus, you see, I and my young people make a fair bargain on both sides; it's no charity. I don't believe in charity."

"No," said Hilary, feeling her spirit rise. She was yet young enough, yet enough unworn by the fight to feel the deliciousness of work—honest work for honest pay. "I think I could do it," she added. "I think, with a little practice, I really could keep a shop."

"At all events, perhaps you could do what I find more difficult to get done, and well done, for it requires a far higher class of women than generally apply: you could keep the accounts of a shop; you should be the head, and it would be easy to find the hands. Let me see; there is a young lady, she has managed my stationer's business at Kensington these two years, and now she is going to be married. Are you good at figures? Do you understand book-keeping?"

And suddenly changing into the woman of business, and one who was evidently quite accustomed both to arrange and command, Miss Balquidder put Hilary through a sort of extempore arithmetical catechism, from which she came off with flying colors.

"I only wish there were more like you. I wish there were more young ladies brought up like—"

"Like boys!" said Hilary, laughing, "for I always used to say that was my case."

"No, I never desire to see young women made into men." And Miss Balquidder seemed a little scandalized. "But I do wish girls were taught fewer accomplishments, and more reading, writing, and arithmetic; were made as accurate, orderly, and able to help themselves as boys are. But to business. Will you take the management of my stationer's shop?"

Hilary's breath came hard and fast. Much as she had longed for work, to get this sort of work—to keep a stationer's shop! What would her sisters say? what would *he* say? But she dared not think of that just now.

"How much should I be able to earn, do you think?"

Miss Balquidder considered a moment, and then said, rather shortly, for it was not exactly acting on her own principles; she knew the pay was above the work. "I will give you a hundred a year."

A hundred a year! actually certain, and over and above any other income. It seemed a fortune to poor Hilary.

"Will you give me a day or two to think about it and consult my sisters?"

She spoke quietly, but Miss Balquidder could see how agitated she was; how she evidently struggled with many feelings that would be best struggled with alone. The good old lady rose.

"Take your own time, my dear; I will keep the situation open for you for one week from this date. And now I must send you away, for I have a great deal to do."

They parted, quite like friends; and Hilary went out, walking quickly, feeling neither the wind nor the rain. Yet when she reached No. 15 she could not bring herself to enter, but took another turn or two round the Crescent, trying to be quite sure of her own mind before she opened the matter to her sisters. And there was one little battle to be fought which the sisters did not know.

It was perhaps foolish, seeing she did not belong to him in any open way, and he had no external right over her life or her actions, that she should go back and back to the question, "What would Robert Lyon say?"

He knew she earned her daily bread; sometimes this had seemed to vex and annoy him, but it must be done; and when a thing was inevitable, it was not Mr. Lyon's way to say much about it. But being a governess was an accredited and customary mode of a young lady's earning her livelihood. This was different. If he should think it too public, too unfeminine: he had such a horror of a woman's being any thing but a woman, as strong and brave as she could, but in a womanly way; doing any thing, however painful, that she was obliged to do, but never out of choice or bravado, or the excitement of stepping out of her own sphere into man's. Would Robert Lyon think less of her, Hilary, because she had to learn to take care of herself, to protect herself, and to act in so many ways for herself, contrary to the natural and right order of things? That old order — God forbid it should ever change! — which ordained that the women should be "keepers at home;" happy rulers of that happy little world, which seemed as far off as the next world from this poor Hilary.

"What if he should look down upon me? What if he should return and find me different from what he expected?" And bitter tears burned in her eyes as she walked rapidly and passionately along the deserted street. Then a revulsion came.

"No; love is worth nothing that is not worth every thing, and to be trusted through every thing. If he *could* forget me—*could* love any one better than me—me myself, no matter what I was—ugly or pretty, old or young, rich or poor—I would not care for his love. It would not be worth my having; I'd let it go. Robert, though it broke my heart, I'd let you go."

Her eyes flashed; her poor little hand clenched itself under her shawl; and then, as a half reproach, she heard in fancy the steady loving voice—which could have calmed her wildest paroxysm of passion and pain—"You must trust me, Hilary."

Yes, he was a man to be trusted. No doubt very much like other men, and by no means such a hero to the world at large as this fond girl made him out to be; but Robert Lyon had, with all people, and under all circumstances, the character of reliableness. He had also—you might read it in his face—a quality equally rare, faithfulness. Not merely sincerity, but faithfulness; the power of conceiving one clear purpose or one strong love—in unity is strength—and of not only keeping true to it at the time, but of holding fast to it with a single-minded persistency that never even takes in the idea of voluntary change, as long as persistency is right or possible.

"Robert, Robert!" sobbed this forlorn girl, as if slowly waking up to a sense of her forlornness, and of the almost universal fickleness—not actual falseness, but fickleness, which prevails in the world and among mankind. "Oh Robert, be faithful! faithful to yourself—faithful to me!"

CHAPTER XIV.

WHEN Miss Hilary reached home, Elizabeth opened the door to her; the parlor was deserted.

Miss Leaf had gone to lie down, and Miss Selina was away to see the Lord Mayor's Show with Mr. Peter Ascott.

"With Mr. Peter Ascott!" Hilary was a little surprised, but on second thoughts she found it natural; Selina was glad of any amusement—to her, not only the narrowness, but the dullness of their poverty was inexpressibly galling. "She will be back to dinner, I suppose?"

"I don't know," said Elizabeth, briefly.

Had Miss Hilary been less preoccupied, she would have noticed something not quite right about the girl — something that at any other time would have aroused the direct question, "What is the matter, Elizabeth?" For Miss Hilary did not consider it beneath her dignity to observe that things might occasionally go wrong with this solitary young woman, away from her friends, and exposed to all the annoyances of London lodgings; that many trifles might happen to worry and perplex her. If the mistress could not set them right, she could, at least give the word of kindly sympathy, as precious to "a poor servant" as to the queen on her throne.

This time, however, it came not, and Elizabeth disappeared below stairs immediately.

The girl was revolving in her own mind a difficult ethical question. To-day, for the first time in her life, she had *not* "told Miss Hilary every thing." Two things had happened, and she could not make up her mind as to whether she ought to communicate them.

Now Elizabeth had a conscience, by nature a very tender one, and which, from circumstances, had been cultivated into a much higher sensitiveness than, alas! is com-

G

mon among her class, or, indeed, in any class. This, 't an error, was Miss Hilary's doing: it probably caused Elizabeth a few more miseries, and vexations, and painful shocks in the world than she would have had had she imbibed only the ordinary tone of morality, especially the morality of ordinary domestic servants; but it was an error upon which, in summing up her life, the Recording Angel would gravely smile.

The first trial had happened at breakfast-time. Ascott, descending earlier than his wont, had asked her, Did any gentleman, short and dirty, with a hooked-nose, inquire for him yesterday?

Elizabeth thought a minute, and recollected that some person answering the above not too flattering description had called, but refused to leave his name, saying he did not know the ladies, but was a particular friend of Mr. Leaf's.

Ascott laughed. "So he is—a very particular friend; but my aunts would not fancy him, and I don't want him to come here. Say, if he calls, that I'm gone out of town."

"Very well, sir. Shall you start before dinner?" said Elizabeth, whose practical mind immediately recurred to that meal, and to the joint, always contrived to be hot on the days that Ascott dined at home.

He seemed excessively tickled. "Bless you, you are the greatest innocent! Just say what I tell you, and never mind—hush! here's Aunt Hilary."

And Miss Hilary's anxious face, white with long wakefulness, had put out of Elizabeth's head the answer that was coming; indeed, the matter slipped from her mind altogether, in consequence of another circumstance which gave her much more perplexity.

During her young mistress's absence, supposing Miss Selina out too, and Miss Leaf up stairs, she had come suddenly into the parlor without knocking. There, to her amazement, she saw Miss Selina and Mr. Ascott standing, in close conversation, over the fire. They were so engrossed that they did not notice her, and she shut the door again immediately. But what confounded her was that she was certain, absolutely certain, Mr. Ascott had his arm round Miss Selina's waist!

Now that was no business of hers, and yet the faithful domestic was a good deal troubled; still more so when, by Miss Leaf's excessive surprise at hearing of the visitor who had come and gone, carrying Miss Selina away to the city, she was certain the elder sister was completely in the dark as to any thing going to happen in the family.

Could it be a wedding? Could Miss Selina really love, and be intending to marry, that horrid little man? For, strange to say, this young servant had, what many a young beauty of rank and fashion has not, or has lost forever—the true, pure, womanly creed, that loving and marrying are synonymous terms; that to let a man put his arm round your waist when you do not intend to marry him, or to intend to marry him for money or any thing else when you do not really love him, are things quite impossible and incredible to any womanly mind. A creed somewhat out of date, and perhaps existing only in stray nooks of the world; but, thank God! it does exist. Hilary had it, and she had taught it to Elizabeth.

"I wonder whether Miss Hilary knows of this? I wonder what she would say to it?"

And now arose the perplexing ethical question aforesaid as to whether Elizabeth ought to tell her.

It was one of Miss Hilary's doctrines—the same for the kitchen as the parlor, nay, preached strongest in the kitchen, where the mysteries of the parlor are often so cruelly exposed — that a secret accidentally found out should be kept as sacred as if actually confided; also, that the secret of an enemy should no more be betrayed than that of a beloved and trusting friend.

"Miss Selina isn't my enemy," smiled Elizabeth, "but I'm not overfond of her, and so I'd rather not tell of her, or vex her if I can help it. Anyhow, I'll keep it to myself for a bit."

But the secret weighed heavily upon her, and, besides,

her honest heart felt a certain diminution of respect for Miss Selina. What could she see to like in that common-looking, commonplace man, whom she could not have met a dozen times, of whose domestic life she knew nothing, and whose personality Elizabeth, with the sharp observation often found in her class, probably because coarse people do not care to hide their coarseness from servants, had speedily set down at her own valuation—"Neither carriage nor horses, nor nothing, will ever make *him* a gentleman!"

He, however, sent Miss Selina home magnificently in the said carriage; Ascott with her, who had been picked up somewhere in the City, and who came into his dinner without the slightest reference to going "out of town."

But in spite of her Lord Mayor's Show, and the great attention which she said she had received from "various members of the Common Council of the City of London," Miss Selina was, for her, meditative, and did not talk quite so much as usual. There was in the little parlor an uncomfortable atmosphere, as if all of them had something on their minds. Hilary felt the ice must be broken, and if she did not do it nobody else would. So she said, stealing her hand into Johanna's, under shelter of the dim firelight,

"Selina, I wanted to have a little family consultation. I have just received an offer."

"An offer!" repeated Miss Selina, with a visible start. "Oh, I forgot; you went to see your friend, Miss Balquidder, this morning. Did you get any thing out of her? Has she any nephews and nieces wanting a governess?"

"She has no relations at all. But I will just tell you the story of my visit."

"I hope it's interesting," said Ascott, who was lying on the sofa, half asleep, his general habit after dinner. He woke, however, during his Aunt Hilary's relation, and when she reached its climax, that the offer was for her to manage a stationer's shop, he burst out, heartily laughing:

"Well, that is a rich idea. I'll come and buy of you. You'll look so pretty standing behind a counter."

But Selina said, angrily, "You can not even think of such a thing. It would be a disgrace to the family."

"No," said Hilary, clasping tightly her eldest sister's hand—they two had already talked the matter over, "I can not see any disgrace. If our family is so poor that the women must earn their living as well as the men, all we have to see is that it should be honestly earned. What do you say, Ascott?"

She looked earnestly at him; she wanted sorely to find out what he really thought.

But Ascott took it, as he did every thing, very easily. "I don't see why Aunt Selina should make such a fuss. Why need you do any thing, Aunt Hilary? Can't we hold out a little longer, and live upon tick till I get into practice? Of course, I shall then take care of you all; I'm the head of the family. How horridly dark this room is!"

He started up, and gave the fire a fierce poke, which consumed in five minutes a large lump of coal that Hilary had hoped—oh, cruel, sordid economy—would have lasted half the evening.

She broke the uneasy silence which followed by asking Johanna to give her opinion.

Johanna roused herself and spoke:

"Ascott says right; he is the head of the family, and by-and-by, I trust, will take care of us all. But he is not able to do it now, and meantime we must live."

"To be sure we must, auntie."

"I mean, my boy, we must live honestly; we must not run into debt;" and her voice sharpened as with the reflected horror of her young days—if, alas! there ever had been any youth for Henry Leaf's eldest daughter. "No, Ascott, out of debt out of danger. For myself"—she laid her thin old fingers on his arm, and looked up at him with a pitiful mixture of reliance and hopelessness—"I would rather see you breaking stones in the road than living like a gentleman, as you call it, and a swindler, as I call it, upon other people's money."

Ascott sprang up, coloring violently. "You use strong

language, Aunt Johanna. Never mind. I dare say you are right. However, it's no business of mine. Good-night, for I have an engagement."

Hilary said, gravely, she wished he would stay and join in the family consultation.

"Oh no; I hate talking over things. Settle it among yourselves. As I said, it isn't my business."

"You don't care, then, what becomes of us all? I sometimes begin to think so."

Struck by the tone, Ascott stopped in the act of putting on his lilac kid gloves. "What have I done? I may be a very bad fellow, but I'm not quite so bad as that, Aunt Hilary."

"She didn't mean it, my boy," said Aunt Johanna, tenderly.

He was moved, more by the tenderness than the reproach. He came and kissed his eldest aunt in that warm-hearted, impulsive way, which had won him forgiveness for many a boyish fault. It did so now.

"I know I'm not half good enough to you, auntie, but I mean to be. I mean to work hard, and be a rich man some day, and then you may be sure I shall not let my Aunt Hilary keep a shop. Now good-night, for I must meet a fellow on business—really business—that may turn out good for us all, I assure you."

He went away whistling, with that air of untroubled, good-natured liveliness peculiar to Ascott Leaf, which made them say continually that he was "only a boy," living a boy's life, as thoughtless and as free. When his handsome face disappeared the three women sat down again round the fire.

They made no comments on him whatever; they were women, and he was their own. But—passing him over as if he had never existed—Hilary began to explain to her sisters all particulars of her new scheme for maintaining the family. She told these details in a matter-of-fact way, as already arranged, and finally hoped Selina would make no more objections.

"It is a thing quite impossible," said Selina, with dignity.

"Why impossible? I can certainly do the work, and it can not make me less of a lady. Besides, we had better not be ladies if we can not be honest ones. And, Selina, where is the money to come from? We have none in the house; we can not get any till Christmas."

"Opportunities might occur. We have friends."

"Not one in London—except, perhaps, Mr. Ascott, and I would not ask him for a farthing. You don't see, Selina, how horrible it would be to be helped, unless by some one dearly loved. I couldn't bear it! I'd rather beg—starve—almost steal!"

"Don't be violent, child."

"Oh, but it's hard!" and the cry of long-smothered pain burst out. "Hard enough to have to earn one's bread in a way one doesn't like; harder still to have to be parted from Johanna from Monday morning till Saturday night. But it must be.. I'll go. It's a case between hunger, debt, and work; the first is unpleasant, the second impossible, the third is my only alternative. You must consent, Selina, for I *will* do it."

"Don't!" Selina spoke more gently, and not without some natural emotion. "Don't disgrace me, child; for I may as well tell you—I meant to do so to-night—Mr. Ascott has made me an offer of marriage, and I—I have accepted it."

Had a thunderbolt fallen in the middle of the parlor at No. 15, its inmates—that is, two of them—could not have been more astounded.

No doubt this surprise was a great instance of simplicity on their part. Many women would have prognosticated, planned the thing from the first; thought it a most excellent match; seen glorious visions of the house in Russell Square, of the wealth and luxury that would be the portion of "dear Selina," and the general benefit that the marriage would be to the whole Leaf family.

But these two were different from others. They only

saw their sister Selina, a woman no longer young, and not
without her peculiarities, going to be married to a man she
knew little or nothing about—a man whom they themselves
had endured rather than liked, and for the sake of gratitude. He was trying enough merely as a chance visitor;
but to look upon Mr. Ascott as a brother-in-law, as a husband—

"Oh, Selina! you can not be in earnest?"

"Why not? Why should I not be married as well as
my neighbors?" said she, sharply.

Nobody arguing that point, both being, indeed, too bewildered to argue at all, she continued, majestically,

"I assure you, sisters, there could not be a more unex-
ceptionable offer. It is true, Mr. Ascott's origin was rather
humble; but I can overlook that. In his present wealth,
and with his position and character, he will make the best
of husbands."

Not a word was answered; what could be answered?
Selina was free to marry if she liked, and whom she liked.
Perhaps, from her nature, it was idle to expect her to marry in any other way than this; one of the thousand and
one unions where the man desires a handsome, lady-like
wife for the head of his establishment, and the woman
wishes an elegant establishment to be mistress of; so
they strike a bargain—possibly as good as most other bar-
gains.

Still, with one faint lingering of hope, Hilary asked if she
had quite decided.

"Quite. He wrote to me last night, and I gave him his
answer this morning."

Selina certainly had not troubled any body with her
"love affairs." It was entirely a matter of business.

The sisters saw at once that she had made up her mind.
Henceforward there could be no criticism of Mr. Peter Ascott.

Now all was told, she talked freely of her excellent prospects.

"He has behaved handsomely—very much so. He makes

a good settlement on me, and says how happy he will be to help my family, so as to enable you always to make a respectable appearance."

"We are exceedingly obliged to him."

"Don't be sharp, Hilary. He means well. And he must feel that this marriage is a sort of—ahem! condescension on my part, which I never should have dreamed of twenty years ago."

Selina sighed: could it be at the thought of that twenty years ago? Perhaps, shallow as she seemed, this woman might once have had some fancy, some ideal man whom she expected to meet and marry; possibly a very different sort of man from Mr. Peter Ascott. However, the sigh was but momentary; she plunged back again into all the arrangements of her wedding, every one of which, down to the wedding-dress, she had evidently decided.

"And therefore you see," she added, as if the unimportant, almost forgotten item of discussion had suddenly occurred to her, "it's quite impossible that my sister should keep a shop. I shall tell Mr. Ascott, and you will see what he says to it."

But when Mr. Ascott appeared next day in solemn state as an accepted lover he seemed to care very little about the matter. He thought it was a good thing for every body to be independent; did not see why young women— he begged pardon, young ladies—should not earn their own bread if they liked. He only wished that the shop were a little farther off than Kensington, and hoped the name of Leaf would not be put over the door.

But the bride-elect, indignant and annoyed, begged her lover to interfere, and prevent the scheme from being carried out.

"Don't vex yourself, my dear Selina," said he, dryly— how Hilary started to hear this stranger use the household name—"but I can't see that it's my business to interfere. I marry you; I don't marry your whole family."

"Mr. Ascott is quite right; we will end the subject," said Johanna, with grave dignity; while Hilary sat with

G 2

burning cheeks, thinking that, miserable as the family had
been, it had never till now known real degradation.

But her heart was very sore that day. In the morning
had come the letter from India, never omitted, never de-
layed; Robert Lyon was punctual as clock-work in every
thing he did. It came, but this month it was a short and
somewhat sad letter—hinting of failing health, uncertain
prospects; full of a bitter longing to come home, and a
dread that it would be years before that longing was realized.

"My only consolation is," he wrote, for once betraying
himself a little, "that, however hard my life out here may
be, I bear it alone."

But that consolation was not so easy to Hilary. That
they two should be wasting their youth apart, when just
a little heap of yellow coins—of which men like Mr. Ascott
had such profusion—would bring them together, and, let
trials be many or poverty hard, give them the unutterable
joy of being once more face to face and heart to heart—
oh, it was sore—sore!

Yet when she went up from the parlor, where the newly-
affianced couple sat together, "making-believe" a passion
that did not exist, and acting out the sham courtship, proper for the gentleman to pay and the lady to receive—when
she shut her bedroom door, and there, sitting in the cold, ·
read again and again Robert Lyon's letter to Johanna, so
good, so honest; so sad, yet so bravely enduring—Hilary
was comforted. She felt that true love, in its most unsatis-
fied longings, its most cruel delays, nay, even its sharpest
agonies of hopeless separation, is sweeter ten thousand times
than the most "respectable" of loveless marriages such as
this.

So, at the week's end, Hilary went patiently to her work
at Kensington, and Selina began the preparations for her
wedding

CHAPTER XV.

In relating so much about her mistresses, I have lately seemed to overlook Elizabeth Hand.

She was a person easy enough to be overlooked. She never put herself forward, not even now, when Miss Hilary's absence caused the weight of housekeeping and domestic management to fall chiefly upon her. She went about her duties as soberly and silently as she had done in her girlhood; even Miss Leaf could not draw her into much demonstrativeness: she was one of those people who never "come out" till they are strongly needed, and then— But it remained to be proved what this girl would be.

Years afterward Hilary remembered with what a curious reticence Elizabeth used to go about in those days: how she remained as old-fashioned as ever; acquired no London ways, no fripperies of dress or flippancies of manner. Also, that she never complained of any thing, though the discomforts of her lodging-house life must have been great— greater than her mistresses had any idea of at the time. Slowly, out of her rough, unpliant girlhood, was forming that character of self-reliance and self-control, which, in all ranks, makes of some women the helpers rather than the helped, the laborers rather than the pleasure-seekers; women whose constant lot it seems to be to walk on the shadowed side of life, to endure rather than to enjoy.

Elizabeth had very little actual enjoyment. She made no acquaintances, and never asked for holidays. Indeed, she did not seem to care for any. Her great treat was when, on a Sunday afternoon, Miss Hilary sometimes took her to Westminster Abbey or St. Paul's, when her pleasure and gratitude always struck her mistress—nay, even soothed her, and won her from her own many anxieties. It is such a blessing to be able to make any other human being, even for an hour or two, entirely happy!

Except these bright Sundays, Elizabeth's whole time was spent in waiting upon Miss Leaf, who had seemed to grow suddenly frail and old. It might be that living without her child six days out of the seven was a greater trial than had at first appeared to the elder sister, who until now had never parted with her since she was born; or it was perhaps a more commonplace and yet natural cause, the living in London lodgings, without even a change of air from room to room, and the want of little comforts and luxuries, which, with all Hilary's care, were as impossible as ever to their limited means.

For Selina's engagement, which, as a matter of decorum, she had insisted should last six months, did not lessen expenses. Old gowns were shabby, and omnibuses impossible to the future Mrs. Ascott of Russell Square; and though, to do her justice, she spent as little as to her self-pleasing nature was possible, still she spent something.

"It's the last; I shall never cost you any more," she would say, complacently; and revert to that question of absorbing interest, her *trousseau*, an extremely handsome one, provided liberally by Mr. Ascott. Sorely had this arrangement jarred upon the pride of the Leaf family; yet it was inevitable. But no personal favors would the other two sisters have accepted from Mr. Ascott, even had he offered them—which he did not—save a dress each for the marriage, and a card for the marriage-breakfast, which, he also arranged, was to take place at a hotel.

So, in spite of the expected wedding, there was little change in the dull life that went on at No. 15. Its only brightness was when Miss Hilary came home from Saturday to Monday. And in those brief glimpses, when, as was natural, she on her side, and they on theirs, put on their best face, so to speak, each trying to hide from the other any special care, it so fell out that Miss Hilary never discovered a thing which, week by week, Elizabeth resolved to speak to her about, and yet never could. For it was not her own affair; it seemed like presumptuously meddling in the affairs of the family. Above all, it involved the necessity of something which looked like tale-bearing and backbiting of a person she disliked, and there was in Elizabeth—servant as she was—an instinctive chivalrous honor which made her especially anxious to be just to her enemies.

Enemy, however, is a large word to use; and yet day by day her feelings grew more bitter toward the person concerned—namely, Mr. Ascott Leaf. It was not from any badness in him: he was the sort of young man always likely to be a favorite with what would be termed his " inferiors;" easy, good-tempered, and gentlemanly, giving a good deal of trouble certainly, but giving it so agreeably that few servants would have grumbled, and paying for it —as he apparently thought every thing could be paid for — with a pleasant word and a handful of silver.

But Elizabeth's distaste for him had deeper roots. The principal one was his exceeding indifference to his aunts' affairs, great and small, from the marriage, which he briefly designated as a "jolly lark," to the sharp economies which, even with the addition of Miss Hilary's salary, were still requisite. None of these latter did he ever seem to notice, except when they pressed upon himself; when he neither scolded nor argued, but simply went out and avoided them.

He was now absent from home more than ever, and apparently tried as much as possible to keep the household in the dark as to his movements—leaving at uncertain times, never saying what hour he would be back, or if he said so, never keeping to his word. This was the more annoying, as there were a number of people continually inquiring for him, hanging about the house, and waiting to see him "on business;" and some of these occasionally commented on the young gentleman in such unflattering terms that Elizabeth was afraid they would reach the ear of Mrs. Jones, and henceforward tried always to attend to the door herself.

But Mrs. Jones was a wide-awake woman. She had not let lodgings for thirty years for nothing. Ere long she discovered, and took good care to inform Elizabeth of her discovery, that Mr. Ascott Leaf was what is euphuistically termed "in difficulties."

And here one word, lest in telling this poor lad's story I may be supposed to tell it harshly or uncharitably, as if there was no crime greater than that which a large portion of society seems to count as none; as if, at the merest mention of the ugly word debt, this rabid author flew out, and made all the ultra-virtuous persons whose history is here told fly out like turkeys after a bit of red cloth, which is a very harmless scrap of red cloth after all.

Most true, some kind of debt deserves only compassion. The merchant suddenly failing; the tenderly reared family who by some strange blunder or unkind kindness have been kept in ignorance of their real circumstances, and been spending pounds for which there was only pence to pay; the individuals, men or women, who, without any laxity of principle, are such utter children in practice that they have to learn the value and use of money by hard experience, much as a child does, and are little better than children in all that concerns l. s. d. to the end of their days.

But these are debtors by accident, not error. The deliberate debtor, who orders what he knows he has no means of paying for; the pleasure-loving debtor, who can not renounce one single luxury for conscience' sake; the well-meaning, lazy debtor, who might make "ends meet," but does not, simply because he will not take the trouble; upon such as these it is right to have no mercy—they deserve none.

To which of these classes young Ascott Leaf belonged his story will show. I tell it, or rather let it tell itself, and point its own moral; it is the story of hundreds and thousands.

That a young fellow should not enjoy his youth would be hard; that it should not be pleasant to him to dress well, live well, and spend with open hand upon himself as well as others, no one will question. No one would ever wish it otherwise. Many a kindly spendthrift of twenty-one makes a prudent paterfamilias at forty, while a man who in his twenties showed a purposeless niggardliness, would at sixty grow into the most contemptible miser alive. There is something even in the thoughtless liberality of youth to which one's heart warms, even while one's wisdom reproves. But what struck Elizabeth was that Ascott's liberalities were always toward himself, and himself only.

Sometimes when she took in a parcel of new clothes, while others yet unpaid for were tossing in wasteful disorder about his room, or when she cleaned indefinite pairs of handsome boots, and washed dozens of the finest cambric pocket-handkerchiefs, her spirit grew hot within her to remember Miss Hilary's countless wants and contrivances in the matter of dress, and all the little domestic comforts which Miss Leaf's frail health required—things which never once seemed to cross the nephew's imagination. Of course not, it will be said; how could a young man be expected to trouble himself about these things?

But they do, though. Answer, many a widow's son; many a heedful brother of orphan sisters; many a solitary clerk living and paying his way upon the merest pittance; is it not better to think of others than one's self? Can a man, even a young man, find his highest happiness in mere personal enjoyment?

However, let me cease throwing these pebbles of preaching under the wheels of my story; as it moves on it will preach enough for itself.

Elizabeth's annoyances, suspicions, and conscience-pricks as to whether she ought or ought not to communicate both, came to an end at last. Gradually she made up her mind that, even if it did look like tale-bearing, on the following Saturday night Miss Hilary must know all.

It was an anxious week, for Miss Leaf had fallen ill. Not seriously; and she never complained until her sister had left, when she returned to her bed and did not again rise. She would not have Miss Hilary sent for, nor Miss Selina, who was away paying a ceremonious prenuptial visit to Mr. Ascott's partner's wife at Dulwich.

"I don't want any thing that you can not do for me. You are becoming a first-rate nurse, Elizabeth," she said, with that passive, peaceful smile which almost frightened the girl; it seemed as if she were slipping away from this world and all its cares into another existence. Elizabeth felt that to tell her any thing about her nephew's affairs was perfectly impossible. How thankful she was that in the quiet of the sick-room her mistress was kept in igno- rance of the knocks and inquiries at the door, and espe- cially of a certain ominous paper which had fallen into Mrs. Jones's hands, and informed her, as she took good care to inform Elizabeth, that any day "the bailiffs" might be aft- er her young master.

"And the sooner the whole set of you clear out of my house the better; I am a decent, respectable woman," said Mrs. Jones, that very morning; and Elizabeth had had to beg her as a favor not to disturb her sick mistress, but to wait one day, till Miss Hilary came home.

Also, when Ascott, ending with a cheerful and careless countenance his ten minutes' after-breakfast chat in his aunt's room, had met Elizabeth on the staircase, he had stopped to bid her say if any body wanted him he was gone to Birmingham, and would not be home till Monday. And on Elizabeth's hesitating, she having determined to tell no more of these involuntary lies, he had been very angry, and then stooped to entreaties, begging her to do as he asked, or it would be the ruin of him—which she under- stood well enough when, all the day, she—grown painful- ly wise, poor girl!—watched a Jewish-looking man hang- ing about the house, and noticing every body that went in or out of it.

Now, sitting at Miss Leaf's window, she fancied she saw this man disappear into the gin-palace opposite, and at the same moment a figure darted hurriedly round the street- corner and into the door of No. 15.

Elizabeth looked to see if her mistress were asleep, and then crept quietly out of the room, shutting the door after her. Listening, she heard the sound of the latch-key, and of some one coming stealthily up stairs.

"Hollo! Oh, it's only you, Elizabeth."

"Shall I light your candle, sir?"

But when she did the sight was not pleasant. Drenched with rain, his collar pulled up, and his hat slouched, so as in some measure to act as a disguise, breathless and trembling—hardly any body would have recognized in this discreditable object that gentlemanly young man, Mr. Ascott Leaf.

He staggered into his room and threw himself across the bed.

"Do you want any thing, sir?" said Elizabeth, from the door.

"No—yes—stay a minute. Elizabeth, are you to be trusted?"

"I hope I am, sir."

"The bailiffs are after me. I've just dodged them. If they know I'm here the game's all up—and it will kill my aunt."

Shocked as she was, Elizabeth was glad to hear him say that—glad to see the burst of emotion with which he flung himself down on the pillow, muttering all sorts of hopeless self-accusations.

"Come, sir, 'tis no use taking on so," said she, much as she would have spoken to a child, for there was something childish rather than manlike in Ascott's distress. Nevertheless, she pitied him with the unreasoning pity a kind heart gives to any creature who, blameworthy or not, has fallen into trouble. "What do you mean to do?"

"Nothing. I'm cleaned out. And I haven't a friend in the world."

He turned his face to the wall in perfect despair.

Elizabeth tried hard not to sit in judgment upon what the Catechism would call her "betters," and yet her own strong instinct of almost indefinite endurance turned with something approaching contempt from this weak, lightsome nature, broken by the first touch of calamity.

"Come, it's no use making things worse than they are. If nobody knows that you are here, lock your door and keep quiet. I'll bring you some dinner when I bring up missis's tea, and not even Mrs. Jones will be any the wiser."

"You're a brick, Elizabeth—a regular brick!" cried the young fellow, brightening up at the least relief. "That will be capital. Get me a good slice of beef, or ham, or something. And, mind you — don't forget! — a regular stunning bottle of pale ale."

"Very well, sir."

The acquiescence was somewhat sullen, and, had he watched Elizabeth's face, he might have seen there an expression not too flattering. But she faithfully brought him his dinner, and kept his secret, even though, hearing from over the staircase Mrs. Jones resolutely deny that Mr. Leaf had been at home since morning, she felt very much as if she were conniving at a lie. With a painful, half-guilty consciousness, she waited for her mistress's usual question, "Is my nephew come home?" but fortunately it was not asked. Miss Leaf lay quiet and passive, and her faithful nurse settled her for the night with a strangely solemn feeling, as if she were leaving her to her last rest, safe and at peace before the overhanging storm broke upon the family.

But all shadow of this storm seemed to have passed away from him who was its cause. As soon as the house was still Ascott crept down and fell to his supper with as good an appetite as possible. He even became free and conversational.

"Don't look so glum, Elizabeth. I shall soon weather through. Old Ascott will fork out; he couldn't help it. I'm to be his nephew, you know. Oh, that was a clever catch of Aunt Selina's. If only Aunt Hilary would try another like it."

"If you please, sir, I'm going to bed."

"Off with you, then, and I'll not forget the gown at Christmas. You're a sharp young woman, and I'm much obliged to you." And for a moment he looked as if he were about to make the usual unmannerly acknowledgment of civility from a young gentleman to a servant-maid, viz., kissing her, but he pulled a face and drew back. He really couldn't; she was so very plain.

At this moment there came a violent ring, and "Fire!" was shouted through the keyhole of the door. Terrified, Elizabeth opened it, when, with a burst of laughter, a man rushed in and laid hands upon Ascott.

It was the sheriff's officer.

When his trouble came upon him Ascott's manliness returned. He turned very white, but he made no opposition; had even enough of his wits about him—or something better than wits—to stop Mrs. Jones from rushing up in alarm and indignation to arouse Miss Leaf.

"No; she'll know it quite soon enough. Let her sleep till morning. Elizabeth, look here." He wrote upon a card the address of the place he was to be taken to. "Give Aunt Hilary this. Say if she can think of a way to get me out of this horrid mess; but I don't deserve—Never mind. Come on, you fellows."

He pulled his hat over his eyes, jumped into the cab, and was gone. The whole thing had not occupied five minutes.

Stupefied, Elizabeth stood and considered what was best to be done. Miss Hilary must be told; but how to get at her in the middle of the night, thereby leaving her mistress to the mercy of Mrs. Jones. It would never do. Suddenly she thought of Miss Balquidder. She might send a message. No, not a message—for the family misery and disgrace must not be betrayed to a stranger—but a letter to Kensington.

With an effort Elizabeth composed herself sufficiently to write one—her first—to her dear Miss Hilary.

"HONORED MADAM,—Mr. Leaf has got himself into trouble, and is taken away somewhere; and I dare not tell missis; and I wish you was at home, as she is not well, but better than she has been, and she shall know nothing about it till you come. Your obedient and affectionate servant,
"ELIZABETH HAND."

Taking Ascott's latch-key, she quitted the house and slipped out into the dark night, almost losing her way among the gloomy squares, where she met not a creature except the solitary policeman plashing steadily along the wet pavement. When he turned the glimmer of his bull's-eye upon her she started like a guilty creature till she remembered that she really was doing nothing wrong, and so need not be afraid of any thing. This was her simple creed, which Miss Hilary had taught her, and it upheld her, even till she knocked at Miss Balquidder's door.

There, poor girl, her heart sank, especially when Miss Balquidder, in an anomalous costume and a severe voice, opened the door herself, and asked who was there, disturbing a respectable family at this late hour.

Elizabeth answered, what she had before determined to say, as sufficiently explaining her errand, and yet betraying nothing that her mistress might wish concealed.

"Please, ma'am, I'm Miss Leaf's servant. My missis is ill, and I want a letter sent at once to Miss Hilary."

"Oh! come in, then. Elizabeth, I think, your name is?"

"Yes, ma'am."

"What made you leave home at this hour of the night? Did your mistress send you?"

"No."

"Is she so very ill? It seems sudden. I saw Miss Hilary to-day, and she knew nothing at all about it."

Elizabeth shrank a little before the keen eye that seemed to read her through.

"There's more amiss than you have told me, young woman. Is it because your mistress is in serious danger that you want to send for her sister?"

"No."

"What is it, then? You had better tell me at once. I hate concealment."

It was a trial; but Elizabeth held her ground.

"I beg your pardon, ma'am; but I don't think missis would like any body to know, and therefore I'd rather not tell you."

Now the honest Scotswoman, as she said, hated any thing underhand, but she respected the right of every human being to maintain silence if necessary. She looked sharply in Elizabeth's face, which apparently reassured her, for she said, not unkindly,

"Very well, child, keep your mistress's secrets by all means. Only tell me what you want. Shall I take a cab and fetch Miss Hilary at once?"

Elizabeth thanked her, but said she thought that would not do; it would be better just to send the note the first thing to-morrow morning, and then Miss Hilary would come home just as if nothing had happened, and Miss Leaf would not be frightened by her sudden appearance.

"You are a good, mindful girl," said Miss Balquidder. "How did you learn to be so sensible?"

At the kindly word and manner, Elizabeth, bewildered and exhausted with the excitement she had gone through, and agitated by the feeling of having, for the first time in her life, to act on her own responsibility, gave way a little. She did not actually cry, but she was very near it.

Miss Balquidder called over the stair-head, in her quick, imperative voice,

"David, is your wife away to her bed yet?"

"No, ma'am."

"Then tell her to fetch this young woman to the kitchen and give her some supper. And afterward, will you see her safe home, poor lassie? She's awfully tired, you see."

"Yes, ma'am."

And following David's gray head, Elizabeth, for the first time since she came to London, took a comfortable meal in a comfortable kitchen, seasoned with such stories of Miss Balquidder's goodness and generosity, that when, an hour after, she went home and to sleep, it was with a quieter and more hopeful spirit than she could have believed possible under the circumstances.

CHAPTER XVI.

NEXT morning, while with that cheerful, unanxious countenance which those about an invalid must learn continually to wear, Elizabeth was trying to persuade her mistress
not to rise, she heard a knock, and made some excuse for
escaping. She well knew what it was, and who had come.

There, in the parlor, sat Miss Hilary, Mrs. Jones talking
at her rather than to her, for she hardly seemed to hear.
But that she had heard every thing was clear enough.
Her drawn white face, the tight clasp of her hands, showed that the ill tidings had struck her hard.

"Go away, Mrs. Jones," cried Elizabeth, fiercely. "Miss
Hilary will call when she wants you."

And with an ingenious movement that just fell short of
a push, somehow the woman was got on the other side of
the parlor door, which Elizabeth immediately shut. Then
Miss Hilary stretched her hands across the table and looked up piteously in her servant's face.

Only a servant; only that poor servant to whom she
could look for any comfort in this sore trouble, this bitter
humiliation. There was no attempt at disguise or concealment between mistress and maid.

"Mrs. Jones has told me every thing, Elizabeth. How
is my sister? She does not know?"

"No; and I think she is a good deal better this morning.
She has been very bad all week; only she would not let me
send for you. She is really getting well now; I'm sure of
that."

"Thank God!" And then Miss Hilary began to weep.

Elizabeth also was thankful, even for the tears, for she
had been perplexed by the hard, dry-eyed look of misery,
deeper than any thing she could comprehend, or than the
circumstances seemed to warrant.

It was deeper. The misery was not only Ascott's ar-

rest; many a lad has got into debt and got out again—
the first taste of the law proving a warning to him for life;
but it was this ominous " beginning of the end." The fatal
end—which seemed to overhang like a hereditary cloud, to
taint as with hereditary disease, the Leaf family.

Another bitterness (and who shall blame it, for when
love is really love, have not the lovers a right to be one
another's first thought?)—what would Robert Lyon say?
To his honest Scotch nature poverty was nothing; honor
every thing. She knew his horror of debt was even equal
to her own. This, and her belief in his freedom from all
false pride, had sustained her against many doubts lest he
might think the less of her because of her present position
—might feel ashamed could he see her sitting at her ledger
in that high desk, or even occasionally serving in the shop.

Many a time things she would have passed over lightly on
her own account she had felt on his; felt how they would
annoy and vex him. The exquisitely natural thought which
Tennyson has put into poetry—

"If I am dear to some one else,
Then I should be to myself more dear"—

had often come, prosaically enough perhaps, into her head,
and prevented her from spoiling her little hands with un-
necessarily rough work, or carelessly passing down ill
streets and by-ways, where she knew Robert Lyon, had he
been in London, would never have allowed her to go. Now
what did such things signify? What need of taking care
of herself? These were all superficial, external disgraces;
the real disgrace was within. The plague-spot had burst
out anew; it seemed as if this day were the recommence-
ment of that bitter life of penury, misery, and humiliation,
familiar through three generations to the women of the
Leaf family.

It appeared like a fate. No use to try and struggle out
of it, stretching her arms up to Robert Lyon's tender, honest, steadfast heart, there to be sheltered, taken care of, and
made happy. No happiness for her! Nothing but to go
on enduring and enduring to the end.

Such was Hilary's first emotion: morbid perhaps, yet excusable. It might have lasted longer—though in her healthy nature it could not have lasted very long—had not the reaction come, suddenly and completely, by the opening of the parlor door and the appearance of Miss Leaf.

Miss Leaf—pale, indeed, but neither alarmed nor agitated, who, hearing somehow that her child had arrived, had hastily dressed herself and come down stairs in order not to frighten Hilary. And as she took her in her arms, and kissed her with those mother-like kisses, which were the sweetest Hilary had as yet ever known, the sharp anguish went out of the poor girl's heart.

"Oh, Johanna! I can bear any thing as long as I have you."

And so in this simple and natural way the miserable secret about Ascott came out.

Being once out, it did not seem half so dreadful; nor was its effect nearly so serious as Miss Hilary and Elizabeth had feared. Miss Leaf bore it wonderfully; she might almost have known it beforehand; they would have thought she had, but that she said decidedly she had not.

."Still you need not have minded telling me; though it was very good and thoughtful of you, Elizabeth. You have gone through a great deal for our sakes, my poor girl."

Elizabeth burst into one smothered sob—the first and the last.

"Nay," said Miss Leaf, very kindly, for this unwonted emotion in their servant moved them both, "you shall tell me the rest another time. Go down now, and get Miss Hilary some breakfast."

When Elizabeth had departed the sisters turned to one another. They did not talk much; where was the use of it? They both knew the worst, both as to facts and fears.

"What must be done, Johanna?"

Johanna, after a long pause, said, "I see but one thing—to get him home."

Hilary started up, and walked to and fro along the room.

"No, not that. I will never agree to it. We can not

help him. He does not deserve helping. If the debts were for food now, or any necessaries; but for mere luxuries— mere fine clothes: it is his tailor who has arrested him, you know. I would rather have gone in rags! I would rather see us all in rags! It's mean, selfish, cowardly, and I despise him for it. Though he is my own flesh and blood, I despise him."

"Hilary!"

"No," and the tears burst from her angry eyes, "I don't mean that I despise him. I'm sorry for him; there is good in him, poor dear lad; but I despise his weakness; I feel fierce to think how much it will cost us all, and especially you, Johanna. Only think what comforts of all sorts that thirty pounds would have brought to you!"

"God will provide," said Johanna, earnestly. "But I know, my dear, this is sharper to you than to me. Besides, I have been more used to it."

She closed her eyes with a half shudder, as if living over again the old days—when Henry Leaf's wife and eldest daughter used to have to give dinner-parties upon food that stuck in their throats, as if every morsel had been stolen; which in truth it was, and yet they were helpless, innocent thieves; when they and the children had to wear clothes that seemed to poison them like the shirt of Dejanira; when they durst not walk along special streets, nor pass particular shops, for the feeling that the shop-people must be staring, and pointing, and jibing at them, "Pay me what thou owest!"

"But things can not again be so bad as those days, Hilary. Ascott is young; he may mend. People *can* mend, my child; and he had such a different bringing-up from what his father had, and his grandfather too. We must not be hopeless yet. You see"—and, making Hilary kneel down before her, she took her by both hands, as if to impart something of her own quietness to this poor heart, struggling as young, honest, upright hearts do struggle with something which their whole nature revolts against, and loathes, and scorns—"you see, the boy is our boy; our

H

own flesh and blood. We were very foolish to let him away from us for so long. We might have made him better if we had kept him at Stowbury. But he is young; that is my hope of him; and he was always fond of his aunts, and is still, I think."

Hilary smiled sadly. "Deeds, not words. I don't believe in words."

"Well, let us put aside believing, and only act. Let us give him another chance."

Hilary shook her head. "Another, and another, and another—it will be always the same. I know it will. I can't tell how it is, Johanna; but whenever I look at you, I feel so stern and hard to Ascott. It seems as if there were circumstances when pity to some, to one, was wicked injustice to others; as if there were times when it is right and needful to lop off, at once and forever, a rotten branch, rather than let the whole tree go to rack and ruin. I would do it! I should think myself justified in doing it."

"But not just yet. He is only a boy—our own boy."

And the two women, in both of whom the maternal passion existed strong and deep, yet in the one never had found, and in the other never might find, its natural channel, wept together over this lad, almost as mothers weep.

"But what can we do?" said Hilary at last. "Thirty pounds, and not a halfpenny to pay it with; must we borrow?"

"Oh no—no," was the answer, with a shrinking gesture; "no borrowing. There is the diamond ring."

This was a sort of heir-loom from eldest daughter to eldest daughter of the Leaf family, which had been kept, even as a sort of superstition, through all temptations of poverty. The last time Miss Leaf looked at it she had remarked, jestingly, it should be given some day to that important personage talked of for many a year among the three aunts—Mrs. Ascott Leaf.

"Who must do without it now," said Johanna, looking regretfully at the ring; "that is, if he ever takes to himself a wife, poor boy."

Hilary answered, beneath her breath, "Unless he alters, I earnestly hope he never may." And there came over her involuntarily a wild, despairing thought, Would it not be better that neither Ascott nor herself should ever be married, that the family might die out, and trouble the world no more?

Nevertheless she rose up to do what she knew had to be done, and what there was nobody to do but herself.

"Don't mind it, Johanna; for indeed I do not. I shall go to a first-rate, respectable jeweler, and he will not cheat me; and then I shall find my way to the sponging-house —isn't that what they call it? I dare say many a poor woman has been there before me. I am not the first, and shall not be the last, and nobody will harm me. I think I look honest, though my name is Leaf."

She laughed—a bitter laugh; but Johanna silenced it in a close embrace; and when Hilary rose up again she was quite her natural self. She summoned Elizabeth, and began giving her all domestic directions, just as usual; finally, bade her sister good-by in a tone as like her usual tone as possible, and left her settled on the sofa in content and peace.

Elizabeth followed to the door. Miss Hilary had asked her for the card on which Ascott had written the address of the place where he had been taken to; and though the girl said not a word, her anxious eyes made piteous inquiry.

Her mistress patted her on the shoulder.

"Never mind about me; I shall come to no harm, Elizabeth."

"It's a bad place; such a dreadful place, Mrs. Jones says."

"Is it?" Elizabeth guessed part, not the whole of the feelings that made Hilary hesitate, shrink even, from the duty before her, turning first so hot, and then so pale. Only as a duty could she have done it at all. "No matter, I must go. Take care of my sister."

She ran down the door-steps, and walked quickly through the Crescent. It was a clear, sunshiny, frosty day—such a day as always both cheered and calmed her. She had, despite all her cares, youth, health, energy; and a holy and constant love lay like a sleeping angel in her heart. Must I tell the truth, and own that before she had gone two streets' length Hilary ceased to feel so very, very miserable?

Love—this kind of love of which I speak—is a wonderful thing, the most wonderful thing in all the world. The strength it gives, the brightness, the actual happiness, even in the hardest times, is often quite miraculous. When Hilary sat waiting in the jeweler's shop, she watched a little episode of high life—two wealthy people choosing their marriage-plate; the bride, so careless and haughty; the bridegroom, so unutterably mean to look at, stamped with that innate smallness and coarseness of soul which his fine clothes only made more apparent. And she thought—oh, how fondly she thought!—of that honest, manly mien; of that true, untainted heart, which, she felt sure, had never loved any woman but herself; of the warm, firm hand, carving its way through the world for her sake, and waiting patiently till it could openly clasp hers, and give her every thing it had won. She would not have exchanged him, Robert Lyon, with his penniless love, his half-hopeless fortunes, or maybe his lot of never-ending care, for the "brawest bridegroom" under the sun.

Under this sun—the common, every-day winter sun of Regent and Oxford Streets—she walked now as brightly and bravely as if there were no trouble before her, no painful meeting with Ascott, no horrid humiliation from which every womanly feeling in her nature shrunk with acute pain. "Robert, my Robert!" she whispered in her heart, and felt him so near to her that she was at rest, she hardly knew why.

Possibly grand, or clever, or happy people who condescend to read this story may despise it, think it unideal, uninteresting; treating of small things and common people—"poor persons," in short. I can not help it. I write for the poor; not to excite the compassion of the rich toward them, but to show them their own dignity and the bright side of their poverty. For it has its bright side; and its very darkest, when no sin is mixed up therewith, is brighter than many an outwardly prosperous life.

"*Better is a dinner of herbs, where love is, than a stalled ox and hatred therewith.*

"*Better is a dry morsel, and quietness therewith, than a house full of sacrifices and strife.*"

With these two sage proverbs—which all acknowledge and scarcely any really believe, or surely they would act a little more as if they did—I leave Johanna Leaf sitting silently in her solitary parlor, knitting stockings for her child; weaving many a mingled web of thought withal, yet never letting a stitch go down; and Hilary Leaf walking cheerily and fearlessly up one strange street and down another to find out the "bad" place, where she once had no idea it would ever have been her lot to go. One thing she knew, and gloried in the knowledge, that if Robert Lyon had known she was going, or known half the cares she had to meet, he would have recrossed the Indian Seas—have risked fortune, competence, hope of the future, which was the only cheer of his hard present—in order to save her from them all.

The minute history of this painful day I do not mean to tell. Hilary never told it till, years after, she wept it out upon a bosom that could understand the whole, and would take good care that, while the life beat in his, *she* never should go through the like again.

Ascott came home—that is, was brought home—very humbled, contrite, and grateful. There was no one to meet him but his Aunt Johanna, and she just kissed him quietly, and bade him come over to the fire; he was shivering, and somewhat pale. He had even two tears in his handsome eyes, the first Ascott had been known to shed since he was a boy. That he felt a good deal, perhaps as much as was in his nature to feel, there could be no doubt. So his two aunts were glad and comforted; gave him his tea and the warmest seat at the hearth; said not a harsh word to him, but talked to him about indifferent things. Tea be-

ing over, Hilary was anxious to get every thing painful
ended before Selina came home—Selina, who, they felt by
instinct, had now a separate interest from themselves, and
had better not be told this sad story if possible; so she
asked her nephew "if he remembered what they had to do
this evening."

"Had to do? Oh, Aunt Hilary, I'm so tired! can't you
let me be quiet? Only this one night. I promise to bring
you every thing on Monday."

"Monday will be too late. I shall be away. And you
know you can't do without my excellent arithmetic," she
added, with a faint smile. "Now, Ascott, be a good boy—
fetch down all those bills, and let us go over them together."

"His debts came to more than the thirty pounds then?"
said his Aunt Johanna, when he was gone.

"Yes. But the ring sold for fifty." And Hilary drew
to the table, got writing materials, and sat waiting, with a
dull, silent patience in her look, at which Johanna sighed
and said no more.

The aunt and nephew spent some time in going over
that handful of papers, and approximating to the sum total, in that kind of awful arithmetic when figures cease to
be mere figures, but grow into avenging monsters, bearing
with them life or death.

"Is that all? You are quite sure it is all?" said Hilary
at last, pointing to the whole amount, and looking steadily into Ascott's eyes.

He flushed up, and asked what she meant by doubting
his word.

"Not that, but you might easily have made a mistake;
you are so careless about money matters."

"Ah! that's it. I'm just careless, and so I come to grief.
But I never mean to be careless any more. I'll be as pre-
cise as you. I'll balance my books every week—every
day, if you like—exactly as you do at that horrid shop,
Aunt Hilary."

So he was rattling on, but Hilary stopped him by pointing to the figures.

"You see, this sum is more than we expected. How is it to be met? Think for yourself. You are a man now."

"I know that," said Ascott, sullenly; "but what's the use of it? Money only makes the man, and I have none. If the ancient Peter would but die now and leave me his heir, though to be sure Aunt Selina might be putting her oar in. Perhaps—considering I'm Aunt Selina's nephew—if I were to walk into the old chap now, he might be induced to fork out! Hurrah! that's a splendid idea."

"What idea?"

"I'll borrow the money from old Ascott."

"That means, because he has already given, you would have him keep on giving—and you would take, and take, and take—Ascott, I'm ashamed of you."

But Ascott only burst out laughing. "Nonsense! he has money and I have none; why shouldn't he give it me?"

"Why?" she repeated, her eyes flashing and her little feminine figure seeming to grow taller while she spoke; "I'll tell you, since you don't seem yourself to understand it. Because a young man, with health and strength in him, should blush to eat any bread but what he himself earns. Because he should work at any thing and every thing, stint himself of every luxury and pleasure, rather than ask or borrow, or, except under rare circumstances, rather than be indebted to any living soul for a single half-penny. I would not, if I were a young man."

"What a nice young man you would make, Aunt Hilary!"

There was something in the lad's imperturbable good-humor at once irritating and disarming. Whatever his faults, they were more negative than positive; there was no malice prepense about him, no absolute personal wickedness. And he had the strange charm of manner and speech which keeps up one's outer surface of habitual affection toward a person long after all its foundations of trust and respect have hopelessly crumbled away.

"Come, now, my pretty aunt must go with me. She will manage the old ogre much better than I. And he

must be managed somehow. It's all very fine talking of
independence, but isn't it hard that a poor fellow should
be living in constant dread of being carried off to that horrid, uncleanly, beastly den—bah! I don't like thinking of
it—and all for want of twenty pounds? You must go to
him, Aunt Hilary."

She saw they must—there was no help for it. Even Johanna said so. It was, after all, only asking for Ascott's
quarterly allowance three days in advance, for it was due
on Tuesday. But what jarred against her proud, honest
spirit was the implication that such a request gave of taking as a right that which had been so long bestowed as a
favor. Nothing but the great strait they were in could
ever have driven her to consent that Mr. Ascott should be
applied to at all; but since it must be done, she felt that
she had better do it herself. Was it from some lurking
doubt or dread that Ascott might not speak the entire
truth, as she had insisted upon its being spoken, before Mr.
Ascott was asked for any thing? since whatever he gave
must be given with a full knowledge on his part of the
whole pitiable state of affairs.

It was with a strange, sad feeling—the sadder because
he never seemed to suspect it, but talked and laughed with
her as usual—that she took her nephew's arm and walked
silently through the dark squares, perfectly well aware that
he only asked her to go with him in order to do an unpleasant thing which he did not like to do himself, and that she
only went with him in the character of watch, or supervi-
sor, to try and save him from doing something which she
herself would be ashamed should be done.

Yet he was ostensibly the head, hope, and stay of the
family. Alas! many a family has to submit to, and smile
under an equally melancholy and fatal sham.

CHAPTER XVII.

MR. ASCOTT was sitting half asleep in his solitary dining-room, his face rosy with wine, his heart warmed also, probably from the same cause. Not that he was in the least "tipsy"—that low word applicable only to low people, and not to men of property, who have a right to enjoy all the good things of this life. He was scarcely even "merry," merely "comfortable," in that cozy, benevolent state which middle-aged or elderly gentlemen are apt to fall into after a good dinner and good wine, when they have no mental resources, and the said good dinner and good wine constitutes their best notion of felicity.

Yet wealth and comfort are not things to be despised. Hilary herself was not insensible to the pleasantness of this warm, well-lit, crimson-atmosphered apartment. She as well as her neighbors liked pretty things about her, soft, harmonious colors to look at and wear, well-cooked food to eat, cheerful rooms to live in. If she could have had all these luxuries with those she loved to share them, no doubt she would have been much happier. But yet she felt to the full that solemn truth that "a man's life consisteth not in the abundance of things that he possesses;" and though hers was outwardly so dark, so full of poverty, anxiety, and pain, still she knew that inwardly it owned many things, one thing especially, which no money could buy, and without which fine houses, fine furniture, and fine clothes—indeed, all the comforts and splendors of existence, would be worse than valueless—actual torment. So, as she looked around her, she felt not the slightest envy of her sister Selina.

Nor of honest Peter, who rose up from his arm-chair, pulling the yellow silk handkerchief from his sleepy face, and, it must be confessed, receiving his future connections very willingly, and even kindly.

Now how was he to be told? How, when she and Ascott sat over the wine and dessert he had ordered for them,
listening to the rich man's complaisant pomposities, were
they to explain that they had come a begging, asking him,
as the climax to his liberalities, to advance a few pounds
in order to keep the young man whom he had for years generously and sufficiently maintained out of prison? This,
smooth it over as one might, was, Hilary felt, the plain English of the matter, and as minute after minute lengthened,
and nothing was said of their errand, she sat upon thorns.

But Ascott drank his wine and ate his walnuts quite
composedly.

At last Hilary said, in a sort of desperation, "Mr. Ascott,
I want to speak to you."

"With pleasure, my dear young lady. Will you come
to my study? I have a most elegantly furnished study, I
assure you. And any affair of yours—"

"Thank you, but it is not mine; it concerns my nephew
here."

And then she braced up all her courage, and while Ascott busied himself over his walnuts—he had the grace to
look excessively uncomfortable—she told, as briefly as possible, the bitter truth.

Mr. Ascott listened, apparently without surprise, and,
anyhow, without comment. His self-important loquacity
ceased, and his condescending smile passed into a sharp,
reticent, business look. He knitted his shaggy brows, contracted that coarsely-hung but resolute mouth, in which lay
the secret of his success in life, buttoned up his coat, and
stuck his hands behind him over his coat-tails. As he stood
there on his own hearth, with all his comfortable splendors
about him—a man who had made his own money, hardly
and honestly, who from the days when he was a poor er-
rand-lad had had no one to trust to but himself, yet had
managed always to help himself, ay, and others too—Hi
lary's stern sense of justice contrasted him with the graceful young man who sat opposite to him, so much his in-
ferior, and so much his debtor. She owned that Peter

Ascott had a right to look both contemptuous and displeased.

"A very pretty story, but I almost expected it," said he.

And there he stopped. In his business capacity he was too acute a man to be a man of many words, and his feelings, if they existed, were kept to himself.

"It all comes to this, young man," he continued, after an uncomfortable pause, in which Hilary could have counted every beat of her heart, and even Ascott played with his wine-glass in a nervous kind of way—"you want money, and you think I'm sure to give it, because it wouldn't be pleasant just now to have discreditable stories going about concerning the future Mrs. Ascott's relatives. You're quite right, it wouldn't. But I'm too old a bird to be caught with chaff for all that. You must rise very early in the morning to take *me* in."

Hilary started up in an agony of shame. "That's not fair, Mr. Ascott. We do not take you in. Have we not told you the whole truth? I was determined you should know it before we asked you for one farthing of your money. If there were the smallest shadow of a chance for Ascott in any other way, we never would have come to you at all. It is a horrible, horrible humiliation!"

It might be that Peter Ascott had a soft place in his heart, or that this time, just before his marriage, was the one crisis which sometimes occurs in a hard man's life, when, if the right touch comes, he becomes malleable ever after; but he looked kindly at the poor girl, and said, in quite a gentle way,

"Don't vex yourself, my dear. I shall give the young fellow what he wants; nobody ever called Peter Ascott stingy. But he has cost me enough already; he must shift for himself now. Hand me over that check-book, Ascott; but remember, this is the last you'll ever see of my money."

He wrote the memorandum of the check inside the page, then tore off the check itself, and proceeded to write the words "Twenty pounds," date it, and sign it, lingering over the signature as if he had a certain pride in the honest name " Peter Ascott," and was well aware of its monetary value on 'Change and elsewhere.

" There, Miss Hilary, I flatter myself that's not a bad signature, nor would be easily forged. One can not be too careful over— What's that? a letter, John?"

By his extreme eagerness, almost snatching it from his footman's hands, it was one of importance. He made some sort of rough apology, drew the writing materials to him, wrote one or two business-looking letters, and made out one or two more checks.

" Here's yours, Ascott; take it, and let me have done with it," said he, throwing it across the table folded up. " Can't waste time on such small transactions. Ma'am, excuse me, but five thousand pounds depends on my getting these letters written and sent off within a quarter of an hour."

Hilary bent her head, and sat watching the pen scratch, and the clock tick on the mantlepiece; thinking if this really was to be the last of his godfather's allowance, what on earth would become of Ascott? For Ascott himself, he said not a word; not even when, the letters dispatched, Mr. Ascott rose, and administering a short, sharp homily, tacitly dismissed his visitors. Whether this silence was sullenness, cowardice, or shame, Hilary could not guess.

She quitted the house with a sense of grinding humiliation almost intolerable. But still the worst was over; the money had been begged and given—there was no fear of a prison. And, spite of every thing, Hilary felt a certain relief that this was the last time Ascott would be indebted to his godfather. Perhaps this total cessation of extraneous help might force the young man upon his own resources, compel his easy temperament into active energy, and bring out in him those dormant qualities that his aunts still fondly hoped existed in him.

" Don't be down-hearted, Ascott," she said; " we will manage to get on somehow till you hear of a practice, and then you must work—work like a ' brick,' as you call it. You will, I know."

He answered nothing.

"I won't let you give in, my boy," she went on, kindly. "Who would ever dream of giving in at your age, with health and strength, a good education, and no encumbrances whatever—not even aunts! for we will not stand in your way, be sure of that. If you can not settle here, you shall try to get out abroad, as you have sometimes wished, as an army-surgeon or a ship's doctor; you say these appointments are easy enough to be had. Why not try? Any thing; we will consent to any thing, if only we can see your life busy, and useful, and happy."

Thus she talked, feeling far more tenderly to him in his forlorn despondency than when they had quitted the house two hours before. But Ascott took not the slightest notice. A strange fit of sullenness or depression seemed to have come over him, which, when they reached home and met Aunt Johanna's silently-questioning face, changed into devil-may-care indifference.

"Oh yes, aunt, we've done it; we've got the money, and now I may go to the dogs as soon as I like."

"No," said Aunt Hilary, "it is nothing of the sort; it is only that Ascott must now depend upon himself, and not upon his godfather. Take courage," she added, and went up to him and kissed him on the forehead; "we'll never let our boy go to the dogs! and as for this disappointment, or any disappointment, why, it's just like a cold bath; it takes away your breath for the time, and then you rise up out of it brisker and fresher than ever."

But Ascott shook his head with a fierce denial. "Why should that old fellow be as rich as Crœsus and I as poor as a rat? Why should I be put into the world to enjoy myself, and can't? Why was I made like what I am, and then punished for it? Whose fault is it?"

Ay, *whose?* The eternal, unsolvable problem rose up before Hilary's imagination. The ghastly spectre of that everlasting doubt, which haunts even the firmest faith sometimes—and which all the nonsense written about that mystery which,

"Binding nature fast in fate,
Leaves free the human will,"

only makes darker than before—oppressed her for the time
being with an inexpressible dread.

Ay, *why* was it that the boy was what he was? From
his inherited nature, his temperament, or his circumstances? What, or, more awful question still, *who* was to blame?

But as Hilary's thoughts went deeper down the question
answered itself—at least as far as it ever can be answered
in this narrow, finite stage of being. Whose will—we dare
not say whose blame—is it that evil must inevitably gen-
erate evil? that the smallest wrong-doing in any human
being rouses a chain of results which may fatally involve
other human beings in an almost incalculable circle of misery? The wages of sin is death. Were it not so, sin would
cease to be sin, and holiness, holiness. If He, the All-holy, .
who for some inscrutable purpose saw fit to allow the existence of evil, allowed any other law than this, in either
the spiritual or material world, would He not be denying
Himself, counteracting the necessities of His own righteous
essence, to which evil is so antagonistic, that we can not
doubt it must be in the end cast into total annihilation—
into the allegorical lake of fire and brimstone, which is the
"second death?" Nay, do they not in reality deny Him
and His holiness almost as much as Atheists do. who preach
that the one great salvation which He has sent into the
world is a salvation *from punishment*—a keeping out of
hell and getting into heaven—instead of a salvation *from
sin*, from the power and love of sin, through the love of
God in Christ?

I tell these thoughts, because like lightning they passed
through Hilary's mind, as sometimes a whole chain of
thoughts do, link after link, and because they helped her
to answer her nephew quietly and briefly, for she saw he
was in no state of mind to be argued with.

"I can not explain, Ascott, why it is that any of us are
what we are, and why things happen to us as they do; it
is a question we none of us understand, and in this world

never shall. But if we know what we ought to be, and how we may make the best of every thing, good or bad, that happens to us, surely that is enough, without perplexing ourselves about any thing more."

Ascott smiled, half contemptuously, half carelessly : he was not a young fellow likely to perplex himself long or deeply about these sort of things.

"Anyhow, I've got £20 in my pocket, so I can't starve for a day or two. Let's see; where is it to be cashed? Hillo! who would have thought the old fellow would have been so stupid? Look there, Aunt Hilary!"

She was so unfamiliar with checks for £20, poor little woman! that she did not at first recognize the omission of the figures "£20" at the left-hand corner. Otherwise the check was correct.

"Ho, ho!" laughed Ascott, exceedingly amused, so easily was the current of his mind changed. "It must have been the £5000 pending that muddled the 'cute old fellow's brains. I wonder whether he will remember it afterward, and come posting up to see that I have taken no ill advantage of his blunder; changed this 'Twenty' into 'Seventy.' I easily could, and put the figures £70 here. What a good joke!"

"Had ye not better go to him at once, and have the matter put right?"

"Rubbish! I can put it right myself. It makes no difference who fills up a check, so that it is signed all correct. A deal you women know of business!"

But still Hilary, with a certain womanish uneasiness about money-matters, and an anxiety to have the thing settled beyond doubt, urged him to go.

"Very well; just as you like. I do believe you are afraid of my turning forger."

He buttoned his coat with a half sulky, half defiant air, left his supper untasted, and disappeared.

It was midnight before he returned. His aunts were still sitting up, imagining all sorts of horrors, in an anxiety too great for words; but when Hilary ran to the door with

the natural " Oh, Ascott, where have you been ?" he pushed
her aside with a gesture that was almost fierce in its repulsion.

"Where have I been? taking a walk round the Park;
that's all. Can't I come and go as I like, without being
pestered by women? I'm horribly tired. Let me alone
—do !"

They did let him alone. Deeply wounded, Aunt Johanna took no further notice of him than to set his chair a little closer to the fire, and Aunt Hilary slipped down stairs
for more coals. There she found Elizabeth, who they
thought had long since gone to bed, sitting on the stairs,
very sleepy, but watching still.

"Is he come in?" she asked; "because there are more
bailiffs after him. I'm sure of it; I saw them."

This, then, might account for his keeping out of the way
till after twelve o'clock, and also for his wild, haggard
look. Hilary put aside her vague dread of some new misfortune; assured Elizabeth that all was right; he had got
wherewithal to pay every body on Monday morning, and
would be safe till then. All debtors were safe on Sunday.

"Go to bed now—there's a good girl; it is hard that
you should be troubled with our troubles."

Elizabeth looked up with those fond gray eyes of hers.
She was but a servant, and yet looks like these engraved
themselves ineffaceably on her mistress's heart, imparting
the comfort that all pure love gives from any one human
being to another.

And love has its wonderful rights and rewards. Perhaps Elizabeth, who thought herself nothing at all to her
mistress, would have marveled to know how much closer
her mistress felt to this poor, honest, loving girl, whose
truth she believed in, and on whose faithfulness she im-
plicitly depended, than toward her own flesh and blood,
who sat there moodily over the hearth; deeply pitied, sed-
ulously cared for, but as for being confided in, relied on, in
great matters or small, his own concerns or theirs—the
thing was impossible.

They could not even ask him—they dared not, in such a strange mood was he—the simple question, Had he seen Mr. Ascott, and had Mr. Ascott been annoyed about the check? It would not have been referred to at all had not Hilary, in holding his coat to dry, taken his pocket-book out of the breast-pocket, when he snatched at it angrily.

"What are you meddling with my things for? Do you want to get at the check, and be peering at it to see if it's all right? But you can't; I've paid it away. Perhaps you'd like to know who to? Then you sha'n't. I'll not be accountable to you for all my proceedings. I'll not be treated like a baby. You'd better mind what you are about, Aunt Hilary."

Never, in all his childish naughtiness or boyish impertinence, had Ascott spoken to her in such a tone. She regarded him at first with simple astonishment, then hot indignation, which spurred her on to stand up for her dignity, and not submit to be insulted by her own nephew. But then came back upon her her own doctrine, taught by her own experience, that character and conduct alone constitutes real dignity or authority. She had, in point of fact, no authority over him; no one can have, not even parents, over a young man of his age, except that personal influence which is the strongest sway of all.

She said only, with a quietness that surprised herself, "You mistake, Ascott; I have no wish to interfere with you whatever; you are your own master, and must take your own course. I only expect from you the ordinary respect that a gentleman shows to a lady. You must be very tired and ill, or you would not have forgotten that."

"I didn't; or, if I did, I beg your pardon," said he, half subdued. "When are you going to bed?"

"Directly. Shall I light your candle also?"

"Oh no, not for the world; I couldn't sleep a wink. I'd go mad if I went to bed. I think I'll turn out and have a cigar."

His whole manner was so strange that his Aunt Johan-

na, who had sat aloof, terribly grieved, but afraid to interfere, was moved to rise up and go over to him.

"Ascott, my dear, you are looking quite ill. Be advised
by your old auntie. Go to bed at once, and forget every
thing till morning."

"I wish I could—I wish I could. Oh, auntie, auntie!"

He caught hold of her hand, which she had laid upon his
head, looked up a minute into her kind, fond face, and burst
into a flood of boyish tears.

Evidently his troubles had been too much for him; he
was in a state of great excitement. For some minutes his
sobs were almost hysterical; then by a struggle he recovered himself, seemed exceedingly annoyed and ashamed,
took up his candle, bade them a hurried good-night, and
went to bed.

That is, he went to his room; but they heard him moving about overhead for a long while after; nor were they
surprised that he refused to rise next morning, but lay
most of the time with his door locked until late in the afternoon, when he went out for a long walk, and did not return till supper, which he ate almost in silence. Then, after going up to his room, and coming down again, complaining bitterly how very cold it was, he crept in to the fireside with a book in his hand, of which Hilary noticed he
scarcely read a line.

His aunts said nothing to him; they had determined
not; they felt that further interference would be not only
useless, but dangerous.

"He will come to himself by-and-by; his moods, good or
bad, never last long, you know," said Hilary, somewhat bitterly. "But, in the mean time, I think we had better just
do as he says—let him alone."

And in that sad, hopeless state they passed the last hours
of that dreary Sunday—afraid either to comfort him or reason with him; afraid, above all, to blame him, lest it might
drive him altogether astray. That he was in a state of
great misery, half sullen, half defiant, they saw, and were
scarcely surprised at it; it was very hard not to be able

to open their loving hearts to him, as those of one family should always do, making every trouble a common care, and every joy a universal blessing. But in his present state of mind—the sudden obstinacy of a weak nature conscious of its weakness, and dreading control—it seemed impossible either to break upon his silence or to force his confidence.

They might have been right in this, or wrong; afterward Hilary thought the latter. Many a time she wished and wished, with a bitter regret, that instead of the quiet " Good-night, Ascott !" and the one rather cold kiss on his forehead, she had flung her arms round his neck, and insisted on his telling out his whole mind to her, his nearest kinswoman, who had been half aunt and half sister to him all his life. But it was not done : she parted from him, as she did Sunday after Sunday, with a sore, sick feeling of how much he might be to her, to them all, and how little he really was.

If this silence of hers was a mistake—one of those mistakes which sensitive people sometimes make—it was, like all similar errors, only too sorrowfully remembered and atoned for.

CHAPTER XVIII.

THE week passed by, and Hilary received no ill tidings from home. Incessant occupation kept her from dwelling too much on anxious subjects ; besides, she would not have thought it exactly right, while her time and her mental powers were for so many hours per diem legally Miss Balquidder's, to waste the one and weaken the other by what is commonly called " fretting." Nor, carrying this conscientious duty to a higher degree and toward a higher Master, would she have dared to sit grieving overmuch over their dark future. And yet it was very dark. She pondered over what was to be done with Ascott, or whether he was still to be left to the hopeless hope of doing something for himself; how long the little establishment at No. 15 could be kept together, or if, after Selina's marriage, it would not be advisable to make some change that should contract expenses, and prevent this hard separation, from Monday to Saturday, between Johanna and herself.

These, with equally anxious thoughts, attacked her in crowds every day and every hour; but she had generally sufficient will to put them aside, at least till after work was done, and they could neither stupefy nor paralyze her. Trouble had to her been long enough familiar to have taught her its own best lesson—that the mind can, in degree, rule itself, even as it rules the body.

Thus, in her business duties, which were principally keeping accounts; in her management of the two young people under her, and of the small domestic establishment connected with the shop, Hilary went steadily on, day after day; made no blunders in her arithmetic, no mistakes in her housekeeping. Being new to all her responsibilities, she had to give her whole mind to them; and she did it; and it was a blessing to her—the sanctified blessing which rests upon labor, almost seeming to neutralize its primeval curse.

But night after night, when work was over, she sat alone at her sewing—the only time she had for it—and her thoughts went faster than her needle. She turned over plan after plan, and went back upon hope after hope, that had risen and broken like waves of the sea—nothing happening that she had expected; the only thing which had happened, or which seemed to have any permanence or reality, being two things which she had never expected at all—Selina's marriage, and her own engagement with Miss Balquidder. It often happens so, in most people's lives, until at last they learn to live on from day to day, doing each day's duty within the day, and believing that it is a righteous as well as a tender hand which keeps the next day's page safely folded down.

So Hilary sat, glad to have a quiet hour, not to grieve in, but to lay out the details of a plan which had been ma-

turing in her mind all week, and which she meant definitely to propose to Johanna when she went home next day.
It would cost her something to do so, and she had had
some hesitations as to the scheme itself, until at last she
threw them all to the winds, as an honest-hearted, faithful,
and faithfully-trusting woman would. Her plan was, that
they should write to the only real friend the family had—
the only good man she believed in—stating plainly their
troubles and difficulties about their nephew; asking his advice, and possibly his help. He might know of something
—some opening for a young surgeon in India, or some temporary appointment for the voyage out and home, which
might catch Ascott's erratic and easily-attracted fancy;
give him occupation for the time being, and at least detach
him from his present life, with all its temptations and dangers.

Also, it might result in bringing the boy again under
that influence which had been so beneficial to him while it
lasted, and which Hilary devoutly believed was the best
influence in the world. Was it unnatural if mingled with
an earnest desire for Ascott's good was an underlying delight that that good should be done to him by Robert
Lyon?

So, when her plan was made, even to the very words in
which she meant to unfold it to Johanna, and the very form
in which Johanna should write the letter, she allowed herself a few brief minutes to think of him—Robert Lyon—
to call up his eyes, his voice, his smile; to count, for the
hundredth time, how many months—one less than twenty-
four, so she could not say years now—it would be before
he returned to England. Also, to speculate when and
where they would first meet, and how he would speak the
one word—all that was needful to change "liking" into
"love," and "friend" into "wife." They had so grown together during so many years, not the less so during these
years of absence, that it seemed as if such a change would
hardly make any difference. And yet—and yet—as she
sat and sewed, wearied with her day's labors, sad and per-

plexed, she thought—if only by some strange magic, Robert Lyon were standing opposite, holding open his arms,
ready and glad to take her and all her cares to his heart,
how she would cling there! how closely she would creep
to him, weeping with joy and content, neither afraid nor
ashamed to let him see how dearly she loved him!

Only a dream! ah, only a dream! and she started from
it at the sharp sound of the door-bell—started, blushing
and trembling, as if it had been Robert Lyon himself, when
she knew it was only her two young assistants whom she
had allowed to go out to tea in the neighborhood. So she
settled herself to her work again; put all her own thoughts
by in their little private corners, and waited for the entrance and the harmless gossip of these two orphan girls,
who were already beginning to love her, and to make a
friend of her, and toward whom she felt herself quite an
elderly and responsible person. Poor little Hilary! It
seemed to be her lot always to take care of somebody or
other. Would it ever be that any body should take care
of her?

So she cleared away some of her needle-work, stirred the
fire, which was dropping hollow and dull, and looked up
pleasantly to the opening door. But it was not the girls:
it was a man's foot and a man's voice.

"Any person of the name of Leaf living here? I wish
to see her, on business."

At another time she would have laughed at the manner
and words, as if it were impossible so great a gentleman
as Mr. Ascott could want to see so small a person as the
"person of the name of Leaf," except on business. But
now she was startled by his appearance at all. She sprang
up only able to articulate "My sister—"

"Don't be frightened; your sisters are quite well. I
called at No. 15 an hour ago."

"You saw them?"

"No; I thought it unadvisable, under the circumstances."

"What circumstances?"

"I will explain, if you will allow me to sit down; bah!

I've brought in sticking to me a straw out of that con-founded shaky old cab. One ought never to be so stupid as to go any where except in one's own carriage. This is rather a small room, Miss Hilary."

He eyed it curiously round; and, lastly, with his most acute look, he eyed herself, as if he wished to find out something from her manner before going into farther explanations.

But she stood before him a little uneasy, and yet not very much so. The utmost she expected was some quarrel with her sister Selina; perhaps the breaking off of the match, which would not have broken Hilary's heart, at all events.

"So you have really no idea what I'm come about?"

"Not the slightest."

"Well!" said Peter Ascott, "I hardly thought it; but when one has been taken in as I have been, and this isn't the first time by your family—"

"Mr. Ascott! will you explain yourself?"

"I will, ma'am. It's a very unpleasant business I come about; any other gentleman but me would have come with a police-officer at his back. Look here, Miss Hilary Leaf—did you ever set eyes on this before?"

He took out his check-book, turned deliberately over the small memorandum halves of the page, till he came to one in particular, then hunted in his pocket-book for something.

"My banker sent in to-day my canceled checks, which I don't usually go over oftener than three months; he knew that, the scamp!"

Hilary looked up.

"Your nephew, to be sure. See!"

He spread before her a check, the very one she had watched him write seven days before, made payable to "Ascott Leaf, or bearer," and signed with the bold, peculiar signature, "Peter Ascott." Only, instead of being a check for twenty pounds, it was for seventy.

Instantly the whole truth flashed upon Hilary; Ascott's remark about how easily the T could be made into an S, and what a "good joke" it would be; his long absence that night; his strange manner; his refusal to let her see the check again; all was clear as daylight.

Unfortunate boy! the temptation had been too strong for him. Under what sudden, insane impulse he had acted —under what delusion of being able to repay in time; or of Mr. Ascott's not detecting the fraud; or, if discovered, of its being discovered after the marriage, when to prosecute his wife's nephew would be a disgrace to himself, could never be known. But there unmistakable was the altered check, which had been presented and paid, the banker, of course, not having the slightest suspicion of any thing amiss.

"Well, isn't this a nice return for all my kindness? So cleverly done, too. But for the merest chance I might not have found it out for three months. Oh, he's a precious young rascal, this nephew of yours. His father was only a fool, but he— Do you know that this is a matter of forgery—forgery, ma'am," added Mr. Ascott, waxing hot in his indignation.

Hilary uttered a bitter groan.

Yes, it was quite true. Their Ascott, their own boy, was no longer merely idle, extravagant, thoughtless—faults bad enough, but capable of being mended as he grew older: he had done that which to the end of his days he could never blot out. He was a swindler and a forger.

She clasped her hands tightly together, as one struggling with sharp physical pain, trying to read the expression of Mr. Ascott's face. At last she put her question into words.

"What do you mean to do? Shall you prosecute him?"

Mr. Ascott crossed his legs, and settled his neckcloth with a self-satisfied air. He evidently rather enjoyed the importance of his position. To be dictator, almost of life and death, to this unfortunate family was worth certainly fifty pounds.

"Well, I haven't exactly determined. The money, you see, is of no moment to me, and I couldn't get it back anyhow. He'll never be worth a halfpenny, that rascal. I might prosecute, and nobody would blame me; indeed, if I were to decline marrying your sister, and cut the whole set of you, I don't see," and he drew himself up, "that any thing could be said against me. But—"

Perhaps, hard man as he was, he was touched by the agony of suspense in Hilary's face, for he added,

"Come, come, I won't disgrace your family; I won't do any thing to harm the fellow."

"Thank you!" said Hilary, in a mechanical, unnatural voice.

"As for my money, he's welcome to it, and much good may it do him. 'Set a beggar on horseback, and he'll ride to the devil,' and in double quick time too. I won't hinder him. I wash my hands of the young scapegrace. But he'd better not come near me again."

"No," acquiesced Hilary, absently.

"In fact," said Mr. Ascott, with a twinkle of his sharp eye, "I have already taken measures to frighten him away, so that he may make himself scarce, and give neither you nor me any farther trouble. I drove up to your door with a policeman, asked to see Mr. Leaf, and when I heard that he was out—a lie, of course—I left word I'd be back in half an hour. Depend upon it," and he winked confidentially, "he will smell a rat, and make a moonlight flitting of it, and we shall never hear of him any more."

"Never hear of Ascott any more?" repeated Hilary; and for an instant she ceased to think of him as what he was—swindler, forger, ungrateful to his benefactors, a disgrace to his home and family. She saw only the boy Ascott, with his bright looks and pleasant ways, whom his aunts had brought up from his cradle, and loved with all his faults—perhaps loved still. "Oh, I must go home. This will break Johanna's heart!"

Mr. Peter Ascott possibly never had a heart, or it had been so stunted in its growth that it had never reached its fair development. Yet he felt sorry in his way for the "young person," who looked so deadly white, yet tried so hard not to make a scene; nay, when her two assistants

I

came into the one little parlor, deported herself with steady composure; told them that she was obliged suddenly to go home, but would be back, if possible, the next morning. Then, in that orderly, accurate way which Peter Ascott could both understand and appreciate, she proceeded to arrange with them about the shop and the house in case she might be detained till Monday.

"You're not a bad woman of business," said he, with a patronizing air. "This seems a tidy little shop; I dare say you'll get on in it."

She looked at him with a bewildered air, and went on speaking to the young woman at the door.

"How much might your weekly receipts be in a place like this? And what salary does Miss—Miss What's-her-name give to each of you? You're the head shop-woman, I suppose?"

Hilary made no answer; she scarcely heard. All her mind was full of but one thing: "Never see Ascott any more!" There came back upon her all the dreadful stories she had ever heard of lads who had committed forgery or some similar offense, and, in dread of punishment, had run away in despair, and never been heard of for years—come to every kind of misery, perhaps even destroyed themselves. The impression was so horribly vivid, that when, pausing an instant in putting her books in their places, she heard the door-bell ring, Hilary with difficulty repressed a scream.

But it was no messenger of dreadful tidings—it was only Elizabeth Hand; and the quiet fashion in which she entered showed Hilary at once that nothing dreadful had happened at home.

"Oh no, nothing has happened," confirmed the girl. "Only Miss Leaf sent me to see if you could come home to-night instead of to-morrow. She is quite well—that is, pretty well; but Mr. Leaf—"

Here, catching sight of Miss Hilary's visitor, Elizabeth stopped short. Peter Ascott was one of her prejudices. She determined in his presence to let out no more of the family affairs.

On his part, Mr. Ascott had always treated Elizabeth as people like him usually do treat servants, afraid to lose an inch of their dignity, lest it should be an acknowledgment of equal birth and breeding with the class from which they are so terribly ashamed to have sprung. He regarded her now with a lorldly air.

"Young woman—I believe you are the young woman who this afternoon told me that Mr. Leaf was out. It was a fib, of course."

Elizabeth turned round indignantly. "No, sir; I don't tell fibs. He was out."

"Did you give him my message when he came in?"

"Yes, sir."

"And what did he say, eh?"

"Nothing."

This was the literal fact; but there was something behind which Elizabeth had not the slightest intention of communicating. In fact, she set herself, physically and mentally, in an attitude of dogged resistance to any pumping of Mr. Ascott; for though, as she had truly said, nothing special had happened, she felt sure that he was at the bottom of something which had gone wrong in the household that afternoon.

It was this. When Ascott returned, and she told him of his godfather's visit, the young man had suddenly turned so ghastly pale that she had to fetch him a glass of water, and his Aunt Johanna—Miss Selina was out—had to tend him and soothe him for several minutes before he was right again. When at last he seemed returning to his natural self, he looked wildly up at his aunt, and clung to her in such an outburst of feeling, that Elizabeth had thought it best to slip out of the room. It was tea-time, but still she waited outside for half an hour or longer, when she gently knocked, and after a minute or two Miss Leaf came out. There seemed nothing wrong, at least not much—not more than Elizabeth had noticed many and many a time after talks betwen Ascott and his aunts.

"I'll take in the tea myself," she said; "for I want you

to start at once for Kensington to fetch Miss Hilary. Don't frighten her — mind that, Elizabeth. Say I am much as usual myself, but that Mr. Leaf is not quite well, and I think she might do him good. Remember the exact words."

Elizabeth did, and would have delivered them accurately if Mr. Ascott had not been present, and addressed her in that authoritative manner. Now, she resolutely held her tongue.

Mr. Ascott might in his time have been accustomed to cringing, frightened, or impertinent servants, but this was a phase of the species with which he was totally unfamiliar. The girl was neither sullen nor rude, yet evidently quite independent; afraid neither of her mistress, nor of himself. He was sharp enough to see that whatever he wanted to get out of Elizabeth must be got in another way.

"Come, my wench, you'd better tell; it'll be none the worse for you, and it sha'n't harm the young fellow, though I dare say he has paid you well for holding your tongue."

"About what, sir?"

"Oh! you know what happened when you told him I had called, eh? Servants get to know all about their master's affairs."

"Mr. Leaf isn't my master, and his affairs are nothing to me; I don't pry into 'em," replied Elizabeth. "If you want to know any thing, sir, hadn't you better ask himself? He's at home to-night. I left him and my missus going to their tea."

"Left them at home, and at tea?"

"Yes, Miss Hilary."

It was an inexpressible relief. For the discovery must have come. Ascott must have known or guessed that Mr. Ascott had found him out; he must have confessed all to his aunt, or Johanna would never have done two things which her sister knew she strongly disliked—sending Elizabeth wandering through London at night, and fetching Hilary home before the time. Yet they had been left sitting quietly at their tea!

Perhaps, after all, the blow had not been so dreadful.

Johanna saw comfort through it all. Vague hopes arose in Hilary also; visions of the poor sinner sitting "clothed and in his right mind," contrite and humbled; comforted by them all, with the inexpressible tenderness with which we yearn over one who "was dead and is alive again, was lost, and is found;" helped by them all in the way that women—some women especially, and these were of them —seem formed to help the erring and unfortunate; for, erring as he was, he had also been unfortunate.

Many an excuse for him suggested itself. How foolish of them, ignorant women that they were, to suppose that seventeen years of the most careful bringing up could, with his temperament, stand against the countless dangers of London life; of any life where a young man is left to him-self in a great town, with his temptations so many, and his power of resistance so small. •

And this might not, could not be a deliberate act. It must have been committed under a sudden impulse, to be repented of for the rest of his days. Nay, in the strange way in which our sins and mistakes are made not only the whips to scourge us, but the sicknesses out of which we oft-en come—suffering and weak indeed, but yet relieved, and fresh, and sound—who could tell but that this grave fault, this actual guilt, the climax of so many lesser errors, might not work out in the end Ascott's complete reformation?

So, in the strange way in which, after a great shock, we begin to revive a little, to hope against hope, to see a slen-der ray breaking through the darkness, Hilary composed herself, at least so far as to enable her to bid Elizabeth go down stairs, and she would be ready directly.

"I think it is the best thing I can do—to go home at once," she said.

"Certainly, my dear," replied Mr. Ascott, rather flattered by her involuntary appeal, and by an inward consciousness of his own exceeding generosity. "And, pray, don't disturb yourselves. Tell your sister from me—your sister Selina, I mean—that I overlook every thing on condition that you keep him out of my sight—that young blackguard!"

"Don't, don't!" cried Hilary, piteously.

"Well, I won't, though it's his right name—a fellow who could— Look you, Miss Hilary, when his father sent to me to beg ten pounds to bury his mother with, I did bury her, and him also, a month after, very respectably too, though he had no claim upon me, except that he came from Stowbury. And I stood godfather to the child, and I've done my duty by him. But mark my words, what's bred in the bone will come in the flesh. He was born in a prison, and he'll die in a prison."

"God forbid!" said Hilary, solemnly. And again she felt the strong conviction, that whatever his father had been, or his mother, of whom they had heard nothing till she was dead, Ascott could not have lived all these years of his childhood and early boyhood with his three aunts at Stowbury without gaining at least some good, which might counteract the hereditary evil; as such evil can be counteracted, even as hereditary disease can be gradually removed by wholesome and careful rearing in a new generation.

"Well, I'll not say any more," continued Peter Ascott; "only, the sooner the young fellow takes himself off the better. He'll only plague you all. Now, can you send out for a cab for me?"

Hilary mechanically rang the bell and gave the order.

"I'll take you to town with me if you like. It'll save you the expense of the omnibus. I suppose you always travel by omnibus?"

Hilary answered something, she hardly knew what, except that it was a declining of all these benevolent attentions. At last she got Mr. Ascott outside the street door, and, returning, put her hand to her head with a moan.

"Oh, Miss Hilary, don't look like that!"

"Elizabeth, do you know what has happened?"

"No."

"Then I don't want you to know. And you must never try to find it out; for it is a secret that ought to be kept strictly within the family. Are you to be trusted?"

" Yes, Miss Hilary."

" Now, get me my bonnet, and let us make haste and go home."

They walked down the gas-lit Kensington High Street, Hilary taking her servant's arm; for she felt strangely weak. As she sat in the dark corner of the omnibus she tried to look things in the face, and form some definite plan; but the noisy rumble at once dulled and confused her faculties. She felt capable of no consecutive thought, but found herself stupidly watching the two lines of faces, wondering, absently, what sort of people they were; what were their lives and histories; and whether they all had, like herself, their own personal burden of woe. Which was, alas! the one fact that never need be doubted in this world.

It was nigh upon eleven o'clock when Hilary knocked at the door of No. 15.

Miss Leaf opened it; but for the first time in her life she had no welcome for her child.

" Is it Ascott? I thought it was Ascott," she cried, peering eagerly up and down the street.

" He is gone out, then? When did he go?" asked Hilary, feeling her heart turn stone-cold.

" Just after Selina came in. She—she vexed him. But he can not be long. Is not that man he?"

And just as she was, without shawl or bonnet, Johanna stepped out into the cold, damp night, and strained her eyes into the darkness; but in vain.

" I'll walk round the Crescent once, and maybe I shall find him. Only go in, Johanna."

And Hilary was away again into the dark, walking rapidly, less with the hope of finding Ascott than to get time to calm herself, so as to meet, and help her sisters to meet, this worst depth of their calamity; for something warned her that this last desperation of a weak nature is more to be dreaded than any overt obstinacy of a strong one. She had a conviction that Ascott never would come home.

After a while they gave up waiting and watching at the front door, and shut themselves up in the parlor. The first explanation past, even Selina ceased talking; and they sat together, the three women, doing nothing, attempting to do nothing, only listening; thinking every sound was a step on the pavement or a knock at the door. Alas! what would they not have given for the fiercest knock, the most impatient, angry footstep, if only it had been their boy's?

About one o'clock Selina had to be put to bed in strong hysterics. She had lashed her nephew with her bitter tongue till he had rushed out of the house, declaring that none of them should ever see his face again. Now she reproached herself as being the cause of all, and fell into an agony of remorse, which engrossed her sisters' whole care; until, her violent emotion having worn itself out, she went to sleep, the only one who did sleep in that miserable family.

For Elizabeth also, having been sent to bed hours before, was found by Miss Hilary sitting on the kitchen stairs, about four in the morning. Her mistress made no attempt at reproach, but brought her into the parlor to share the silent watch, never broken except to make up the fire or light a fresh candle; till candles burned up, and shutters were opened, and upon their great calamity stared the broad unwelcome day.

CHAPTER XIX.

"Missing"—"Lost"—"To—"—all the initials of the alphabet—we read these sort of advertisements in the newspapers; and unless there happens to be in them something intensely pathetic, comical, or horrible, we think very little about them. Only those who have undergone all that such an advertisement implies can understand its depth of misery: the sudden missing of the person out of the home-circle, whether going away in anger or driven away by terror or disgrace; the hour after hour and day after day of agonized suspense; the self-reproach, real or imaginary, lest any thing might have been said or done that was not

said or done—any thing prevented that was not prevented;
the gnawing remorse for some cruel, or careless, or bitter
word, that could so easily have been avoided.

Alas! if people could only be made to feel that every
word, every action carries with it the weight of an eterni-
ty; that the merest chance may make something said or
done quite unpremeditatedly, in vexation, sullenness, or
spite, the *last* action, the *last* word; which may grow into
an awful remembrance, rising up between them and the
irredeemable past, and blackening the future for years!

Selina was quite sure her unhappy nephew had committed suicide, and that she had been the cause of it. This
conviction she impressed incessantly on her two sisters as
they waited upon her, or sat talking by her bedside during
that long Saturday, when there was nothing else to be
done.

That was the misery of it. There was nothing to be
done. They had not the slightest clew to Ascott's haunts
or associates. With the last lingering of honest shame, or
honest respect for his aunts, he had kept all these things to
himself. To search for him in wide London was altogether
impossible.

Two courses suggested themselves to Hilary—one, to go
and consult Miss Balquidder; the other—which came into
her mind from some similar case she had heard of—to set
on foot inquiries at all police-stations. But the first idea
was soon rejected: only at the last extremity could she
make patent the family misery—the family disgrace. To
the second, similar and even stronger reasons applied.
There was something about the cool, matter-of-fact, business-like act of setting a detective officer to hunt out their
nephew from which these poor women recoiled. Besides,
impressed as he was—he had told his Aunt Johanna so—
with the relentlessness of Mr. Ascott, might not the chance
of his discovering that he was hunted drive him to desperation?

Hardly to suicide. Hilary steadfastly disbelieved in
that. When Selina painted horrible pictures of his throw-

I 2

ing himself off Waterloo Bridge; or being found hanging to a tree in one of the parks; or locking himself in a hotel bedchamber and blowing out his brains, her younger sister only laughed—laughed as much as she could—if only to keep Johanna quiet.

Yet she herself had few fears; for she knew that Ascott was, in a sense, too cowardly to kill himself. He so disliked physical pain, physical unpleasantness of all kinds. She felt sure he would stop short, even with the razor or the pistol in his hand, rather than do a thing so very disagreeable.

Nevertheless, in spite of herself, while she and her sisters sat together, hour after hour, in a stillness almost like that when there is a death in the house, these morbid terrors took a double size. Hilary ceased to treat them as ridiculous impossibilities, but began to argue them out rationally. The mere act of doing so made her recoil; for it seemed an acknowledgment that she was fighting, not with chimeras, but realities.

"It is twenty-four hours since he went," she reasoned. "If he had done any thing desperate he would have done it at once, and we should have heard of it long before now; ill news always travels fast. Besides, his name was marked on all his clothes in full. I did it myself. And his coat-pockets were always stuffed with letters; he used to cram them in as soon as he got them, you know."

And at this small remembrance of one of his "ways," even though it was an unkind way, and had caused them many a pain, from the want of confidence it showed, his poor, fond aunts turned aside to hide their starting tears. The very phrase "he used to" seemed such an unconscious admission that his life with them was over and done—that he never would either please them or vex them any more.

Yet they took care that during the whole day every thing should be done as if he were expected minute by minute: that Elizabeth should lay the fourth knife and fork at dinner, the fourth cup and saucer at tea. Elizabeth, who throughout had faithfully kept her pledge; who went about silently and unobservantly, and by every means in her power put aside the curiosity of Mrs. Jones as to what could be the reason that her lodgers had sat up all night, and what on earth had become of young Mr. Leaf.

After tea, Johanna, quite worn out, consented to go to bed; and then Hilary, left to her own responsibility, set herself to consider how long this dreadful quietness was to last, whether nothing could be done. She could endure whatever was inevitable, but it was against her nature as well as her conscience to sit down tamely to endure any thing whatsoever till it did become inevitable.

In the first place, she determined on that which a certain sense of honor, as well as the fear of vexing him should he come home, had hitherto prevented—the examining of Ascott's room, drawers, clothes, and papers. It was a very dreary business—almost like doing the like to a person who was dead, only without the sad sanctity that belongs to the dead, whose very errors are forgotten and forgiven, who can neither suffer nor make others suffer any more.

Many things she found, and more she guessed at—things which stabbed her to the heart, things that she never told, not even to Johanna; but she found no clew whatever to Ascott's whereabouts, intentions, or connections. One thing, however, struck her—that most of his clothes, and all his somewhat extensive stock of jewelry, were gone; every thing, in short, that could be convertible into money. It was evident that his flight, sudden as it was, had been premeditated as at least a possibility.

This so far was satisfactory. It took away the one haunting fear of his committing suicide, and made it likely that he was still lingering about, hiding from justice and Mr. Ascott, or perhaps waiting for an opportunity to escape from England—from the fear that his godfather, even if not prosecuting him, had the power and doubtless the will completely to crush his future, wherever he was known.

Where could he go? His aunt tried to think over every word he had ever let fall about America, Australia, or any

other place to which the hopeless outlaws of this country
fly; but she could recollect nothing to enable her to form
any conclusion. One thing only she was sure of—that if
once he went away, his own words would come true; they
would never see his face again. The last tie, the last con-
straint that bound him to home and a steady, righteous life
would be broken : he would go all adrift, be tossed hither
and thither on every wave of circumstance—what *he* called
circumstance—till Heaven only knew what a total wreck
he might speedily become, or in what forlorn and far-off
seas his ruined life might go down. He, Ascott Leaf, the
last of the name and family.

"It can not be; it shall not be!" cried Hilary. A sharp,
bitter cry of resistance to the death; and her heart seemed
to go out to the wretched boy, and her hands to clutch at
him, as if he were drowning, and she were the only one to
save him. How could she do it?

If she could only get at him by word or letter! But
that seemed impossible, until, turning over scheme after
scheme, she suddenly thought of the one which so many
people had tried in similar circumstances, and which she
remembered they had talked over and laughed over, they
and Ascott, one Sunday evening not so very long ago.
This was—a *Times* advertisement.

The difficulty how to word it, so as to catch his attention
and yet escape publicity, was very great, especially as his
initials were so common. Hundreds of "A. L.'s" might be
wandering away from home, to whom all that she dared
say to call Ascott back would equally apply. At last a
bright thought struck her.

"A. leaf" (with a small *l*) "will be quite safe wherever
found. Come. Saturday. 15."

As she wrote it—this wretched double-entendre—she
was seized with that sudden sense of the ludicrous which
sometimes intrudes in such a ghastly fashion in the very
midst of great misery. She burst into uncontrollable laughter, fit after fit; so violent that Elizabeth, who came in by

chance, was terrified out of her wits, and, kneeling beside her mistress, implored her to be quiet. At last the paroxysm ended in complete exhaustion. The tension of the last twenty-four hours had given way, and Hilary knew her strength was gone. Yet the advertisement ought to be taken to the *Times* office that very night, in order to be inserted without fail on Monday morning.

There was but one person whom she could trust—Elizabeth.

She looked at the girl, who was kneeling beside the sofa, rubbing her feet, and sometimes casting a glance round, in the quiet way of one well used to nursing, who can find out how the sufferer is without "fussing" with questions. She noticed, probably because she had seen little of her of late, a curious change in Elizabeth. It must have been gradual, but yet its result had never been so apparent before. Her brusqueness had softened down, and there had come into her and shone out of her, spite of all her natural uncomeliness of person, that beautiful, intangible something, common alike to peasant and queen, as clear to see and as sad to miss in both—womanliness. Added thereto · was the gentle composure of mien which almost invariably accompanied it, which instinctively makes you feel that in great things or small, whatever the woman has to do, she will do it in the womanliest, wisest, and best way.

So thought Miss Hilary as she lay watching her servant, and then explained to her the errand upon which she wished to send her.

Not much explanation, for she merely gave her the advertisement to read, and told her what she wished done with it. And Elizabeth, on her part, asked no questions, but simply listened and obeyed.

After she was gone Hilary lay on the sofa passive and motionless. Her strength and activity seemed to have collapsed at once into that heavy quietness which comes when one has endured to the utmost limit of endurance, when one feels as if to speak a word or to lift a finger would be as much as life was worth.

"Oh, if I could only go to sleep!" was all she thought.

By-and-by sleep did come, and she was taken far away out of these miseries. By the strange peculiarity of dreams, that we so seldom dream about any grief that oppresses us at the time, but generally of something quite different, she thought she was in some known unknown land, lovely and beautiful, with blue hills rising in the distance, and blue seas creeping and curling on to the shore. On this shore she was walking with Robert Lyon, just as he used to be, with his true face and honest voice. He did not talk to her much; but she felt him there, and knew they had but "one heart between them." A heart which had never once swerved, either from the other; a heart whole and sound, into which the least unfaith had never come—that had never known, or recognized even as a possibility, the one first doubt, the ominous

> "Little rift within the lute,
> That by-and-by will make the music mute,
> And, ever widening, slowly silence all."

Is it ever so in this world? Does God ever bring the faithful man to the faithful woman, and make them love one another with a righteous, holy, persistent tenderness, which dare look in His face, nor be ashamed; which sees in this life only the beginning of the life to come; and in the closest, most passionate human love something to be held with a loose hand, something frail as glass and brittle as straw, unless it is perfected and sanctified by the love divine?

Hilary at least believed so. And when, at Elizabeth's knock, she woke with a start, and saw—not the sweet seashore and Robert Lyon, but the dull parlor, and the last flicker of the fire, she thanked God that her dream was not all a dream—that, sharp as her misery was, it did not touch this—the love of her heart: she believed in Robert Lyon still.

And so she rose and spoke quite cheerfully, asking Elizabeth how she had managed, and whether the advertisement would be sure to be in on Monday morning.

"Yes, Miss Hilary; it is sure to be all right."

And then the girl hung about the room in an uneasy way, as if she had something to tell, which was the fact.

Elizabeth had had an adventure. It was a new thing in her monotonous life; it brightened her eyes, and flushed her cheeks, and made her old nervousness of manner return. More especially as she was somewhat perplexed, being divided in her mind between the wish she had to tell her mistress every thing, and the fear to trouble her, at this troublous time, with any small matter that merely concerned herself.

The matter was this. When she had given in her advertisement at the *Times* office, and was standing behind the counter waiting for her change and receipt, there stood beside her a young man, also waiting. She had hardly noticed him, till on his talking to the clerk about some misprint in his advertisement, apparently one of the great column of "Want Places," her ear was caught by the unmistakable Stowbury accent.

It was the first time she had heard it since she left home, and to Elizabeth's tenacious nature home in absence had gained an additional charm, had grown to be the one place in the world about which her affections clung. In these dreary wilds of London, to hear a Stowbury tongue, to catch sight of a Stowbury person, or even one who might know Stowbury, made her heart leap up with a bound of joy. She turned suddenly, and looked intently at the young man, or rather the lad, for he seemed a mere lad, small, slight, and whiskerless.

"Well, miss, I hope you'll know me again next time," said the young fellow. At which remark Elizabeth saw that he was neither so young nor so simple as she had at first thought. She drew back, very much ashamed, and coloring deeply.

Now, if Elizabeth ever looked any thing like comely, it was when she blushed; for she had the delicate skin peculiar to the young women of her district, and when the blood rushed through it, no cheek of lady fair ever assumed

a brighter rose. That, or the natural vanity of man in being noticed by woman, caught the youth's attention.

"Come, now, miss, don't be shy or offended. Perhaps
I'm going your way? Would you like company home?"

"No, thank you," said Elizabeth, with great dignity.

"Well, won't you even tell a fellow your name? Mine's
Tom Cliffe, and I live—"

"Cliffe! Are you little Tommy Cliffe, and do you come
from Stowbury?"

And all Elizabeth's heart was in her eyes.

As has been said, she was of a specially tenacious nature.
She liked few people, but those she did like she held very
fast. Almost the only strong interest of her life, except
Miss Hilary, had been the little boy whom she had snatched
from under the horse's heels; and though he was rather a
scapegrace, and cared little for her, and his mother was a
decidedly objectionable woman, she had clung to them
both firmly till she lost sight of them.

Now it was not to be expected that she should recognize
in this London stranger the little lad whose life she had
saved—a lad, too, from her beloved Stowbury—without
a certain amount of emotion, at which the individual in
question broadly stared.

"Bless your heart, I am Tommy Cliffe from Stowbury,
sure enough. Who are you?"

"Elizabeth Hand."

Whereupon ensued a most friendly greeting. Tom declared he should have known her any where, and had never
forgotten her—never! How far that was true or not, he
certainly looked as if it were; and two great tears of
pleasure dimmed Elizabeth's kind eyes.

"You've grown a man now, Tommy," said she, looking
at him with a sort of half-maternal pride, and noticing his
remarkably handsome and intelligent face; so intelligent
that it would have attracted notice, though it was set upon
broad, stooping shoulders, and a small, slight body. "Let
me see—how old are you?"

"I'm nineteen, I think."

"And I'm two-and-twenty. How aged we are growing!" said Elizabeth with a smile.

Then she asked after Mrs. Cliffe, but got only the brief answer, "Mother's dead," given in a tone as if no more inquiries would be welcome. His two sisters, also, had died of typhus in one week, and Tom had been "on his own hook," as he expressed it, for the last three years.

He was extremely frank and confidential; told how he had begun life as a printer's "devil," afterwards become a compositor, and his health failing, had left the trade, and gone as a servant to a literary gentleman.

"An uncommon clever fellow is master; keeps his carriage, and has dukes to dinner, all out of his books. Maybe you've heard of them, Elizabeth?" and he named a few, in a patronizing way; at which Elizabeth smiled, for she knew them well. But she nevertheless regarded with a certain awe the servant of so great a man, and "little Tommy Cliffe" took a new importance in her eyes.

Also, as he walked with her along the street to find an omnibus, she could not help perceiving what a sharp little fellow he had grown into; how, like many another printer's boy, he had caught the influence of the atmosphere of letters, and was educated—self-educated, of course—to a degree far beyond his position. When she looked at him, and listened to him, Elizabeth involuntarily thought of Benajamin Franklin, and of many more who had raised themselves from the ink-pot and the compositor's desk to fame and eminence, and she fancied that such might be the lot of "little Tommy Cliffe." Why not? If so, how excessively proud she should be!

For the moment she had forgotten her errand; forgotten even Miss Hilary. It was not till Tom Cliffe asked her where she lived that she suddenly recollected her mistress might not like, under present circumstances, that their abode or any thing concerning them should be known to a Stowbury person.

It was a struggle. She would have liked to see the lad again; have liked to talk over with him Stowbury things and Stowbury people; but she felt she ought not, and she would not.

"Tell me where you live, Tom, and that will do just as well—at least till I speak to my mistress. I never had a visitor before, and my mistress might not like it."

"No followers allowed, eh?"

Elizabeth laughed. The idea of little Tommy Cliffe as her "follower" seemed so very funny.

So she bade him good-by; having, thanks to his gay frankness, been made acquainted with all about him, but leaving him in perfect ignorance concerning herself and her mistress. She only smiled when he declared contemptuously, and with rather a romantic emphasis, that he would hunt her out, though it were half over London.

This was all her adventure. When she came to tell it, it seemed very little to tell, and Miss Hilary listened to it rather indifferently, trying hard to remember who Tommy Cliffe was, and to take an interest in him because he came from Stowbury. But Stowbury days were so far off now —with such a gulf of pain between.

Suddenly the same fear occurred to her that had occurred to Elizabeth.

"The lad did not see the advertisement, I hope? You did not tell him about us?"

"I told him nothing," said Elizabeth, speaking softly, and looking down. "I did not mention even any body's name."

"That was right: thank you."

But oh, the bitterness of knowing, and feeling sure Elizabeth knew too, the thing for which she thanked her; and that not to mention Ascott's name was the greatest kindness the faithful servant could show toward the family.

CHAPTER XX.

Ascott Leaf never came home.

Day after day appeared the advertisement, sometimes slightly altered, as hope or fear suggested; but no word, no letter, no answer of any kind reached the anxious women.

By-and-by, moved by their distress, or perhaps feeling that the scapegrace would be safer got rid of if found and dispatched abroad in some decent manner, Mr. Ascott himself took measures for privately continuing the search. Every outward-bound ship was examined; every hospital visited; every case of suicide investigated; but in vain. The unhappy young man had disappeared, suddenly and completely, as many another has disappeared, out of the home-circle, and been never heard of more.

It is difficult to understand how a family can possibly bear such a sorrow, did we not know that many have had to bear it, and have borne it, with all its load of agonizing suspense, slowly dying hope,

"The hope that keeps alive despair," .

settling down into a permanent grief, compared to which the grief for loss by death is light and endurable.

The Leaf family went through all this. Was it better or worse for them that their anguish had to be secret? that there were no friends to pity, inquire, or console? that Johanna had to sit hour by hour and day by day in the solitary parlor, Selina having soon gone back to her old ways of "gadding about" and her marriage preparations; and that, hardest of all, Hilary had on the Monday morning to return to Kensington, and work, work, work, as nothing were amiss?

But it was natural that all this should tell upon her; and one day Miss Balquidder said, after a long covert observation of her face. "My dear, you look ill. Is there any

thing troubling you? My young people always tell me
their troubles, bodily or mental. I doctor both."

"I am sure of it," said Hilary, with a sad smile, but entered into no explanation, and Miss Balquidder had the
wise kindliness to inquire no further. Nevertheless, on
some errand or other she came to Kensington nearly every evening, and took Hilary back with her to sleep at
No. 15.

"Your sister Selina must wish to have you with her as
much as possible till she is married," she said, as a reason
for doing this.

And Hilary acquiesced, but silently, as we often do ac-
quiesce in what ought to be a truth, but which we know to
be the saddest, most painful falsehood.

For Selina, it became plain to see, was one of the family
no more. After her first burst of self-reproachful grief she
took Mr. Ascott's view of her nephew's loss—that it was a
good riddance; went on calmly with her bridal preparations, and seemed only afraid lest any thing should interfere to prevent her marriage.

But the danger was apparently tided over. No news
of Ascott came. Even the daily inquiries for him by his
creditors had ceased. His aunt Selina was beginning to
breathe freely, when, the morning before the wedding-day,
as they were all sitting in the midst of white finery, but as
sadly and silently as if it were a funeral, a person was suddenly shown in "on business."

It was a detective officer sent to find out from Ascott
Leaf's aunts whether a certain description of him, in a
printed hand-bill, was correct; for his principal creditor,
exasperated, had determined on thus advertising him in
the public papers as having "absconded."

Had a thunderbolt fallen in the little parlor the three
aunts could not have been more utterly overwhelmed.
They made no "scene"—a certain sense of pride kept these
poor gentlewomen from betraying their misery to a strange
man; though he was a very civil man, and having delivered
himself of his errand, like an automaton, sat looking into

his hat, and taking no notice of aught around him. He was accustomed to this sort of thing.

Hilary was the first to recover herself. She glanced round at her sisters, but they had not a word to say. In any crisis of family difficulty they always left her to take the helm.

Rapidly she ran over in her mind all the consequences that would arise from this new trouble—the public disgrace; Mr. Ascott's anger and annoyance—not that she cared much for this, except so far as it would affect Selina; lastly, the death-blow it was to any possible hope of reclaiming the poor prodigal, who she did not believe was dead, but still fondly trusted would return one day from his wanderings and his swine's husks to have the fatted calf killed for him and glad tears shed over him. But after being advertised as "absconded," Ascott never would, never could come home any more.

Taking as cool and business-like a tone as she could, she returned the paper to the detective.

"This is a summary proceeding. Is there no way of avoiding it?"

"One, miss," replied the man, very respectfully. "If the family would pay the debt."

"Do you know how much it is?"

"Eighty pounds."

"Ah!"

That hopeless sigh of Johanna's was sufficient answer, though no one spoke.

But in desperate cases some women acquire a desperate courage, or rather it is less courage than faith—the faith which is said to "remove mountains"—the belief that to the very last there must be something to be done, and, if it can be done, they will have strength to do it. True, the mountain may not be removed, but the mere act of faith or courage sometimes teaches how to climb over it.

"Very well. Take this paper back to your employer. He must be aware that his only chance of payment is by suppressing it. If he will do that, in two days he shall

hear from us, and we will make arrangements about paying the debt."

Hilary said this to her sisters' utter astonishment; so
utter that they let her say it, and let the detective go
away with a civil "Good-morning," before they could interfere or contradict by a word.

"Paying the debt! Hilary, what have you promised!
It is an impossibility."

"Like the Frenchman's answer to his mistress—'Ma-
dame, if it had been possible it would have been done already; if it is impossible, it shall be done.' It shall, I
say."

"I wonder you can jest about our misfortunes," said Selina, in her most querulous voice.

"I'm not jesting. But where is the use of sitting down
to moan! I mean what I say. The thing must be done."

Her eyes glittered—her small, red lips were set tightly
together.

"If it is not done, sisters—if his public disgrace is not
prevented, don't you see the result? Not as regards your
marriage, Selina—the man must be a coward who would
refuse to marry a woman he cared for, even though her
nearest kinsman had been hanged at the Old Bailey—but
Ascott himself. The boy is not a bad boy, though he has
done wickedly; but there is a difference between a wicked act and a wicked nature. I mean to save him if I can."

"How?"

"By saving his good name; by paying the debt."

"And where on earth shall you get the money?"

"I will go to Miss Balquidder and—"

"Borrow it?"

"No, never! I would as soon think of stealing it."

Then controlling herself, Hilary explained that she meant
to ask Miss Balquidder to arrange for her with the creditor
to pay the eighty pounds by certain weekly or monthly in-
stallments, to be deducted from her salary at Kensington.

"It is not a very great favor to ask of her—merely that
she should say, 'This young woman is employed by me;

I believe her to be honest, respectable, and so forth; also, that when she makes a promise to pay, she will to the best of her power perform it.' A character which is at present rather a novelty in the Leaf family."

"Hilary!"

"I am growing bitter, Johanna, I know I am. Why should we suffer so much? Why should we be always dragged down — down — in this way? Why should we never have had any one to cherish and take care of us, like other women? Why—"

Miss Leaf laid her finger on her child's lips—

"Because it is the will of God."

Hilary flung herself on her dear old sister's neck, and burst into tears.

Selina too cried a little, and said that she should like to help in paying the debt if Mr. Ascott had no objection. And then she turned back to her white splendors, and became absorbed in the annoyance of there being far too much clematis and far too little orange-blossom in the bridal bonnet—which it was now too late to change. A little, also, she vexed herself about the risk of confiding in Miss Balquidder, lest by any chance the story might get round to Russell Square; and was urgent that at least nothing should be said or done until after to-morrow. She was determined to be married, and dreaded any slip between the cup and the lip.

But Hilary was resolute. "I said that in two days the matter should be arranged, and so it must be, or the man will think we too break our promises."

"You can assure him to the contrary," said Selina, with dignity. "In fact, why can't you arrange with him without going at all to Miss Balquidder?"

Again the fierce, bitter expression returned to Hilary's face.

"You forget, Miss Balquidder's honest name is his only guarantee against the dishonesty of ours."

"Hilary, you disgrace us — disgrace me — speaking in such a way. Are we not gentlewomen?"

"I don't know, Selina. I don't seem to know or to feel any thing, except that I would live on bread and water in order to live peaceably and honestly. Oh! will it ever, ever be?"

She walked up and down the parlor, disarranging the white draperies which lay about, feeling unutterable contempt for them and for her sister. Angry and miserable, with every nerve quivering, she was at war with the whole world.

This feeling lasted even when, after some discussion, she gained her point, and was on her way to call on Miss Balquidder. She went round and round the square many times, trying to fix in her mind word for word what she meant to say; revealing no more of the family history than was absolutely necessary, and stating her business in the briefest, hardest, most matter-of-fact way—putting it as a transaction between employer and employed, in which there was no more favor asked or bestowed than could possibly be avoided. And as the sharp east wind blew across her at every corner, minute by minute she felt herself growing more fierce, and hard, and cold.

"This will never do. I shall be wicked by-and-by. I must go in and get it over."

Perhaps it was as well. Well for her, morally as physically, that there should have been that sudden change from the blighting weather outside to the warm, well-lighted room, where the good rich woman sat at her early and solitary tea.

Very solitary it looked—the little table in the centre of that large, handsome parlor, with the one cup and saucer, the one easy-chair. And as Hilary entered she noticed, amid all this comfort and luxury, the still, grave, almost sad expression which solitary people always get to wear.

But the next minute Miss Balquidder had turned round, and risen, smiling.

"Miss Leaf, how very kind of you to come and see me! Just the day before the wedding, too, when you must be so busy! Sit down and tell me all about it. But first, my dear, how wet your boots are! Let me take them off at once."

Which she did, sending for her own big slippers, and putting them on the tiny feet with her own hands.

Hilary submitted—in truth, she was too much surprised to resist.

Miss Balquidder had, like most folk, her opinions or "crotchets"—as they might be—and one of them was, to keep her business and friendly relations entirely distinct and apart. Whenever she went to Kensington or her other establishments she was always emphatically "the mistress"—a kindly and even motherly mistress certainly, but still authoritative, decided. Moreover, it was her invariable rule to treat all her *employés* alike—"making no stepbairns" among them. Thus for some time it had happened that Hilary had been, and felt herself to be, just Miss Leaf, the book-keeper, doing her duty to Miss Balquidder, her employer, and neither expecting nor attaining any closer relation.

But in her own house, or it might be from the sudden apparition of that young face at her lonely fireside, Miss Balquidder appeared quite different.

A small thing touches a heart that is sore with trouble. When the good woman rose up—after patting the little feet, and approving loudly of the woolen stockings—she saw that Hilary's whole face was quivering with the effort to keep back her tears.

There are some women of whom one feels by instinct that they were, as Miss Balquidder had once jokingly said of herself, specially meant to be mothers. And though, in its strange providence, Heaven often denies the maternity, it can not, and does not mean to shut up the well-spring of that maternal passion—truly a passion to such women as these, almost as strong as the passion of love—but lets the stream, which might otherwise have blessed one child or one family, flow out wide and far, blessing wherever it goes.

In a tone that somehow touched every fibre of Hilary's

K

heart, Miss Balquidder said, placing her on a low chair be‑
side her own,

"My dear, you are in trouble. I saw it a week or two
ago, but did not like to speak. Couldn't you say it out,
and let me help you? You need not be afraid. I never
tell any thing, and every body tells every thing to me."

That was true. Added to this said motherliness of hers,
Miss Balquidder possessed that faculty, which some peo‑
ple have in a remarkable degree, and some—very good peo‑
ple too—are totally deficient in, of attracting confidence.
The secrets she had been trusted with, the romances she
had been mixed up in, the Quixotic acts she had been called
upon to perform during her long life, would have made a
novel—or several novels—such as no novelist could dare
to write, for the public would condemn them as impossible
and unnatural. But all this experience—though happily
it could never be put into a book—had given to the wom‑
an herself a view of human nature at once so large, lenient,
and just, that she was the best person possible to hear the
strange and pitiful story of young Ascott Leaf.

How it came out Hilary hardly knew; she seemed to
have told very little, and yet Miss Balquidder guessed it
all. It did not appear to surprise or shock her. She nei‑
ther began to question nor preach; she only laid her hand
—her large, motherly, protecting hand, on the bowed head,
saying,

"How much you must have suffered, my poor bairn!"

The soft Scotch tone and word—the grave, quiet Scotch
manner, implying more than it even expressed—was it
wonderful if underlying as well as outside influences made
Hilary completely give way?

Robert Lyon had had a mother, who died when he was
seventeen, but of whom he kept the tenderest remembrance,
often saying that of all the ladies he had met with in the
world there was none equal to her—the strong, tender, wom‑
anly peasant woman—refined in mind, and word, and ways
—though to the last day of her life she spoke broad Scotch,
and did the work of her cottage with her own hands. It

seems as if that mother—toward whom Hilary's fancy had clung, lovingly as a woman ought to cling, above all others, to the mother of the man she loves—were speaking to her now, comforting her and helping her—comfort and help that it would have been sweeter to receive from her than from any woman living.

A mere fancy; but in her state of long uncontrolled excitement it took such possession of her that Hilary fell on her knees, and hid her face in Miss Balquidder's lap, sobbing aloud.

The other was a little surprised; it was not her Scotch way to yield to emotion before folk; but she was a wise woman, she asked no questions, merely held the quivering hands and smoothed the throbbing head, till composure returned. Some people have a magical, mesmeric power of soothing and controlling: it was hers. When she took the poor face between her hands, and looked straight into the eyes, with, "There, you are better now," Hilary returned the gaze as steadily, nay, smilingly, and rose.

"Now, may I tell you my business?"

"Certainly, my dear. When one's friends are in trouble, the last thing one ought to do is to sit down beside them and moan. Did you come to ask my advice, or had you any definite plan of your own?"

"I had." And Hilary told it.

"A very good plan, and very generous in you to think of it. But I see two strong objections: first, whether it can be carried out; secondly, whether it ought."

Hilary shrank, sensitively.

"Not on my account, my dear, but your own. I often see people making martyrs of themselves for some worthless character on whom the sacrifice is utterly wasted. I object to this, as I would object to throwing myself or my friend into a blazing house, unless I were morally certain there was a life to be saved. Is there in this case?"

"I think there is! I trust in Heaven there is!" said Hilary, earnestly.

There was both pleasure and pity expressed in Miss Bal-

quidder's countenance as she replied, "Be it so: that is a
matter on which no one can judge except yourself. But
on the other matter you ask my advice, and I must give
it. To maintain two ladies and pay a debt of eighty pounds
out of one hundred a year is simply impossible."

"With Johanna's income and mine it will be a hundred
and twenty pounds and some odd shillings a year."

"You accurate girl! But even with this it can not be
done, unless you were to live in a manner so restricted in
the commonest comforts that at your sister's age she would
be sure to suffer. You must look on the question from all
sides, my dear. You must be just to others as well as to
that young man, who seems never to— But I will leave
him unjudged."

They were both silent for a minute, and then Miss Balquidder said: "I feel certain there is but one rational way
of accomplishing the thing, if you are bent upon doing it,
if your own judgment and conscience tell you it ought to
be done. Is it so?"

"Yes," said Hilary, firmly.

The old Scotswoman took her hand with a warm press-
ure. "Very well. I don't blame you. I might have done
the same myself. Now to my plan. Miss Leaf, have you
known me long enough to confer on me the benediction—
one of the few that we rich folk possess—'It is more blessed to give than to receive?'"

"I don't quite understand."

"Then allow me to explain. I happen to know this creditor of your nephew's. He being a tailor and an outfitter,
we have had dealings together in former times, and I know
him to be a hard man, an unprincipled man, such a one as
no young woman should have to do with, even in business
relations. To be in his power, as you would be for some
years if your scheme of gradual payment were carried out,
is the last thing I should desire for you. Let me suggest
another way. Take me for your creditor instead of him.
Pay him at once, and I will write you a check for the
amount."

The thing was put so delicately, in such an ordinary manner, as if it were a mere business arrangement, that at first Hilary hardly perceived all it implied. When she did —when she found that it was in plain terms a gift or loan of eighty pounds offered by a person almost a stranger, she was at first quite bewildered. Then (ah! let us not blame her if she carried to a morbid excess that noble independence which is the foundation of all true dignity in man or woman) she shrunk back into herself, overcome with annoyance and shame. At last she forced herself to say, though the words came out rather coldly,

"You are very good, and I am exceedingly obliged to you; but I never borrowed money in my life. It is quite impossible."

"Very well; I can understand your feelings. I beg your pardon," replied Miss Balquidder, also somewhat coldly.

They sat silent and awkward, and then the elder lady took out a pencil and began to make calculations in her memorandum-book.

"I am reckoning what is the largest sum per month that you could reasonably be expected to spare, and how you may make the most of what remains. Are you aware that London lodgings are very expensive? I am thinking that if you were to exchange out of the Kensington shop into another I have at Richmond, I could offer you the first floor above it for much less rent than you pay Mrs. Jones, and you could have your sister living with you."

"Ah! that would make us both so much happier! How good you are!"

"You will see I only wish to help you to help yourself, not to put you under any obligation, though I can not see any thing so very terrible in your being slightly indebted to an old woman who has neither chick nor child, and is at perfect liberty to do what she likes with her own."

There was a pathos in the tone which smote Hilary into quick contrition.

"Forgive me! But I have such a horror of borrowing

money—you must know why after what I have told you
of our family. You must surely understand—"

"I do, fully; but there are limits even to independence.
A person who, for his own pleasure, is ready to take money
from any body and every body, without the slightest pros-
pect or intention of returning it, is quite different from a
friend who in a case of emergency accepts help from another friend, being ready and willing to take every means
of repayment, as I knew you were, and meant you to be.
I meant, as you suggested, to stop out of your salary so
much per month, till I had my eighty pounds safe back
again."

"But suppose you never had it back? I am young and
strong; still I might fall ill—I might die, and you never
be repaid."

"Yes, I should," said Miss Balquidder, with a serious
smile. "You forget, my dear bairn, '*Inasmuch as ye have
done it to one of these little ones, ye have done it unto* ME.'
'*He that giveth to the poor lendeth to the* LORD.' I have lent
Him a good deal at different times, and He has always paid
me back with usury."

There was something at once solemn and a little sad in
the way the old lady spoke. Hilary forgot her own side
of the subject—her pride, her humiliation.

"But do you not think, Miss Balquidder, that one ought
to work on, struggle on, to the last extremity, before one
accepts an obligation, most of all a money obligation?"

"I do, as a general principle. Yet money is not the greatest thing in this world, that a pecuniary debt should be the
worst to bear. And sometimes one of the kindest acts you
can do to a fellow-creature—one that touches and softens
his heart, nay, perhaps wins it to you for life, is to accept a
favor from him."

Hilary made no reply.

"I speak a little from experience. I have not had a very
happy life myself—at least most people would say so if
they knew it; but the Lord has made it up to me by giving me the means of bringing happiness, in money as well

as other ways, to other people. Most of us have our favorite luxuries; this is mine. I like to do people good; I
like, also—though maybe that is a mean weakness—to feel
that I do it. If all whom I have been made instrumental
in helping had said to me, as you have done, ' I will not be
helped, I will not be made happy,' it would have been rather hard for me."

And a smile, half humorous, half sad, came over the hard-
featured face, spiritualizing its whole expression.

Hilary wavered. She compared her own life, happy still,
and hopeful, for all its cares, with that of this lonely woman, whose only blessing was her riches, except the generous heart which sanctified them, and made them such.
Humbled, nay, ashamed, she took and kissed the kindly
hand which had succored so many, yet which, in the inscrutable mystery of Providence, had been left to go down
to the grave alone; missing all that is personal, dear, and
precious to a woman's heart, and getting instead only what
Hilary now gave her—the half-sweet, half-bitter payment
of gratitude.

" Well, my bairn, what is to be done ?"

" I will do whatever you think right," murmured Hilary.

CHAPTER XXI.

It was not a cheerful morning on which to be married.
A dense, yellow, London fog, the like of which the Misses
Leaf had never yet seen, penetrated into every corner of
the parlor at No. 15, where they were breakfasting dreari-
ly by candle-light, all in their wedding attire. They had
been up since six in the morning, and Elizabeth had dressed
her three mistresses one after the other, taking exceeding
pleasure in the performance; for she was still little more
than a girl, to whom a wedding was a wedding, and this
was the first she had ever had to do with in her life.

True, it disappointed her in some things. She was a little surprised that last evening had passed off just like all

other evenings. The interest and bustle of packing soon subsided—the packing consisting only of the traveling trunk, for the rest of the *trousseau* went straight to Russell Square, every means having been taken to ignore the very existence of No. 15; and then the three ladies had supper as usual, and went to bed at their customary hour, without any special demonstration of emotion or affection. To Elizabeth this was strange. She had not yet yet learned the unspeakable bitterness of a parting where nobody has any grief to restrain.

On a wedding morning, of course, there is no time to be spared for sentiment. The principal business appeared to be—dressing. Mr. Ascott had insisted on doing his part in making his new connections appear " respectable" at his marriage, and for Selina's sake they had consented. Indeed, it was inevitable: they had no money whatever to clothe themselves withal. They must either have accepted Mr. Ascott's gifts—in which, to do him justice, he was both thoughtful and liberal—or they must have staid away from the wedding altogether, which they did not like to do " for the sake of the family."

So, with a sense of doing their last duty by the sister, who would be, they felt, henceforward a sister no more, Miss Leaf attired herself in her violet silk and white China shawl, and Miss Hilary put on her silver-gray poplin, with a cardinal cape, as was then in fashion, trimmed with white swan's-down. It was rather an elderly costume for a bridemaid; but she was determined to dress warmly, and not risk, in muslins and laces, the health which to her now was money, life—nay, honor.

For Ascott's creditor had been already paid: Miss Balquidder never let grass grow under her feet. When Hilary returned to her sisters that day there was no longer any fear of public exposure; she had the receipted bill in her hand, and she was Miss Balquidder's debtor to the extent of eighty pounds.

But it was no debt of disgrace or humiliation, nor did she feel it as such. She had learned the lesson which the large-hearted rich can always teach the poor, that, while there is sometimes, to some people, no more galling chain, there is to others—and these are the highest natures too —no more firm and sacred bond than gratitude. But still the debt was there; and Hilary would never feel quite easy till it was paid—in money, at least. The generosity she never wished to repay. She would rather feel it wrapping her round. like an arm that was heavy only through its exceeding tenderness, to the end of her days.

Nevertheless she had arranged that there was to be a regular monthly deduction from her salary; and how, by retrenchment, to make this monthly payment as large as she could, was a question which had occupied herself and Johanna for a good while after they retired to rest, for there was no time to be lost. Mrs. Jones must be given notice to; and there was another notice to be given, if the Richmond plan were carried out; another sad retrenchment, foreboding which, when Elizabeth brought up supper, Miss Hilary could hardly look the girl in the face, and, when she bade her good-night, had felt almost like a secret conspirator.

For she knew that, if the money to clear this debt was to be saved, they must part with Elizabeth.

No doubt the personal sacrifice would be considerable, for Hilary would have to do the work of their two rooms with her own hands, and give up a hundred little comforts in which Elizabeth, now become a most clever and efficient servant, had made herself necessary to them both. But the two ladies did not think of that at the moment; they only thought of the pain of parting with her. They thought of it sorely, even though she was but a servant, and there was a family parting close at hand. Alas! people must take what they earn. It was a melancholy fact that, of the two impending losses, the person they should miss most would be, not their sister, but Elizabeth.

Both regrets combined made them sit at the breakfast table—the last meal they should ever take together as a family—sad and sorry, speaking about little else than the

K 2

subject which presented itself as easiest and uppermost,
namely, clothes.

Finally, they stood all completely arrayed, even to bon-
nets; Hilary looking wonderfully bewitching in hers, which
was the very pattern of one that may still be seen in a
youthful portrait of our gracious queen—a large round
brim, with a wreath of roses inside; while Miss Leaf's was
somewhat like it, only with little bunches of white ribbon,
"for," she said, "my time of roses has gone by." But her
sweet faded face had a peace that was not in the other
two—not even in Hilary's.

But the time arrived; the carriage drew up at the door.
Then nature and sisterly feeling asserted themselves for a
minute. Miss Selina "gave way," not to any loud or in-
decorous extent, to nothing that could in the least harm
her white satin, or crumple her laces and ribbons; but she
did shed a tear or two—real honest tears—kissed her sisters affectionately, hoped they would be very happy at
Richmond, and that they would often come to see her at
Russell Square.

"You know," said she, half apologetically, "it is a great
deal better for one of us at least to be married and settled.
Indeed, I assure you, I have done it all for the good of my
family."

And for the time being she devoutly believed she had.

So it was all over. Elizabeth herself, from the aisle of
St. Pancras Church, watched the beginning and ending of
the show; a very fine show, with a number of handsomely
dressed people, wedding guests, who seemed to stare about
them a good deal, and take little interest in either bride or
bridegroom. The only persons Elizabeth recognized were
her mistresses—Miss Leaf, who kept her veil down and
never stirred; and Miss Hilary, who stood close behind the
bride, listening with downcast eyes to the beautiful marriage service. It must have touched her more than on her
sister's account, for a tear, gathered under each eyelash,
silently rolled down the soft cheek and fell.

"Miss Hilary's an angel, and he'll be a lucky man that

gets *her*," meditated her faithful "bower-maiden" of old,
as, a little excited by the event of the morning, she stood
by the mantlepiece and contemplated a letter which had
come after the ladies had departed; one of these regular
monthly Indian letters, after which, Elizabeth was sharp
enough to notice, Miss Hilary's step always grew lighter
and her eye brighter for many days.

"It must be a nice thing to have somebody fond of one,
and somebody to be fond of," meditated she. And "old-
fashioned piece of goods" as she was—according to Mrs.
Jones (who now, from the use she was in the Jones's *mé-
nage*, patronized and confided in her extremely)—some little bit of womanly craving after the woman's one hope
and crown of bliss crept into the poor maid-servant's heart.
But it was not for the maid-servant's usual necessity—a
"sweetheart"—somebody to "keep company with;" it was
rather for somebody to love, and perhaps take care of a
little. People love according to their natures, and Elizabeth's was a strong nature; its principal element being a
capacity for passionate devotedness, almost unlimited in
extent. Such women, who love most, are not always, indeed very rarely, loved best. And so it was perhaps as
well that poor Elizabeth should make up her mind, as she
did very composedly, that she herself should never be married; but after that glorious wedding of Miss Hilary's to
Mr. Lyon, should settle down to take care of Miss Leaf all
her days.

"And if I turn out only half as good and contented as
my mistress, it can't be such a dreadful thing to be an old
maid, after all," stoically said Elizabeth Hand.

The words were scarcely out of her mouth when her attention was caught by some one in the passage inquiring
for her—yes, actually for her. She could hardly believe
her eyes when she perceived it was her new-found old acquaintance, Tom Cliffe. He was dressed very well, out of
livery; indeed, he looked so extremely like a gentleman
that Mrs. Jones's little girl took him for one, called him
"Sir," and showed him into the parlor.

"All right. I thought this was the house. Uncommon sharp of me to hunt you out, wasn't it, Elizabeth?"

But Elizabeth was a little stiff, flurried, and perplexed. Her mistresses were out; she did not know whether she ought to ask Tom in, especially as it must be into the parlor: there was no other place to take him to.

However, Tom settled the matter with a conclusive "Oh, gammon!"—sat himself down, and made himself quite comfortable. And Elizabeth was so glad to see him—glad to have another chance of talking about dear old Stowbury. It could not be wrong; she would not say a word about the family, not even tell him she lived with the Misses Leaf if she could help it. And Tom did not seem in the least curious.

"Now, I call this quite a coincidence. I was stopping at St. Pancras Church to look at a wedding—some old city fogy who lives in Russell Square, and is making a great splash; and there I see you, Elizabeth, standing in the crowd, and looking so nice and spicy—as fresh as an apple and as brisk as a bee. I hummed, and hawed, and whistled, but I couldn't catch your eye; then I missed you, and was vexed above a bit, till I saw some one like you going in at this door, so I just knocked and asked; and here you are! 'Pon my life, I am very glad to see you."

"Thank you, Tom," said Elizabeth, pleased, even grateful for the trouble he had taken about her: she had so few friends—in truth, actually none.

They began to talk, and Tom Cliffe talked exceedingly well. He had added to his natural cleverness a degree of London sharpness, the result of much "knocking about" ever since childhood. Besides, his master, the literary gentleman, who had picked him out of the printing-office, had taken a deal of pains with him. Tom was, for his station, a very intelligent and superior young man. Not a boy, though he was still under twenty, but a young man: that precocity of development which often accompanies a delicate constitution, making him appear, as he was indeed, in mind and character, fully six or seven years older than his real age.

He was a handsome fellow, too, though small; dark-haired, dark-eyed, with regular and yet sensitive and mo-bile features. Altogether Tom Cliffe was decidedly•inter-esting, and Elizabeth took great pleasure in looking at him, and in thinking, with a certain half motherly, half romantic satisfaction, that but for her, and her carrying him home from under the horse's heels, he might, humanly speaking, have been long ago buried in Stowbury church-yard.

"I have a 'church-yard cough' at times still," said he, when speaking of this little episode of early life. "I don't think I shall ever live to be a middle-aged man." And he shook his head, and looked melancholy and poetical; nay, even showed Elizabeth some poetry that he himself had written on the subject, which was clever enough in its way.

Elizabeth's interest grew. An ordinary baker or butcher boy would not have attracted her in the least; but here was something in the shape of a hero, somebody who at once touched her sympathies and roused her admiration; for Tom was quite as well informed as she was herself—more so, indeed. He was one of the many shrewd and clever working-men who were then beginning to rise up and think for themselves, and educate themselves. He at-tended classes at mechanics' institutions, and young men's debating societies, where every topic of the day, religion, politics, political economy, was handled freely, as the young do handle these serious things. He threw himself, heart and soul, into the new movement, which, like all revolu-tions, had at first its great and fatal dangers, but yet re-sulted in much good; clearing the political sky, and bring-ing all sorts of hidden abuses under the sharp eyes of that great scourge of evil-doers—public opinion.

Yet Elizabeth, reared under the wing of the conservative Misses Leaf, was a little startled when Tom Cliffe, who ap-parently liked talking and being listened to, gave her a long dissertation on the true principles of the Charter, and how Frost, Williams, and Jones—names all but forgotten now—were very ill-used men, actual martyrs. She was more than startled—shocked indeed—until there came a reaction of the deepest pity—when he confessed that he never went to church. He saw no use in going, he said; the parsons were all shams, paid largely to chatter about what they did not understand; the only real religion was that which a man thought out for himself, and acted out for himself; which was true enough, though only a half truth; and innocent Elizabeth did not see the other half.

But she was touched and carried away by the earnestness and enthusiasm of the lad, wild, fierce iconoclast as he was, ready to cast down the whole fabric of Church and State, though without any personal hankering after lawless rights and low pleasures. His sole idol was, as he said, intellect, and that was his preservation.

Also, the fragile health which was betrayed in every flash of his eye, every flush of his sallow cheek, made Tom Cliffe, even in the two hours he staid with her, come very close to Elizabeth's heart. It was such a warm heart, such a liberal heart, thinking so little of itself or of its own value.

So here began to be told the old story, familiar in kitchens as parlors; but, from the higher bringing-up of the two parties concerned, conducted in this case more after the fashion of the latter than the former.

Elizabeth Hand was an exceptional person, and Tom had the sense to see that at once. He paid her no coarse attentions, did not attempt to make love to her; but he liked her, and he let her see that he did. True, she was not pretty, and she was older than he; but that, to a boy of nineteen, is rather flattering than otherwise. Also, for there is a law even under the blind mystery of likings and fallings in love—a certain weakness in him, that weakness which generally accompanies the poetical nature, clung to the quiet, solid, practical strength of hers. He liked to talk and be listened to by those silent, admiring, gentle gray eyes; and he thought it very pleasant when, with a motherly prudence, she warned him to be careful over his cough, and gave him a flannel breastplate to protect his chest against the cold.

When he went away Tom was so far in love that, following the free and easy ways of his class, he attempted to give Elizabeth a kiss; but she drew back so hotly that he begged her pardon, and slipped away rather confounded.

"That's an odd sort of young woman; there's something in her," said he to himself. "I'll get a kiss, though, by-and-by."

Meanwhile Elizabeth, having forgotten all about her dinner, sat thinking, actually doing nothing but thinking, until within half an hour of the time when her mistresses might be expected back. They were to go direct to the hotel, breakfast, wait till the newly-married couple had departed, and then come home. They would be sure to be weary, and want their tea.

So Elizabeth made every thing ready for them, steadily putting Tom Cliffe out of her mind. One thing she was glad of, that, talking so much about his own affairs, he had forgotten to inquire concerning hers, and was still quite ignorant even of her mistresses' name. He therefore could tell no tales of the Leaf family at Stowbury. Still she determined at once to inform Miss Hilary that he had been here, but that, if she wished it, he should never come again. And it spoke well for her resolve that, while resolving, she was startled to find how very sorry she should feel if Tom Cliffe never came again.

I know I am painting this young woman with a strangely tender conscience, a refinement of feeling, and a general moral sensitiveness which people say is seldom or never to be found in her rank of life. And why not? Because mistresses treat servants as servants, and not as women; because in the sharp, hard line they draw, at the outset, between themselves and their domestics, they give no chance for any womanliness to be developed; and therefore, since human nature is weak, and without help from without, a long degraded class can never rise; sweethearts will still come crawling through back entries and down at area doors; mistresses will still have to dismiss helpless and fallen, or brazen in iniquity, many a wretched girl who once was innocent; or, if nothing actually vicious results, may have many a good, respectable servant, who left to get married, return, complaining that her "young man," whom she knew so little about, has turned out a drunken scoundrel of a husband, who drives her back to her old comfortable "place" to beg for herself and her starving babies a morsel of bread.

When, with a vivid blush that she could not repress, Elizabeth told her mistress that Tom Cliffe had been to see her, the latter replied at first carelessly, for her mind was preoccupied. Then, her attention caught by the aforesaid blush, Miss Hilary asked,

"How old is the lad?"

"Nineteen."

"That's a bad age, Elizabeth. Too old to be a pet, and rather too young for a husband."

"I never thought of such a thing," said Elizabeth, warmly—and honestly, at the time.

"Did he want to come and see you again?"

"He said so."

"Oh, well, if he is a steady, respectable lad, there can be no objection. I should like to see him myself next time."

And then a sudden sharp reflection that there would likely be no next time, in their service at least, made Miss Hilary feel quite a hypocrite.

"Elizabeth," said she, "we will speak about Tom Cliffe —is not that his name?—by-and-by. Now, as soon as tea is over, my sister wants to talk to you. When you are ready, will you come up stairs?"

She spoke in an especially gentle tone, so that by no possibility could Elizabeth fancy they were displeased with her.

Now, knowing the circumstances of the family, Elizabeth's conscience had often smitten her that she must eat a great deal; that her wages, paid regularly month by month, must make a great hole in her mistress's income. She was, alack! a sad expense, and she tried to lighten her cost in every possible way. But it never struck her that they could do without her, or that any need would arise for their doing so.   So she went into the parlor quite un-suspiciously, and found Miss Leaf lying on the sofa, and Miss Hilary reading aloud the letter from India.   But it was laid quietly aside as she said,

"Johanna, Elizabeth is here."

Then Johanna, rousing herself to say what must be said, but putting it as gently and kindly as she could, told Eliz-abeth, what mistresses often think it below their dignity to tell to servants, the plain truth—namely, that circum-stances obliged herself and Miss Hilary to retrench their expenses as much as they possibly could.   That they were going to live in two little rooms at Richmond, where they would board with the inmates of the house.

"And so, and so—" Miss Leaf faltered.   It was very hard to say it with those eager eyes fixed upon her.

Hilary took up the word—

"And so, Elizabeth, much as it grieves us, we shall be obliged to part with you.   We can not any longer afford to keep a servant."

No answer.

"It is not even as it was once before, when we thought you might do better for yourself.   We know, if it were possible, you would rather stay with us, and we would rather keep you.   It is like parting with one of our own family."   And Miss Hilary's voice too failed.   "However, there is no help for it; we must part."

Elizabeth, recovered from her first bewildered grief, was on the point of bursting out into entreaties that she might do like many another faithful servant, live without wages, put up with any hardships, rather than be sent away.   But something in Miss Hilary's manner told her it would be useless—worse than useless, painful; and she would do any thing rather than give her mistress pain.   When, ut-terly unable to control it, she gave vent to one loud sob, the expression of acute suffering on Miss Hilary's counte-nance was such that she determined to sob no more.   She felt that, for some reason or other, the thing was inevita-ble; that she must take up her burden, as her mistress had done, even though it were the last grief of all—leaving that beloved mistress.

"That's right, Elizabeth," said Miss Hilary, softly. "All these changes are very bitter to us also, but we must bear them. There is nothing lasting in this world except doing right, and being good, and faithful, and helpful to one another."

She sighed. Possibly there had been sad tidings in the letter which she still held in her hand, clinging to it as we do to something which, however sorely it hurts us, we would not part with for the whole world. But there was no hopelessness or despair in her tone, and Elizabeth caught the influence of that true courageous heart.

"Perhaps you may be able to take me back again soon, ma'am," said she, looking toward Miss Leaf. "And meantime I might get a place; Mrs. Jones has told me of several;" and she stopped, afraid lest it might be found out how often Mrs. Jones had urged her to "better herself," and she had indignantly refused. "Or" (a bright idea occurred) "I wonder if Miss Selina, that is, Mrs. Ascott, would take me in at Russell Square?"

Hilary looked hard at her.

"Would you really like that?"

"Yes, I should; for I should see and hear of you. Miss Hilary, if you please, I wish you would ask Mrs. Ascott to take me."

And Hilary, much surprised—for she was well acquainted with Elizabeth's sentiments toward both Mr. Ascott and the late Miss Selina—promised.

CHAPTER XXII.

And now I leave Miss Hilary for a time—leave her in, if not happiness, great peace—peace which, after these stormy months, was an actual paradise of calm to both herself and Johanna.

Their grief for Ascott had softened down. Its very hope-

lessness gave it resignation. There was nothing more to
be done; they had done all they could, both to find him
out and to save him from the public disgrace which might
blight any hope of reformation. Now the result must be
left in higher hands.

Only at times fits of restless trouble would come; times
when a sudden knock at the door would make Johanna
shake nervously for minutes afterward; when Hilary walked about every where with her mind preoccupied, and her
eyes open to notice every chance passer-by; nay, she had
sometimes secretly followed down a whole street some figure which, in its light, jaunty step, and long, fashionably-
cut hair, reminded her of Ascott.

Otherwise they were not unhappy, she and her dearest
sister. Poor as they were, they were together, and their
poverty had no sting. They knew exactly how much they
would receive monthly, and how much they ought to spend.
Though obliged to calculate every penny, still their income
and their expenses were alike certain; there was no anxiety about money matters, which of itself was an indescriba-
ble relief. Also, there was that best blessing—peace at
home. Never in all her days had Johanna known such an
easy life; sitting quietly in her parlor while Hilary was
engaged in the shop below; descending to dinner, where
she took the head of the table, and the young people soon
learned to treat her with great respect and even affection;
then waiting for the happy tea in their own room, and the
walk afterward in Richmond Park or along the Thames
banks toward Twickenham. Perhaps it was partly from
the contrast to that weary year in London; but never, in
any spring, had the air seemed so balmy, or the trees so
green. They brought back to Hilary's face the youthful
bloom which she had begun to lose, and, in degree, her
youthful brightness, which had also become slightly over-
clouded. Again she laughed and made her little domestic
jokes, and regained her pretty way of putting things, so
that every thing always appeared to have a cheerful, and
even a comical side.

Also—for while we are made as we are, with capacity for happiness, and especially the happiness of love, it is sure to be thus—she had a little private sunbeam in her own heart which brightened outside things. After that sad letter from India which came on Selina's wedding-day, every succeeding one grew more cheerful, more demonstrative, nay, even affectionate; though still with that queer Scotch pride of his, that would ask for nothing till it could ask and have every thing, and give every thing in return —the letters were all addressed to Johanna.

"What an advantage it is to be an old woman!" Miss Leaf would sometimes say, mischievously, when she received them. But more often she said nothing, waiting in peace for events to develop themselves. She did not think much about herself, and had no mean jealousy over her child; she knew that a righteous and holy love only makes all natural affections more sacred and more dear.

And Hilary? She held her head higher and prouder; and the spring trees looked greener, and the river ran brighter in the sunshine. Ah, Heaven pity us all! it is a good thing to have love in one's life; it is a good thing, if only for a time, to be actually *happy* — not merely contented, but *happy!*

And so I will leave her, this little woman; and nobody need mourn over her because she is working too hard, or pity her because she is obliged to work; has to wear common clothes, and live in narrow rooms, and pass on her poor weary feet the grand carriages of the Richmond gentry, who are not a bit more well-born or well-educated than she; who never take the least notice of her, except sometimes to peer curiously at the desk where she sits in the shop-corner, and wonder who "that young person with the rather pretty curls" can be. No matter, she is happy.

How much happiness was there in the large house at Russell Square?

The Misses Leaf could not tell; their sister never gave them an opportunity of judging.

"My son's my son till he gets him a wife,
But my daughter's my daughter all her life."

And so, most frequently, is "my sister." But not in this case. It could not be; they never expected it would.

When, on her rare visits to town, Hilary called at Russell Square, she always found Mrs. Ascott handsomely dressed, dignified, and gracious. Not in the slightest degree uncivil or unsisterly, but gracious — perhaps a thought too gracious. Most condescendingly anxious that she should stay to luncheon, and eat and drink the best the house afforded, but never by any chance inviting her to stay to dinner. Consequently, as Mr. Ascott was always absent in the city until dinner, Hilary did not see him for months together, and her brother-in-law was, she declared, no more to her than any other man upon 'Change, or the man in the moon, or the Great Mogul.

His wife spoke little about him. After a few faint, formal questions concerning Richmond affairs, somehow her conversation always recurred to her own—the dinners she had been at, those she was going to give, her carriages, clothes, jewelry, and so on. She was altogether a very great lady, and Hilary, as she avouched laughingly — it was, in this case, better to laugh than to grieve—felt an exceedingly small person beside her.

Nevertheless, Mrs. Ascott showed no unkindness—nay, among the various changes that matrimony had produced in her, her temper appeared rather to have improved than otherwise; there was now seldom any trace of that touchy sharpness which used to be called "poor Selina's way." And yet Hilary never quitted the house without saying to herself, with a sigh, the old phrase, "Poor Selina!"

Thus, in the inevitable consequences of things, her visits to Russell Square became fewer and fewer; she kept them up as a duty, not exacting any return, for she felt that was impossible, though still keeping up the ghostly shadow of sisterly intimacy. Nevertheless, she knew well it was but a shadow; that the only face that looked honest, glad welcome, or that she was honestly glad to see in her

brother-in-law's house, was the under house-maid, Elizabeth Hand.

Contrary to all expectations, Mrs. Ascott had consented
to take Elizabeth into her service. With many stipula-
tions and warnings never to presume on past relations,
never even to mention Stowbury on pain of instant dismissal, still she did take her, and Elizabeth staid. At every
one of Miss Hilary's visits, lying in wait in the bedchamber,
or on the staircase, or creeping up at the last minute to
open the hall door, was sure to appear the familiar face,
beaming all over. Little conversation passed between
them — Mrs. Ascott evidently disliked it; still Elizabeth
looked well and happy, and when Miss Hilary told her so
she always silently smiled.

But this story must tell the whole truth which lay beneath that fond, acquiescing smile.

Elizabeth was certainly in good health, being well fed,
well housed, and leading, on the whole, an easy life; happy,
too, when she looked at Miss Hilary. But her migration
from Mrs. Jones's lodgings to this grand mansion had not
been altogether the translation from Purgatory to Paradise
that some would have supposed.

The author of this simple story having—unfortunately
for it—never been in domestic service, especially in the
great houses of London, does not pretend to describe the
ins and outs of their "high life below stairs;" to repeat
kitchen conversations, to paint the humors of the servants'
hall—the butler and housekeeper getting tipsy together,
the cook courting the policeman, and the footman making
love successively to every house-maid and lady's-maid.
Some writers have depicted all this, whether faithfully or
not they know best; but the present writer declines to attempt any thing of the kind. Her business is solely with
one domestic, the country girl who came unexpectedly into
this new world of London servant-life—a world essentially
its own, and a life of which the upper classes are as ignorant as they are of what goes on in Madagascar and Ota-
heite.

This fact was the first which struck the unsophisticated Elizabeth. She, who had been brought up in a sort of feudal relationship to her dear mistresses, was astonished to find the domestics of Russell Square banded together into a community which, in spite of their personal bickerings and jealousies, ended in alliance offensive and defensive against the superior powers, whom they looked upon as their natural enemies. Invisible enemies certainly; for "master" they hardly ever saw, and, excepting the lady's-maid, were mostly as ignorant of "missis." The housekeeper was the middle link between the two estates—the person with whom all business was transacted, and to whom all complaints had to be made. Beyond being sometimes talked over, generally in a quizzical, depreciatory, or condemnatory way, the heads of the establishment were no more to their domestics than the people who paid wages, and exacted in return certain duties, which most of them made as small as possible, and escaped whenever they could.

If this be an exaggerated picture of a state of things perhaps in degree inevitable—and yet it should not be, for it is the source of incalculable evil, this dividing of a house against itself—if I have in any way said what is not true, I would that some intelligent "voice from the kitchen" would rise up and tell us what is true, and whether it be possible on either side to find means of amending what so sorely needs reformation.

Elizabeth sometimes wanted Tom Cliffe to do this—to " write a book," which he, eager young malcontent, was always threatening to do, upon the evils of society, and especially the tyranny of the upper classes. Tom Cliffe was the only person to whom she imparted her troubles and perplexities : how different her life was from that she had been used to; how among her fellow-servants there was not one who did not seem to think and act in a manner totally opposed to every thing she had learned from Miss Hilary; how, consequently, she herself was teased, bullied, threatened, or, at best, "sent to Coventry" from morning till night.

"I'm quite alone, Tom—I am, indeed," said she, almost crying, the first Sunday night when she met him accidentally in going to church, and, in her dreary state of mind, was exceedingly glad to see him. He consoled her, and even went to church with her, half promising to do the same next Sunday, and calling her "a good little Christian, who almost inclined him to be a Christian too."

And so, with the vague feeling that she was doing him good and keeping him out of harm—that lad who had so much that was kindly and nice about him—Elizabeth consented, not exactly to an appointment, but she told him what were her "Sundays out," and the church she usually attended, if he liked to take the chance of her being there.

Alack! she had so few pleasures; she so seldom got even a breath of outside air—it was not thought necessary for servants. The only hour she was allowed out was the church-going on alternate Sunday evenings. How pleasant it was to creep out then, and see Tom waiting for her under the opposite trees, dressed so smart and gentlemanlike, looking so handsome and so glad to see her—her, the poor countrified Elizabeth, who was quizzed incessantly by her fellow-servants on her oddness, plainness, and stupidity.

Tom did not seem to think her stupid, for he talked to her of all his doings and plannings, vague and wild as those of the young tailor in "Alton Locke," yet with a romantic energy about them that strongly interested his companion; and he read her his poetry, and addressed a few lines to herself, beginning,

> "Dearest and best, my long familiar friend;"

which was rather a poetical exaggeration, since he had altogether forgotten her in the interval of their separation. But she never guessed this, and so they both clung to the early tie, making it out to be ten times stronger than it really was, as people do who are glad of any excuse for being fond of one another.

.Tom really was getting fond of Elizabeth. She touched the higher half of his nature—the spiritual and imagina-

tive half. That he had it, though only a working-man, and
she too, though only a domestic servant, was most true:
probably many more of their class have it than we are at
all aware of. Therefore these two, being special individuals, were attracted by each other; she by him because he
was so clever, and he by her because she was so good. For
he had an ideal, poor Tom Cliffe! and, though it had been
smothered and laid to sleep by a not too regular life, it
woke up again under the kind, sincere eyes of this plain,
simple-minded, honest Elizabeth Hand.

He knew she was plain, and so old-fashioned in her
dress, that Tom, who was particular about such things, did
not always like walking with her; but she was so interesting and true; she sympathized with him so warmly—he
found her so unfailingly and unvaryingly good to him
through all the little humors and pettishnesses that almost always accompany a large brain, a nervous temperament, and delicate health. Her quietness soothed him, her
strength of character supported him; he at once leaned
on her and ruled over her.

As to Elizabeth's feelings toward Tom, they will hardly
bear analyzing; probably hardly any strong emotion will,
especially one that is not sudden, but progressive. She
admired him extremely, and yet she was half sorry for
him. Some things in him she did not at all like, and tried
heartily to amend. His nervous fancies, irritations, and
vagaries she was exceedingly tender over; she looked up
to him, and yet took care of him; this thought of him,
and anxiety over him, became by degrees the habit of her
life. People love in so many different ways; and perhaps that was the natural way in which a woman like Elizabeth would love, or creep into love without knowing it,
which is either the safest or the saddest form which the
passion can assume.

Thus things went on, till one dark, rainy Sunday night,
walking round and round the inner circle of the square,
Tom expressed his feelings, at first in somewhat high-
flown and poetical phrases, then melting into the one eter-

ually old and eternally new "Do you love me?" followed
by a long, long kiss, given under shelter of the umbrella,
and in mortal fear of the approaching policeman, who,
however, never saw them, or saw them only as "a pair of
sweethearts"—too common an occurrence on his beat to
excite any attention.

But to Elizabeth the whole thing was new, wonderful;
a bliss so far beyond any thing that had ever befallen her
simple life, and so utterly unexpected therein, that when
she went to her bed that night she cried like a child over
the happiness of Tom loving her, and her exceeding un-
worthiness of the same.

Then difficulties arose in her mind. "No followers allowed" was one of the strict laws of the Russell Square
dynasty. Like many another law of that and of much
higher dynasties, it was only made to be broken; for stray
sweethearts were continually climbing down area railings,
or over garden walls, or hiding themselves behind kitchen
doors. Nay, to such an extent was the system carried out,
each servant being, from self-interest, a safe co-conspirator,
that very often, when Mr. and Mrs. Ascott went out to dinner, and the old housekeeper retired to bed, there were regular symposia held below stairs—nice little supper-parties,
where all the viands in the pantry and the wines in the
cellar were freely used; where every domestic had his or
her "young man" or "young woman," and the goings-on,
though not actually discreditable, were of the most lively
kind.

To be cognizant of these, and yet to feel that, as there
was no actual wickedness going on, she was not justified
in "blabbing," was a severe and perpetual trial to Elizabeth. To join them, or bring Tom among them as her
"young man," was impossible.

"No, Tom," she said, when he begged hard to come in
one evening—for it was raining fast, and he had a bad
cough—"No, Tom, I can't let you. If other folk break
the laws of the house, I won't; you must go. I can only
meet you out of doors."

And yet to do this surreptitiously, just as if she were ashamed of him, or as if there were something wrong in their being fond of one another, jarred upon Elizabeth's honest nature. She did not want to make a show of him, especially to her fellow-servants: she had the true woman's instinct of liking to keep her treasures all to herself, but she had also her sex's natural yearning for sympathy in the great event of a woman's life. She would have liked to have somebody unto whom she could say, "Tom has asked me to marry him," and who would have answered cordially, " It's all right; he is a good fellow: you are sure to be happy."

Not that she doubted this; but it would have been an additional comfort to have a mother's blessing, or a sister's, or even a friend's, upon this strange and sweet emotion which had come into her life. So long as it was thus kept secret there seemed a certain incompleteness and unsanctity about even their happy love.

Tom did not comprehend this at all. He only laughed at her for feeling so " nesh" (that means tender, sensitive; but the word is almost unexplainable to other than Stowbury ears) on the subject. He liked the romance and excitement of secret courtship—men often do; rarely women, unless there is something in them not quite right, not entirely womanly.

But Tom was very considerate, and though he called it " silly," and took a little fit of crossness on the occasion, he allowed Elizabeth to write to her mother about him, and consented that on her next holiday she should go to Richmond, in order to speak to Miss Hilary on the same subject, and ask her also to write to Mrs. Hand, stating how good and clever Tom was, and how exceedingly happy was Tom's Elizabeth.

" And won't you come and fetch me, Tom ?" asked she, shyly. " I am sure Miss Hilary would not object, nor Miss Leaf neither."

Tom protested he did not care two straws whether they objected or not; he was a man of twenty, in a good trade

—he had lately gone back to the printing, and being a clever workman, earned capital wages. He had a right to choose whom he liked, and marry when he pleased. If Elizabeth didn't care for him, she might leave him alone.

"Oh, Tom!" was all she answered, with a strange gentleness that no one could have believed would ever have come into the manner of South Sea Islander. And quitting the subject then, she afterward persuaded him, and not for the first time, into consenting to what she thought right. There is something rather touching in a servant's holiday. It comes so seldom. She must count on it for so long beforehand, and remember it for so long afterward. This present writer owns to a strong sympathy with the holiday-makers on the grand gala-days of the English calendar. It is a pleasure to watch the innumerable groups of family folk, little children, and 'prentice lads,

> "Dressed in all their best,
> To walk abroad with Sally."

And the various "Sallys" and their corresponding swains can hardly feel more regret than she when it happens to be wet weather on Easter week or at Whitsuntide.

Whit-Monday, the day when Tom escaped from the printing-office, and Elizabeth got leave of absence for six hours, was as glorious a June day as well could be. As the two young people perched themselves on the top of the Richmond omnibus, and drove through Kensington, Hammersmith, Turnham Green, and over Kew Bridge—Tom pointing out all the places, and giving much curious information about them—Elizabeth thought there never was a more beautiful country or a more lovely summer day: she was, she truly said, "as happy as a queen."

Nevertheless, when the omnibus stopped, she, with great self-denial, insisted on getting rid of Tom for a time. She thought Miss Hilary might not quite like Tom's knowing where she lived, or what her occupation was, lest he might gossip about it to Stowbury people; so she determined to pay her visit by herself, and appointed to meet him at a certain hour on Richmond Bridge, over which bridge she

watched him march sulkily, not without a natural pleasure
that he should be so much vexed at losing her company for
an hour or two. But she knew he would soon come to himself—as he did, before he had been half a mile on the road
to Hampton Court, meeting a young fellow he knew, and
going with him over that grand old palace, which furnished
them with a subject at their next debating society, where
they both came out very strong on the question of hypo-
critical priests and obnoxious kings, with especial reference
to Henry VIII. and Cardinal Wolsey.

Meanwhile Elizabeth went in search of the little shop—
which nobody need expect to find at Richmond now—bearing the well-known name "Janet Balquidder." Entering
it, for there was no private door, she saw, in the far corner
above the curtained desk, the pretty curls of her dear Miss
Hilary.

Elizabeth had long known that her mistress "kept a
shop," and with the notions of gentility which are just as
rife in her class as in any other, had mourned bitterly over
this fact. But when she saw how fresh and well the young
lady looked, how busily and cheerfully she seemed to work
with her great books before her, and with what a composed
grace and dignity she came forward when asked for, Elizabeth secretly confessed that not even keeping a shop had
made or could make the smallest difference in Miss Hilary.

She herself was much more changed.

"Why, Elizabeth, I should hardly have known you!"
was the involuntary exclamation of her late mistress.

She certainly did look very nice; not smart—for her so-
ber taste preferred quiet colors—but excessively neat and
well dressed. In her new gown of gray "coburg," her one
handsome shawl, which had been honored several times by
Miss Hilary's wearing, her white straw bonnet and white
ribbons, underneath which the smooth black hair and soft
eyes showed to great advantage, she appeared, not "like
a lady"—a servant can seldom do that, let her dress be
ever so fine—but like a thoroughly respectable, intelligent,
and pleasant-faced young woman.

And her blushes came and went so fast, she was so nervous and yet so beamingly happy, that Miss Hilary soon suspected there was more in this visit than at first appeared.
Knowing that with Elizabeth's great shyness the mystery
would never come out in public, she took an opportunity
of asking her to help her in the-bedroom, and there, with
the folding-doors safely shut, discovered the whole secret.

Miss Hilary was a good deal surprised at first. She had
never thought of Elizabeth as likely to get married at all
—and to Tom Cliffe.

"Why, isn't he a mere boy; ever so much younger than
you are?"

"Three years."

"That is a pity—a great pity; women grow old so much
faster than men."

"I know that," said Elizabeth, somewhat sorrowfully.

"Besides, did you not tell me he was very handsome and
clever?"

"Yes; and I'm neither the one nor the other. I have
thought all that over too, many a time; indeed I have, Miss
Hilary. But Tom likes me—or fancies he does. Do you
think"—and the intense humility which true love always
has, struck into Miss Hilary's own conscious. heart a conviction of how very true this poor girl's love must be. "Do
you think he is mistaken? that his liking me—I mean in
that sort of way—is quite impossible?"

"No, indeed, and I never said it—never thought it," was
the earnest reply. "But consider; three years younger
than yourself; handsomer and cleverer than you are—"

Miss Hilary stopped; it seemed so cruel to say such
things, and yet she felt bound to say them. She knew
her former "bower-maiden" well enough to be convinced
that if Elizabeth were not happy in marriage she would
be worse than unhappy—might grow actually bad.

"He loves you now; you are sure of that; but are you
sure that he is a thoroughly stable and reliable character?
Do you believe he will love you always?"

"I can't tell. Perhaps—if I deserved it," said poor Elizabeth.

And, looking at the downcast eyes, at the thorough womanly sweetness and tenderness which suffused the whole face, Hilary's doubts began to melt away. She thought how sometimes men, captivated by inward rather than outward graces, have fallen in love with plain women, or women older than themselves, and actually kept to their attachment through life with a fidelity rare as beautiful. Perhaps this young fellow, who seemed, by all accounts, superior to his class, having had the sense to choose that pearl in an oyster-shell, Elizabeth Hand, might also have the sense to appreciate her, and go on loving her to the end of his days. Anyhow, he loved her now, and she loved him, and it was useless reasoning any more about it.

"Come, Elizabeth," cried her mistress, cheerfully, "I have said all my say, and now I have only to give my good wishes. If Tom Cliffe deserves you, I am sure you deserve him, and I should like to tell him so."

"Should you, Miss Hilary?" and with a visible brightening up Elizabeth betrayed Tom's whereabouts, and her little conspiracy to bring him here, and her hesitation lest it might be "intruding."

"Not at all. Tell him to come at once. I am not like my sister; we always allow 'followers.' I think a mistress stands in the relation of a parent for the time being, and that can not be a right or good love which is concealed from her, as if it were a thing to be ashamed of."

"I think so too. And I'm not a bit ashamed of Tom, nor he of me," said Elizabeth, so energetically that Miss Hilary smiled.

"Very well; take him to have his tea in the kitchen, and then bring him up stairs to speak to my sister and me."

At that interview, which of course was rather trying, Tom acquitted himself to every body's satisfaction. He was manly, modest, self-possessed; did not say much—his usual talkativeness being restrained by the circumstances of the case, and the great impression made upon him by Miss Hilary, who, he afterward admitted to Elizabeth, "was a real angel, and he should write a poem upon her."

But the little he did say gave the ladies a very good impression of the intelligence and even refinement of Elizabeth's sweetheart. And though they were sorry to see him look so delicate, still there was a something better than handsomeness in his handsome face, which made them not altogether surprised at Elizabeth's being so fond of him.

As she watched the young couple down Richmond Street in the soft summer twilight—Elizabeth taking Tom's arm, and Tom drawing up his stooping figure to its utmost extent, both a little ill matched in height as they were in some other things, but walking with that air of perfect confidence and perfect contentedness in each other which always betrays, to a quick eye, those who have agreed to walk through the world together—Miss Hilary turned from the window and sighed.

CHAPTER XXIII.

FOLLOWING Miss Hilary's earnest advice that every thing should be fair and open, Elizabeth, on the very next day after that happy Whit-Monday, mustered up her courage, asked permission to speak to her mistress, and told her she was going to be married to Tom Cliffe; not immediately, but in a year's time or so, if all went well.

Mrs. Ascott replied sharply that it was no affair of hers, and she could not be troubled about it. For her part, she thought, if servants knew their own advantages, they would keep a good place when they had it, and never get married at all. And then, saying she had heard a good character of her from the housekeeper, she offered Elizabeth the place of upper house-maid, a young girl, a *protégée* of the house-keeper's, being substituted in hers.

"And when you have sixteen pounds a year, and somebody to do all your hard work for you, I dare say you'll think better of it, and not be so foolish as to go and get married."

But Elizabeth had her own private opinion on that matter. She was but a woman, poor thing! and two tiny
rooms of her own, with Tom to care for and look after,
seemed a far happier home than that great house, where she
had not only her own work to do, but the responsibility
of teaching and taking charge of that careless, stupid, pretty Esther, who had all the forwardness, untidiness, and un-
conscientiousness of a regular London maid-servant, and
was a sore trial to the staid, steady Elizabeth.

Tom consoled her, in his careless but affectionate way;
and another silent consolation was the "little bits of things,"
bought out of her additional wages, which she began to
put by in her box—sticks and straws for the new sweet
nest that was a-building: a metal tea-pot, two neat glass
salt-cellars, and—awful extravagance!—two real second-
hand silver spoons—Tom did so like having things nice
about him! These purchases, picked up at stray times,
were solid, substantial, and useful; domestic rather than
personal; and all with a view to Tom rather than herself.
She hid them with a magpie-like closeness, for Esther and
she shared the same room; but sometimes when Esther
was asleep she would peep at them with an anxious, lingering tenderness, as if they made more of an assured reality what even now seemed so very like a dream.

—Except, indeed, on those Sunday nights when Tom and
she went to church together, and afterward took a walk,
but always parted at the corner of the square. She never
brought him in to the house, nor spoke of him to her fellow-servants. How much they guessed of her engagement
she neither knew nor cared.

Mrs. Ascott, too, had apparently quite forgotten it. She
seemed to take as little interest in her servants' affairs as
they in hers.

Nevertheless, ignorant as the lower regions were in general of what was passing in the upper, occasionally rumors
began to reach the kitchen that "master had been a-blow-
ing up missis, rather!" And once, after the solemn dinner,
with three footmen to wait on two people, was over, Eliza-

beth, passing through the hall, caught the said domestics laughing together, and saying it was "as good as a play; cat and dog was nothing to it." After which "the rows up stairs" became a favorite joke in the servants' hall.

But still Mr. Ascott went out daily after breakfast, and came home to dinner; and Mrs. Ascott spent the morning in her private sitting-room or "boudoir," as she called it; lunched, and drove out in her handsome carriage, with her footman behind; dressed elegantly for dinner, and presided at her own table with an air of magnificent satisfaction in all things. She had perfectly accommodated herself to her new position; and if under her satins and laces beat a solitary, dissatisfied, or aching heart, it was nobody's business but her own. At least, she kept up the splendid sham with a most creditable persistency.

But all shams are dangerous things. Be the surface ever so smooth and green, it will crack sometimes, and a faint wreath of smoke betray the inward volcano. The like had happened once or twice, as on the day when the men-servants were so intensely amused. Also Elizabeth, when putting in order her mistress's bedroom, which was about the hour Mr. Ascott left for the city, had several times seen Mrs. Ascott come in there suddenly, white and trembling. Once, so agitated was she, that Elizabeth had brought her a glass of water; and instead of being angry or treating her with the distant dignity which she had always kept up, her mistress had said, almost in the old Stowbury tone, "Thank you, Elizabeth."

However, Elizabeth had the wisdom to take no notice, but to slip from the room, and keep her own counsel.

At last, one day, the smouldering domestic earthquake broke out. There was "a precious good row," the footman suspected, at the breakfast-table; and after breakfast, master, without waiting for the usual attendance of that functionary with his hat, and gloves, and a Hansom cab, had flung himself out at the hall door, slamming it after him with a noise that startled the whole house. Shortly afterward "missis's" bell had rung violently, and she had been found lying on the floor of her bedroom in a dead faint, her maid, a foolish little Frenchwoman, screaming over her.

The frightened servants gathered round in a cluster, but nobody attempted to touch the poor lady, who lay rigid and helpless, hearing none of the comments that were freely made upon her, or the conjectures as to what master had done or said that produced this state of things. Mistress she was, and these four or five women, her servants, had lived in her house for months, but nobody loved her; nobody knew any thing about her; nobody thought of doing aught for her, till a kitchen-maid, probably out of former experience in some domestic emergency, suggested, "Fetch Elizabeth."

The advice was eagerly caught at, every body being so thankful to have the responsibility shifted to some other body's shoulders; so in five minutes Elizabeth had the room cleared, and her mistress laid upon the bed, with nobody near except herself and the French maid.

By-and-by Mrs. Ascott opened her eyes.

"Who's that? What are you doing to me?"

"Nothing, ma'am. It's only me—Elizabeth."

At the familiar soothing voice the poor woman—a poor, wretched, forlorn woman she looked, lying there, in spite of all her grandeur—turned feebly round.

"Oh, Elizabeth, I'm so ill! take care of me." And she fainted away once more.

It was some time before she came quite to herself, and then the first thing she said was to bid Elizabeth bolt the door and keep every body out.

"The doctor, ma'am, if he comes?"

"I'll not see him. I don't want him. I know what it is. I—"

She pulled Elizabeth closer to her, whispered something in her ear, and then burst into a violent fit of hysterical weeping.

Amazed, shocked, Elizabeth at first did not know what to do; then she took her mistress's head on her shoulder, and quieted her by degrees almost as she would a child. The sobbing ceased, and Mrs. Ascott lay still a minute, till suddenly she clutched Elizabeth's arm.

"Mind you don't tell. *He* doesn't know, and he shall not; it would please him so. It does not please me. Sometimes I almost think I shall hate it because it is his child."

She spoke with a fierceness that was hardly credible either in the dignified Mrs. Peter Ascott or the languid Miss Selina. To think of Miss Selina's expecting a baby! The idea perfectly confounded poor Elizabeth.

"I don't know very much about such matters," said she, deprecatingly; "but I'm sure, ma'am, you ought to keep yourself quiet, and I wouldn't hate the poor little baby if I were you. It may be a very nice little thing, and turn out a great comfort to you."

Mrs. Ascott lifted her heavy eyes to the kindly, sympathetic, womanly face—thorough woman, for, as Elizabeth went on, her heart warmed with the strong instinct which comes almost of itself.

"Think, to have a tiny little creature lying here beside you; something your very own, with its pretty face looking so innocent and sweet at you, and its pretty fingers touching you." Here Elizabeth's voice quite faltered over the picture she had drawn. "Oh, ma'am, I'm sure you would be so fond of it."

Human nature is strong. This cold, selfish woman, living her forty years without any strong emotion, marrying without love, and reaping, not in contrition, but angry bitterness, the certain punishment of such a marriage, even this woman was not proof against the glorious mystery of maternity, which should make every daughter of Eve feel the first sure hope of her first-born child to be a sort of divine annunciation.

Mrs. Ascott lay listening to Elizabeth. Gradually through her shut eyelids a few quiet tears began to flow.

"Do you mind me talking to you this way, ma'am?"

"No, no! Say what you like. I'm glad to have any body to speak to. Oh, I am a very miserable woman!"

Strange that Selina Ascott should come to betray, and to Elizabeth Hand, of all people, that she was a "miserable woman." But circumstances bring about unforeseen confidences; and the confidence once given is not easily recalled. Apparently the lady did not wish to recall it. In the solitude of her splendid house, in her total want of all female companionship—for she refused to have her sisters sent for—"he would only insult them, and I'll not have my family insulted"—poor Selina clung to her old servant as the only comfort she had.

During the dreary months that followed, when, during the long, close summer days, the sick lady scarcely stirred from her bedroom, and, fretful, peevish, made the very most of what to women in general are such patiently borne and sacred sufferings, Elizabeth was her constant attendant. She humored all her whims, endured all her ill tempers, cheered her in her low spirits, and was, in fact, her mistress's sole companion and friend.

This position no one disputed with her. It is not every woman who has, as Miss Leaf used to say of Elizabeth, "a genius for nursing;" and very few patients make nursing a labor of love. The whole household were considerably relieved by her taking a responsibility for which she was so well fitted and so little envied. Even Mr. Ascott, who, when his approaching honors could no longer be concealed from him, became for the nonce a most attentive husband, and succumbed dutifully to every fancy his wife entertained, openly expressed his satisfaction in Elizabeth, and gave her one or two bright golden guineas in earnest of his gratitude.

How far she herself appreciated her new and important position; whether her duties were done from duty, or pity, or that determined self-devotedness which some women are always ready to carry out toward any helpless thing that needs them, I can not say, for she never told. Not even to Miss Hilary, who at last was permitted to come and pay a formal visit; nor to Tom Cliffe, whom she now saw very rarely, for her mistress, with characteristic selfishness, would hardly let her out of her sight for half an hour.

Tom at first was exceedingly savage at this; by degrees he got more reconciled, and met his sweetheart now and then for a few minutes at the area gate, or wrote her long poetical letters, which he confided to some of her fellow-servants, who thereby got acquainted with their secret. But it mattered little, as Elizabeth had faithfully promised that, when her mistress's trial was over, and every thing smooth and happy, she would marry Tom at once. So she took the jokes below stairs with great composure, feeling, indeed, too proud and content to perplex herself much about any thing.

Nevertheless, her life was not easy, for Mrs. Ascott was very difficult to manage. She resisted angrily all the personal sacrifices entailed by impending motherhood, and its terrors and forebodings used to come over her—poor weak woman that she was!—in a way that required all Elizabeth's reasonings to counteract, and all her self-control to hide the presentiment of evil, not unnatural under the circumstances.

Yet sometimes poor Mrs. Ascott would take fits of pathetic happiness, when she busied herself eagerly over the preparations for the new-comer; would make Elizabeth take out, over and over again, the little clothes, and examine them with childish delight. Sometimes she would gossip for hours over the blessing that was sent to her so late in life—half regretting that it had come so late; that she should be almost an old woman before her little son or daughter was grown up.

"Still, I may live to see it, you know: to have a pretty girl to take on my arm into a ballroom, or a big fellow to send to college: the Leafs always went to college in old times. He shall be Henry Leaf Ascott, that I am determined on; and if it's a girl, perhaps I may call her Johanna. My sister would like it—wouldn't she?"

For more and more, in the strange softening of her nature, did Selina go back to the old ties.

"I am not older than my mother was when Hilary was born. She died, but that was because of trouble. Women do not necessarily die in childbirth even at forty; and in twenty years more I shall only be sixty—not such a very old woman. Besides, mothers never are old; at least not to their children. Don't you think so, Elizabeth?"

And Elizabeth answered as she best could. She too, out of sympathy or instinct, was becoming wondrous wise.

But I am aware all this will be thought very uninteresting, except by women and mothers. Let me hasten on.

By degrees, as Mrs. Ascott's hour approached, a curious tranquillity and even gentleness came over her. Her fretful dislike of seeing any face about her but Elizabeth's became less. She even endured her husband's company for an hour of an evening, and at last humbled her pride enough to beg him to invite her sisters to Russell Square from Saturday to Monday, the only time when Hilary could be spared.

"For we don't know what may happen," said she to him, rather seriously.

And though he answered, "Oh, nonsense!" and desired her to get such ridiculous fancies out of her head, still he consented, and himself wrote to Miss Leaf, giving the formal invitation.

The three sisters spent a happy time together, and Hilary made some highly appreciated family jokes about the handsome Christmas box that Selina was going to be so kind as to give them, and the small probability that she would have much enjoyment of the Christmas dinner to which Mr. Ascott, in the superabundance of his good feeling, had invited his sisters-in-law. The baby, blessed innocent! seemed to have softened down all things—as babies often do.

Altogether, it was with great cheerfulness, affectionateness, and hope that they took leave of Selina; she, with unwonted consideration, insisting that the carriage should convey them all the way to Richmond.

"And," she said, "perhaps some of these days my son, if he is a son, may have the pleasure of escorting his aunts home. I shall certainly call him 'Henry Leaf,' and bring him up to be in every way a credit to our family."

When the ladies were away, and Mrs. Ascott had retired to bed, it was still only nine o'clock, and a bright moonlight night. Elizabeth thought she could steal down stairs and try to get a breath of fresh air round the square. Her long confinement made her almost sick sometimes for a sight of the outer world, a sight of—let me tell the entire truth—her own faithful Tom.

She had not seen him now for fourteen days, and though his letters were very nice and exceedingly clever, still she craved for a look at his face, a grasp of his hand, perhaps even a kiss, long, and close, and tender, such as he would sometimes insist upon giving her, in spite of all policemen. His love for her, demonstrative as was his nature, had become to this still, quiet girl inexpressibly sweet—far sweeter than she knew.

It was a clear winter night, and the moon went climbing over the fleecy white clouds in a way that made beauty even in Russell Square. Elizabeth looked up at the sky, and thought how Tom would have enjoyed it, and wished he were beside her, and was so glad to think he would soon be beside her always, with all his humors and weaknesses, all his little crossnesses and complainings; she could put up with all, and be happy through all, if only she had him with her and loving her.

His love for her, though fitful and fanciful, was yet so warm and real that it had become a necessity of her life. As he always told her—especially after he had had one of his little quarrels with her—hers was to him.

"Poor Tom, I wonder how he gets on without me! Well, it won't be for long."

And she wished she could have let him know she was out here, that they might have had a chat for just ten minutes.

Unconsciously she walked toward their usual trysting-place, a large, overhanging plane-tree on the Keppel Street corner of the square.

Surely, surely, that could not be Tom! Quite impossible, for he was not alone. Two people, a young man and a young woman, stood at the tryst, absorbed in conversation: evidently sweethearts, for he had one arm around her, and he kissed her unresisted several times.

Elizabeth gazed, fascinated, almost doubting the evidence of her own senses. For the young man's figure was so excessively like Tom's. At length, with the sort of feeling that makes one go steadily up to a shadow by the roadside, some ugly spectre that we feel sure, if we stare it out, will prove to be a mere imagination, she walked deliberately up to and past these "sweethearts."

They did not see her; they were far too much occupied with one another; but she saw them, and saw at once that it was Tom, Tom's own self, and with him her fellow-servant Esther.

People may write volumes on jealousy, and volumes will still remain to be written. It is, next to remorse for guilt, the sharpest, sorest, most maddening torment that human nature can endure.

We may sit and gaze from the boxes at our *Othellos* and *Biancas;* we may laugh at the silly heart-burnings between Cousin Kate and Cousin Lucy in the ballroom, or the squabbles of Mary and Sally in the kitchen over the gardener's lad, but there the thing remains. A man can not make love to two women, a woman can not coquette with two men, without causing in degree that horrible agony, cruel as death, which is at the root of half the tragedies, and the cause of half the crimes of this world.

The complaint comes in different forms; sometimes it is a case of slow poisoning, or of ordeal by red-hot irons, which, though not fatal, undermines the whole character, and burns ineffaceable scars into the soul. And people take it in various ways—some fiercely, stung by a sense of wounded self-love; others haughtily:

> "Pride's a safe robe, I'll wear it; but no rags."

Others, again, humble, self-distrustful natures, whose only

pride came through love, have nothing left them except
rags.   In a moment all their thin robes of happiness are
torn off; they stand shivering, naked, and helpless before
the blasts of the bitter world.

This was Elizabeth's case. After the first instant of
stunned bewilderment and despair she took it all quite naturally, as if it were a thing which she ought all along to
have known was sure to happen, and which was no more
than she expected and deserved.

She passed the couple, still unobserved by them, and
then walked round the other side of the square deliberately home.

I am not going to make a tragic heroine of this poor
servant-girl. Perhaps, people may say, there is nothing
tragic about the incident.   Merely a plain, quiet, old-fashioned woman, who is so foolish as to like a handsome young
swain, and to believe in him, and to be surprised when he
deserts her for a pretty girl of eighteen.   All quite after
the way things go on in the world, especially in the serv-
ant-world; and the best she can do is to get over it, or take
another sweetheart as quickly as possible.   A very common
story after all, and more of a farce than a tragedy.

But there are some farces which, if you look underneath
the surface, have a good many of the elements of tragedy.

I shall neither paint Elizabeth tearing her own hair nor
Esther's, nor going raging about the square in moonlight
in an insane fit of jealousy.   She was not given to "fits"
under any circumstances or about any thing.   All she felt
went deep down into her heart, rooted itself, and either
blossomed or cankered there.

On this night she, as I said, walked round the square to
her home, then quietly went up stairs to her garret, locked
the door, and sat down upon her bed.

She might have sat there for an hour or more, her bonnet and shawl still on, without stirring, without crying, altogether cold and hard like a stone, when she fancied she
heard her mistress's bell ring, and mechanically rose up
and went down stairs to listen.   Nothing was wanted,

so she returned to her garret and crept to bed in the dark.

When, soon afterward, Esther likewise came up to bed, Elizabeth pretended to be asleep. Only once, taking a stealthy glance at the pretty girl who stood combing her hair at the looking-glass, she was conscious of a sick sense of repulsion, a pain like a knife running through her at sight of the red young lips which Tom had just been kissing, of the light figure which he had clasped as he used to clasp her. But she never spoke, not one word.

Half an hour after she was roused by the nurse coming to her bedside. Mrs. Ascott was very ill, and was calling for Elizabeth. Soon the whole establishment was in confusion, and in the sharp struggle between birth and death Elizabeth had no time to think of any thing but her mistress.

Contrary to every expectation, all ended speedily and happily; and before he went off to the City next day, the master of the house, who, in the midst of his anxiety and felicity, had managed to secure a good night's sleep and a good breakfast, had the pleasure of sending off a special messenger to the *Times* office with the notification, "The Lady of Peter Ascott, Esq., of a son and heir."

CHAPTER XXIV.

A FORTNIGHT's time rather increased than diminished the excitement incident on the event at Russell Square.

Never was there such a wonderful baby, and never was there such a fuss made over it. Unprejudiced persons might have called it an ugly, weakly little thing; indeed, at first there were such apprehensions of its dying that it had been baptized in a great hurry, "Henry Leaf Ascott," according to the mother's desire, which in her critical position nobody dared to thwart. Even at the end of fourteen days the "son and heir" was still a puling, sickly, yellow-faced baby. But to the mother it was every thing.

From the moment she heard its first cry Mrs. Ascott's whole nature seemed to undergo a change. Her very eyes —those cold blue eyes of Miss Selina's—took a depth and tenderness whenever she turned to look at the little bundle that lay beside her. She never wearied of touching the tiny hands and feet, and wondering at them, and showing—to every one of the household who was favored with a sight of it—"my baby," as if it had been a miracle of the universe. She was so unutterably happy and proud.

Elizabeth, too, seemed not a little proud of the baby. To her arms it had first been committed; she had stood by at its first washing and dressing, and had scarcely left it or her mistress since. Nurse, a very grand personage, had been a little jealous of her at first, but soon grew condescending, and made great use of her in the sick-room, alleging that such an exceedingly sensible young person, so quiet and steady, was almost as good as a middle-aged married woman. Indeed, she once asked Elizabeth if she was a widow, since she looked as if she had "seen trouble;" and was very much surprised to learn she was single, and only twenty-three years old.

Nobody else took any notice of her. Even Miss Hilary was so engrossed by her excitement and delight over the baby that she only observed, "Elizabeth, you look rather worn-out; this has been a trying time for you." And Elizabeth had just answered "Yes"—no more.

During the fortnight she had seen nothing of Tom. He had written her a short note or two, and the cook told her he had been to the kitchen door several times asking for her, but, being answered that she was with her mistress up stairs, had gone away.

"In the sulks, most like, though he didn't look it. He's a pleasant-spoken young man, and I'm sure I wish you luck with him," said Cookie, who, like all the other servants, was now exceedingly civil to Elizabeth.

Her star had risen; she was considered in the household a most fortunate woman. It was shortly understood that nurse—majestic nurse, had spoken so highly of her, that at the month's end the baby was to be given entirely into her charge, with, of course, an almost fabulous amount of wages.

"Unless," said Mrs. Ascott, when this proposition was made, suddenly recurring to a fact which seemed hitherto to have quite slipped from her mind—"unless you are still willing to get married, and think you would be happier married. In that case I won't hinder you. But it would be such a comfort to me to keep you a little longer."

"Thank you, ma'am," answered Elizabeth, softly, and busied herself with walking baby up and down the room, hushing it on her shoulder. If in the dim light tears fell on its puny face, God help her, poor Elizabeth!

Mrs. Ascott made such an excellent recovery that in three weeks' time nobody was the least anxious about her, and Mr. Ascott arranged to start on a business journey to Edinburg, promising, however, to be back in three days for the Christmas dinner, which was to be a grand celebration. Miss Leaf and Miss Hilary were to appear thereat in their wedding-dresses; and Mrs. Ascott herself took the most vital interest in Johanna's having a new cap for the occasion. Nay, she insisted upon ordering it from her own milliner, and having it made of the most beautiful lace— the "sweetest" old lady's cap that could possibly be invented.

Evidently this wonderful baby had opened all hearts, and drawn every natural tie closer. Selina, lying on the sofa, in her graceful white wrapper, and her neat close cap, looked so young, so pretty, and, above all, so exceedingly gentle and motherly, that her sisters' hearts were full to overflowing. They acknowledged that happiness, like misery, was often brought about in a fashion totally unforeseen and incredible. Who would have thought, for instance, on that wretched night when Mr. Ascott came to Hilary at Kensington, or on that dreary, heartless wedding-day, that they should ever have been sitting in Selina's room so merry and comfortable, admiring the baby, and on the friendliest terms with baby's papa?

"Papa" is a magical word, and let married people have fallen ever so wide asunder, the thought, "my child's mother," "my baby's father," must in some degree bridge the gulf between them. When Peter Ascott was seen stooping, awkwardly enough, over his son's cradle, poking his dumpy fingers into each tiny cheek in a half alarmed, half investigating manner, as if he had wondered how it had all come about, but, on the whole, was rather pleased than otherwise, the good angel of the household might have stood by and smiled, trusting that the ghastly skeleton therein might in time crumble away into harmless' dust, under the sacred touch of infant fingers.

The husband and wife took a kindly, even affectionate leave of one another. Mrs. Ascott called him "Peter," and begged him to take care of himself, and wrap up well that cold night. And when he was gone, and her sisters also, she lay on her sofa with her eyes open, thinking. What sort of thoughts they were, whether repentant or hopeful, solemn or tender, whether they might have passed away and been forgotten, or how far they might have influenced her life to come, none knew, and none ever did know.

When there came a knock at the door, and a message for Elizabeth, Mrs. Ascott suddenly overheard it and turned round.

"Who is wanting you — Tom Cliffe? Isn't that the young man you are to be married to? Go down to him at once. And stay, Elizabeth, as it's such a bitter night, take him for half an hour into the housekeeper's room. Send her up stairs, and tell her I wished it, though I don't allow 'followers.'"

"Thank you, ma'am," said Elizabeth once more, and obeyed. She must speak to Tom some time, it might as well be done to-night as not. Without pausing to think, she went down with dull, heavy steps to the housekeeper's room.

Tom stood there alone. He looked so exactly his own old self, he came forward to meet her so completely in his old familiar way, that for the instant she thought she must be under some dreadful delusion; that the moonlight night in the square must have been all a dream; Esther, still the silly little Esther, whom Tom had often heard of and laughed at; and Tom, her own Tom, who loved nobody but her.

"Elizabeth, what an age it is since I've had a sight of you!"

But, though the manner was warm as ever,

> "In his tone
> A something smote her, as if Duty tried
> To mock the voice of Love, how long since flown,"

and quiet as she stood, Elizabeth shivered in his arms.

"Why, what's the matter? Aren't you glad to see me? Give me another kiss, my girl, do!"

He took it; and she crept away from him and sat down.

"Tom, I've got something to say to you, and I'd better say it at once."

"To be sure. 'Tisn't any bad news from home, is it? Or"—looking uneasily at her—"I haven't vexed you, have I?"

"*Vexed* me," she repeated, thinking what a small, foolish word it was to express what had happened and what she had been suffering. "No, Tom, not vexed me exactly. But I want to ask you a question. Who was it that you stood talking with, under our tree in the square, between nine and ten o'clock this night three weeks ago?"

Though there was no anger in the voice, it was so serious and deliberate that it made Tom start.

"Three weeks ago; how can I possibly tell?"

"Yes, you can; for it was a fine moonlight night, and you stood there a long time."

"Under the tree, talking to somebody?" What nonsense! Perhaps it wasn't me at all."

"It was, for I saw you."

"The devil you did!" muttered Tom.

"Don't be angry, only tell me the plain truth. The young woman that was with you was our Esther here, wasn't she?"

For a moment Tom looked altogether confounded. Then he tried to recover himself, and said, crossly, " Well, and if it was, where's the harm? Can't a man be civil to a pretty girl without being called over the coals in this way?"

Elizabeth made no answer, at least not immediately. At last she said, in a very gentle, subdued voice,

"Tom, are you fond of Esther? You would not kiss her if you were not fond of her. Do you like her as—as you used to like me?"

And she looked right up into his eyes. Hers had no reproach in them, only a piteous entreaty, the last clinging to a hope which she knew to be false.

"Like Esther? Of course I do. She's a nice sort of girl, and we're very good friends."

" Tom, a man can't be 'friends,' in that sort of way, with a pretty girl of eighteen, when he is going to be married to somebody else. At least, in my mind, he ought not."

Tom laughed in a confused manner. "I say, you're jealous, and you'd better get over it."

Was she jealous? was it all fancy, folly? Did Tom stand there, true as steel, without a feeling in his heart that she did not share, without a hope in which she was not united, holding her, and preferring her, with that individuality and unity of love which true love ever gives and exacts, as it has a right to exact?

Not that poor Elizabeth reasoned in this way, but she felt the thing by instinct without reasoning.

"Tom," she said, "tell me outright, just as if I was somebody else, and had never belonged to you at all, do you love Esther Martin?"

Truthful people enforce truth. Tom might be fickle, but he was not deceitful; he could not look into Elizabeth's eyes and tell her a deliberate lie; somehow he dared not.

"Well, then—since you will have it out of me—I think I do."

So Elizabeth's "ship went down." It might have been a very frail vessel, that nobody in their right senses would have trusted any treasure with, still she did; and it was all she had, and it went down to the bottom like a stone.

It is astonishing how soon the sea closes over this sort of wreck, and how quietly people take—when they must take, and there is no more disbelieving it—the truth which they would have given their lives to prove was an impossible lie.

For some minutes Tom stood facing the fire, and Elizabeth sat on her chair opposite without speaking. Then she took off her brooch, the only love-token he had given her, and put it into his hand.

"What's this for?" asked he, suddenly.

"You know. You'd better give it to Esther. It's Esther, not me, you must marry now."

And the thought of Esther, giddy, flirting, useless Esther, as Tom's wife, was almost more than she could bear. The sting of it put even into her crushed humility a certain honest self-assertion.

"I'm not going to blame you, Tom, but I think I'm as good as she. I'm not pretty, I know, nor lively, nor young —at least I'm old for my age; but I was worth something. You should not have served me so."

Tom said, the usual excuse, that he "couldn't help it." And suddenly turning round, he begged her to forgive him, and not forsake him.

She forsake Tom! Elizabeth almost smiled.

"I do forgive you; I'm not a bit angry with you. If I ever was I have got over it."

"That's right. You're a dear soul. Do you think I don't like you, Elizabeth?"

"Oh yes," she said, sadly, "I dare say you do, a little, in spite of Esther Martin. But that's not my way of liking, and I couldn't stand it."

"What couldn't you stand?"

"Your kissing me to-day, and another girl to-morrow; your telling me I was every thing to you one week, and saying exactly the same thing to another girl the next. It would be hard enough to bear if we were only friends, but

M

as sweethearts, as husband and wife, it would be impossible. No, Tom, I tell you the truth, I could not stand it."

She spoke strongly, unhesitatingly, and for an instant there flowed out of her soft eyes that wild, fierce spark, latent even in these quiet humble natures, which is dangerous to meddle with.

Tom did not attempt it. He felt all was over. Whether he had lost or gained—whether he was glad or sorry, he hardly knew.

"I'm not going to take this back, anyhow," he said, "fiddling" with the brooch; and then going up to her, he attempted, with trembling hands, to refasten it in her collar.

The familiar action, his contrite look, were too much. People who have once loved one another, though the love is dead (for love *can* die), are not able to bury it all at once, or if they do, its pale ghost will still come knocking at the door of their hearts, "Let me in, let me in!"

Elizabeth ought, I know, in proper feminine dignity, to have bade Tom farewell without a glance or a touch. But she did not. When he had fastened her brooch she looked up in his familiar face a sorrowful, wistful, lingering look, and then clung about his neck:

"Oh Tom, Tom, I was so fond of you!"

And Tom mingled his tears with hers, and kissed her many times, and even felt his old affection returning, making him half oblivious of Esther; but mercifully—for love rebuilt upon lost faith is like a house founded upon sands —the door opened, and Esther herself came in.

Laughing, smirking, pretty Esther, who, thoughtless as she was, had yet the sense to draw back when she saw them.

"Come here, Esther!" Elizabeth called, imperatively; and she came.

"Esther, I've given up Tom; you may take him if he wants you. Make him a good wife, and I'll forgive you. If not—"

She could not say another word. She shut the door upon them, and crept up stairs, conscious only of one thought—

if she only could get away from them, and never see either of their faces any more!

And in this Fate was kind to her, though in that awful way in which Fate—say rather Providence—often works; cutting, with one sharp blow, some knot that our poor, feeble, mortal fingers have been long laboring at in vain, or making that which seemed impossible to do the most natural, easy, and only thing to be done.

How strangely often in human life "one woe doth tread upon the other's heel!" How continually, while one of those small private tragedies that I have spoken of is being enacted within, the actors are called upon to meet some other tragedy from without, so that external energy counteracts inward emotion, and holy sympathy with another's sufferings stifles all personal pain. That truth about sorrows coming "in battalions" may have a divine meaning in it—may be one of those mysterious laws which guide the universe—laws that we can only trace in fragments, and guess at the rest, believing, in deep humility, that one day we shall "know even as we are known."

Therefore I ask no pity for Elizabeth, because ere she had time to collect herself, and realize in her poor confused mind that she had indeed said good-by to Tom, given him up and parted from him forever, she was summoned to her mistress's room, there to hold a colloquy outside the door with the seriously-perplexed nurse.

One of those sudden changes had come which sometimes, after all seems safe, strike terror into a rejoicing household, and end by carrying away, remorseless, the young wife from her scarcely tasted bliss, the mother of many children from her close circle of happy duties and yearning loves.

Mrs. Ascott was ill. Either she had taken cold, or been too much excited, or, in the over-confidence of her recovery, some slight neglect had occurred—some trifle which nobody thinks of till afterward, and which yet proves the fatal cause, the "little pin" that

"Bores through the castle wall"

of mortal hope, and King Death enters in all his awful state.

Nobody knew it or dreaded it; for, though Mrs. Ascott was certainly ill, she was not at first very ill; and there being no telegraphs in those days, no one thought of sending for either her husband or her sisters. But that very hour, when Elizabeth went up to her mistress, and saw the flush on her cheek and the restless expression of her eye, King Death had secretly crept in at the door of the mansion in Russell Square.

The patient was carefully removed back into her bed. She said little, except once, looking up uneasily—

" I don't feel quite myself, Elizabeth."

And when her servant soothed her in the long-familiar way, telling her she would be better in the morning, she smiled contentedly, and turned to go to sleep.

Nevertheless, Elizabeth did not go to her bed, but sat behind the curtain, motionless, for an hour or more.

Toward the middle of the night, when her baby was brought to her, and the child instinctively refused its natural food, and began screaming violently, Mrs. Ascott's troubled look returned.

" What is the matter? What are you doing, nurse? I won't be parted from my baby—I won't, I say !"

And when, to soothe her, the little thing was again put into her arms, and again turned from her, a frightful expression came into the mother's face.

" Am I going to be ill? Is baby—"

She stopped; and as nurse determinately carried it away, she attempted no resistance, only followed it across the room with eager eyes. It was the last glimmer of reason there. From that time her mind began to wander, and before morning she was slightly delirious.

Still nobody apprehended danger. Nobody really knew any thing about the matter except nurse, and she, with a selfish fear of being blamed for carelessness, resisted sending for the doctor till his usual hour of calling. In that large house, as, in many other large houses, every body's business was nobody's business, and a member of the family, even the mistress, might easily be sick or dying in some room therein, while all things else went on just as usual, and no one was any the wiser.

About noon even Elizabeth's ignorance was roused up to the conviction that something was very wrong with Mrs. Ascott, and that nurse's skill could not counteract it. On her own responsibility she sent, or rather she went to fetch the doctor. He came; and his fiat threw the whole household into consternation.

Now they knew that the poor lady whose happiness had touched the very stoniest hearts in the establishment hovered upon the brink of the grave. Now all the women-servants, down to the little kitchen-maid with her dirty apron at her eyes, crept up stairs, one after the other, to the door of what had been such a silent, mysterious room, and listened, unhindered, to the ravings that issued thence. "Poor missis," and the "poor little baby," were spoken of softly at the kitchen dinner-table, and confidentially sympathized over with inquiring tradespeople at the area gate. A sense of awe and suspense stole over the whole house, gathering thicker hour by hour of that dark December day.

When her mistress was first pronounced "in danger," Elizabeth, aware that there was no one to act but herself, had taken a brief opportunity to slip from the room and write two letters, one to her master in Edinburg, and the other to Miss Hilary. The first she gave to the footman to post; the second she charged him to send by special messenger to Richmond. But he, being lazily inclined, or else thinking that, as the order was only given by Elizabeth, it was of comparatively little moment, posted them both. So vainly did the poor girl watch and wait; neither Miss Leaf nor Miss Hilary came.

By night Mrs. Ascott's delirium began to subside, but her strength was ebbing fast. Two physicians—three—stood by the unconscious woman, and pronounced that all hope was gone, if, indeed, the case had not been hopeless from the beginning.

"Where is her husband? Has she no relations—no mother or sisters?" asked the fashionable physician, Sir —— ——, touched by the sight of this poor lady dying alone, with only a nurse and a servant about her. "If she has, they ought to be sent for immediately."

Elizabeth ran down stairs, and rousing the old butler from his bed, prevailed on him to start immediately in the carriage to bring back Miss Leaf and Miss Hilary. It would be midnight before he reached Richmond; still it must be done.

"I'll do it, my girl," said he, kindly; "and I'll tell them as gently as I can. Never fear."

When Elizabeth returned to her mistress's room the doctors were all gone, and nurse, standing at the foot of Mrs. Ascott's bed, was watching her with the serious look which even a hireling or a stranger wears in the presence of that sight which, however familiar, never grows less awful—a fellow-creature slowly passing from this life into the life unknown.

Elizabeth crept up to the other side. The change, undescribable yet unmistakable, which comes over a human face when the warrant for its dissolution has gone forth, struck her at once.

Never yet had Elizabeth seen death. Her father's she did not remember, and among her few friends and connections none other had occurred. At twenty-three years of age she was still ignorant of that solemn experience which every woman must go through some time, often many times, during her life. For it is to women that all look in their extreme hour. Very few men, even the tenderest-hearted, are able to watch by the last struggle and close the eyes of the dying.

For the moment, as she glanced round the darkened room, and then at the still figure on the bed, Elizabeth's courage failed. Strong love might have overcome this fear—the natural recoil of youth and life from coming into contact with death and mortality; but love was not exactly the bond between her and Mrs. Ascott. It was rather

duty, pity, the tenderness that would have sprung up in
her heart toward any body she had watched and tended
so long.

"If she should die, die in the night, before Miss Hilary
comes!" thought the poor girl, and glanced once more round
the shadowy room, where she was now left quite alone.
For nurse, thinking with true worldly wisdom of the preservation of the "son and heir," which was decidedly the
most important question now, had stolen away, and was
busy in the next room, seeing various young women whom
the doctors had sent, one of whom was to supply to the infant the place of the poor mother whom it would never
know.

There was nobody left but herself to watch this dying
mother, so Elizabeth took her lot upon her, smothered
down her fears, and sat by the bedside waiting for the
least expression of returning reason in the sunken face,
which was very quiet now.

Consciousness did return at last, as the doctors had said
it would. Mrs. Ascott opened her eyes; they wandered
from side to side, and then she said, feebly,

"Elizabeth, where's my baby?"

What Elizabeth answered she never could remember;
perhaps nothing, or her agitation betrayed her, for Mrs.
Ascott said again,

"Elizabeth, am I going to—to leave my baby?"

Some people might have considered it best to reply with
a lie—the frightened, cowardly lie that is so often told at
death-beds to the soul passing direct to its God. But this
girl could not and dared not.

Leaning over her mistress, she whispered as softly as she
could, choking down the tears that might have disturbed
the peace which, mercifully, seemed to have come with
dying,

"Yes, you are going very soon—to God. He will watch
over baby, and give him back to you again some day quite
safe."

"Will He?"

The tone was submissive, half inquiring, like that of a child learning something it had never learned before—as Selina was now learning. Perhaps even those three short weeks of motherhood had power so to raise her whole nature that she now gained the composure with which even the weakest soul can sometimes meet death, and had grown not unworthy of the dignity of a Christian's dying.

Suddenly she shivered. "I am afraid; I never thought of—this. Will nobody come and speak to me?"

Oh, how Elizabeth longed for Miss Hilary, for any body, who would have known what to say to the dying woman; who perhaps, as her look and words implied, till this hour had never thought of dying. Once it crossed the servant's mind to send for some clergyman; but she knew none, and was aware that Mrs. Ascott did not either. She had no superstitious feeling that any clergyman would do, just to give a sort of spiritual extreme unction to the departing soul. Her own religious faith was of such an intensely personal, silent kind, that she did not believe in any good to be derived from a strange gentleman coming and praying by the bedside of a stranger, repeating set sayings with a set countenance, and going away again. And yet with that instinct which comes to almost every human soul, fast departing, Mrs. Ascott's white lips whispered, "Pray."

Elizabeth had no words except those which Miss Leaf used to say night after night in the little parlor at Stowbury. She knelt down, and in a trembling voice repeated in her mistress's ear, "*Our father which art in heaven,*" to the end.

After it Mrs. Ascott lay very quiet. At length she said, "Please—bring—my—baby." It had been from the first, and was to the last, "*my*" baby.

The small face was laid close to hers, that she might kiss it.

"He looks well; he does not miss me much yet, poor little fellow!" And the strong natural agony came upon her, conquering even the weakness of her last hour. "Oh, it's hard, hard! Will nobody teach my baby to remember me?"

And then lifting herself up on her elbow she caught hold of nurse.

"Tell Mr. Ascott that Elizabeth is to take care of baby. Promise, Elizabeth. Johanna is old—Hilary may be married—*you* will take care of my baby?"

"I will—as long as I live," said Elizabeth Hand.

She took the child in her arms, and for almost another hour stood beside the bed thus, until nurse whispered, "Carry it away; its mother doesn't know it now."

But she did; for she feebly moved her fingers as if in search of something. Baby was still asleep, but Elizabeth contrived, by kneeling down close to the bed, to put the tiny hand under those cold fingers; they closed immediately upon it, and remained so till the last.

When Miss Leaf and Miss Hilary came in Elizabeth was still kneeling there, trying softly to take the little hand away; for the baby had wakened and began its piteous wail. But it did not disturb the mother now.

"Poor Selina" was no more. Nothing of her was left to her child except the name of a mother. It may have been better so.

CHAPTER XXV.

"IN MEMORY OF
SELINA,
THE BELOVED WIFE OF PETER ASCOTT, ESQ.,
OF RUSSELL SQUARE, LONDON,
AND DAUGHTER OF
THE LATE HENRY LEAF, ESQ.,
OF THIS TOWN.
DIED DECEMBER 24, 1839,
AGED 41 YEARS."

SUCH was the inscription which now, for six months, had met the eyes of the inhabitants of Stowbury, on a large, dazzlingly-white marble monument, the first that was placed in the church-yard of the New Church.

What motive induced Mr. Ascott to inter his wife here

M 2

—whether it was a natural wish to lay her, and some day lie beside her, in their native earth; or the less creditable desire of showing how rich he had become, and of joining his once humble name, even on a tomb-stone, with one of the oldest names in the annals of Stowbury—nobody could find out.   Probably nobody cared.

The Misses Leaf were content that he should do as he pleased in the matter: he had shown strong but not exaggerated grief at his loss; if any remorse mingled therewith, Selina's sisters happily did not know it.   Nobody ever did know the full history of things except Elizabeth, and she kept it to herself.   So the family skeleton was buried quietly in Mrs. Ascott's grave.

Peter Ascott showed, in his coarse fashion, much sympathy and consideration for his wife's sisters.   He had them staying in the house till a week after the funeral was over, and provided them with the deepest and handsomest mourning.   He even, in a formal way, took counsel with them as to the carrying out of Mrs. Ascott's wishes, and the retaining of Elizabeth in charge of the son and heir, which was accordingly settled.   And then they went back to their old life at Richmond, and the widower returned to his solitary bachelor ways.   He looked as usual; went to and from the City as usual; and his brief married life seemed to have passed away from him like a dream.

Not altogether a dream.   Gradually he began to wake up to the consciousness of an occasional child's cry in the house—that large, silent, dreary house, where he was once more the sole, solitary master.   Sometimes, when he came in from church on Sundays, he would mount another flight of stairs, walk into the nursery at the top of the house, and stare with distant curiosity at the little creature in Elizabeth's arms, pronounce it a "fine child, and did her great credit!" and walk down again.   He never seemed to consider it as *his* child, this poor old bachelor of so many years' standing; he had outgrown apparently all sense of the affections or the duties of a father.   Whether they ever would come into him; whether, after babyhood was passed, he would begin to take an interest in the little creature who throve and blossomed into beauty—which, as if watched by guardian angels, dead mothers' children seem often to do—was a source of earnest speculation to Elizabeth.

In the mean time he treated both her and the baby with extreme consideration, allowed her to do just as she liked, and gave her indefinite sums of money to expend upon the nursery.

When summer came, and the doctor ordered change of air, Mr. Ascott consented to her suggestion of taking a lodging for herself and baby near baby's aunts at Richmond; only desiring that the lodging should be as handsome as could be secured, and that every other Sunday she should bring up his son to spend the day at Russell Square.

And so, during the long summer months, the motherless child, in its deep mourning—which looks so pathetic on a very young baby—might be seen carried about in Elizabeth's arms every where. When, after the first six weeks, the wet-nurse left—in fact, two or three wet-nurses successively were abolished—she took little Henry solely under her own charge. She had comparatively small experience, but she had common sense, and the strong motherly instinct which comes by nature to some women. Besides, her whole soul was wrapped up in this little child.

From the hour when, even with her mistress dying before her eyes, Elizabeth had felt a strange thrill of comfort in the new duty which had come into her blank life, she took to this duty as women only can whose life *has* become a blank. She received the child as a blessing sent direct from God; by unconscious hands—for Mrs. Ascott knew nothing of what happened; something that would heal her wounded heart, and make her forget Tom.

And so it did. Women and mothers well know how engrossing is the care of an infant; how each minute of the day is filled up with something to be done or thought of; so that "fretting" about extraneous things becomes quite impossible. How gradually the fresh life growing up and expanding puts the worn-out or blighted life into the background, and all the hopes and fancies cling around the small, beautiful present, the ever-developing, ever-marvelous mystery of a young child's existence! Why. it should be so we can only guess; but that it is so, many a wretched wife, many a widowed mother, many a broken-hearted, forlorn aunt, has thankfully proved.

Elizabeth proved it likewise. She did not exactly lose all memory of her trouble, but it seemed lighter; it was swallowed up in this second passion of adopted motherhood. And so she sank, quietly and at once, into the condition of a middle-aged woman, whose life's story—and her sort of women have but one—was a mere episode, told and ended.

For Esther had left and been married to Tom Cliffe within a few weeks of Mrs. Ascott's funeral. Of course, the household knew every thing; but nobody condoled with Elizabeth. There was a certain stand-off-ishness about her which made them hold their tongues. They treated her with much respect, as her new position demanded. She took this, as she took every thing, with the grave quietness which was her fashion from her youth up; assumed her place as a confidential upper servant; dressed well, but soberly, like a woman of forty, and was called "Mrs. Hand."

The only trace her "disappointment" left upon her was a slightly bitter way of speaking about men in general, and a dislike to any chatter about love-affairs and matrimony. Her own story she was never known to refer to in the most distant way except once.

Miss Hilary—who, of course, had heard all, but delicately kept silence—one night, when little Henry was not well, remained in the lodgings on Richmond Hill, and slept in the nursery, Elizabeth making up for herself a bed on the floor close beside baby and cradle. In the dead of night the two women, mistress and maid, by some chance, said a few things to one another which never might have been said in the daylight, and which, by tacit consent, were never afterward referred to by either, any more than if they had been spoken in a dream.

Elizabeth told briefly, though not without emotion, all that had happened between herself and Tom, and how he was married to Esther Martin. And then both women went back, in a moralizing way, to the days when they had both been " young" at Stowbury, and how different life was from what they then thought and looked forward to—Miss Hilary and her " bower-maiden."

" Yes," answered the former, with a sigh, " things are, indeed, not as people fancy when they are girls. We dream, and dream, and think we see very far into the future, which nobody sees but God. I often wonder how my life will end."

Elizabeth said, after a pause, " I always felt sure you would be married, Miss Hilary. There was one person— is he alive still ? Is he ever coming home ?"

" I don't know."

" I am sure he was very fond of you. And he looked like a good man."

" He was the best man I ever knew."

This was all Miss Hilary said, and she said it softly and mournfully. She might never have said it at all; but it dropped from her unawares in the deep feeling of the moment, when her heart was tender over Elizabeth's own sad, simply-told story. Also because of a sudden and great darkness which had come over her own.

Literally, she did not now know whether Robert Lyon were alive or dead. Two months ago his letters had suddenly ceased, without any explanation, his last being exactly the same as the others—as frank, as warmly affectionate, as cheerful and brave.

One solution to this was his possible coming home. But she did not, after careful reasoning on the subject, believe that likely. She knew exactly his business relations with his employers; that there was a fixed time for his return to England, which nothing except the very strongest necessity could alter. Even in the chance of his health breaking, so as to incapacitate him for work, he should, he always said, have to go to the hills rather than take the voyage home prematurely. And, in that case, he certainly would have informed his friends of his movements. There was nothing erratic, or careless, or eccentric about Robert Lyon; he was a practical, business-like Scotchman —far too cautious and too regular in all his habits to be guilty of those accidental negligences by which wanderers abroad sometimes cause such cruel anxieties to friends at home.

For the same reason, the other terrible possibility—his death — was not likely to have happened without their hearing of it. Hilary felt sure, with the strong confidence of love, that he would have taken every means to leave her some last word—some farewell token—which would reach her after he was gone, and comfort her with the assurance of what, living, he had never plainly told. Sometimes, when a wild terror of his death seized her, this settled conviction drove it back again. He must be living, or she would have heard.

There was another interpretation of the silence, which many would have considered the most probable of all—he might be married. Not deliberately, but suddenly; drawn into it by some of those impelling trains of circumstance which are the cause of so many marriages, especially with men; or impelled by one of those violent passions which occasionally seize on an exceedingly good man, fascinating him against his conscience, reason, and will, until he wakes up to find himself fettered and ruined for life. Such things do happen, strangely, pitifully often. The like might have happened to Robert Lyon.

Hilary did not actually believe it, but still her common sense told her that it was possible. She was not an inexperienced girl now; she looked on the world with the eyes of a woman of thirty; and though, thank Heaven! the romance had never gone out of her—the faith, and trust, and tender love—still it had sobered down a little. She knew it was quite within the bounds of possibility that a young man, separated from her for seven years, thrown into all kinds of circumstances and among all sorts of people, should have changed very much in himself, and, consequently, toward her; that, without absolute faithlessness, he might suddenly have seen some other woman he liked better, and have married at once. Or if he came back unmarried — she had taught herself to look this probability also steadily in the face—he might find the reality of her, Hilary Leaf, different from his remembrance of her; and so, without actual falseness to the old true love, might not love her any more.

These fears made her resolutely oppose Johanna's wish to write to the house of business at Liverpool, and ask what had become of Mr. Lyon. It seemed like seeking after him, trying to hold him by the slender chain which he had never attempted to make any stronger, and which, already, he might have broken, or desired to break.

She could not do it. Something forbade her; that something in the inmost depths of a woman's nature which makes her feel her own value, and exact that she shall be sought; that, if her love be worth having, it is worth seeking; that, however dear a man may be to her, she refuses to drop into his mouth like an overripe peach from a garden wall. In her sharpest agony of anxiety concerning him, Hilary felt that she could not, on her part, take any step that seemed to compel love, or even friendship, from Robert Lyon. It was not pride — she could hardly be called a proud woman—it was an innate sense of the dignity of that love which, as a free gift, is precious as " much fine gold," yet becomes the merest dross—utterly and insultingly poor—when paid as a debt of honor, or offered as a benevolent largess.

And so, though oftentimes her heart felt breaking, Hilary labored on—sat the long day patiently at her desk, interested herself in the young people over whom she ruled, became Miss Balquidder's right hand in all sorts of schemes which that good woman was forever carrying out for the benefit of her fellow-creatures, and, at leisure times, occupied herself with Johanna, or with Elizabeth and the baby, trying to think it was a very beautiful and happy world,

with love still in it, and a God of love ruling over it—
only, only—

Women are very humble in their cruelest pride. Many
a day she felt as if she could have crawled a hundred
miles in the dust, like some Catholic pilgrim, just to get
one sight of Robert Lyon.

Autumn came—lovely, and lingering late. It was November, and yet the air felt mild as May, and the sunshine
had that peculiar genial brightness which autumnal sunshine alone possesses; even as, perhaps, late happiness has
in it a holy calm and sweetness which no youthful ecstasy
can ever boast.

The day happened to be Hilary's birthday. She had
taken a holiday, which she, Johanna, Elizabeth, and the
baby had spent in Richmond Park, watching the rabbits
darting about under the brown fern, and the deer grazing
contentedly hard by. They had sat a long time under one
of the oak-trees with which the park abounds, listening
for the sudden drop, drop of an occasional acorn among
the fallen leaves, or making merry with the child, as a
healthy, innocent, playful child always can make good
women merry.

Still Master Henry was not a remarkable specimen of
infanthood, and had never occupied more than his proper
nepotal corner in Hilary's heart. She left him chiefly to
Elizabeth, and to his aunt Johanna, in whom the grand-
motherly character had blossomed out in full perfection.
And when these two became engrossed in his infant maj-
esty, Hilary sat a little apart, unconsciously folding her
hands and fixing her eyes on vacancy, becoming fearfully
alive to the sharp truth that, of all griefs, a strong love un-
returned or unfulfilled is the grief which most blights a
woman's life—say, rather, any human life; but it is worst
to a woman, because she must necessarily endure passive-
ly. So enduring, it is very difficult to recognize the good
hand of God therein. Why should He ordain longings,
neither selfish nor unholy, which yet are never granted;
tenderness which expends itself in vain; sacrifices which

are wholly unneeded; and sufferings which seem quite thrown away? That is, if we dared allege of any thing in the moral or in the material world, where so much loveliness, so much love, appear continually wasted, that it is really "thrown away." We never know through what divine mysteries of compensation the Great Father of the universe may be carrying out His sublime plan; and those three words, "God is love," ought to contain, to every doubting soul, the solution of all things.

As Hilary rose from under the tree there was a shadow on her sweet face, a listless weariness in her movements, which caught Johanna's attention. Johanna had been very good to her child. When, do what she would, Hilary could not keep down fits of occasional dullness or impatience, it was touching to see how this woman of over sixty years slipped from her due pedestal of honor and dignity, to be patient with her younger sister's unspoken bitterness and incommunicable care.

She now, seeing how restless Hilary was, rose when she rose, put her arm in hers, and accompanied her, speaking or silent, with quick steps or slow, as she chose, across the beautiful park, than which, perhaps, all England can not furnish a scene more thoroughly sylvan, thoroughly English. They rested on that high ground near the gate of Pembroke Lodge, where the valley of the Thames lies spread out like a map, stretching miles and miles away in luxuriant greenery.

"How beautiful! I wonder what a foreigner would think of this view? Or any one who had been long abroad? How inexpressibly sweet and homelike it would seem to him!"

Hilary turned sharply away, and Johanna saw at once what her words had implied. She felt so sorry, so vexed with herself; but it was best to leave it alone. So they made their way homeward, speaking of something else; and then that happened which Johanna had been almost daily expecting would happen, though she dared not communicate her hopes to Hilary, lest they should prove fallacious.

The two figures, both in deep mourning, might have attracted any one's attention; they caught that of a gentleman who was walking quickly, and looking about him as if in search of something. He passed them at a little distance, then repassed, then turned, holding out both his hands.

"Miss Leaf; I was sure it was you."

Only the voice; every thing else about him was so changed that Hilary herself would certainly have passed him in the street, that brown, foreign-looking, middle-aged man, nor recognized him as Robert Lyon. But for all that it was himself; it was Robert Lyon.

Nobody screamed, nobody fainted. People seldom do that in real life, even when a friend turns up suddenly from the other end of the world. They only hold out a warm hand, and look silently in one another's faces, and try to believe that all is real, as these did.

Robert Lyon shook hands with both ladies, one after the other, Hilary last, then placed himself between them.

"Miss Leaf, will you take my arm?"

The tone, the manner, were so exactly like himself, that in a moment all these intervening years seemed crushed into an atom of time. Hilary felt certain, morally and absolutely certain, that, in spite of all outward change, he was the same Robert Lyon who had bade them all good-by that Sunday night in the parlor at Stowbury. The same, even in his love for herself, though he had simply drawn her little hand under his arm, and never spoken a single word.

Hilary Leaf, down, secretly, on your heart's lowest knees, and thank God! Repent of all your bitternesses, doubts, and pains; be joyful, be joyful! But, oh, remember to be so humble withal.

She was. As she walked silently along by Robert Lyon's side she pulled down her veil to hide the sweetest, most contrite, most childlike tears. What did she deserve, more than her neighbors, that she should be so very, very happy? And when, a good distance across the park, she saw the dark, solitary figure of Elizabeth carrying baby, she quietly guided her companions into a different path, so as to avoid meeting, lest the sight of her happiness might in any way hurt poor Elizabeth.

"I only landed last night at Southampton," Mr. Lyon explained to Miss Leaf, after the fashion people have, at such meetings, of falling upon the most practical and uninteresting details. "I came by the Overland Mail. It was a sudden journey. I had scarcely more than a few hours' notice. The cause of it was some very unpleasant defalcations in our firm."

Hilary might have smiled under any other circumstances; maybe she did smile, and tease him many a time afterward, because the first thing he could find to talk about, after seven years' absence, was "defalcations in our firm." But now she listened gravely, and by-and-by took her part in the unimportant conversation which always occurs after a meeting such as this.

"Were you going home, Miss Leaf? They told me at your house you were expected to dinner. May I come with you? for I have only a few hours to stay. To-night I must go on to Liverpool."

"But we shall hope soon to see you again?"

"I hope so. And I trust, Miss Leaf, that I do not intrude to-day?"

He said this with his Scotch shyness, or pride, or whatever it was; so like his old self, that it made somebody smile! But somebody loved it. Somebody lifted up to his face eyes of silent welcome; sweet, soft brown eyes, where never, since he knew them, had he seen one cloud of anger darken, one shadow of unkindness rise.

"This is something to come home to," he said in a low voice, and not over lucidly. Ay, it was.

"I am by no means disinterested in the matter of dinner, Miss Leaf, for I have no doubt of finding good English roast beef and plum-pudding on your sister's birthday. Happy returns of the day, Miss Hilary."

She was so touched by his remembering this, that, to

hide it, she put on a spice of her old mischievousness, and
asked him if he was aware how old she was.

"Yes: you are thirty; I have known you for fifteen
years."

"It is a long time," said Johanna, thoughtfully.

Johanna would not have been human had she not been
a little thoughtful and silent on the way home, and had
she not many times, out of the corners of her eyes, sharply
investigated Mr. Robert Lyon.

He was much altered; there was no doubt of that.
Seven years of Indian life would change any body—take
the youthfulness out of any body.   It was so with Robert
Lyon.   When, coming into the parlor, he removed his hat,
many a white thread was visible in his hair, and, besides
the spare, dried-up look which is always noticeable in people who have lived long in hot climates, there was an "old"
expression in his face, indicating many a worldly battle
fought and won, but not without leaving scars behind.

Even Hilary, as she sat opposite to him at table, could
not but feel that he was no longer a young man either in
appearance or reality.

We ourselves grow old, or older, without knowing it;
but when we suddenly come upon the same fact in another,
it startles us.   Hilary had scarcely recognized how far she
herself had left her girlish days behind till she saw Robert
Lyon.

"You think me very much changed?" said he, guessing
by his curiously swift intuition of old what she was thinking of.

"Yes, a good deal changed," she answered, truthfully,
at which he was silent.

He could not read—perhaps no man's heart could—all
the emotion that swelled in hers as she looked at him, the
love of her youth, no longer young.   How the ghostly likeness of the former face gleamed out under the hard, worn
lines of the face that now was touching her with ineffable
tenderness.   Also, with solemn content came a sense of
the entire indestructibleness of that love which through

all decay or alteration traces the ideal image still, clings
to it, and cherishes it with a tenacity that laughs to scorn
the grim dread of "growing old."

In his premature and not specially comely middle age,
in his gray hairs, in the painful, anxious, half-melancholy
expression which occasionally flitted across his features, as
if life had gone hard with him, Robert Lyon was a thousand
times dearer to her than when the world was all before
them both in the early days at Stowbury.

There is a great deal of a sentimental nonsense talked
about people having been "young together." Not necessarily is that a bond. Many a tie formed in youth dwindles
away and breaks off naturally in maturer years. Characters alter, circumstances divide. No one will dare to allege
that there may not be loves and friendships formed in middle life as dear, as close, as firm as any of those of youth;
perhaps, with some temperaments, infinitely more so. But
when the two go together, when the calm election of ma-
turity confirms the early instinct, and the lives have run
parallel, as it were, for many years, there can be no bond
like that of those who say, as these two did, "We were
young together."

He said so when, after dinner, he came and stood by the
window where Hilary was sitting sewing. Johanna had
just gone out of the room, whether intentionally or not
this history can not avouch. Let us give her the benefit
of the doubt; she was a generous woman.

During the three hours that Mr. Lyon had been with
her Hilary's first agitation had subsided. That exceeding
sense of rest which she had always felt beside him—the
sure index of people who, besides loving, are meant to
guide, and help, and bless one another—returned as strong
as ever. That deep affection which should underlie all
love revived and clung to him with a childlike confidence,
strengthening at every word he said, every familiar look
and way.

He was by no means so composed as she was, especially
now when, coming up to her side and watching her hands

moving for a minute or so, he asked her to tell him, a little more explicitly, of what had happened to her since they parted.

"Things are rather different from what I thought;" and he glanced with a troubled air round the neat but very humbly furnished parlor. "And about the shop?"

"Johanna told you."

"Yes; but her letters have been so few, so short—not that I could expect more. Still—now, if you will trust me, tell me all."

Hilary turned to him, her friend for fifteen years. He was that if he was nothing more. And he had been very true; he deserved to be trusted. She told him, in brief, the history of the last year or two, and then added,

"But, after all, it is hardly worth the telling, because, you see, we are very comfortable now. Poor Ascott, we suppose, must be in Australia. I earn enough to keep Johanna and myself, and Miss Balquidder is a good friend to us. We have repaid her, and owe nobody any thing. Still we have suffered a great deal. Two years ago—oh! it was a dreadful time."

She was hardly aware of it, but her candid tell-tale face betrayed more even than her words. It cut Robert Lyon to the heart.

"You suffered, and I never knew it."

"I never meant you to know."

"Why not?" He walked the room in great excitement. "I ought to have been told; it was cruel not to tell me. Suppose you had sunk under it; suppose you had died, or been driven to do what many a woman does for the sake of mere bread and a home—what your poor sister did— married. But I beg your pardon."

For Hilary had started up with her face all aglow.

"No," she cried; "no poverty would have sunk me as low as that. I might have starved, but I should never have married."

Robert Lyon looked at her, evidently uncomprehending, then said humbly, though rather formally,

"I beg your pardon once more. I had no right to allude to any thing of the kind."

Hilary replied not. It seemed as if now, close together, they were farther apart than when the Indian Seas rolled between them.

Mr. Lyon's brown cheek turned paler and paler; he pressed his lips hard together; they moved once or twice, but still he did not utter a word. At last, with a sort of desperate courage, and in a tone that Hilary had never heard from him in her life before, he said,

"Yes, I believe I have a right—the right that every man has when his whole happiness depends upon it, to ask you one question. You know every thing concerning me; you always have known; I meant that you should—I have taken the utmost care that you should. There is not a bit of my life that has not been as open to you as if—as if— But I know nothing whatever concerning you."

"What do you wish to know?" she faltered.

"Seven years is a long time. Are you free? I mean, are you engaged to be married?"

"No."

"Thank God!"

He dropped his head down between his hands and did not speak for a long time.

And then with difficulty—for it was always hard to him to speak out—he told her, at least he somehow made her understand, how he had loved her. No light fancy of sentimental youth, captivated by every fresh face it sees, putting upon each one the coloring of its own imagination, and adorning not what is, but what itself creates: no sudden, selfish, sensuous passion, caring only to attain its object, irrespective of reason, right, or conscience; but the strong, deep love of a just man, deliberately choosing one woman as the best woman out of all the world, and setting himself resolutely to win her. Battling for her sake with all hard fortune; keeping, for her sake, his heart pure from all the temptations of the world; never losing sight of her; watching over her so far as he could, consistently with the

sense of honor (or masculine pride—which was it? but Hilary forgave it, anyhow) which made him resolutely compel
himself to silence; holding her perfectly free, while he held
himself bound.   Bound by a faithfulness perfect as that of
the knights of old—asking nothing, and yet giving all.

Such was his love—this brave, plain-spoken, single-heart-
ed Scotsman.   Would that there were more such men and
more such love in the world!

Few women could have resisted it, certainly not Hilary,
especially with a little secret of her own lying perdu at the
bottom of her heart; that "sleeping angel" whence half
her strength and courage had come; the noble, faithful,
generous love of a good woman for a good man.   But this
secret Robert Lyon had evidently never guessed, or deemed
himself wholly unworthy of such a possession.

He took her hand at last, and held it firmly.

"And now that you know all, do you think in time—I'll
not hurry you—but in time, do you think I could make you
love me?"

She looked up in his face with her honest eyes.   Smiling
as they were, there was pathos in them; the sadness left
by those long years of hidden suffering, now forever ended.

"I have loved you all my life," said Hilary.

CHAPTER XXVI.

Let us linger a little over this chapter of happy love, so
sweet, so rare a thing.   Ay, most rare; though hundreds
continually meet, love, or fancy they do, engage themselves,
and marry; and hundreds more go through the same proceeding, with the slight difference of the love omitted—
Hamlet, with the part of Hamlet left out.   But the real
love, steady and true; tried in the balance, and not found
wanting; tested by time, silence, separation; by good and
ill fortune; by the natural and inevitable change which
years make in every character—this is the rarest thing to
be found on earth, and the most precious.

I do not say that all love is worthless which is not exactly this sort of love. There have been people who have succumbed instantly and permanently to some mysterious attraction, higher than all reasoning; the same which made Hilary "take an interest" in Robert Lyon's face at church, and made him, he afterward confessed, the very first time he gave Ascott a lesson in the parlor at Stowbury, say to himself, "If I did marry, I think I should like such a wife as that brown-eyed bit lassie." And there have been other people, who, choosing their partners from accidental circumstances, or from mean worldly motives, have found Providence kinder to them than they deserved, and settled down into happy, affectionate husbands and wives.

But none of these loves can possibly have the sweetness, the completeness of such a love as that between Hilary Leaf and Robert Lyon.

There was nothing very romantic about it. From the moment when Johanna entered the parlor, found them standing hand-in-hand at the fireside, and Hilary came forward and kissed her, and after a slight hesitation Robert did the same, the affair proceeded in most mill-pond fashion:

> "Unruffled by those cataracts and breaks,
> That humor interposed too often makes."

There were no lovers' quarrels; Robert Lyon had chosen that best blessing next to a good woman, a sweet-tempered woman; and there was no reason why they should quarrel more as lovers than they had done as friends. And, let it be said to the eternal honor of both, now, no more than in their friendship days, was there any of that hungry engrossment of each other's society, which is only another form of selfishness, and by which lovers so often make their own happy courting-time a season of never-to-be-forgotten bitterness to every body connected with them.

Johanna suffered a little; all people do when the new rights clash with the old ones; but she rarely betrayed it. She was exceedingly good: she saw her child happy, and she loved Robert Lyon dearly. He was very mindful of

N

her, very tender; and as Hilary still persisted in doing her daily duty in the shop, he spent more of his time with the elder sister than he did with the younger, and sometimes declared solemnly that if Hilary did not treat him well he intended to make an offer to Johanna!

Oh, the innumerable little jokes of those happy days! Oh, the long, quiet walks by the river-side, through the park, across Ilam Common—any where—it did not matter —the whole world looked lovely, even on the dullest winter day! Oh, the endless talks; the renewed mingling of two lives, which, though divided, had never been really apart, for neither had any thing to conceal—neither had ever loved any but the other.

Robert Lyon was, as I have said, a good deal changed, outwardly and inwardly. He had mixed much in society, taken an excellent position therein, and this had given him not only a more polished manner, but an air of decision and command, as of one used to be obeyed. There could not be the slightest doubt, as Johanna once laughingly told him, that he would always be "master in his own house."

But he was very gentle with his "little woman," as he called her. He would sit for hours at the "ingle-neuk"— how he did luxuriate in the English fires!—with Hilary on a footstool beside him, her arm resting on his knee, or her hand fast clasped in his. And sometimes, when Johanna went out of the room, he would stoop and gather her close to his heart. But I shall tell no tales; the world has no business with these sort of things.

Hilary was very shy of parading her happiness; she disliked any demonstrations thereof, even before Johanna. And when Miss Balquidder, who had, of course, been told of the engagement, came down one day expressly to see her "fortunate fellow-countryman," this Machiavelian little woman actually persuaded her lover to have an important engagement in London! She could not bear him to be "looked at."

"Ah! well, you must leave me, and I will miss you terribly, my dear," said the old Scotchwoman. "But it's an ill

wind that blows nobody good, and I have another young
lady quite ready to step into your shoes. When shall you
be married?"

" I don't know—hush! we'll talk another time," said Hilary, glancing at Johanna.

Miss Balquidder took the hint and was silent.

That important question was indeed beginning to weigh
heavily on Hilary's mind. She was fully aware of what
Mr. Lyon wished, and, indeed, expected; that when, the
business of the firm being settled, in six months hence he
returned to India, he should not return alone. When he
said this, she had never dared to answer, hardly even to
think. She let the peaceful present float on, day by day,
without recognizing such a thing as the future.

But this could not be always. It came to an end one
January afternoon, when he had returned from a second
absence in Liverpool. They were walking up Richmond
Hill. The sun had set frostily and red over the silver
curve of the Thames, and Venus, large and bright, was
shining like a great eye in the western sky. Hilary long
remembered exactly how every thing looked, even to the
very tree they stood under when Robert Lyon asked her
to fix definitely the day that she would marry him.

" Would she consent—there seemed no special reason to
the contrary—that it should be immediately? Or would
she like to remain with Johanna as she was, till just before
they sailed? He wished to be as good as possible to Johanna; still—"

And something in his manner impressed Hilary more than
ever before with the conviction of all she was to him; likewise all he was to her—more, much more than even a few
short weeks since. Then, intense as it was, the love had a
dream-like unreality; now it was close, homelike, familiar.
Instinctively she clung to his arm; she had become so used
to being Robert's darling now. She shivered as she thought
of the wide seas rolling between them; of the time when
she should look for him at the daily meal and daily fireside,
and find him no more.

"Robert, I want to talk to you about Johanna."

"I guess what it is," said he, smiling; "you would like her to go out to India with us. Certainly, if she chooses. I hope you did not suppose I should object?"

"No; but it is not that. She would not live six months in a hot climate: the doctor tells me so."

"You consulted him?"

"Yes, confidentially, without her knowing it. But I thought it right. I wanted to make quite sure before— before— Oh, Robert—"

The grief of her tone caused him to suspect what was coming. He started.

"You don't mean that? Oh no, you can not! My little woman—my own little woman—she could not be so unkind."

Hilary turned sick at heart. The dim landscape, the bright sky, seemed to mingle and dance before her, and Venus to stare at her with a piercing, threatening, baleful lustre.

"Robert, let me sit down on the bench, and sit you beside me. It is too dark for people to notice us, and we shall not be very cold."

"No, my darling;" and he slipped his plaid round her shoulders, and his arm with it.

She looked up pitifully. "Don't be vexed with me, Robert, dear; I have thought it all over; weighed it on every side; nights and nights I have been awake pondering what was right to do, and it always comes to the same thing."

"What?"

"It's the old story," she answered, with a feeble smile. "'I canna leave my minnie.' There is nobody in the world to take care of Johanna but me, not even Elizabeth, who is engrossed in little Henry. If I left her I am sure it would kill her. And she can not come with me. Dear!" (the only fond name she ever called him) "for these three years—you say it need only be three years—you will have to go back to India alone!"

Robert Lyon was a very good man, but he was only a

man, not an angel; and though he made comparatively little show of it, he was a man very deeply in love. With
that jealous tenacity over his treasure, hardly blamable,
since the love is worth little which does not wish to have
its object "all to itself," he had, I am afraid, contemplated,
not without pleasure, the carrying off of Hilary to his Indian home; and it had cost him something to propose that
Johanna should go too. He was very fond of Johanna;
still—

If I tell what followed, will it forever lower Robert Lyon
in the estimation of all readers? He said, coldly, "As you
please, Hilary;" rose up, and never spoke another word till
they reached home.

It was the first dull tea-table they had ever known; the
first time Hilary had ever looked at that dear face, and seen
an expression there which made her look away again. He
did not sulk; he was too gentlemanly for that; he even ex-
erted himself to make the meal pass pleasantly as usual;
but he was evidently deeply wounded — nay, more, displeased. The strong, stern man's nature within him had
rebelled; the sweetness had gone out of his face, and something had come into it which the very best of men have
sometimes: alas for the woman who can not understand
and put up with it!

I am not going to preach the doctrine of tyrants and
slaves; but when two walk together they *must* be agreed,
or if by any chance they are not agreed, one *must* yield.
It may not always be the weaker, or in weakness may lie
the chiefest strength; but it must be one or other of the
two who has to be the first to give way; and, save in very
exceptional cases, it is, and it ought to be, the woman.
God's law and nature's, which is also God's, ordains this;
instinct teaches it; Christianity enforces it.

Will it inflict a death-blow upon any admiration she may
have excited, this brave little Hilary, who fought through
the world by herself; who did not shrink from traversing
London streets alone at seemly and unseemly hours; from
going into sponging-houses and debtors' prisons; from

earning her own livelihood, even in a shop—if I confess
that Robert Lyon, being angry with her, justly or unjust-
ly, and she, looking upon him as her future husband, her
"lord and master" if you will, whom she would one day
promise, and intended literally to "obey"—she thought it
her duty—not only her pleasure, but her *duty*—to be the
first to make reconciliation between them? ay, and at every sacrifice except that of principle.

And I am afraid, in spite of all that "strong-minded"
women may preach to the contrary, that all good women
will have to do this to all men who stand in any close relation toward them, whether fathers, husbands, brothers, or
lovers, if they wish to preserve peace, and love, and holy
domestic influence; and that so it must be to the end of
time.

Miss Leaf might have discovered that something was
amiss, but she was too wise to take any notice, and being
more than usually feeble that day, immediately after tea
she went to lie down. When Hilary followed her, arranged her pillows, and covered her up, Johanna drew her
child's face close to her and whispered,

"That will do, love. Don't stay with me. I would not
keep you from Robert on any account."

Hilary all but broke down; and yet the words made her
stronger, firmer; set more clearly before her the solemn
duty which young folks in love are so apt to forget, that
there can be no blessing on the new tie if for any thing
short of inevitable necessity they let go one link of the
old.

Yet Robert— It was such a new and dreadful feeling
to be standing outside the door and shrink from going in
to him; to see him rise up formally, saying, "Perhaps he
had better leave," and have to answer with equal formality, "Not unless you are obliged;" and for him then, with
a shallow pretense of being at ease, to take up a book and
offer to read aloud to her while she worked — he who
used always to set his face strongly against all sewing
of evenings, because it deprived him temporarily of the

sweet eyes and the little soft hand—oh, it was hard—hard!

Nevertheless, she sat still and tried to listen; but the words went in at one ear and out at the other—she retained nothing. By-and-by her throat began to swell, and she could not see her needle and thread. Yet still he went on reading. It was only when, by some blessed chance, turning to reach a paper-cutter, he caught sight of her, that he closed the book and looked discomposed—not softened, only discomposed.

Who shall be first to speak? Who shall catch the passing angel's wing? One minute, and it may have passed over.

I am not apologizing for Hilary the least in the world. I do not know even if she considered whether it was her place or Robert's to make the first advance. Indeed, I fear she did not consider it at all, but just acted upon impulse, because it was so cruel, so heart-breaking, to be at variance with him. But if she had considered it I doubt not she would have done from duty exactly what she did by instinct—crept up to him as he sat at the fireside, and laid her little hand on his.

"Robert, what makes you so angry with me still?"

"Not angry; I have no right to be."

"Yes, you would have if I had really done wrong. Have I?"

"You must judge for yourself. For me—I thought you loved me better than I find you do, and I made a mistake; that is all."

Ay, he had made a mistake, but it was not that one. It was the other mistake that men continually make about women; they can not understand that love is not worth having, that it is not love at all, but merely a selfish carrying out of selfish desires, if it blinds us to any other duty, or blunts in us any other sacred tenderness. They can not see how she who is false in one relation may be false in another; and that, true as human nature's truth, ay, and often fulfilling itself, is Brabantio's ominous warning to Othello—

"Look to her, Moor! have a good eye to see;
She has deceived her father, and may thee."

.Perhaps, as soon as he had said the bitter word, Mr. Ly-on was sorry; anyhow, the soft answer which followed it thrilled through every nerve of the strong-willed man—a man not easily made angry, but when he was, very hard to move.

"Robert, will you listen to me for two minutes?"

"For as long as you like, only you must not expect me to agree with you. You can not suppose I shall say it is right for you to forsake me."

"I forsake you? oh, Robert!"

Words are not always the wisest arguments. His "lit-tle woman" crept closer, and laid her head on his breast; he clasped her convulsively.

"Oh, Hilary, how could you wound me so?"

And, in lieu of the discussion, a long silence brooded over the fireside—the silence of exceeding love.

"Now, Robert, may I talk to you?"

"Yes. Preach away, my little conscience!"

"It shall not be preaching, and it is not altogether for conscience," said she, smiling. "You would not like me to tell you I did not *love* Johanna?"

"Certainly not. I love her very much myself, only I pre-fer you, as is natural. Apparently you do *not* prefer me, which may be also natural."

"Robert!"

There are times when a laugh is better than a reproach; and something else, which need not be more particularly explained, is safer than either. It is possible Hilary tried the experiment, and then resumed her "say."

"Now, Robert, put yourself in my place, and try to think for me. I have been Johanna's child for thirty years; she is entirely dependent upon me. Her health is feeble; every year of her life is at least doubtful. If she lost me I think she would never live out the next three years. You would not like that?"

"No."

"In all divided duties like this, somebody must suffer; the question is, which can suffer best. She is old and frail, we are young; she is alone, we are two; she never had any happiness in her life except perhaps me; and we—oh, how happy we are! I think, Robert, it would be better for us to suffer than poor Johanna."

"You little Jesuit," he said; but the higher nature of the man was roused; he was no longer angry.

"It is only for a short time, remember—only three years."

"And how can I do without you for three years?"

"Yes, Robert, you can." And she put her arms round his neck, and looked at him eye to eye. "You know I am your very own, a piece of yourself, as it were; that when I let you go it is like tearing myself from myself; yet I can bear it rather than do, or let you do, in the smallest degree, a thing which is not right."

Robert Lyon was not a man of many words; but he had the rare faculty of seeing a case clearly, without reference to himself, and of putting it clearly also, when necessary.

"It seems to me, Hilary, that this is hardly a matter of abstract right or wrong, or a good deal might be argued on my side the subject. It is more a case of personal conscience. The two are not always identical, though they look so at first; but they both come to the same result."

"And that is—"

"If my little woman thinks it right to act as she does, I also think it right to let her. And let this be the law of our married life, if we ever are married," and he sighed, "that when we differ each should respect the other's conscience, and do right, in the truest sense, by allowing the other to do the same."

"Oh, Robert! how good you are."

"So these two, an hour after, met Johanna with cheerful faces, and she never knew how much both had sacrificed for her sake. Once only, when she was for a few minutes absent from the parlor, did Robert Lyon renew the subject, to suggest a medium course.

But Hilary resolutely refused. Not that she doubted

N 2

him—she doubted herself. She knew quite well, by the pang that darted through her like a shaft of ice, as she felt his warm arm round her, and thought of the time when she would feel it no more, that, after she had been Robert Lyon's happy wife for three months, to let him go to India without her would be simply and utterly impossible.

Fast fled the months; they dwindled into weeks, and then into days. I shall not enlarge upon this time. Now, when the ends of the world are drawn together, and every family has one or more relatives abroad, a grief like Hilary's has become so common that nearly every one can, in degree, understand it. How bitter such partings are, how much they take out of the brief span of mortal life, and, therefore, how far they are justifiable for any thing short of absolute necessity, Heaven knows.

In this case it was an absolute necessity. Robert Lyon's position in "our firm," with which he identified himself with the natural pride of a man who has diligently worked his way up to fortune, was such that he could not, without sacrificing his future prospects, and likewise what he felt to be a point of honor, refuse to go back to Bombay until such time as his senior partner's son, the young fellow whom he had "coached" in Hindostanee, and nursed through a fever years ago, could conveniently take his place abroad.

"Of course," he said, explaining this to Hilary and her sister, "accidental circumstances might occur to cause my return home before the three years were out, but the act must be none of mine; I must do my duty."

"Yes, you must," answered Hilary, with a gleam lighting up her eyes. She loved so in him this one great principle of his life—the back-bone of it, as it were—duty before all things.

Johanna asked no questions. Once she had inquired, with a tremulous, hardly concealed alarm, whether Robert wished to take Hilary back with him, and Hilary had kissed her, smilingly, saying, "No, that was impossible." Afterward the subject was never revived.

And so these two lovers, both stern in what they thought their duty, went on silently together to the last day of parting.

It was almost as quiet a day as that never-to-be-forgotten Sunday at Stowbury. They went a long walk together, in the course of which Mr. Lyon forced her to agree to what hitherto she had steadfastly resisted, that she and Johanna should accept from him enough, in addition to their own fifty pounds a year, to enable them to live comfortably without her working any more.

"Are you ashamed of my working?" she asked, with something between a tear and a smile. "Sometimes I used to be afraid you would think the less of me because circumstances made me an independent woman, earning my own bread. Do you?"

"My darling! no. I am proud of her. But she must never work any more. Johanna says right; it is a man's place, and not a woman's. I will not allow it."

When he spoke in that tone Hilary always submitted.

He told her another thing while arranging with her all the business part of their concerns, and to reconcile her to this partial dependence upon him, which, he urged, was only forestalling his rights—that, before he first quitted England seven years ago, he had made his will, leaving her, if still unmarried, his sole heir and legatee—indeed, in exactly the position that she would have been had she been his wife.

"This will exists still, so that in any case you are safe. No farther poverty can ever befall my Hilary."

His—his own—Robert Lyon's own. Her sense of this was so strong that it took away the sharpness of the parting; made her feel, up to the very last minute, when she clung to him—was pressed close to him—heart to heart and lip to lip—for a space that seemed half a lifetime of mixed anguish and joy—that he was not really going; that, somehow or other, next day or next week he would be back again, as in his frequent reappearances, exactly as before.

When he was really gone—when, as she sat with her tearless eyes fixed on the closed door, Johanna softly touched her, saying, "My child!" then Hilary learned it all.

The next twenty-four hours will hardly bear being written about. Most people know what it is to miss the face out of the house—the life out of the heart. To come and go, to eat and drink, to lie down and rise, and find all things the same, and gradually to recognize that it must be the same, indefinitely, perhaps always. To be met continually by small trifles—a dropped glove, a book, a scrap of handwriting that yesterday would have been thrown into the fire, but to-day is picked up and kept as a relic; and at times, bursting through the quietness which must be gained, or at least assumed, the cruel craving for one word more—one kiss more—for only one five minutes of the eternally ended yesterday!

All this hundreds have gone through; so did Hilary. She said afterward it was good for her that she did; it would make her feel for others in a way she had never felt before. Also, because it taught her that such a heart-break can be borne and lived through when help is sought where only real help can be found; and where, when reason fails, and those who, striving to do right irrespective of the consequences, cry out against their torments, and wonder why they should be made so to suffer, child-like faith comes to their rescue. For, let us have all the philosophy at our fingers' ends, what are we but children? We know not what a day may bring forth. All wisdom resolves itself into the simple hymn which we learned when we were young:

> "Deep in unfathomable mines
>   Of never-failing skill,
> He treasures up His vast designs,
>   And works His sovereign will.
>
> "Blind unbelief is sure to err,
>   And scan His work in vain:
> God is His own interpreter,
>   And He will make it plain."

The night after Robert Lyon left, Hilary and Johanna were sitting together in their parlor. Hilary had been writing a long letter to Miss Balquidder, explaining that she would now give up, in favor of the other young lady, or any other of the many to whom it would be a blessing, her position in the shop; but that she hoped still to help her—Miss Balquidder—in any way she could point out that would be useful to others. She wished, in her humble way, as a sort of thank-offering from one who had passed through the waves and been landed safe ashore, to help those who were still struggling, as she herself had struggled once. She desired, as far as in her lay, to be Miss Balquidder's "right hand" till Mr. Lyon came home.

This letter she read aloud to Johanna, whose failing eyesight refused all candle-light occupation, and then came and sat beside her in silence. She felt terribly worn and weary, but she was very quiet now.

"We must go to bed early," was all she said.

"Yes, my child."

And Johanna smoothed her hair in the old, fond way, making no attempt to console her, but only to love her—always the safest consolation. And Hilary was thankful that never, even in her sharpest agonies of grief, had she betrayed that secret which would have made her sister's life miserable, have blotted out the thirty years of motherly love, and caused the other love to rise up like a cloud between her and it, never to be lifted until Johanna sank into the possibly not far-off grave.

"No, no," she thought to herself, as she looked on that frail old face, which even the secondary grief of this last week seemed to have made frailer and older. "No, it is better as it is; I believe I did right. The end will show."

The end was nearer than she thought. So, sometimes —not often, lest self-sacrifice should become a less holy thing than it is—Providence accepts the will for the act, and makes the latter needless.

There was a sudden knock at the hall door.

"It is the young people coming in to supper."

"It's not," said Hilary, starting up: "it's not their knock. It is—"

She never finished the sentence, for she was sobbing in Robert Lyon's arms.

"What does it all mean?" cried the bewildered Johanna, of whom, I must confess, for once nobody took the least notice.

It meant that, by one of these strange accidents, as we call them, which in a moment alter the whole current of things, the senior partner had suddenly died, and his son, not being qualified to take his place in the Liverpool house, had to go out to India instead of Robert Lyon, who would now remain permanently, as the third senior partner, in England.

This news had met him at Southampton. He had gone thence direct to Liverpool, arranged affairs so far as was possible, and returned, traveling without an hour's intermission, to tell his own tidings, as was best — or as he thought it was.

Perhaps at the core of his heart lurked the desire to come suddenly back, as, it is said, if the absent or the dead could come, they would find all things changed: the place filled up in home and hearth — no face of welcome — no heart leaping to heart in the ecstasy of reunion.

"Well, if Robert Lyon had any misgivings—and being a man, and in love, perhaps he had—they were ended now.

"Is she glad to see me?" was all he could find to say when, Johanna having considerately vanished, he might have talked as much as he pleased.

Hilary's only answer was a little, low laugh of inexpressible content.

He lifted up between his hands the sweet face, neither so young nor so pretty as it had been, but oh! so sweet, with the sweetness that long outlives beauty—a face that a man might look on all his lifetime and never tire of—so infinitely loving, so infinitely true! And he knew it was his wife's face, to shine upon him day by day, and year by year, till it faded into old age—beautiful and beloved even then. All the strong nature of the man gave way; he wept almost like a child in his " little woman's" arms.

Let us leave them there, by that peaceful fireside—these two, who are to sit by one fireside as long as they live. Of their further fortune we know nothing—nor do they themselves—except the one fact, in itself joy enough for any mortal cup to hold, that it will be shared together. Two at the hearth, two abroad; two to labor, two to re joice; or, if so it must be, two to weep, and two to com- fort one another; the man to be the head of the woman, and the woman the heart of the man. This is the ordina- tion of God; this is the perfect life; none the less perfect that so many fall short of it.

So let us bid them good-by: Robert Lyon and Hilary Leaf, " Good-by; God be with ye !" for we shall see them no more.

CHAPTER XXVII.

ELIZABETH stood at the nursery window, pointing out to little Henry how the lilacs and laburnums were coming into flower in the square below, and speculating with him whether the tribes of sparrows which they had fed all win- ter from the mignonnette boxes on the window-sill would be building nests in the tall trees of Russell Square; for she wished, with her great aversion to London, to make her nursling as far as possible a " country" child.

Master Henry Leaf Ascott was by no means little now. He would run about on his tottering fat legs, and he could say "Mammy Lizzie," also " Pa-pa," as had been carefully taught him by his conscientious nurse. At which papa had been at first excessively surprised, then gratified, and had at last taken kindly to the appellation as a matter of course.

It inaugurated a new era in Peter Ascott's life. At first twice a week, and then every day, he sent up for " Master Ascott" to keep him company at dessert; he then changed his dinner-hour from half past six to five, because Eliza-

beth, with her stern sacrifice of every thing to the child's
good, had suggested to him, humbly but firmly, that late
hours kept little Henry too long out of his bed.   He gave
up his bottle of port and his after-dinner sleep, and took
to making water-lilies and caterpillars out of oranges, and
boats out of walnut-shells, for his boy's special edification.
Sometimes when, at half past six, Elizabeth, punctual as
clock-work, knocked at the dining-room door, she heard
father and son laughing together in a most jovial manner,
though the decanters were in their places and the wine-
glasses untouched.

And even after the child disappeared the butler declared
that master usually took quietly to his newspaper, or rang
for his tea, or perhaps dozed harmlessly in his chair till
bedtime.

I do not allege that Peter Ascott was miraculously
changed; people do not change, especially at his age; ex-
ternally he was still the same pompous, overbearing, coarse
man, with whom, no doubt, his son would have a tolerably sore bargain in years to come.   But still the child
had touched a soft corner in his heart, the one soft corner
which in his youth had yielded to the beauty of Miss Selina Leaf, and the old fellow was a better old fellow than
he had once been.   Probably, with care, he might be for
the rest of his life at least manageable.

Elizabeth hoped so, for his boy's sake; and, little as she
liked him, she tried to conquer her antipathy as much as
she could.   She always took care to treat him with extreme respect, and to bring up little Henry to do the
same.   And, as often happens, Mr. Ascott began gradually
to comport himself in a manner deserving of respect.   He
ceased his oaths and his coarse language; seldom flew into
a passion; and last, not least, the butler avouched that
master hardly ever went to bed "muzzy" now.   Toward
all his domestics, and especially to his son's nurse, he behaved himself more like a master and less like a tyrant,
so that the establishment at Russell Square went on in a
way more peaceful than had ever been known before.

There was no talk of his giving it a new mistress; he seemed to have had enough of matrimony. Of his late wife he never spoke; whether he loved her or not, whether he had regretted her or not, the love and regret were now alike ended.

Poor Selina! It was Elizabeth only, who, with a sacred sense of duty, occasionally talked to little Henry about "mamma up there"—pointing to the blank bit of blue sky over the trees of Russell Square, and hoped in time to make him understand something about her, and how she had loved him, her "baby." This love—the only beautiful emotion her life had known, was the one fragment that remained of it after her death, the one remembrance she left to her child.

Little Henry was not in the least like her, nor yet like his father. He took after some forgotten type, some past generation of either family, which reappeared in this as something new. To Elizabeth he was a perfect revelation of beauty and infantile fascination. He filled up every corner of her heart. She grew fat and flourishing, even cheerful; so cheerful that she bore with equanimity the parting with her dear Miss Hilary, who went away in glory and happiness as Mrs. Robert Lyon, to live in Liverpool, and Miss Leaf with her. Thus both Elizabeth's youthful dreams ended in nothing, and it was more than probable that for the future, their lives and hers being so widely apart, she would see very little of her beloved mistresses any more. But they had done their work in her and for her, and it had borne fruit a hundred-fold, and would still.

"I know you will take care of this child—he is the hope of the family," said Miss Leaf, when she was giving her last kiss to little Henry. "I could not bear to leave him if I were not leaving him with you."

And Elizabeth had taken her charge proudly in her arms, knowing she was trusted, and inwardly vowing to be worthy of that trust.

Another dream was likewise ended—so completely that she sometimes wondered if it was ever real; whether she had ever been a happy girl, looking forward as girls do to wifehood and motherhood, or whether she had not been always the staid middle-aged person she was now, whom nobody ever suspected of any such things.

She had been once back to her old home, to settle her mother comfortably upon a weekly allowance, to 'prentice her little brother, to see one sister married, and the other sent off to Liverpool to be servant to Mrs. Lyon. While at Stowbury, she had heard by chance of Tom Cliffe's passing through the town as a Chartist lecturer, or something of the sort, with his pretty, showy London wife, who, when he brought her there, had looked down rather contemptuously upon the street where Tom was born.

This was all Elizabeth knew about them. They, too, had passed from her life as phases of keen joy and keener sorrow do pass, like a dream and the shadows of a dream. It may be, life itself will seem at the end to be nothing more.

But Elizabeth Hand's love-story was not so to end.

One morning, the same morning when she had been pointing out the lilacs to little Henry, and now came in from the square with a branch of them in her hand, the postman gave her a letter, the handwriting of which made her start as if it had been a visitation from the dead.

"Mammy Lizzie, Mammy Lizzie!" cried little Henry, plucking at her gown, but for once his nurse did not notice him. She stood on the door-step, trembling violently; at length she put the letter into her pocket, lifted the child, and got up stairs somehow. When she had settled her charge to his midday sleep, then, and not till then, did she take out and read the few lines, which, though written on shabby paper, and with more than one blot, were so like—yet so terribly unlike—Tom's caligraphy of old:

"Dear Elizabeth,—I have no right to ask any kindness of you; but if you would like to see an old friend alive, I wish you would come and see me. I have been long of asking you, lest you might fancy I wanted to get something out of you; for I'm as poor as a rat; and once lately

I saw you, looking so well and well-to-do. But it was the same kind old face, and I should like to get one kind look from it before I go where I sha'n't want any kindness from any body. However, do just as you choose.

"Yours affectionately,   T. CLIFFE.

"Underneath is my address."

It was in one of those wretched nooks in Westminster, now swept away by Victoria Street and other improvements. Elizabeth happened to have read about it in one of the many charitable pamphlets, reports, etc., which were sent continually to the wealthy Mr. Ascott, and which he sent down stairs to light fires with. What must not poor Tom have sunk to before he had come to live there? His letter was like a cry out of the depths, and the voice was that of her youth, her first love.

Is any woman ever deaf to that? The love may have died a natural death: many first loves do: a riper, completer, happier love may have come in its place; but there must be something unnatural about the woman, and man likewise, who can ever quite forget it—the dew of their youth—the beauty of their dawn.

"Poor Tom! poor Tom!" sighed Elizabeth; "my own poor Tom!"

She forgot Esther, either from Tom's not mentioning her, or in the strong return to old times which his letter produced; forgot her for the time being as completely as if she had never existed. Even when the recollection came it made little difference. The sharp jealousy, the dislike and contempt, had all calmed down; she thought she could now see Tom's wife as any other woman—especially if, as the letter indicated, they were so very poor and miserable.

Possibly Esther had suggested writing it? Perhaps, though Tom did not, Esther did "want to get something out of her"—Elizabeth Hand, who was known to have large wages, and to be altogether a thriving person? Well, it mattered little. The one fact remained: Tom was in distress; Tom needed her; she must go.

Her only leisure time was of an evening, after Henry

was in bed. The intervening hours, especially the last one, when the child was down stairs with his father, calmed her; subdued the tumult of old remembrances that came surging up and beating at the long-shut door of her heart. When her boy returned, leaping and laughing, and playing all sorts of tricks as she put him to bed, she could smile too. And when, kneeling beside her in his pretty white night-gown, he stammered through the prayer she had thought it right to begin to teach him, though of course he was too young to understand it, the words "Thy will be done;" "Forgive us our trespasses, as we forgive those who trespass against us;" and, lastly, "Lead us not into temptation, but deliver us from evil," struck home to his nurse's inmost soul.

"Mammy—Mammy Lizzie's 'tying!"

Yes, she was crying, but it did her good. She was able to kiss her little boy, who slept like a top in five minutes; then she took off her good silk gown, and dressed herself soberly and decently, but so that people should not suspect, in that low and dangerous neighborhood, the sovereigns that she carried in an under-pocket, ready to use as occasion required. Thus equipped, she started without a minute's delay for Tom's lodging.

It was poorer than even she expected. One attic room, bare almost as when it was built. No chimney or grate, no furniture except a box which served as both table and chair; and a heap of straw, with a blanket thrown over it. The only comfort about it was that it was clean: Tom's innate sense of refinement had abided with him to the last.

Elizabeth had time to make all these observations, for Tom was out—gone, the landlady said, to the druggist's shop round the corner.

"He's very bad, ma'am," added the woman, civilly, probably led thereto by Elizabeth's respectable appearance, and the cab in which she had come, lest she should lose a minute's time. "Can't last long; and Lord knows who's to bury him."

With that sentence knelling in her ears Elizabeth waited till she heard the short cough and the hard breathing of some one toiling heavily up the stair.

Tom—Tom himself. But oh! so altered; with every bit of youth gone out of him; with death written on every line of his haggard face, the death he had once prognosticated with a sentimental pleasure, but which now had come upon him in all its ghastly reality.

He was in the last stage of consumption. The disease was latent in his family, Elizabeth knew: she had known it when she had belonged to him, and fondly thought that, as his wife, her incessant care might save him from it; but nothing could save him now.

"Who's that?" said he, in his own sharp, fretful voice.

"Me, Tom. But don't speak. Sit down till your cough's over."

Tom grasped her hand as she stood by him, but he made no farther demonstration, nor used any expression of gratitude. He seemed far too ill. Sick people are always absorbed in the sad present; they seldom trouble themselves much about the past. Only there was something in the way Tom clung to her hand, helplessly, imploringly, that moved the inmost heart of Elizabeth.

"I'm very bad, you see. This cough—oh, it shakes me dreadfully, especially of nights."

"Have you any doctor?"

"The druggist close by, or rather the druggist's shopman. He's a very kind young fellow, from our county, I fancy, for he asked me once if I wasn't a Stowbury man; and ever since he has doctored me for nothing, and given me a shilling too, now and then, when I've been a'most clemmed to death in the winter."

"Oh, Tom, why didn't you write to me before? Have you actually wanted food?"

"Yes, many a time. I've been out of work this twelve-month."

"But Esther?"

"Who?" screamed Tom.

"Your wife."

"My wife? I've got none! She spent every thing till I fell ill, and then she met a fellow with lots o' money. Curse her!"

The fury with which he spoke shook him all over, and sent him into another violent fit of coughing, out of which he revived by degrees, but in a state of such complete exhaustion that Elizabeth hazarded no more questions. He must evidently be dealt with exactly like a child.

She made up her mind in her own silent way, as indeed she had done ever since she came into the room.

"Lie down, Tom, and keep yourself quiet for a little. I'll be back as soon as I can—back with something to do you good. You won't object?"

"No, no; you can do any thing you like with me. You always could."

Elizabeth groped her way down stairs strangely calm and self-possessed. There was need. Tom, dying, had come to her as his sole support and consolation—thrown himself helplessly upon her, never doubting either her will or her power to help him. Neither must fail. The inexplicable woman's strength, sometimes found in the very gentlest, quietest, and apparently the weakest character, nerved her now.

She went up and down street after street, looking for lodgings, till the evening darkened, and the Abbey towers rose grimly against the summer sky. Then she crossed over Westminster Bridge, and on a little street on the Surrey side she found what she wanted—a decent room, half sitting, half bedroom, with what looked like a decent landlady. There was no time to make many inquiries; any thing was better than to leave Tom another night w'.ere he was.

She paid a week's rent in advance; bought firing and provisions; every thing she could think of to make him comfortable, and then she went to fetch him in a cab.

The sick man offered no resistance; indeed, he hardly seemed to know what she was doing with him. She discovered the cause of this half-insensibility when, in making a bundle of his few clothes, she found a packet labeled "opium."

"Don't take it from me," he said, pitifully. "It's the only comfort I have."

But when he found himself in the cheerful room, with the fire blazing and the tea laid out, he woke up like a person out of a bad dream.

"Oh, Elizabeth, I'm so comfortable!"

Elizabeth could have wept.

Whether the wholesome food and drink revived him, or whether it was one of the sudden flashes of life that often occur in consumptive patients, but he seemed really better, and began to talk, telling Elizabeth about his long illness, and saying over and over again how very kind the druggist's young man had been to him.

"I'm sure he's a gentleman, though he has come down in the world; for, as he says, 'Misery makes a man acquainted with strange bedfellows, and takes the nonsense out of him.' I think so too; and if ever I get better, I don't mean to go about the country speaking against born gentlefolks any more. They're much of a muchness as ourselves—bad and good; a little of all sorts; the same flesh and blood as we are. Aren't they, Elizabeth?"

"I suppose so."

"And there's another thing I mean to do—I mean to try and be good like you. Many a night, when I've lain on that straw, and thought I was dying, I've remembered you and all the things you used to say to me. You are a good woman; there never was a better."

Elizabeth smiled, a faint, rather sad smile; for, as she was washing up the tea-things, she had noticed Tom's voice grow feebler, and his features sharper and more wan.

"I'm very tired," he said. "I'm afraid to go to bed, I get such wretched nights; but I think, if I lay down in my clothes, I could go to sleep."

Elizabeth helped him to the small pallet, shook his pillow, and covered him up as if he had been a child.

"You're very good to me," he said, and looked up at

her—Tom's bright, fond look of years ago. But it passed away in a moment, and he closed his eyes, saying he was so terribly tired.

"Then I'll bid you good-by, for I ought to have been at home by now. You'll take care of yourself, Tom, and I'll come and see you again the very first hour I can be spared. And if you want me you'll send to me at once? You know where?"

"I will," said Tom. "It's the same house, isn't it, in Russell Square?"

"Yes." And they were both silent.

After a minute Tom asked, in a troubled voice,

"Have you forgiven me?"

"Yes, Tom, quite."

"Won't you give me one kiss, Elizabeth?"

She turned away. She did not mean to be hard, but somehow she could not kiss Esther's husband.

"Ah! well, it's all the same. Good-by!"

"Good-by, Tom."

But as she stood at the door, and looked back at him lying with his eyes shut, and as white as if he were dead, Elizabeth's heart melted. He was her Tom, her own Tom, of whom she had been so fond, so proud; whose future she had joyfully anticipated long before she thought of herself as mixed up with it; and he was dying—dying at four-and-twenty; passing away to the other world, where, perhaps, she might meet him yet, with no cruel Esther between.

"Tom," she said, and knelt beside him, "Tom, I didn't mean to vex you. I'll try to be as good as a sister to you. I'll never forsake you as long as you live."

"I know you never will."

"Good-by, then, for to-night."

And she did kiss him, mouth to mouth, quietly and tenderly. She was so glad of it afterward.

It was late enough when she reached Russell Square; but nobody ever questioned the proceedings of Mrs. Hand, who was a privileged person. She crept in beside her little Henry, and as the child turned in his sleep and put his arms about her neck, she clasped him tight, and thought there was still something to live for in this weary world.

All night she thought over what best could be done for Tom. Though she never deceived herself for a moment as to his state, still she thought, with care and proper nursing, he might live a few months, especially if she could get him into the Consumption Hospital, newly started in Chelsea, of which she was aware Mr. Ascott—who dearly liked to see his name in a charity-list—was one of the governors.

There was no time to be lost; she determined to speak to her master at once.

The time she chose was when she brought down little Henry, who was now always expected to appear, and say, "Dood morning, papa," before Mr. Ascott went into the city.

As they stood, the boy laughing in his father's face, and the father beaming all over with delight, the bitter, almost fierce thought smote Elizabeth, Why should Peter Ascott be standing there fat and flourishing, and poor Tom dying? It made her bold to ask the only favor she ever had asked of the master whom she did not care for, and to whom she had done her duty simply as duty, without, until lately, one fragment of respect.

"Sir, if you please, might I speak with you a minute before you go out?"

"Certainly, Mrs. Hand. Any thing about Master Henry? Or perhaps yourself? You want more wages? Very well. I shall be glad, in any reasonable way, to show my satisfaction at the manner in which you bring up my son."

"Thank you, sir," said Elizabeth, courtesying. "But it is not that."

And in the briefest language she could find she explained what it was.

Mr. Ascott knitted his brows and looked important. He never scattered his benefits with a silent hand, and he dearly liked to create difficulties, if only to show how he could smooth them down.

O

"To get a patient admitted at the Consumptive Hospital is, you should be aware, no easy matter, until the building at Queen's Elm is complete. But I flatter myself I have influence. I have subscribed a deal of money. Possibly the person may be got in in time. Who did you say he was?"

"Thomas Cliffe. He married one of the servants here, Esther—"

"Oh, don't trouble yourself about the name; I shouldn't recollect it. The housekeeper might. Why didn't his wife apply to the housekeeper?"

The careless question seemed hardly to expect an answer, and Elizabeth gave none. She could not bear to make public Tom's misery and Esther's shame.

"And you say he is a Stowbury man? That is certainly a claim. I always feel bound, somewhat as a member of Parliament might be, to do my best for any one belonging to my native town. So be satisfied, Mrs. Hand; consider the thing settled."

And he was going away; but time being of such great moment, Elizabeth ventured to detain him till he had written the letter of recommendation, and found out what days the application for admittance could be received. He did it very patiently, and even took out his purse and laid a sovereign on the top of the letter.

"I suppose the man is poor; you can use this for his benefit."

"There is no need, thank you, sir," said Elizabeth, putting it gently aside. She could not bear that Tom should accept any body's money but her own.

At her first spare moment she wrote him a long letter explaining what she had done, and appointing the next day but one, the earliest possible, for taking him out to Chelsea herself. If he objected to the plan he was to write and say so; but she urged him as strongly as she could not to let slip this opportunity of obtaining good nursing and first-rate medical care.

Many times during the day the thought of Tom alone

in his one room—comfortable though it was, and though she had begged the landlady to see that he wanted nothing—came across her with a sudden pang. His face, feebly lifted up from the pillow, with its last affectionate smile, the sound of his cough as she stood listening outside on the stair-head, haunted her all through that sunshiny June day; and mingled with it came ghostly visions of that other day in June—her happy Whitsun holiday—her first and her last.

No letter coming from Tom on the appointed morning, she left Master Harry in the charge of the house-maid, who was very fond of him—as indeed he bade fair to be spoiled by the whole establishment at Russell Square—and went down to Westminster.

There was a long day before her, so she took a minute's breathing space on Westminster Bridge, and watched the great current of London life ebbing and flowing—life on the river and life on the shore; every body so busy, and active, and bright.

"Poor Tom! poor Tom!" she sighed, and wondered whether his ruined life would ever come to any happy ending except death.

She hurried on, and soon found the street where she had taken his lodging. At the corner of it was, as is too usual in London streets, a public house, about which more than the usual number of disreputable idlers were hanging. There were also one or two policemen, who were ordering the little crowd to give way to a group of twelve men, coming out.

"What is that?" asked Elizabeth.

"Coroner's inquest; jury proceeding to view the body."

Elizabeth, who had never come into contact with any thing of the sort, stood aside with a sense of awe, to let the little procession pass, and then followed it up the street.

It stopped—oh no! not at that door! But it was; there was no mistaking the number, nor the drawn-down blind in the upper room—Tom's room.

"Who is dead?" she asked, in a whisper that made the policeman stare.

"Oh! nobody particular; a young man, found dead in his bed; supposed to be a case of consumption; verdict will probably be, 'Died by the visitation of God.'"

Ay, that familiar phrase, our English law's solemn recognition of our national religious feeling, was true here. God had "visited" poor Tom; he suffered no more.

Elizabeth leaned against the doorway, and saw the twelve jurymen go up stairs with a clatter of feet, and come down again, one after the other, less noiselessly, and some of them looking grave. Nobody took any notice of her until the lodging-house mistress appeared.

"Oh, here she is, gentlemen. This is the young woman as saw him last alive. She'll give her evidence. She'll tell you I'm not a bit to blame."

And, pulling Elizabeth after her, the landlady burst into a torrent of explanation—how she had done her very best for the poor fellow; how she had listened at his door several times during the first day, and heard him cough, that is, she thought she had, but toward night all was so very quiet; and there having come a letter by post, she thought she would take it up to him.

"And I went in, gentlemen, and I declare, upon my oath, I found him lying just as he is now, and as cold as a stone."

"Let me pass; I'm a doctor," said somebody behind; a young man, very shabbily dressed, with a large beard. He pushed aside the landlady and Elizabeth till he saw the latter's face.

"Give that young woman a chair and a glass of water, will you?" he called out; and his authoritative manner impressed the jurymen, who gathered round him, ready and eager to hear any thing he could say.

He gave his name as John Smith, druggist's assistant; said that the young man who lodged up stairs, whose death he had only just heard of, had been his patient for some months, and was in the last stage of consumption. He had no doubt the death had ensued from perfectly natural

causes, as he explained in such technical language as completely to overpower the jury, and satisfy them accordingly. They quitted the parlor, and proceeded to the public
house, where, after a brief consultation, they delivered their
verdict, as the astute policeman had foretold, "Died by the
visitation of God;" took pipes and brandy all round at the
bar, and then adjourned to their several homes, gratified at
having done their duty to their country.

Meantime Elizabeth crept up stairs. Nobody hindered
or followed her; nobody cared any thing for the solitary
dead.

There he lay—poor Tom!—almost as she had left him;
the counterpane was hardly disturbed, the candle she had
placed on the chair had burned down to a bit of wick,
which still lay in the socket. Nobody had touched him,
or any thing about him, as, in all cases of "Found dead,"
English law exacts.

Whether he had died soon after she quitted him that
night, or whether he had lingered through the long hours
of darkness, or of daylight following, alive and conscious
perhaps, yet too weak to call any one, even had there been
any one he cared to call—when or how the spirit had
passed away unto Him who gave it were mysteries that
could never be known.

But it was all over now; he lay at rest with the death
smile on his face. Elizabeth, as she stood and looked at
him, could not, dared not weep.

"My poor Tom, my own dear Tom," was all she thought,
and knew that he was all her own now; that she had loved
him through every thing, and loved him to the end.

CHAPTER XXVIII.

ELIZABETH spent the greatest part of her holiday in that
house, in that room. Nobody interfered with her; nobody
asked in what relation she stood to the deceased, or what
right she had to take upon herself the arrangements for his

funeral. Every body was only too glad to let her assume
a responsibility which would otherwise have fallen on the
parish.

The only person who appeared to remember either her
or the dead man was the druggist's assistant, who sent in
the necessary medical certificate as to the cause of death.
Elizabeth took it to the Registrar, and thence proceeded
to an undertaker hard by, with whom she arranged all
about the funeral, and that it should take place in the new
cemetery at Kensal Green. She thought she should like
that better than a close, noisy London church-yard.

Before she left the house she saw poor Tom laid in his
coffin, and covered up forever from mortal eyes. Then, and
not till then, she sat herself down beside him and wept.

Nobody contested with her the possession of the few
things that had belonged to him, which were scarcely more
than the clothes he had on when he died; so she made
them up into a parcel and took them away with her. In
his waistcoat pocket she found one book, a little Testament,
which she had given him herself. It looked as if it had
been a good deal read. If all his studies, all his worship
of " pure intellect," as the one supreme good, had ended in
that, it was a blessed ending.

When she reached home Elizabeth went at once to her
master, returned him his letter of recommendation, and explained to him that his kindness was not needed now.

Mr. Ascott seemed a good deal shocked, inquired from
her a few particulars, and again took out his purse, his one
panacea for all mortal woes. But Elizabeth declined; she
said she would only ask him for an advance of her next
half-year's wages. She preferred burying her old friend
herself.

She buried him, herself the only mourner, on a bright
summer's day, with the sun shining dazzlingly on the white
grave-stones in Kensal Green. The clergyman appeared,
read the service, and went away again. A few minutes
ended it all. When the undertaker and his men had also
departed she sat down on a bench near to watch the sex-

ton filling up the grave—Tom's grave. She was very quiet, and none but a closely-observant person watching her face could have penetrated into the truth of what your impulsive characters, always in the extremes of mirth or misery, never understand about quiet people, that "still waters run deep."

While she sat there some one came past her and turned round. It was the shabby-looking chemist's assistant, who had appeared at the inquest and given the satisfactory evidence which had prevented the necessity of her giving hers.

Elizabeth rose and acknowledged him with a respectful courtesy; for under his threadbare clothes was the bearing of a gentleman, and he had been so kind to Tom.

"I am too late," he said; "the funeral is over. I meant to have attended it, and seen the last of the poor fellow."

"Thank you, sir," replied Elizabeth, gratefully.

The young man stood before her, looking at her earnestly for a minute or two, and then exclaimed, with a complete change of voice and manner, "Elizabeth! don't you know me? What has become of my Aunt Johanna?"

It was Ascott Leaf.

But no wonder Elizabeth had not recognized him. His close-cropped hair, his large beard hiding half his face, and a pair of spectacles which he had assumed, were a sufficient disguise. Besides, the great change from his former "dandy" appearance to the extreme of shabbiness—his clothes being evidently worn as long as they could possibly hold together, and his generally depressed air giving the effect of one who had gone down in the world—made him, even without the misleading "John Smith," most unlikely to be identified with the Ascott Leaf of old.

"I never should have known you, sir!" said Elizabeth, truthfully, when her astonishment had a little subsided; "but I am very glad to see you. Oh, how thankful your aunts will be!"

"Do you think so? I thought it was quite the contrary. But it does not matter; they will never hear of me, unless you tell them—and I believe I may trust you. You would not betray me, if only for the sake of that poor fellow yonder ?"

"No, sir."

"Now tell me something about my aunts, especially my Aunt Johanna."

And sitting down in the sunshine, with his arm upon the back of the bench, and his hand hiding his eyes, the poor prodigal listened in silence to every thing Elizabeth told him; of his Aunt Selina's marriage and death, and of Mr. Lyon's return, and of the happy home at Liverpool.

"They are all quite happy, then ?" said he, at length; "they seem to have begun to prosper ever since they got rid of me. Well, I'm glad of it. I only wanted to hear of them from you. I shall never trouble them any more. You'll keep my secret, I know. And now I must go, for I have not a minute more to spare. Good-by, Elizabeth."

With a humility and friendliness, strange enough in Ascott Leaf, he held out his hand—empty, for he had nothing to give now—to his aunt's old servant. But Elizabeth detained him.

"Don't go, sir; please don't—not just yet." And then she added, with an earnest respectfulness that touched the heart of the poor, shabby man, "I hope you'll pardon the liberty I take. I'm only a servant, but I knew you when you were a boy, Mr. Leaf; and if you would trust me—if you would let me be of use to you in any way—if only because you were so good to *him* there."

"Poor Tom Cliffe; he was not a bad fellow; he liked me rather, I think; and I was able to doctor him, and help him a little. Heigh-ho; it's a comfort to think I ever did any good to any body."

Ascott sighed, drew his rusty coat-sleeve across his eyes, and sat contemplating his boots, which were any thing but dandy boots now.

"Elizabeth, what relation was Tom to you? If I had known you were acquainted with him I should have been afraid to go near him; but I felt sure, though he came from

Stowbury, he did not guess who I was; he only knew me as Mr. Smith; and he never once mentioned you. Was he your cousin, or what?"

Elizabeth considered a moment, and then told the simple fact; it could not matter now.

"I was once going to be married to him, but he saw somebody he liked better, and married her."

"Poor girl! poor Elizabeth!"

Perhaps nothing could have shown the great change in Ascott more than the tone in which he uttered these words; a tone of entire respect and kindly pity, from which he never once departed during that conversation, and many, many others, so long as their confidential relations lasted.

"Now, sir, would you be so kind as to tell me something about yourself? I'll not repeat any thing to your aunts, if you don't wish it."

Ascott yielded. He had been so long, so utterly forlorn. He sat down beside Elizabeth, and then, with eyes often averted, and with many breaks between, which she had to fill up as best she could, he told her all his story, even to the sad secret of all, which had caused him to run away from home, and hide himself in the last place where they would have thought he was, the safe wilderness of London. There, carefully disguised, he had lived decently while his money lasted, and then, driven step by step to the brink of destitution, he had offered himself for employment in the lowest grade of his own profession, and been taken as assistant by the not overscrupulous chemist and druggist in that not too respectable neighborhood of Westminster, with a salary of twenty pounds a year.

"And I actually live upon it!" added he, with a bitter smile. "I can't run into debt; for who would trust me? And I dress in rags almost, as you see. And I get my meals how and where I can; and I sleep under the shop-counter. A pretty life for Mr. Ascott Leaf, isn't it, now? What would my aunts say if they knew it?"

"They would say it was an honest life, and that they were not a bit ashamed of you."

Ascott drew himself up a little, and his chest heaved visibly under the close-buttoned, threadbare coat.

"Well, at least it is a life that makes nobody else miserable."

Ay, that wonderful teacher, Adversity,

> "Which, like the toad, ugly and venomous,
> Wears yet a precious jewel in its head,"

had left behind this jewel in the young man's heart. A disguised, beggared outcast, he had found out the value of an honest name; forsaken, unfriended, he had learned the preciousness of home and love; made a servant of, tyrannized over, and held in low esteem, he had been taught by hard experience the secret of true humility and charity—the esteeming of others better than himself.

Not with all natures does misfortune so work, but it did with his. He had sinned; he had paid the cost of his sin in bitter suffering; but the result was cheaply bought, and he already began to feel that it was so.

"Yes," said he, in answer to a question of Elizabeth's, "I really am, for some things, happier than I used to be. I feel more like what I was in the old days, when I was a little chap at Stowbury. Poor old Stowbury! I often think of the place in a way that's perfectly ridiculous. Still, if any thing happened to me, I should like my aunts to know it, and that I didn't forget them."

"But, sir," asked Elizabeth, earnestly, "do you never mean to go near your aunts again?"

"I can't say; it all depends upon circumstances. I suppose," he added, "if, as is said, one's sin is sure to find one out, the same rule goes by contraries. It seems poor Cliffe once spoke of me to a district visitor, the only visitor he ever had; and this gentleman, hearing of the inquest, came yesterday to inquire about him of me; and the end was that he offered me a situation with a person he knew, a very respectable chemist in Tottenham Court Road."

"And shall you go?"

"To be sure. I've learned to be thankful for small mer-

cies. Nobody will find me out or recognize me. You
didn't. Who knows? I may even have the honor of dis-
pensing drugs to Uncle Ascott of Russell Square."

"But," said Elizabeth, after a pause, "you will not always remain as John Smith, druggist's shopman, throwing
away all your good education, and position, and name?"

"Elizabeth," said he, in a humbled tone, "how dare I
ever resume my own name and get back my rightful position while Peter Ascott lives? Can you or any body point
out a way?"

She thought the question over in her clear head; clear
still, even at this hour, when she had to think for others,
though all personal feeling and interest were buried in that
grave over which the sexton was now laying the turf that
would soon grow smoothly green.

"If I might advise, Mr. Leaf, I should say, save up all
your money, and then go, just as you are, with an honest,
bold front, right into my master's house, with the fifty
pounds in your hand—"

"By Jove, you've hit it!" cried Ascott, starting up.
"What a thing a woman's head is! I've turned over
scheme after scheme, but I never once thought of any so
simple as that. Bravo, Elizabeth! You're a remarkable
woman."

She smiled—a very sad smile—but still she felt glad.
Any thing that she could possibly do for any creature belonging to her dear mistresses seemed to this faithful servant the natural and bounden duty of her life.

Long after the young man, whose mercurial temperament
no trouble could repress, had gone away in excellent spirits,
leaving her an address where she could always find him,
and give him regular news of his aunts, though he made
her promise to give them, as yet, no tidings in return, Elizabeth sat still, watching the sun decline and the shadows
lengthen over the field of graves. In the calmness and
beauty of this solitary place an equal calm seemed to come
over her; a sense of how wonderfully events had linked
themselves together and worked themselves out; how even

poor Tom's mournful death had brought about this meeting, which might end in restoring to her beloved mistresses their lost sheep, their outcast, miserable boy. She did not reason the matter out, but she felt it, and felt that in making her in some degree his instrument God had been very good to her in the midst of her desolation.

It seemed Elizabeth's lot always to have to put aside her own troubles for the trouble of somebody else. Almost immediately after Tom Cliffe's death her little Henry fell ill with scarlatina, and remained for many months in a state of health so fragile as to engross all her thought and care. It was with difficulty that she contrived a few times to go for Henry's medicines to the shop where "John Smith" served.

She noticed that every time he looked healthier, brighter, freer from that aspect of broken-down respectability which had touched her so much. He did not dress any better, but still "the gentleman" in him could never be hidden or lost, and he said his master treated him "like a gentleman," which was apparently a pleasant novelty.

"I have some time to myself also. Shop shuts at nine, and I get up at 5 A.M.—bless us! what would my aunt Hilary say! And it's not for nothing. There are more ways than one of turning an honest penny, when a young fellow really sets about it. Elizabeth, you used to be a literary character yourself; look into the —— and the ——" (naming two popular magazines), "and if you find a series of especially clever papers on sanitary reform, and so on, I did 'em!"

He slapped his chest with Ascott's merry laugh of old. It cheered Elizabeth for a long while afterward.

By-and-by she had to take little Henry to Brighton, and lost sight of "John Smith" for some time longer.

It was on a snowy February day, when, having brought the child home quite strong, and received unlimited gratitude and guineas from the delighted father, Master Henry's faithful nurse stood in her usual place at the dining-room door, waiting for the interminable grace of "only five minutes more" to be over, and her boy carried ignominiously but contentedly to bed.

The footman knocked at the door. "A young man wanting to speak to master on particular business."

"Let him send in his name."

"He says you wouldn't know it, sir."

"Show him in, then. Probably a case of charity, as usual. Oh!"

And Mr. Ascott's opinion was confirmed by the appearance of the shabby young man with the long beard, whom Elizabeth did not wonder he never recognized in the least.

She ought to have retired, and yet she could not. She hid herself partly behind the door, afraid of passing Ascott, dreading alike to wound him by recognition or non-recognition. But he took no notice. He seemed excessively agitated.

"Come a-begging, young man, I suppose? Wants a situation, as hundreds do, and think that I have half the clerkships in the city at my disposal, and that I am made of money besides. But it's no good, I tell you, sir; I never give nothing to strangers, except—Here, Henry, my son, take that person there this half crown."

And the little boy, in his pretty purple velvet frock and his prettier face, trotted across the room and put the money into poor Ascott's hand. He took it; and then, to the astonishment of Master Henry, and the still greater astonishment of his father, lifted up the child and kissed him.

"Young man, young fellow—"

"I see you don't know me, Mr. Ascott, and it's not surprising. But I have come to repay you this—" he laid a fifty-pound note down on the table. "Also, to thank you earnestly for not prosecuting me, and to say—"

"Good God!"—the sole expletive Peter Ascott had been heard to use for long—"Ascott Leaf, is that you? I thought you were in Australia, or dead, or something."

"No, I'm alive and here, more's the pity perhaps, except that I have lived to pay you back what I cheated you out of. What you generously gave me I can't pay, though I

may some time. Meantime I have brought you this. It's
honestly earned. Yes"—observing the keen doubtful look
—"though I have hardly a coat to my back, I assure you
it's honestly earned."

Mr. Ascott made no reply. He stooped over the bank-
note, examined it, folded it, and put it into his pocket-book;
then, after another puzzled investigation of Ascott, cleared
his throat.

"Mrs. Hand, you had better take Master Henry up stairs."

An hour after, when little Henry had long been sound
asleep, and she was sitting at her usual evening sewing in
her solitary nursery, Elizabeth learned that the "shabby
young man" was still in the dining-room with Mr. Ascott,
who had rung for tea and some cold meat with it. And
the footman stated, with undisguised amazement, that the
shabby young man was actually sitting at the same table
with master!

Elizabeth smiled to herself, and held her tongue. Now,
as ever, she always kept the secrets of the family.

About ten o'clock she was summoned to the dining-room.

There stood Peter Ascott, pompous as ever, but with a
certain kindly good-humor lightening his heavy face, looking condescendingly around him, and occasionally rubbing
his hands slowly together, as if he were exceedingly well
pleased with himself. There stood Ascott Leaf, looking
bright and handsome in spite of his shabbiness, and quite
at his ease—which small peculiarity was never likely to
be knocked out of him under the most depressing circumstances.

He shook hands with Elizabeth warmly.

"I wanted to ask you if you have any message for Liverpool. I go there to-morrow on business for Mr. Ascott,
and afterward I shall probably go and see my aunts." He
faltered a moment, but quickly shook the emotion off. "Of
course I shall tell them all about you, Elizabeth. Any
special message, eh?"

"Only my duty, sir, and Master Henry is quite well
again," said Elizabeth, formally, and dropping her old-fash-

ioned courtesy; after which, as quickly as she could, she slipped out of the dining-room.

But long, long after, when all the house was gone to bed, she stood at the nursery window, looking down upon the trees of the square, that stretched their motionless arms up into the moonlight sky—just such a moonlight as it was once, more than three years ago, the night little Henry was born. And she recalled all the past, from the day when Miss Hilary hung up her bonnet for her in the house-place at Stowbury; the dreary life at No. 15; the Sunday nights when she and Tom Cliffe used to go wandering round and round the square.

"Poor Tom!" said she to herself, thinking of Ascott Leaf, and how happy he had looked, and how happy his aunts would be to-morrow. "Well, Tom would be glad too if he knew all."

But, happy as every body was, there was nothing so close to Elizabeth's heart as the one grave over which the snow was now lying, white and peaceful, out at Kensal Green.

Elizabeth is still living—which is a great blessing, for nobody could well do without her. She will probably attain a good old age, being healthy and strong, very equable in temper now, and very cheerful too, in her quiet way. Doubtless she will yet have Master Henry's children climbing her knees, and calling her "Mammy Lizzie."

But she will never marry. She never loved any body but Tom.

THE END.

VALUABLE AND INTERESTING WORKS

FOR

PUBLIC & PRIVATE LIBRARIES

PUBLISHED BY HARPER & BROTHERS, NEW YORK.

BOSWELL'S LIFE OF JOHNSON, Including Boswell's Journal of a Tour to the Hebrides, and Johnson's Diary cf a Journey into North Wales. Edited by GEORGE BIRKBECK HILL, D.C.L., Pembroke College, Oxford. *Édition de Luxe.* In Six Volumes. Large 8vo, Half Vellum, Uncut Edges and Gilt Tops, with many Portraits, Fac-similes, etc., $30 00. *Popular Edition.* 6 vols., Cloth, Uncut Edges and Gilt Tops, $10 00.

THE JOURNAL OF SIR WALTER SCOTT, 1825-1832. From the Original Manuscript at Abbotsford. With Two Portraits and Engraved Title-pages. Two volumes, 8vo, Cloth, Uncut Edges and Gilt Tops, $7 50; Half Calf, $12 00. *Popular Edition.* One volume, Crown 8vo, Cloth, $2 50.

STUDIES IN CHAUCER: His Life and Writings. By THOMAS R. LOUNSBURY, Professor of English in the Sheffield Scientific School of Yale University. With a Portrait of Chaucer. 3 vols., 8vo, Cloth, Uncut Edges and Gilt Tops, $9 00. *(In a Box.)*

PHARAOHS, FELLAHS, AND EXPLORERS. By AMELIA B. EDWARDS. Illustrated. 8vo, Cloth, Ornamental, Uncut Edges and Gilt Top, $4 00.

INDIKA. The Country and the People of India and Ceylon. By JOHN F. HURST, D.D., LL.D. With 6 Maps and 250 Illustrations. 8vo, Cloth, $5 00; Half Morocco, $7.00. *(Sold by Sub-scription only.)*

MOTLEY'S LETTERS. The Correspondence of John Lothrop Motley, D.C.L. Edited by GEORGE WILLIAM CURTIS. With Portrait. 2 vols., 8vo, Cloth, $7 00; Sheep, $8 00; Half Calf, $11 50.

MACAULAY'S ENGLAND. The History of England from the Accession of James II. By THOMAS BABINGTON MACAULAY. 5 vols., in a Box, 8vo, Cloth, with Paper Labels, Uncut Edges and Gilt Tops, $10 00; Sheep, $12 50; Half Calf, $21 25. (*Sold only in Sets.*) Cheap Edition, 5 vols., 12mo, Cloth, $2 50; Sheep, $3 75.

MACAULAY'S MISCELLANEOUS WORKS. The Miscellaneous Works of Lord Macaulay. 5 vols., in a Box, 8vo, Cloth, with Paper Labels, Uncut Edges and Gilt Tops, $10 00; Sheep, $12 50; Half Calf, $21 25. (*Sold only in Sets.*)

HUME'S ENGLAND. History of England, from the Invasion of Julius Cæsar to the Abdication of James II., 1688. By DAVID HUME. 6 vols., in a Box, 8vo, Cloth, with Paper Labels, Uncut Edges and Gilt Tops, $12 00; Sheep, $15 00; Half Calf, $25 50. (*Sold only in Sets.*) Popular Edition, 6 vols., in a Box, 12mo, Cloth, $3 00; Sheep, $4 50.

THE WORKS OF OLIVER GOLDSMITH. Edited by PETER CUNNINGHAM, F.S.A. 4 vols., 8vo, Cloth, Paper Labels, Uncut Edges and Gilt Tops, $8 00; Sheep, $10 00; Half Calf, $17 00.

THE RISE OF THE DUTCH REPUBLIC. A History. By JOHN LOTHROP MOTLEY, LL.D., D.C.L. With a Portrait of William of Orange. 3 vols., in a Box. 8vo, Cloth, with Paper Labels, Uncut Edges and Gilt Tops, $6 00; Sheep, $7 50; Half Calf, $12 75. (*Sold only in Sets.*)

HISTORY OF THE UNITED NETHERLANDS: From the Death of William the Silent to the Twelve Years' Truce—1548–1609. With a full View of the English-Dutch Struggle against Spain, and of the Origin and Destruction of the Spanish Armada. By JOHN LOTHROP MOTLEY, LL.D., D.C.L. Portraits. 4 vols., in a Box, 8vo, Cloth, with Paper Labels, Uncut Edges and Gilt Tops, $8 00; Sheep, $10 00; Half Calf, $17 00. (*Sold only in Sets.*)

THE LIFE AND DEATH OF JOHN OF BARNEVELD, Advocate of Holland. With a View of the Primary Causes and Movements of the "Thirty Years' War." By JOHN LOTHROP MOTLEY, LL.D., D.C.L. Illustrated. 2 vols., in a Box, 8vo, Cloth, with Paper Labels, Uncut Edges and Gilt Tops, $4 00; Sheep, $5 00; Half Calf, $8 50. (*Sold only in Sets.*)

GIBBON'S ROME. The History of the Decline and Fall of the Roman Empire. By EDWARD GIBBON. With Notes by Dean MILMAN, M. GUIZOT, and Dr. WILLIAM SMITH. 6 vols., in a Box, 8vo, Cloth, with Paper Labels, Uncut Edges and Gilt Tops, $12 00; Sheep, $15 00; Half Calf, $25 50. Popular Edition, 6 vols., in a Box, 12mo, Cloth, $3 00; Sheep, $4 50. (*Sold only in Sets.*)

A DICTIONARY OF THE ENGLISH LANGUAGE. Pronouncing, Etymological, and Explanatory: embracing Scientific and other Terms, Numerous Familiar Terms, and a Copious Selection of Old English Words. By the Rev. JAMES STORMONTH. The Pronunciation Revised by the Rev. P. H. PHELP, M.A. Imperial 8vo, Cloth, $5 00; Half Roan, $6 50; Full Sheep, $6 50.

A MANUAL OF HISTORICAL LITERATURE, comprising Brief Descriptions of the most Important Histories in English, French, and German, together with Practical Suggestions as to Methods and Courses of Historical Study, for the Use of Students, General Readers, and Collectors of Books. By CHARLES KENDALL ADAMS, LL.D. Third Edition, Revised and Enlarged. Crown 8vo, Cloth, $2 50.

ART AND CRITICISM. Monographs and Studies. By THEODORE CHILD. Richly Illustrated. Large 8vo, Cloth, Ornamental, Uncut Edges and Gilt Top, $6 00. (*In a Box.*)

THE SPANISH–AMERICAN REPUBLICS. By THEODORE CHILD. Illustrated by T. DE THULSTRUP, FREDERIC REMINGTON, WILLIAM HAMILTON GIBSON, W. H. ROGERS, and other Eminent Artists. Large 8vo, Cloth, Ornamental, $3 50.

ILIOS, the City and Country of the Trojans. A Narrative of the Most Recent Discoveries and Researches made on the Plain of Troy. By Dr. HENRY SCHLIEMANN. Maps, Plans, and Illustrations. Imperial 8vo, Illuminated Cloth, $7 50; Half Morocco, $10 00.

TROJA. Results of the Latest Researches and Discoveries on the Site of Homer's Troy, and in the Heroic Tumuli and other Sites, made in the Year 1882, and a Narrative of a Journey in the Troad in 1881. By Dr. HENRY SCHLIEMANN. Preface by Professor A. H. Sayce. With Wood-cuts, Maps, and Plans. 8vo, Cloth, $5 00; Half Morocco, $7 50.

HISTORY OF THE UNITED STATES. By RICHARD HIL-
DRETH. FIRST SERIES: From the Discovery of the Continent
to the Organization of the Government under the Federal Con-
stitution. SECOND SERIES: From the Adoption of the Federal
Constitution to the end of the Sixteenth Congress. Popular
Edition, 6 vols., in a Box, 8vo, Cloth, with Paper Labels, Uncut
Edges and Gilt Tops, $12 00; Sheep, $15 00; Half Calf, $25 00
(*Sold only in Sets.*)

RECOLLECTIONS OF PRESIDENT LINCOLN and His Ad-
ministration. By LUCIUS E. CHITTENDEN. With Portrait.
8vo, Cloth, Uncut Edges and Gilt Top, $2 50; Half Calf,
$4 75.

MEMOIR OF THE LIFE OF LAURENCE OLIPHANT and of
Alice Oliphant, his wife. By MARGARET OLIPHANT W. OLI-
PHANT. 2 vols., 8vo, Cloth, Uncut Edges and Gilt Tops, $7 00.
(*In a Box.*)

EPISODES IN A LIFE OF ADVENTURE; or, Moss from a
Rolling Stone. By LAURENCE OLIPHANT. 12mo, Cloth, $1 25.

HAIFA; OR, LIFE IN MODERN PALESTINE. By LAURENCE
OLIPHANT. Edited, with Introduction, by CHARLES A. DANA.
12mo, Cloth, $1 75.

CONSTITUTIONAL HISTORY OF THE UNITED STATES
from their Declaration of Independence to the Close of their
Civil War. By GEORGE TICKNOR CURTIS. Two Volumes.
Vol. I., 8vo, Cloth, Uncut Edges and Gilt Top, $3 00.

OUR ITALY. An Exposition of the Climate and Resources of
Southern California. By CHARLES DUDLEY WARNER. Illustrated. 8vo, Cloth, Uncut Edges and Gilt Top, $2 50.

LONDON LETTERS, and Some Others. By GEORGE W.
SMALLEY, London Correspondent of the *New York Tribune.*
Two Volumes. Vol I. Personalities—Two Midlothian Cam-
paigns. Vol. II. Notes on Social Life—Notes on Parliament—
Pageants — Miscellanies. 8vo, Cloth, Uncut Edges and Gilt
Tops, $6 00.

LIFE AND LETTERS OF GENERAL THOMAS J. JACKSON
(Stonewall Jackson). By His Wife, MARY ANNA JACKSON.
With an Introduction by HENRY M. FIELD, D.D. Illustrated.
8vo, Cloth, $2 00.

'POLITICAL HISTORY OF RECENT TIMES (1816-1875). With Special Reference to Germany. By WILLIAM MÜLLER. Translated, with an Appendix covering the Period from 1876 to 1881, by the Rev. JOHN P. PETERS, Ph.D. 12mo, Cloth, $2 00.

THE LIFE AND LETTERS OF LORD MACAULAY. By his Nephew, GEORGE OTTO TREVELYAN, M.P. With Portrait on Steel. 2 vols., 8vo, Cloth, Uncut Edges and Gilt Tops, $5 00; Sheep, $6 00; Half Calf, $9 50. *Popular Edition*, two vols. in one, 12mo, Cloth, $1 75.

THE EARLY HISTORY OF CHARLES JAMES FOX. By GEORGE OTTO TREVELYAN. 8vo, Cloth, Uncut Edges and Gilt Tops, $2 50; Half Calf, $4 75.

WRITINGS AND SPEECHES OF SAMUEL J. TILDEN. Edited by JOHN BIGELOW. 2 vols., 8vo, Cloth, Uncut Edges and Gilt Tops, $6 00 per set.

MEMOIRS OF JOHN ADAMS DIX. Compiled by his Son, MORGAN DIX. With Five Steel-plate Portraits. 2 vols., 8vo, Cloth, Uncut Edges and Gilt Tops, $5 00.

THROUGH THE DARK CONTINENT; or, The Sources of the Nile, Around the Great Lakes of Equatorial Africa, and Down the Livingstone River to the Atlantic Ocean. 149 Illustrations and 10 Maps. By H. M. STANLEY. 2 vols., 8vo, Cloth, $7 50; Sheep, $9 50; Half Morocco, $12 00.

THE CONGO and the Founding of its Free State, a Story of Work and Exploration. With over One Hundred Full-page and smaller Illustrations, Two Large Maps, and several smaller ones. By H. M. STANLEY. 2 vols., 8vo, Cloth, $7 50; Sheep, $9 50; Half Morocco, $12 00.

HISTORY OF THE ENGLISH PEOPLE. By JOHN RICHARD GREEN, M.A. With Maps. 4 vols., 8vo, Cloth, $2 50 per vol. Volumes sold separately. Complete sets, Sheep, $12 00; Half Calf, $19 00.

THE MAKING OF ENGLAND. By JOHN RICHARD GREEN. With Maps. 8vo, Cloth, $2 50; Sheep, $3 00; Half Calf, $4 75.

THE CONQUEST OF ENGLAND. By JOHN RICHARD GREEN. With Maps. 8vo, Cloth, $2 50; Sheep, $3 00; Half Calf, $4 75.

A SHORT HISTORY OF THE ENGLISH PEOPLE. By JOHN RICHARD GREEN, M.A. Revised and Enlarged. With Colored Maps and Tables. 8vo, Cloth, $1 20.

THE LAND OF THE MIDNIGHT SUN. Summer and Winter Journeys in Sweden, Norway, Lapland, and Northern Finland. By PAUL B. DU CHAILLU. Illustrated. 2 vols., 8vo, Cloth, $7 50; Half Calf, $12 00.

CYCLOPÆDIA OF UNITED STATES HISTORY. From the Aboriginal Period to 1876. By BENSON J. LOSSING. Illustrated by 2 Steel Portraits and over 1000 Engravings. 2 vols., Royal 8vo, Cloth, $10 00; Sheep, $12 00; Half Morocco, $15 00.

PICTORIAL FIELD-BOOK OF THE REVOLUTION; or, Illustrations by Pen and Pencil of the History, Biography, Scenery, Relics, and Traditions of the War for Independence. By BENSON J. LOSSING. 2 vols., 8vo, Cloth, $14 00; Sheep or Roan, $15 00; Half Calf, $18 00.

PICTORIAL FIELD-BOOK OF THE WAR OF 1812; or, Illustrations by Pen and Pencil of the History, Biography, Scenery, Relics, and Traditions of the last War for American Independence. By BENSON J. LOSSING. 8vo, Cloth, $7 00; Sheep or Roan, $8 50; Half Calf, $10 00.

ENGLISH MEN OF LETTERS. Edited by JOHN MORLEY. The following volumes are now ready:

JOHNSON. By L. Stephen.—GIBBON. By J. C. Morison.—SCOTT. By R. H. Hutton.—SHELLEY. By J. A. Symonds.—GOLDSMITH. By W. Black.—HUME. By Professor Huxley.—DEFOE. By W. Minto.—BURNS. By Principal Shairp. —SPENSER. By R. W. Church.—THACKERAY. By A. Trollope.—BURKE. By J. Morley.—MILTON. By M. Pattison.—SOUTHEY. By E. Dowden.—CHAUCER. By A. W. Ward.—BUNYAN. By J. A. Froude.—COWPER. By G. Smith.—POPE. By L. Stephen.—BYRON. By J. Nichols.—LOCKE. By T. Fowler.—WORDSWORTH. By F. W. H. Myers.—HAWTHORNE. By Henry James, Jr.—DRYDEN. By G. Saintsbury.—LANDOR. By S. Colvin.—DE QUINCEY. By D. Masson.—LAMB. By A. Ainger.—BENTLEY. By R. C. Jebb.—DICKENS. By A. W. Ward.—GRAY. By E. W. Gosse.—SWIFT. By L. Stephen.—STERNE. By H. D. Traill. — MACAULAY. By J. C. Morison.— FIELDING. By A. Dobson.— SHERIDAN. By Mrs. Oliphant.—ADDISON. By W. J. Courthope.—BACON. By R. W. Church.—COLERIDGE. By H. D. Traill.—SIR PHILIP SIDNEY. By J. A. Symonds.—KEATS. By S. Colvin. 12mo, Cloth, 75 cents per volume.

Popular Edition. 36 volumes in 12, Cloth, $12 00; Half Leather, $21 00.

HISTORY OF THE INQUISITION OF THE MIDDLE AGES. By HENRY CHARLES LEA. 3 vols., 8vo, Cloth, Uncut Edges and Gilt Tops, $3 00 per vol.

THE MIKADO'S EMPIRE. Book I. History of Japan, from 660 B.C. to 1872 A.D. Book II. Personal Experiences, Observations, and Studies in Japan, from 1870 to 1874. With Two Supplementary Chapters: Japan in 1883, 1886, and 1890. By W. E. GRIFFIS. Copiously Illustrated. 8vo, Cloth, $4 00, Half Calf, $6 25.

A SHORT HISTORY OF THE ENGLISH COLONIES IN AMERICA. By HENRY CABOT LODGE. With Colored Map. 8vo, Half Leather, $3 00.

THE LAND AND THE BOOK. Biblical Illustrations drawn from the Manners and Customs, the Scenes and Scenery, of the Holy Land. By WILLIAM M. THOMSON, D.D., Forty-five Years a Missionary in Syria and Palestine. In Three Volumes. Copiously Illustrated. Square 8vo, Ornamental Cloth, per volume, $6 00; Sheep, $7 00; Half Morocco, $8 50; Full Morocco, Gilt Edges, $10 00.
　　Volume I. SOUTHERN PALESTINE AND JERUSALEM.—Volume II. CENTRAL PALESTINE AND PHŒNICIA.—Volume III. LEBANON, DAMASCUS, AND BEYOND JORDAN.
　　Also, Handsome *Popular Edition* in Three Vols., Cloth, $9 00 per Set; Half Leather, $12 00. (*Sold only in Sets.*)

THE INVASION OF THE CRIMEA: its Origin, and an Account of its Progress down to the Death of Lord Raglan. By ALEXANDER WILLIAM KINGLAKE. With Maps and Plans. Six vols. 12mo, Cloth, $2 00 per vol. ; Half Calf, $22 50 per set.

FIFTY YEARS AGO. By WALTER BESANT. With a Portrait and Characteristic Illustrations by Cruikshank and others. 8vo, Cloth, $2 50.

THE TSAR AND HIS PEOPLE; or, Social Life in Russia. Papers by THEODORE CHILD, EUGÈNE MELCHIOR DE VOGÜÉ, CLARENCE COOK, and VASSILI VERESTCHAGIN. Illustrated. Square 8vo, Cloth, Uncut Edges and Gilt Top, $3 00.

THE CAPITALS OF SPANISH AMERICA. By WILLIAM ELEROY CURTIS. With a Colored Map and 358 Illustrations 8vo, Cloth, $3 50.

JINRIKISHA DAYS IN JAPAN. By ELIZA RUHAMAH SKIDMORE. Illustrated. Post 8vo, Cloth, Ornamental, $2 00.

LIFE OF BISHOP MATTHEW SIMPSON, of the Methodist Episcopal Church. By GEORGE R. CROOKS, D.D. Illustrated. 8vo, Cloth, $3 75; Gilt Edges, $4 25; Half Morocco, $5 25. (*Sold by Subscription.*)

SERMONS BY BISHOP MATTHEW SIMPSON, of the Methodist Episcopal Church. Edited by GEORGE R. CROOKS, D.D. 8vo, Cloth, $2 50.

LITERARY INDUSTRIES. By HUBERT HOWE BANCROFT. With Steel-Plate Portrait. Post 8vo, Cloth $1 50.

CURIOSITIES OF THE AMERICAN STAGE. By LAURENCE HUTTON. With Copious and Characteristic Illustrations. Crown 8vo, Cloth, Uncut Edges and Gilt Top, $2 50.

STUDIES IN THE WAGNERIAN DRAMA. By HENRY E. KREHBIEL. Post 8vo, Cloth, $1 25.

HISTORY OF MEDLÆVAL ART. By Dr. FRANZ VON REBER. Translated and Augmented by Joseph Thacher Clarke. With 422 Illustrations, and a Glossary of Technical Terms. 8vo, Cloth, $5 00.

HISTORY OF ANCIENT ART. By Dr. FRANZ VON REBER. Revised by the Author. Translated and Augmented by Joseph Thacher Clarke. With 310 Illustrations and a Glossary of Technical Terms. 8vo, Cloth, $3 50.

OUTLINES OF INTERNATIONAL LAW, with an Account of its Origin and Sources, and of its Historical Development. By GEORGE B. DAVIS, U.S.A. Crown 8vo, Cloth, $2 00.

CYPRUS: its Ancient Cities, Tombs, and Temples. A Narrative of Researches and Excavations during Ten Years' Residence in that Island. By L. P. DI CESNOLA. With Portrait, Maps, and 400 Illustrations. 8vo, Cloth, Extra, Uncut Edges and Gilt Top, $7 50.

THE ANCIENT CITIES OF THE NEW WORLD: Being Voyages and Explorations in Mexico and Central America, from 1857 to 1882. By DÉSIRÉ CHARNAY. Translated by J. Gonino and Helen S. Conant. Illustrations and Map. Royal 8vo, Ornamental Cloth, Uncut Edges, Gilt Top, $6 00.